ALSO BY
PHILLIP QUINN MORRIS

Mussels

Thirsty City

Thirsty City

PHILLIP QUINN MORRIS

Random House ⌂ New York

All rights reserved under International and Pan-American
Copyright Conventions. Published in the United States
by Random House, Inc., New York and simultaneously
in Canada by Random House of Canada Limited, Toronto.

Library of Congress Cataloging-in-Publication Data
Morris, Phillip Quinn.
Thirsty City/by Phillip Quinn Morris.
p. cm.
ISBN 0-394-57581-4
I. Title.
PS3563.O874465T48   1990
813'.54—dc20   89-43410

Manufactured in the United States of America
24689753

FIRST EDITION

Book design by Carole Lowenstein

To Susan, Jimmy, Erin, Debbie,
and especially to Mama

A special thanks to
Michael V. Carlisle
and to
David Rosenthal

Contents

The War Between the States Had Been Good to Cordelle Remington Reynolds

| | Wendell Laves reached his arms to the clear blue sky. Cordelle looked up, as it seemed Wendell was pointing for everyone to look up at the sky. But of the funeral congregation, Cordelle was the only one who looked upward. Everyone else, the forty-odd men, were looking at Cordelle or Wendell Laves or Jenny's casket, but mostly at Cordelle.

Wendell Laves jerked his arms back down and hollered at the top of his lungs in a fire-and-brimstone cadence, "Jenny was a good bitch!"

The six pallbearers lowered the small casket down into the grave.

Cordelle kept staring up at the sky, thinking about Winn. She would be home soon from LSU and would spend two weeks at Big House before going with her roommate to Europe for the major part of the summer. Cordelle wanted Winn's two weeks at Big House to be as special as possible.

Olan Massey and Red Stinnett were standing to the back of the crowd. They were dressed somewhat alike: both wore starched khakis, an open-collar shirt, and brogans. Ever since the moon shot, neither one of them had worn a suit, even to funerals. They both figured things hadn't been right from the day Armstrong had taken that giant step for mankind, and they didn't want to be caught during rapture wearing coat and tie. Not knowing how long it would take for God to judge every man, woman, and child that had ever existed, a stiff collar could get uncomfortable.

Olan looked at Cordelle, then said to Red, low-like so nobody else could overhear, "Bennie J.'s wife all the time come."

Red said, "Somebody got to bring Mama Dog Midnight, Queen of the Coon Dogs."

"Bennie J.'s too busy. Look like his boy bring Mama Dog?"

"Wright?" Red said, like Olan didn't know what he was talking about. "He too damn harum-scarum to come to a funeral. Like his sister. Hell, Bennie J.'s wife has to bring Mama Dog."

"I feel skittish," Olan said. "A woman at a coon dog funeral."

Red said, "She's born, raised a Republican," like that explained the whole matter.

"Naw!" Olan cried in disbelief.

"Yeah!"

"I'll be dogged! And I knowed Bennie J. all these here years."

"Yeah. She's from Campbell County."

"No wonder they younguns act so different. It does strange things to an offspring to be mixing blood like that. If the blood not kept pure, strange things can happen, just like in a coon dog."

"They come out tolerable types. Pure life is one day going to be a rare thing," Red commented, feeling pleased that he had summed up the condition of the world.

Cordelle's family had been in Alabama long before the Civil War, but in Campbell, a county whose border was sixty miles from the border of Sumpter County. Campbell County was mountainous, sandy, and rocky. It grew no cotton nor had any slaves. When the South seceded from the Union, Campbell County seceded from Alabama, going Republican and forming its own state. The county had a lot of timber and grew a little corn and made a lot of whiskey. Its unique political position in the Civil War put it in the situation of not having to serve on either side but being able to sell whiskey to both. Campbell County would forevermore remain Republican and up until now, 1970, was probably the only place in the real Deep South that wasn't Democrat.

Cordelle was born in 1925 but unlike everyone else other than the aristocracy hadn't seen hard times in the Depression. Her father, Lucius, was a mechanic in an era and area new to automobiles. And Prohibition pushed Lucius into a position as one of the first high-performance engine builders in the South.

The Depression, like the Civil War, had been good to Cordelle.

Cordelle had a sister five years younger, Coleen. Lucius intended to send both through boarding school at Sumpter College for Women in Sumpter County. When Cordelle reached sixteen she was sent.

Sumpter College for Women was founded in 1802 and had been spared in the Civil War. When Sherman's troops came through burning everything, they marched upon the Sumpter College for Women. All the young ladies of the college stood firmly along the upper veranda of the main building. The mistress of the college gave a speech to the colonel, a plea to be spared as it was a learning

institution. The colonel held off, sent a line to President Lincoln himself. The president granted that the college be saved.

On through the years Sumpter College for Women would always be receptive to liberals, Republicans, and bright young girls whose families had enough money to pay the high tuition. Sumpter College promoted and dramatized its unique and rich heritage at every opportunity. In the mistress's office, which later became the president's office when the board of directors voted in a man to head the women's college, Lincoln's letter was displayed in a glass case. There was also a bust of Lincoln until Bennie J. blew the head off with the right barrel of a sawed-off double-barrel twelve-gauge shotgun.

It happened like this.

After completing her first year at Sumpter, Cordelle experienced severe financial difficulty. During the year she had been away from home, Lucius had drunk and gambled himself into monetary ruin. The only other person in the world who had been able to keep Lucius in line, other than Cordelle, was Cordelle and Coleen's mother, Ana. Ana had passed away of pneumonia when Cordelle was in the eighth grade. Somehow, Lucius figured boarding school would help make up to his daughters for having been motherless during their adolescent years.

Cordelle, of course, had to leave the college but remained in Sumpter, renting a room in town and getting a job at the Sumpter County Bank with dreams of reentering Sumpter College in a couple of years. Though Lucius began to curb his drinking and gambling, most of his money went toward the debts he had incurred. Meanwhile, Cordelle pinched dimes, nickels, and dollars from her small paycheck, hoping to save enough for board and tuition, hoping her father would perhaps recover enough financially to pay three fourths. Every penny counted, but still she sent money to Coleen in order that she might continue dressing in the manner to which she was accustomed.

Working at the bank, Cordelle met Bennie J. Reynolds, one of the bank's more colorful and increasingly important customers. A year later they were married. After two years of marriage, they sat one hot summer night on a front porch and talked of life and the kids they would have. Bennie J. explained that the kids were going to get an education, a college education. He talked at length of how if he were to die, even a sizable estate could be taken away or squandered. But an education was something no one could take away from the children they someday were going to have, Bennie J. proudly enjoyed explaining on that hot Alabama summer night.

After a moment of silence while Bennie J. gloated in his foresightedness, Cordelle began to express her regret at not having a diploma from Sumpter College for Women. That's when Bennie J. first worried should something bad happen to him, Cordelle would not have the security of a college education to fall back on. He told her there on the front porch, "You're going back to Sumpter and get your degree." She told Bennie J. that only unmarried women under twenty-five years of age could attend Sumpter College for Women.

One month after that night, Bennie J. confessed to Greer Yarborough, "I've tried a lot of nice approaches. Boy, have I been nice. Just been bending over backwards explaining things and circumstances to that president out at the college. He just don't seem to give in to understanding." The next day Bennie J. walked into the college president's office with a sack of twenty-dollar bills and a sawed-off double-barrel twelve-gauge shotgun. He let himself into the office and walked up to the president, who was sitting at his desk. Bennie J. threw the sack down on the desk. He said, "There's enough cash money in there for three years' tuition and boarding for Cordelle Remington Reynolds. And she won't even be living on campus. In two more years she's got a sister that's goin' to be attending here. I'll bring you some more money then."

The president glanced up at Bennie J. like he was being terribly disturbed, not even noticing the shotgun, not even letting the sack of money get his attention, and said, "Mr. Reynolds, I'm afraid we've been over this before quite extensively. I don't think you seem to understand . . ."

Bennie J. raised up the shotgun and blew off Lincoln's head. When the resonance quieted, fragments settled to rest, Bennie J. said through the smell of gunpowder, "Shit, it's hard to miss with these things up close. Lookie here, I got one more barrel left." That's when Cordelle got enrolled again in the Sumpter College for Women.

Bennie J. wasn't necessarily given to violence, but he was adamantly given to obtaining results.

Meanwhile, back in Campbell County, Cordelle's family on both sides were holding their own, though Lucius had resumed some of his drinking and gambling but now in a more subdued manner. The other side of Cordelle's family was into corn farming and illegal whiskey business in Campbell County. The rest of Alabama had experienced a boom after the world war; yet, as Campbell County always seemed to be independent of the State—it had even called itself the Free State of Campbell during the War Between the States—

it was not now sharing in that economic boom. But that was soon to change.

Three of Cordelle's uncles were the political bosses of Campbell County, which meant nothing outside the county until Big Jim Folsum decided he wanted to be governor of the State of Alabama. State candidates never gave any attention to Campbell County, it being Republican. But Big Jim had the perfect plan. If he could get Campbell County to vote Democrat, and to vote for him, he could take the gubernatorial race.

In an old hunting cabin on Sipsey River and over a gallon of the finest sippin' moonshine available, Big Jim Folsum and Cordelle's three uncles quickly came to an agreement. Campbell County would surprise the state by voting Democrat and for Big Jim. And Big Jim promised to pork-barrel to the county and to further its own financial interests.

For the first time in its history, Campbell County voted Democrat.

Big Jim was elected governor and soon charmed the press as the epitome of Southern politicians. He openly declared that he saw it as his duty to steal everything he could while in office. He confessed unashamedly to having a mistress in southern California whom he shuttled to in a private state plane. He fell out of a jeep drunk while inspecting the Alabama National Guard on national television. He even forgot the names of his own children as he was introducing them on state television.

When Big Jim took power, Campbell County got more than its share. All Cordelle's uncles were appointed as state cabinet heads and every cousin that wanted a state job got one. Campbell County roads were paved and widened, parks were put in. The lumber mills got contracts to sell timber to the state. Rightly or wrongly, Cordelle's uncles had brought Campbell County into a boom.

Lucius was named the head of the Alcoholic Beverage Control Board. Bennie J. had commented, "Lucius figured the best way to handle and control the alcohol problems of the state was to try to drink it all up himself."

Lucius had had a wild life, but his last four years were the wildest. The days after his financial demise were his roughest. For a couple years his drinking was limited to that which he snuck during long work hours as a mechanic at a local garage; his gambling came to a halt. He spent his other hours at home, idle and depressed.

But his appointment by Big Jim changed all that, making his last years his most glorious. He had access to the National Guard Armories and state trooper units—if he wasn't hot-rodding a patrol car for fun, he was shooting something up with a Thompson machine gun. The state and especially Campbell County were Lucius's playground, where he wasted thousands of taxpayers' dollars.

At age sixty-nine, five days before Big Jim was to go out of office and Patterson took a short term as governor before the Little Judge, George Wallace, was to begin his infamous reign, Lucius took a state trooper car and lost it off the Sipsey River bridge going a hundred and fifty miles an hour, plunging down the ravine to his death.

Bennie J. had said his going off the bridge had marked the end of "fun politics." He had meant it was the end of a governor of Alabama openly drinking, womanizing, admitting to personal political paybacks, and the beginning of the nation putting their eyes to Alabama. Almost overnight, the Alabama playground of political bedfellows turned into a battleground of racial and social issues.

Whether Lucius's plunging down the ravine was a mere accident or a foreboding of the coming political affairs of the State of Alabama was unclear. What was clear was that one of Lucius's greatest pleasures was seeing both Cordelle and later Coleen winning Miss Maid of Cotton. (Being married, Cordelle was an illegal contestant, but her enrollment at Sumpter College for Women made her appear still a maiden.) Cordelle had a knack for benefiting from heritages she had nothing to do with. She was from a county that grew no cotton, yet managed, along with her sister and later her daughter, to win the Miss Maid of Cotton title.

Changing history around for her convenience was one of Cordelle's most effortless attributes. She was so adept at conveying her impression of history that her son, Wright, was in the fourth grade before he learned that the War Between the States was not when a bunch of "carpet-trackers" would come into nice Southern homes and steal all of the silver service, thus causing the "Silver War." And the grammar school textbooks of Alabama were so written that not until he was in the seventh grade did he learn that the South had lost the war.

Cordelle had her right hand clasped over her Patek Phillipe as if she'd been wiping a smudge from the crystal, and she still stared toward the sky, pondering Winn's homecoming. Cordelle wore three rings: her wedding band and a two-carat D-grade blue-white solitaire on her left ring finger, a baguette-cut sapphire on her right.

On her right wrist she wore the gold ID bracelet Bennie J. had given her when she was eighteen. Lapping over the bracelet was a gold wrist stamp that connected to a leash made of eight fine pieces of black, tightly braided leather. At the other end of the leash was a gold mesh collar that was around the twenty-five-inch neck of Mama Dog Midnight, who was lying down asleep.

Then it all of a sudden came clear to Cordelle. Something had been bothering her, something about Winn's coming home she couldn't put her finger on, something she'd been unable to prepare for sufficiently. It was so obvious that she had never thought of it: Winn's homecoming, her two-week celebration of being at Big House before she went abroad, was for Bennie J. It was Bennie J.'s celebration. That was it. Now it all could make sense. Now everything could take its proper perspective.

Cordelle looked down from the sky and back to Wendell Laves. Cordelle was proud she had put her finger on it, proud of her capability of keeping order to Big House.

Midnight woke as if telepathically connected to Cordelle's process, having slept so as to allow that process to make its calculations, evaluations, and deductions unhampered. Mama Dog Midnight stood up slowly, stretched, and shook herself. The shoulders of the jet black Plott hound came almost to the top of Cordelle's hipbone.

Mama Dog Midnight started howling; then all the other coon dogs there began howling. That meant the breakup of the funeral.

Cordelle pulled on the leash and Mama Dog Midnight followed Cordelle to her black Eldorado Cadillac. The congregation's eyes followed Cordelle, staring mostly at her black cotton dress. She opened the passenger door. Mama Dog crawled into the front seat and sat up on her haunches. Cordelle shut the door and walked around the car. Grit Adams opened the door for her, Cordelle thanked him kindly, he shut the door, and she drove away.

Olan and Red watched the brand-new Cadillac as it crawled up onto the paved county road and drove out of sight.

Red said, "I's hoping Wright would run for representative."

"Maybe he will."

"I's thinking he'd git further than J.C. done."

"Probably will. J.C. give it all up after one term as senator."

"You don't reckon Wright'd be sympathetic to Republican views, do ye?"

"Naw, naw. Only so much Bennie J. put up with. Mixed blood or no mixed blood."

Red took another cut of Day's Work and paused before he stuck it in his mouth to say, "I wonder if Cordelle votes Republican?"

Olan replied, "You know Sumpter County don't allow no Republicans on the ballot. If she vote Republican she votes it somewheres else."

2 The sun was coming through the large French glass windows of the two adjacent walls. Prisms hung down over the windows, making rainbows on the walls and furniture. Wright and Hanna were lying in bed together, Hanna asleep, Wright awake, gazing about the room. An hour before they had woken up and talked. Hanna told stories about living with her mother, Coleen, in that one-bedroom apartment in old New Orleans. Wright and Hanna talked about when they were nine years old and rode the train together from New Orleans to Sumpter, dressing up and telling everyone they were married.

Hanna had gone back to sleep, but Wright was unable to, thinking how Winn would come to Big House tonight. He had talked to her the night before. She'd told him that they wouldn't have to slip gin into Big House this summer. She had found a strong malt liquor called Right Time that looked and smelled just like the popular Sumpter County soft drink, Sun-Drop. She had bought a bottle capper. They could put the malt liquor in the soda bottles, and as neither Cordelle nor Bennie J. drank soda, the young folk could just walk around Big House drinking Right Time, everybody else thinking it was Sun-Drop.

Wright lay awake pondering how he didn't have the balls his sister had. If he ever got as close to the edge as Winn liked to live, he would probably just go ahead and jump, just go ahead and jump because he didn't have the balls to stand there and teeter on the edge. Wright knew he had a lot of natural charisma that might allow him to live on the edge and get away with it—but he didn't like the feel of risk.

There was a knock at the door. Wright said, "Come in" before he realized that there had been a knock at the door and that he had invited the knocker in; he had been so in his own thoughts of Winn. He pulled the covers up high on himself and Hanna and scooted away from her. She remained asleep, breathing shallow breaths, her figure almost masked by the rumples in the covers. Wright stared at her door, praying Hanna had locked it last night. But the door slowly cracked open. Cordelle walked in, then looked surprised. She said to Wright, "What are you and Hanna doing in bed together?!"

Wright yawned, said, "Uh," to have time to think some more. It came to him what to say as he noticed the empty fifth of Gilbey's gin on the dresser. "Uh—Hanna had another one of her nightmares last night. And she was scared. So I had to come in here and stay with her." After he had said that it sounded so good he wondered if it were true; then he started worrying Cordelle would see the liquor bottle.

But Cordelle changed her mood, saying, "Aw, poor thing. Last night I woke up and just had to look in Winn's room one more time to make sure everything is ready for her. When I walked by the room here I thought I heard her moaning."

"Yeah. She had a hard time getting back to sleep. I had to stay up with her two or three hours. That's why we're sleeping in so late. I wanted to get up at the crack of dawn, go to the marina with Doddy, but I knew I wouldn't do anybody any good walking around sleepy all day."

"B.J. called up mad that y'all weren't down at the marina yet. I'll call him and tell him Hanna had trouble last night. That y'all had to sleep in."

Hanna grunted and wiggled but remained asleep.

Cordelle continued, "Now, y'all have to help me with the coming-home party.

"Mama! Quit worrying. Everything is going to be all right."

"That's what you always say. You and your sister both. Winn is the very same way. I hope Hanna doesn't pick that up from y'all. What would happen if B.J. and I weren't all the time worrying about y'all?"

Wright grunted. Cordelle added rhetorically, "Huh?" while she adjusted the belt on her dress. "I've got to go up to Mr. Bernstein's and get a pair of shoes for the Coon-on-a-log today," she said mostly to herself, then added, "Now, your sister is only going to be here a few short weeks before she goes to Europe, and I want it to to be special for her."

Wright was saying, "All right, all right," in an annoyed tone when Cordelle turned around and saw the gin bottle. She gasped and said, "What's this?" She only got stern like that about whisky, dope, God, and Southern heritages.

Wright said, "A whiskey bottle." He hadn't thought up anything, would have to make it up as he went. He had already done well, he thought, by calling it a whiskey bottle instead of a gin bottle, that implying he didn't know much about whiskey or gin drinking.

"What is a whiskey bottle doing in my house?" Cordelle demanded. When Cordelle began enforcing discipline Big House suddenly became "my house," a point Winn liked to observe.

"Uh." Wright wiped his eyes like he was sleepy. "I found it on the side of the road and I was going to give it to Kathy Lee for her to découpage. It's such a pretty bottle."

Satisfied about the gin bottle, Cordelle said, "Why don't you take Kathy Lee out? Lou Ann and J.C. are crazy about you."

"Aw, Mama," Wright said. This was more aggravating than the gin bottle. The subject of Kathy Lee was not as easily diverted as the subject of liquor bottles or being found in the bathroom at the same time with Hanna. The subject of Kathy Lee probably fell under the category of Southern heritage. "That was junior high. She goes with Eddie now. And anyway, she's going off to Rutgers in a month or so."

"I don't see what Eddie or Rutgers has to do with anything," Cordelle said and then thought a moment. "Maybe we should give Kathy Lee a party."

"Mama!"

"I saw Lou Ann uptown yesterday. She said they were going to invite you over for a visit soon because they haven't seen you in a while. And I want you to go over there. They're crazy about you."

"All right, all right," he said, like he was sacrificing himself. It so happened he enjoyed going over to the Thomases', talking with J.C., but he felt the need to act as though he were being greatly put out. He recognized this and sometimes wondered if it were something he'd picked up from Bennie J., treating every interaction as a bargain or a deal.

Hanna grunted and rolled over, her crotch settling up against Wright's thigh. Wright shook Hanna and said, "Hanna. Wake up. You're dreaming."

Hanna opened her eyes, catching a glimpse of Cordelle, and inconspiciously scooted away from Wright.

Cordelle said, singsongy, "Good morning, Hanna."

Hanna propped up on her elbow and said, "Morning, Cordelle," in a droggy voice. She lay back flat on her back, still looking at Cordelle.

"Did you have a rough night, honey?" Cordelle asked.

"Yes, ma'am. Pretty rough."

"Now, we can send you to a doctor for some help if you need it," Cordelle assured her.

Hanna replied quickly, "No, ma'am. I'm okay." Wright had told her the story of Lanny Jones. At the time Wright was five and Lanny about forty, Lanny had managed and sharecropped Bennie J.'s farmland. Lanny had been buddy-buddy with Wright, letting him ride up on his big Case tractors and taking him down to the crossroads for Dr. Peppers. Lanny had gotten in a bad way and had gone to a doctor, seeking help. He'd gotten sent down to Brice's Mental Institute in Tuscaloosa and given some shock treatments. When he'd come home he'd stuck the end of a twelve-gauge Winchester automatic shotgun in his mouth and blown his brains out. Wright and Winn had concluded emotional help and doctors didn't belong in the same breath together.

Cordelle looked at her watch and then back to Wright and Hanna. "I'd like to stay and chat but I've got to get going. I'll see y'all gators later."

Hanna and Wright said, "Later, gator."

Cordelle turned to go out and saw the bottle again. She said, "If y'all ever started drinking or taking drugs they'd just have to take me on down to Tuscaloosa to the funny house."

Cordelle left, closing the door behind her.

When Wright thought he could hear her walking across Big Room downstairs, he kicked the covers up in the air and said, "If you went to Tuscaloosa you could get Alabama-Auburn tickets."

3 Bennie J. said, "If they went to Tuscaloosa they could get Alabama-Auburn tickets. If I's a young man with the opportunity to get a college education wouldn't but one place I'd go. University of Alabama. Can't get Alabama-Auburn tickets going to LSU. Shit. I don't know what them kids want to go off to Baton Rouge for."

Bennie J. was dipping the dead minnows out of the minnow pools at the back of the bait shop. Wendell Laves was leaned up against a post, sucking his teeth.

Wendell Laves said, "Winn goes to LSU, don't she?"

Bennie J. didn't especially give a shit about Wendell Laves but liked him all right for somebody who stopped in to hang around the marina. Wendell liked trying to be buddies with Bennie J., liked to tell people how he had just come from Bennie J.'s Bait Shop talking with Bennie J. But that really didn't make for much clout because Bennie J. would complain about his kids to anybody who would listen and sympathize.

Bennie J. said, "Yeah. Winn been to seven colleges and universities in the South. Alabama. Florida State. Auburn. Tennessee. Ole Miss. Vanderbilt. And now LSU. Don't know why she didn't want to stay at Tuscaloosa. Hell, I told her she was going to college, not on a damn tour. I ain't letting Wright and Hanna shit around transferring and changing their majors like Winn done. Bless her heart." Bennie J. laughed. "Poor little girl can't make up her mind where she wants to go. She'll be home tonight. I sure do miss my little girl."

"What kin is Hanna? She's a Remington, ain't she?"

Bennie J. slung a dead minnow out onto the dirt service road that came up to the back of the bait shop. He said, "Hanna is Cordelle's sister Coleen's little girl."

"Aw."

"Yeah. She just finished Sumpter College. Wright just finished high school. Tryin' to git some work out of 'em but all they do is lay up sleep, go to the picture show, and ride around in them skitters."

"Wright's all right," Wendell Laves assured him, even though he only knew what Wright looked like and hadn't been around him much in five years. "He don't take no shit off'n nobody."

"Yeah. But he won't stand hitched. Here one minute. Off in them skitters with Hanna next minute. Got a farm, house need tended to, trailer courts. And now it's the big season for the bait shop and grill, the whole marina here. Bennie J. needs help. He can't do all this by hisself," Bennie J. said, referring to himself in the third person as he often did.

Wendell agreed, "Yeah," took out a knife, and started picking one of his back molars.

"And can't git him out of bed in the mornings. He ought to took Mama Dog Midnight to Howard's dog's funeral. Cordelle had to take her."

Wendell said, "Looks like you'd take Mama Dog Midnight to the coon dog funeral."

"Me?" Bennie J. responded quickly like Wendell was stupid. "I guess I'm gone have to go to my own funeral someday but, by God, I'm gone be late for it."

Bennie J. set the minnow net down and propped his knee up on one of the pool walls. He took a top-bound spiral notebook, where he kept a record of money owed him, out of his hip pocket. He rested the notebook on his thigh, and while chewing feverishly on a wooden match he wrote down on a clean page all the whiskey that would be needed for the Coon-on-a-log.

Even as he was scribbling away with Wendell Laves ten feet away making conversation, Bennie J. was preoccupied. A troublesome thought had been festering in his mind for over a year, and especially since Wright had graduated high school.

He wondered if he'd made his money too fast. He got annoyed with himself for thinking such a thing, for coming to so irrational a conclusion to explain everything that was wrong. He knew there was no way to make too much money nor to make it too fast. But he had done something too fast, or skipped some kind of steps. Maybe he let Cordelle spend too much money. Not that it cut into their empire. "Take a look at Terrel and them," he would say aloud to himself as he pondered all this, driving to the marina in his pickup. Terrel was a moonshiner, bootlegger, and antique dealer who lived on the other side of the Tennessee state line. He might not be as wealthy as Bennie J., but Bennie J. figured he was worth a couple of million anyway. Terrel had personally confided to Bennie J. that he had a hundred thousand dollars in lard cans full of 1923 silver dollars buried out around in the hills. And his kids, two sons and a daughter, weren't transferring from college to college. They were staying around, getting married when they turned twenty and building three-bedroom brick houses on Terrel's land. Terrel and his wife lived in a three-bedroom, one-story brick house with a basement. Not any of this damn Parthenon shit. Maybe that was part of the trouble. And Terrel's kids, they went up to Nashville and bought nice clothes. Where did Wright and Winn shop—up at the hardware store, bought navy bellbottom jeans and denim work shirts. Shit.

Here he was, he had built an empire and already it had started to decay down to the way the Thomas family had. Wealthiest, most aristocratic family in Sumpter County for two hundred years, and now Bennie J. bet he could match two dollars for every one of J.C.'s. All that was left of the family was J.C. and Lou Ann. They had two kids and one of them got killed in war when he was eighteen. Shit, J.C. couldn't even keep all his family alive. Only Kathy

Lee was left, and J.C. and Lou Ann were about to ship her way off North to college.

And damn if his own family wasn't turning out worse than J.C.'s. He was going to have to stay on top of Wright. Wright wouldn't have no more damn sense than to get drafted and go over and get killed in some shit war. Bennie J. couldn't figure Wright out. He made straight As he didn't have to half-ass study for; and everybody was always trying to kiss his ass. But did Wright appreciate it? Hell, naw. Wright didn't hunt, fish, wouldn't stand hitched at the marina, didn't give a shit about farming, didn't even know what he would major in in college, didn't give a shit. All Bennie J. knew was that Wright better let the citizens of Sumpter County and its district elect him to the U.S. House of Representatives or, by God, he wouldn't have a job. If Wright didn't start applying himself to something he was going to turn out worse than J.C. The people of Sumpter had put a lot of stock in Wright, given him a lot of attention, adored him. He had better, by God, be thinking about putting something back. He had better think twice about transferring around colleges, getting himself killed in a shit war, or not coming back to Sumpter long enough to get elected to go to Washington.

Bennie J. was thinking how he had bust his ass all his life to what—in three months him and Cordelle would be sitting by themselves in a damn Parthenon in the middle of a thousand-acre estate. And what could they do? Get in Cordelle's black hearse-looking Cadillac and drive a few miles over to J.C. and Lou Ann's, who were sitting by themselves in a damn three-story medieval antebellum mansion in the middle of a thousand-acre estate. They could all sit and drink coffee and talk about their children touring around the world doing a semester at every college in the world, but wouldn't ever come back to Sumpter to do any damn work.

Wendell Laves said, "You got to git 'em while they still cryin'."

"What?" Bennie J. said, looking over at Wendell, wondering for a moment what that had to do with anything he was thinking. He put the notebook back into his pocket.

"Six months ago Buford Adams spent four hundred dollars burying his brother and then last month spent five hundred dollars burying his coon dog. Got to git 'em while they still cryin'. What most folks don't understand is when they burying that coon dog they burying him for everybody they ever knowed to die. They just ain't burying that coon dog, hell naw," Wendell said and then spit.

"I try to tell my boy. I say, Wright, you got to figure what people want and git it right then. People got money and all they wantin' is some reason to give it to ya. This I'll-have-it-later ain't worth a shit. Folks want things right now. But Wright won't listen."

A red MGA with the stereo blaring out a Doors song came barreling up to the back of the bait shop.

Bennie J. said, "The longer his hair gets I think the deafer he gits."

The music was cut, then the engine. Mama Dog Midnight was sitting up in the passenger's seat of the small two-seater convertible.

Bennie J. looked through the chicken wire that encaged the back area of the bait shop. He hollered, "There's my man! Finally." Bennie J. smiled and watched Wright let Mama Dog out of the car.

Wright opened the back door that was made of two-by-fours and chicken wire. He and Midnight walked through. Wright said, "Mornin', Doddy!"

"Mornin', Wright!"

Mama Dog came up to Bennie J. and sat down, raised up her right paw. Bennie J. started shaking her paw. "Mama Dog. You git to ride in the skitter this morning?" Then Bennie J. asked Wright, "Where's Hanna?"

"She coming up behind me." Wright said to Wendell, "Mornin'."

Wendell said, "Hell, boy. It ain't mornin'. Damn near afternoon. I already had a funeral. And Coon-on-a-log ain't but a couple a hours away."

Wright stared at Wendell, gave him the evil eye. There were supposedly two and a half billion people on the planet and out of that two and a half billion there was only one that Wright let get away with talking smart to him—Bennie J. When a green MGA came barreling around to the back of the building it gave Wendell an excuse to give a little grin and say, "This must be your cousin."

Bennie J. said, almost singing, "Yeah. Here comes old Hanna Belle. Old Hanna Belle."

Hanna got out, came through the back door, said "Hello" to Wendell, and then walked on over to Bennie J. They hugged each other.

Bennie J. said, "How's my sweetheart doing? I heard you had a rough night."

Hanna said, kind of whining, "I'm okay. We came downstairs and Mae Emma wasn't there."

"Mae Emma's got to run the concession for the Coon-on-a-log."

"I tried to cook something but I burned the eggs. Mama Dog Midnight wouldn't even eat them. It was terrible."

There was a pause in the conversation. Wendell interjected, "I'm goin' in here git me a Co-Cola. Anybody want one?"

Bennie J. said, "Naw, thanks, Wendell."

Wendell liked hearing Bennie J. say his name. He walked through the heavy wooden door into the bait shop.

Bennie J. was rocking Hanna as he kept on hugging her. He said, "Winn'll be home about eight tonight. Hot dig. We'll have a shindig. I'll have all my younguns home. Just wisht I could keep 'em home." Bennie J. let go of Hanna and said to her and Wright, "Y'all go on over to the grill and get you a good breakfast. A body needs a good breakfast. And move y'all skitters from the back here. Old man Finney's bringing some minnow and worms in a little while. Some of the Redstone Arsenal Yankees don't have any better sense than to fish with minnows this time of year."

After Hanna had hopped into her car, Bennie J. reached into his dress pants pockets. There were splatters of minnow pool water across the front and legs of his pants. Bennie J. worked in, fished in, rode around the farm in dress pants. He'd worn all the denim he cared to during the Depression. He pulled out a roll of cash, started peeling off hundreds and twenties, handing them to Wright. He gave him the little notepaper. "I want you and Hanna to take you skitters up to Terrel's and git a coupla loads a whiskey."

There was little Wright liked to do more than drive across the Alabama-Tennessee line hauling a load of whiskey, but every time he did he liked to remind Bennie J. it was a federal offense. It was some kind of bargaining point, Wright didn't exactly know how. He said, "Doddy, you know it's a federal offense to take untaxed alcohol across state lines. Me and Hanna plan on goin' to New Orleans and stay at Aunt Coleen's a week or so for a vacation before we start at LSU. And we won't be able to go to the French Quarter if we in the penitentiary."

"Wright! This is a thirsty city!" Bennie J. hollered.

Midnight looked up, panting and smiling at Bennie J. She had heard this plenty. She lay down up against the cool concrete minnow pool.

"I can get anything in this town fixed. You know that," Bennie J. said.

Most people referred to "town" as Sumpter City, the county seat of Sumpter. Sumpter City had a population of 12,000, was ten miles northeast of Big House, which was three miles north of the marina.

But Bennie J. referred to the whole county this side of the Tennessee River and even a little ways into Tennessee as "this town." Bennie J. continued, "This is a thirsty city! Everbody got money they want to give you. Only trouble is you have to git out and be there to be the one they give they money to."

"I know, Doddy. I know," Wright said before Bennie J. finished. Wright knew Bennie J. didn't like to be cut off when he was giving a talking-to, but Wright was hungry and wanted to look at Hanna some more. He couldn't get enough of looking at her long black hair that came down straight to the top of her butt. He accidently sat on it sometimes, one of the only few things he did that made Hanna snap at him. She looked very tall to Wright, though they were the same height. They, plus Cordelle and Coleen, were all five eight and a half. Since Bennie J. was six foot, Wright hoped he would soon grow another couple inches.

Bennie J. looked at Wright seriously for the first time this morning and asked, "What's wrong with you cousin?"

"Nothing," Wright said, surprised, wondering what Bennie J. was getting at and if Bennie J. knew what he was thinking.

"Somethin's eatin' at her. I can tell. She ain't said nothing to you?"

"No, sir."

Bennie J. looked down at Mama Dog and then back up to Wright. "You sister be home soon. Maybe she can find out what's matter with Hanna."

"She act the same to me, Doddy. I don't think nothing the matter with her," Wright said. Cordelle and especially Winn made Wright speak proper English, but when he was with his daddy alone for five minutes he slipped back into dialect.

"Naw," said Bennie J. as he spat out the wooden match he had gnawed to a pulp. "Somethin's eatin' at her. I can tell." He took out a pack of Doublemint and motioned a piece to Wright, but Wright shook his head.

"Doddy, she just graduate at Sumpter College for Women. Guess she glad to be done with that. Guess she glad to be done with that boardin' school stuff."

"Naw, naw." Bennie J. was chomping the gum like he was trying to get the flavor out of it as fast as he could. "You mama, you auntie, you sister graduate from Sumpter College for Women. They don't act different when they finish." Bennie J. stopped talking to lean up and scratch his back on one of the four-by-four posts. "But she is actin'

a little bit like her mama acted one time. Her mama started drinkin',
then tried to kill herself. Hanna Belle ain't been doin' anything funny,
has she? Beside havin' them nightmares?"

"Doddy! You startin' to worry worse than Mama Cordelle."

"I reckon you right, Wright," Bennie J. sighed. "Her having those
nightmares sure worries me. You got to stay on top of things. That's
how come Doddy Bennie J. have him an empire. That how come you
an' Hanna an' Winn can run around town do what you want, go out
with who you want, associate with who you want, act like little darlings. How come? Cause Doddy Bennie J. work hard and stay on top
of things. Wright, it's a thirsty city."

Bennie J. spit his chewed-out chewing gum into the minnow pool
on the right. One of Bennie J.'s five-pound pet catfishes, Dude or
Dandy, boiled up and hit the chewing gum. Bennie J. reached into
his pocket, pulled out two more fifties, and handed them to Wright.
Bennie J. said, "Here, give Hanna one of these, it's for gas money, and
use the rest to buy yourselves something. Maybe go up to Mr. Bernstein and get some clothes. "Speakin' of Mr. Bernstein, where's
Mama Cordelle?"

Wright had begun to go out the back door. He turned and said,
"She went up to Bernstein's to get some new shoes."

"New shoes. Hell, I'm gone git Mr. Bernstein out the house sell
him some shoes. Mama Cordelle got more shoes than all the stores
in town put together."

Wright waved and walked on to his car as Bennie J. was saying,
"The kids I can't git to buy new clothes, but Mama Cordelle, can't
stop her. Shit. Shit. Shit."

Wendell walked back out with a six-ounce Coca-Cola and a couple
of big Jackson cookies. He said, "I ran into Marlow Jacobs," like he
was apologizing for having been gone so long.

"I reckon old Marlow be after them Shellcrackers today," Bennie
J. said.

Wendell watched Wright's car pull away. "What does Wright's car
tag say?"

"Wild-1. Hanna's says Wild-2. And Winn's says Fast-1. When
Winn had that skitter that Hanna's driving now, she had me call
down to Senator Haggard, git him to pass a bill so Alabama would
make specialty plates. Sometimes Winn's political minded."

Wendell nodded and asked, "Where'd they git them little foreign-
looking cars anyhow?"

"Jerry Lee found them somewhere."

"Jerry Lee's all right."

"I kept Jerry Lee out of the penitentary five times. He don't ever start no trouble. But if somebody wantin' to git beat to a thread of they life, they have a way of findin' Jerry Lee."

"He's one of them good McAllisters. Not one of the sorry bunch," Wendell said, as if Jerry Lee had overcome insurmountable odds.

"Yeah. He was the best whiskey runner there ever was."

"What's he do now?"

"Who? Jerry Lee?" Bennie J. said like Wendell was being stupid. "Jerry Lee can do anything he wants to."

"But mostly?"

"All kind of jobs. But mostly rebuilding Chevy engines in the old shed back of his house."

"Oh," Wendell said. "Well, his fingernails are never dirty, to be rebuilding engines."

"I guess he knows how to clean them," Bennie J. almost hollered. He was getting tired of Wendell's dumb-ass comments. That and the fact Bennie J. didn't have any immediate need to complain about his kids to anybody now, he was ready for Wendell to go on.

4   At the Coon-on-a-log there must have been over two hundred people milling around, talking, laughing, most of them drinking. The air was charged with excitement over the gambling that was about to occur. At the backwaters of the Tennessee River was a clearing on the bank that made an arch, almost a natural water arena. Out in the four-foot-deep water two fence posts were fixed six feet apart. Loosely lashed to the posts was a big log, floating on the water. On that log a chained raccoon ran back and forth. He jumped off the log, but the chain only allowed him a couple of yards. He swam back, climbed onto the log, and shook off like a dog. Fifty feet away two men sat in a flat-bottom wooden boat.

Jerry Lee was walking around with a whiskey glass full of gin and tonic. He wore his sporting dress clothes: Levi's, cowboy boots, long-sleeved white cotton shirt with open collar, and a brown suede western-cut blazer that accentuated his hard muscular build. He was tanned and clean shaven. His shoulder-length hair was raven black and shone in the sun.

Jerry Lee sauntered to the water's edge and stared at the raccoon walking back and forth on the log, annoyed with the chain. Nothing had happened yet. Jerry Lee walked back through the crowd. A man, short, fat, and half-drunk, pushed at him and yelled, "You a hippie? I thank you need a haircut."

Jerry Lee just stood firm and said in a bored manner, "Oh, mister, you got me mixed up with somebody else."

"Who's that I got you mixed up with?"

"You got me mixed up with somebody that gives a shit what you think." Jerry Lee walked on aimlessly, until he heard someone call his name.

It was Cordelle, decked out in white. She didn't look an hour over forty and looked worth every penny of the five million bucks she could have scraped up any week of the year. He said to himself, like daughter, like mother, like younger sister. Hold on, J.L. You don't need gittin' killed off just yet.

Cordelle walked up to Jerry Lee, and they exchanged kisses. Jerry Lee said, "Cordelle, you must be the loveliest lady in all of Sumpter County." He knew he meant the world, but knew Sumpter County sounded more flattering.

"More, J.L. You are such a charmer."

"Gin does tend to loosen up my social graces."

Cordelle thought it was cute the way Jerry Lee drank gin. But if she had seen one of her kids with a can of beer she would have thought they had found it on the side of the road, scalded out the can, and were drinking water out of it to be play-acting. If she had found out it was really beer they would have to send her down to Tuscaloosa.

She said, "I love your hair. It looks like a recording star. Wright is letting his hair grow out a bit now that he's not in school. It's driving B.J. crazy."

"Yeah, there comes a time in a young man's life he got to let his hair flow. But I'm getting to be an old man. Not like Wright."

"Oh, Jerry Lee. You're just a child. Got a whole lifetime of living ahead of you. Don't give me this old man stuff."

Jerry Lee took another sip of gin to see if it would pacify him from wanting to throw her dress up. He smiled at Cordelle.

"Jer, sweetheart, I've got to get over there," Cordelle said and started walking away. "Now you're going to be there on time tonight, aren't you?"

"Oh, yes, ma'am."

"I don't know exactly when Winn will arrive, but I need you to stay long enough for us to do 'Summertime.' Then you go on if you have a date. Oh, just bring your date over to Big House."

"No, ma'am. I don't have a date."

"And all those girls out there just dying for you. You're such a devil, Jerry Lee," Cordelle said, and scampered on away to where the people were crowding around the waterside.

Jerry Lee watched her until she was lost in among the crowd. Then he heard a man hollering, "Goddammit, Blue! Attack! Come straight in. Don't circle!" Others began hollering. Jerry Lee walked over to the edge of the bank and looked. A coon dog was swimming around the log. It came up to the log. The raccoon jumped onto the dog's head, starting to drown it. The two men in the boat paddled to the log. The man at the bow slipped on large black electrician's gloves.

Jerry Lee turned around and headed toward the concession Mae Emma ran. He had tried gambling, legally and illegally, and though he was fairly lucky at winning he never got much excitement out of it. He had given it every chance to take hold of him. He had fucked, fought, and raised hell till he had won medals, but gambling just never took his interest.

He walked up to the concession, laid his glass on the table. "Hey, Mae Emma. Could you fill me up?"

"Hey, baby," Mae Emma said. She was selling barbecue sandwiches. While Jerry Lee waited, he watched Mama Dog Midnight. She was under the concession table eating a baked chicken. Another coon dog came up sniffing. Midnight snapped at him, and he scurried away.

Mae Emma pulled a bottle of gin out of a washtub full of ice, Nesbit Oranges, and NuGrape Sodas. She poured some in Jerry Lee's glass and began pulling out Nesbit Oranges for some kids.

"See you when my glass is empty," Jerry Lee said and walked on, Mae Emma hollering to him he best just take the bottle if he was going to be bothering the shit out of her every time he slugged down four ounces of gin. He noticed a kid taking a bite out of a barbecue sandwich, then a slug of his Nesbit, spilling most of it down the front of his T-shirt that had a picture of a skunk on it that read "I'm a little stinker." The kid held out his sandwich to look down at his shirt, and the dog Midnight ran up and snatched the sandwich out of his hand. Jerry Lee figured the kid could use a taste of his gin but spared himself the temptation.

For thirty minutes he walked around, watching them pull new coons out of the cage to put on the log. Watched people make bets. Some cool, some in a wild frenzy, a few in despair. Ordinarily the dog wouldn't have had a chance against a coon, but somehow chaining it to a log put the coon to a disadvantage. But still folks would bet on the coon.

Finally he ran into Bennie J., who ambled away from the crowd along a swampy creek that emptied into the slough. Jerry Lee followed in silence. Then Bennie J. stopped and looked at Jerry Lee. Bennie J. said, "Got that ready for Hanna yet?"

"Just about, Bennie J." Jerry Lee knew Bennie J. like a book, knew he was worried about something, He knew Bennie J. would be cryptic, but Jerry Lee wouldn't pry the matter.

"Good. Good." Bennie J. looked off into the creek and then said, "Listen, Jerry Lee. It's time we told the kids the whole truth. Before they go off to college. You know, they deserve to know. It's not right not letting them know the whole truth."

Jerry Lee didn't see the big deal about it. He said, "You right, Bennie J.. But they probably already know."

"How?" Bennie J. asked quickly, looking up at Jerry Lee.

"I don't know." Jerry Lee knew Bennie J. to be a very smart man, a wizard in fact. He was a self-taught mathematical genius, knew the ways of the woods, knew the workings of political power. But when it came to his own kids, Bennie J. was naïve, downright dumb sometimes.

When Bennie J. kept staring at him, Jerry Lee added, "Maybe not, but you know how some of the busybodies in this town can talk. Over the years they might have got wind of something."

Bennie J. nodded, then reached up and gripped Jerry Lee's shoulder. He turned and walked back toward the crowd. Jerry Lee walked alongside, knowing that was all Bennie J. would say of the matter.

Bennie J. said in a lighter tone. "What a day, Jerry Lee. Hot damn. Two dogs drownt." He motioned to Jerry Lee. "You hear the money Cordelle puttin' down?"

"Heard she won a couple Gs already."

"Yeah. She's got the touch," Bennie J. said and smiled.

"That's for sure," Jerry Lee agreed. So has her daughter, he thought to himself but tried not to think about it with Bennie J. right there, for Jerry Lee sometimes believed his thoughts were too loud and his imagination too vivid to hide.

5 It's a thirsty city!" Hanna hollered. She had drunk a third of a pint of gin in the last hour.

Terrel said, "It is. And thank God Sumpter's a dry county!" He giggled.

The green MGA was parked in the barn. A man in overalls was loading the trunk with cases of whiskey, pints of moonshine, and fifths of Jack Daniel's Black Label. Another man had the hose to an air compressor, filling the air shocks Jerry Lee had put on the back of the MGAs. Terrel, Wright, and Hanna were standing at the barn door watching. Hanna was holding on to Wright's arm. She had all her hair stuffed up in a fedora, and had a pink scarf fixed into an ascot around her neck. She let go of Wright and got into her car.

The man loading the car said to the other, "You kin git more in the trunks of these little scampers than you'd thank." Then he closed the trunk lid cautiously, tipped his hat to Hanna. He said to Terrel, "I'm goin' out to still number two. I be in 'bout sundown."

"Aright, Jess. I'll have Scutter bring ye some dinner."

Jess and the other man left out the back of the barn. Hanna cranked her car, eased out the barn, then slowly cruised down the dirt road. Wright peeled off some money, gave it to Terrel. Terrel stuffed it down in his pocket without counting it. They watched Hanna disappear around the bend.

Terrel said, "Yeah. All the Reynolds womenfolk got the good looks. Didn't leave nothing for you and old Bennie J." Terrel giggled like he had just said the funniest possible of all things.

"Well, Terrel, I think you got your share of that ugly stick beatin' yourself. Don't be talking about me," Wright said, though he knew himself not to be ugly, and Terrel was handsome in his own rugged sort of way. Terrel was seventy-two, been making whiskey since he was ten. He didn't look a day over sixty. His left knee didn't bend well, making him walk with a slight gimp. But other than that Terrel moved like a man of forty. It was almost an honor just to know Terrel; Wright could sense that it pleased Bennie J. that he took a liking to Wright and spoke highly of him. As Bennie J. put it, Terrel was a legend. Wright had often seriously wondered why Terrel's picture was never on the cover of *Newsweek* or something like that.

Terrel laughed. "Yeuh. I done got whooped up side de head with that ugly stick. But you know—beauty's only skin deep, ugly's to the bone, beauty fades away, but ugly holds its own."

Wright chuckled. They walked toward Wright's loaded-up MGA.

Terrel put his arm around Wright's shoulder as they walked. "You gone be going off the end of the summer."

Wright didn't feel like telling him that the end of the summer seemed like a lifetime away, that he didn't want to go off to college, that he didn't know if he could ever really leave Big House. Wright just said, "Yes, sir?"

"You gone go to college. Probably end up in Washington. Who knows? But one thang's for shore. You the cream of the crop. Yessir-ree. Never let it be said that Wright Reynolds ain't the cream of the crop." Terrel stopped walking, took his hand off Wright's shoulder. "Wright, don't ever forget your friends."

Wright stood there, kind of confused, wondering what that had to do with anything. Wanting to ask how you *could* forget your friends. But Terrel turned and headed back to his house. Wright could have sworn Terrel had started to cry.

The car was light, but backheavy with the load; still Wright took the curves at over fifty miles an hour on the narrow winding Tennessee road. Often he and Hanna played chase here, but right now he didn't care if he caught up to her or not. His mind was pondering this House of Representatives thing, trying to get to the genus of it. Every year he was voted president of his class, though he had no leadership attributes to his knowledge. Two incidents from his childhood stuck out in his mind. In each one he had been surrounded by the town's fathers. Once in the early sixties he had sat on top of a parking meter, eating an ice cream sandwich and staring up at the top of the courthouse steps. The sidewalks were crowded, the streets were crowded. Everyone's eyes and ears were on a small man who was giving a speech. The man yelled now and then, the crowd yelled and clapped and roared often. The speaker's name was George Wallace, a judge with plans of being governor. Wright had finished his ice cream, hopped down off the parking meter, and found Bennie J. with a group of political figures all witnessing this little man's speech and the fervor he was creating in the crowd. Wright had said matter-of-factly, "That man's going to be famous." The crowd around Bennie J. stood silent, staring at Wright, like the Holy Ghost had spoken from his mouth.

The other incident made an even bigger impression on Wright. He was only five at the time. Again, he was with Bennie J. and a group of state politicians. They were at a large private affair for Big Jim Folsum. Big Jim was sitting down. Wright happened to walk by and Big Jim stuck out his hand. Wright, dressed in a suit, shook it. Big

Jim had said, "Senator Reynolds. Yes, sir, you are going to make one fine senator." A quiet fell over the place. Everyone's attention went to Wright and the seemingly divine premonition pronounced by a drunk but still credible Big Jim.

Wright took a sharp curve doing forty-five. He could see the road go down the mountainside in front of him and stretch across a valley for about a mile before it climbed another mountain. But he didn't see Hanna.

All this representative and senator stuff didn't really add up for Wright. He sometimes thought there was a Heart of Dixie Book of the Dead in which it was stated, "And there will be a young man born of a wealthy family, surrounded by beautiful kin, and his name will be Wright. And he shall become Representative of the House. It is the will of God." If folks of Sumpter wanted him to go to Washington, that was fine with him. He just wished they knew he hardly had the guts to leave Big House.

As Wright was crossing the Alabama-Tennessee state line, he looked in his rearview mirror. Hanna was on his tail. She was holding her hat to keep it from blowing off. She took it off and her hair exploded out with the wind. Wright kept glancing into his rearview. Now she had both hands fixing her hair into a ponytail, obviously steering the car with her left knee the way she so expertly could do. Soon they were on the flat dirt roads near the backwaters. Wright could see the clearing and the people. He spotted Hawk Higgins pacing behind the trunk of his '59 Pontiac. He could tell Hawk was down to his last couple of bottles. Hawk was worried he would run out and then have to hear Bennie J.'s speech about not running out of stuff, of having things when people wanted them, not later. Bennie J. didn't believe in missing any sales.

Wright whipped around on one side of the Pontiac and parked, Hanna on the other. A huge cloud of dust rolled between Hawk and his Pontiac and drifted out across the slough.

Wright and Hanna were opening up their trunks when Hawk grinned and said, "Boss, you just in time. I's down to the last bottle of Jack Black." Hawk was about to carry on some more about how Wright was always just in time, but Judy Yarborough walked up and said, "Hey, Hawk. Gimme a bottle a Jack Black." Judy was a man; people who had known Judy all his life wondered why other people would name a girl Judy.

Hawk asked, "Jack Black?" questioning not Judy so much as what he had just heard. Judy had always drunk shine.

Judy said, "Yeuh, Hawk. I's dranking that wildcat whiskey and it come to me like a streak out of the blue. I deserve me some Jack Daniel's Black Label. It come to me right over there." Judy pointed out the location where he had received his awakening.

Hawk put a fifth of Jack Black in a brown paper bag and sold it to Judy. Hanna and Wright were putting the cases of whiskey over in Hawk's faded green trunk. All of a sudden they heard yelping from over toward the creek. Shortly a coon dog ran out of the thicket, hollering and yelping. He ran for about a hundred yards and fell down. A crowd soon was gathering around the dog.

Judy said, "Much obliged, Hawk. I'm goin' over here see what's a matter."

Hawk started unloading Hanna's car, mumbling, "Everybody drinkin' Jack Black. Nobody wants any good corn squeezings anymore."

Wright and Hanna stopped unloading to stare at the large crowd that had now gathered. Wright said, "Hey, Hawk. We'll be back later." He and Hanna walked over to the crowd, then edged around the outside of it, but couldn't tell anything. Wright took Hanna's hand and worked through the people. Hanna spotted Bennie J. and they went over and stood on either side of him.

Wright asked, "What happened?"

Bennie J. said, "Thangs gone crazy. Two dogs got drownt. One coon been killed. Jerry Lee done beat hell out of two men. You Mama won three thousand dollars aready. And now Teke Stanton's dog done got out wandering in the swamp, got bit by some cottonmouths. Don't know why come he to git wandering off like that. Dead."

They stared at Teke's dog. He was starting to bloat. Teke Stanton was kneeled over him in misery, stroking his neck.

Wright had often heard stories about someone waterskiing in the backwaters, dropping to let someone else ski, and sinking down into a bed of cottonmouths. Or someone going swimming in the backwaters and diving into a bed of cottonmouths. The stories started out different but ended up identical. At first the victim hollered he was tangled up in some barbed wire. Soon discovered he was in a bed of snakes. Yelled for everyone else to stay out of the water. Was pulled out. But died before anyone could get him in the boat or to the hospital.

No one was saying much, just staring at the dog and at Teke. Wright said low to Bennie J., "We got the haul to Hawk."

"Good," Bennie J. replied. He walked away from the gathering, Wright and Hanna at his sides. "Look, I come over in *Fast Boat.*"

Bennie J. said. "She's up in those willows the other side of Hawk. Go to the marina and get some more barbecue and Nesbit Oranges." He threw up his arms. "Nesbit Orange. Nesbit Orange. Everthang is Nesbit Orange. Can't give a damn Grape away. It's funny. Got to have what folks want. And got to have it right then."

Several people were trickling away from the dog and going over to the concession. In the midst of the small group, Wright saw a tall, black, slim body which was Mae Emma, and started walking toward her.

Hanna tugged at Bennie J., who was looking at the crowd. He looked back to her and gave her a hug. "What, sweetheart?"

"When I get back with Wright from the marina, I want to talk to you."

Bennie J. smiled and nodded, almost certain she was going to tell him what had been eating at her. They stood there in silence, their arms around each other.

The crowd around Teke's dog had dispersed now, moving over to the water's edge for another event. But Bennie J. and Hanna stood looking at Teke, in the distance, sitting in his pickup truck. The door was open; his hands were on the upper part of the steering wheel, his head down on his hands. Wendell Laves was standing before Teke, talking.

Bennie J. said, "That son of a bitch is selling another hole to put a dog in."

6 | Hanna taxied the eighteen-foot inboard-outboard ski boat into the marina. Wright stepped up through the walk-through windshield to the bow of the boat, even though Hanna was carefully easing *Fast Boat* up broadside to the slip near the back of the bait shop, where they kept *Fast Boat* or Bennie J.'s bass fishing boat, *Croppie 1*, when they were about to use either one.

Wright and Hanna got out and walked along the dock beside the bait shop. Two guys Wright had graduated high school with were in a ski boat that was waiting up near the pumps, fueling. Daughtery Adams weighed 240 and had been all-state. He was University of

Alabama–bound to play football for Bear Bryant. Eddie Young was six foot, but only a little heavier than Wright. He had been going out with Kathy Lee since last September. He was headed to Ole Miss, supposedly going to play baseball there, but Eddie was going to do a lot of things Wright never saw happen.

Wright noticed their neat shorts, knit shirts, haircuts. They almost looked like a couple of Redstone Arsenal Yankees. He said, "Hey, Daughtery. Eddie," and Hanna said hi to them both.

Eddie and Daughtery looked up as if they were being disturbed. Eddie said, "Oh, hi. It's the"—he paused, gave a little smirk—"cousins."

Daughtery said, "I heard y'all were having a fund-raiser for the humane society today."

Hanna and Wright were right alongside the boat now. Wright stopped. Hanna couldn't tell if he was going to stare a hole through Daughtery or jump down on him in the boat.

Finally Eddie said, "We're going out skiing."

Wright said, "All y'all gone do is shit and fall back in it." He stood there a few seconds in case they wanted to start anything and walked on finally with Hanna beside him. Wright imagined Eddie chiding Daughtery, "Why didn't you whip his ass? You can take him." As he held the door of the Grill open for Hanna, he imagined Daughtery starting at his back, taking the fuel nozzle out of the gas tank, saying, "Yeah, I can whip his ass. But I want a lot of people I know to see me do it. And I might just do it before I go off to football training." Sometimes Wright picked up on stuff like that, and every time he wondered if it was just his imagination inventing a scenario, or if that thing was really happening. According to Greer, it was probably really happening. But Greer Yarborough lived with one foot in this plane, whatever that was, and one foot in some twilight zone where ninety-year-old black moonshine cookers got free admission.

The Grill was on the opposite side of the marina from the bait shop. A straight line between the two would have cut the harbor of boats in half. The Grill, a wooden-frame building, sat dockside. Running the length inside was a twenty-two-stool counter. Seven booths and two tables filled the rest of the customer area.

Now about half the stools and four booths were taken. Several people waved or nodded at Wright and Hanna, and a big teenage black boy walked out from the back to greet them. "Hey, man, Hanna. How's it going, gang?"

After Hanna assured Jake things were just fine, Wright handed him the order.

Wright and Hanna sat down at the corner booth by the window. Wright stared at Daughtery and Eddie cruising out of the marina. "In elementary school," Wright said, "me and Daughtery were big buddies. He'd come out to Big House, we'd ride horses and shit. Daughtery's always been big. He'd take up for me at school. Then come along junior high, he turned into a pure-D shitass."

Hanna nodded. "Daughtery seems nice enough. But that Eddie. Something about him seems slimy. He reminds me of those con men and pimps and such in New Orleans."

Wright nodded. They stared silently at the boats in the marina, neither thinking anymore of Daughtery or Eddie. Jake slid a plate onto their table with a couple of cheeseburgers and two Sun-Drops, and had walked away before they realized it. Jake must have snuck two burgers off the grill that were meant for someone else.

They began eating, still quiet, staring out at the boats. Wright thought of when he was a kid. Just like he could invent what Daughtery had been saying, he could look out at the marina and turn back time twelve years. It was night. Commercial fishing boats coming in loaded down with moonshine. Brand-new fast '57 Chevys being loaded up. Old Fords being loaded up. Moonshine upriver, moonshine downriver. There in the middle is Doddy Bennie J., sitting in his old unpainted office in the bait shop, hundred-watt light bulb shining. Small smoke-filled office. (Back then Bennie J. smoked.) Smell of cigarettes mixed with that of pipes, Prince Albert, and cigars, Tampa Nuggets mostly. Stacks of twenties, stacks of fives, flour sacks of old silver dollars. Some of the old moonshiners up in the hills only traded in silver, didn't trust paper money. Bennie J. buying, Bennie J. selling, Bennie J. raking in the dough. Bootleggers bringing Bennie J. presents: cured hams, Civil War buckles, automatic pistols, shotguns, collector edition Winchester pocket knives.

Wright flipped to another scene. Daytime. Big Pete. (Bennie J. hadn't talked about him much in the last couple of years.) Some called Bennie J. the last of the breed. But Bennie J. called Big Pete one of a kind, and the last of the breed, and the last of the era. Unlike Bennie J., his protégé, Pete was flamboyant. Six-five, 300 pounds, seersucker suit, gold watch chain, Panama hat, Tampa Nugget cigar, ten carats of D-grade diamonds on his fingers, spit-shined shoes, a barber shop shave, an ice-blue Cadillac. Going to be at the bait shop an hour, no need to cut off the engine. Just leave the Cadillac outside purring. Pete, owner of Sumpter Wholesale Groceries, had just stuffed Bennie J.'s order for the bait shop in his pocket. Bennie J. paces back and forth along the minnow pools. Pete sits on a wooden stool, wipes his forehead with a handkerchief, puts his handkerchief up, spits, then brings his diamond-studded hand up to his mouth for a puff of Tampa Nugget. Two Cuban cigars are in his front pocket, but they are presents to hand out; his personal taste in cigars has remained cheap. Wright views all this from the shallow minnow pool. He is *in* the minnow pool, minnows tickling him as they swim by. Pete says, "Johnny doubled up his order. He wants ten thousand gallons of white lightning. Wants to know if we want to buy five thousand fifths of Scotch this haul?" Bennie J. paces. "Yeah, I can get rid of five thousand, between Birmingham, Miami Beach, and Havana."

Wright was only five at the time, and nobody knew how smart he was and how he had figured it all out. The liquor would be hauled on what Pete and Bennie J. called "the Train." They owned, rented, or somehow had control of three boxcars, which constantly traveled the freight line. In Miami their cars were loaded with bales of sugar from Cuba and citrus fruit from Ocala. The fruit was unloaded in Sumpter County, near the cotton docks by the river, and sent up to Pete's. They sold the sugar to moonshiners to make whiskey. The boxcars would later be loaded up with moonshine, live chickens in coops, and bales of cotton, sent to New York, and sold to a man Pete knew named Johnny. The circle was completed when untaxed Scotch whiskey and cloth were loaded on in New York to be shipped to Birmingham and on down to Miami, some of it sold to Cuba.

Bennie J. bought sugar from Cuba, Scotch from New York, sold moonshine to New York, Scotch to Cuba. Never left Sumpter County. It was a thirsty city.

The next day Pete comes to the bait shop in his Cadillac. He's dressed in fresh clothes but looks the same, the same style, the same color. He brings a whole box of M&Ms for Wright, a whole box of Hershey bars for Winn, and an expensive box of chocolates for Cordelle. Wright is at the bait shop playing. Winn is at school, Cordelle at home or uptown shopping. Pete fishes ten silver dollars out of his pockets and gives them to Wright, but Wright is to give five of them to Winn when she comes from school. Wright doesn't like all the silver dollars bulging out of his four pants pockets, so takes all but three and puts them with the candy. Wright goes out the back door to find Pete, Doddy Bennie J., and Jerry Lee standing by the minnow pond. Jerry Lee, in his early twenties, is looking at the ground, kicking pebbles, and smoking Marlboros. Bennie J. smokes a Lucky and paces. Pete smokes a Tampa Nugget and talks loudly about nothing in particular. Wright gets into the Cadillac with Pete. Bennie J. gets into Jerry Lee's brand-new '57 Chevy with Jerry Lee at the wheel. Wright likes it that Pete drives fast and his car smells of Tampa Nugget smoke. Near the cotton docks Hawk oversees the unloading. Two trucks finally pull away, one full of fruit, the other full of sugar. Jerry Lee steps up into one of the boxcars and watches Terrel's men load on cases of moonshine. In front of the moonshine in each boxcar they stack coops of live chickens while the rest of the train is loading at the cotton docks. Finally the three boxcars are linked back into the middle of the train. Jerry Lee goes to his car, gets a change of clothes and a coat, an automatic pistol, and a sawed-off shotgun to bring with him as he rides in one of the boxcars to accompany the load. Wright wants to go with Jerry Lee. He wants to see New York and he wants to see Johnny. He met Johnny before, likes to look at his olive skin and listen to his funny accent. Johnny smokes a cigar, pats Wright on the shoulder, and gives him silver dollars like Pete. Unlike Pete or Bennie J., Johnny likes to have a glass of wine. When Johnny says he is ready for another glass of wine Wright says, "Whiskey is for selling, not for drinking." Johnny laughs, tells Wright he is a smart man, even though Wright is not six years old yet, and gives him another silver dollar. Johnny knows to drink a glass of wine in front of Wright costs him a silver dollar, and this is a penalty for some reason he likes to pay. Wright has never been to New York. Johnny and his wife sometimes go to Miami Beach, and Wright sees them when they stop on the way and spend a couple of days with Pete.

Within the next four years, three significant events happened. Johnny retired and moved back with his wife to the country he was from. Castro took over Cuba and the sugar import stopped. Pete had a heart attack and six months later a stroke that took his life. To the best of Wright's knowledge "the Train" ceased to exist.

Bennie J. was certain Wright could not remember "the Train." Bennie J. himself could not remember a moment of his childhood earlier than nine years of age. Anyone who said he or she could remember something when five years old, Bennie J. thought they were delusional.

But now, as Wright ate his cheeseburger and looked out at the dock, he thought how things had changed. As if what he remembered hadn't really happened. Bennie J. was known across Sumpter County as the hard-working man who owned the marina and a nice farm. No one thought of him as a bootlegger, most likely no one ever knew he was. What Wright couldn't figure out was why Bennie J. felt he still had to get Hawk to hustle a few cases of whiskey at the Coon-on-a-logs. Why Bennie J. had to stay at the bait shop all the time acting like his life depended on hustling every dozen minnows, every bag of potato chips, every T-bone steak he possibly could (the bait shop had the best full-service meat market in Sumpter County).

Hanna touched him on the arm. He was going to turn and look at her, and once Wright looked at Hanna he wouldn't want to take his eyes off her, so he paused for a moment. Paused to think how everything was so different. Not even eighteen years old yet, and his early childhood was a completely different culture. Sugar, moonshine, trains, seersucker suits, silver dollars. It all flashed before him.

Just like the War between the States had been good to Cordelle, Cuba and New York had been good to Bennie J. Reynolds.

7   Wright looked at Hanna. Just like he had invented what Daughtery was saying, just like he could roll back his past and view it like a movie, right now he could tell what Hanna was thinking. She was thinking about "the incident." Of all the things they talked about, which included almost everything, they never talked about the incident. But they both almost telepathically knew when the other was thinking of it.

Wright knew he shouldn't have let his childhood roll before him, because whatever mechanism it was he could activate was now warmed up.

"The incident." New Orleans. Hanna's bedroom. They have a crush on each other. They are eleven years old. It is summer. They sit cross-legged like Indians, facing each other. A Ouija board sits on their knees. They have their fingers very lightly on the pointer. Even though they barely touch it, it responds to their questions. Wright knows he is not pushing the thing around. He can tell Hanna isn't either. It has told Wright he is going to be a famous senator, that he is going to live to be very old, that he will marry and have a son. Wright laughs and accuses Hanna of moving the pointer. She swears she is not. Wright gets nervous, but he was feeling a bit funny even before he accused Hanna of moving the pointer. Wright asks the board if Hanna will be famous also. The pointer moves around to answer that Hanna will have the biggest funeral Sumpter County has ever seen. Wright takes his fingers off the pointer and smiles. This datum seems pleasurable, for Wright invents in his own mind the following information: He will be a famous senator and Hanna will be a famous movie star. They will marry, have a son, return to Sumpter County to live out a full and long life together. At an old age, but before bad health sets in, Hanna dies one night in her sleep. Hollywood and the country will remember her by having the biggest and most flamboyant funeral Sumpter County has ever seen.

Wright looks up at Hanna but cannot tell her reaction to the notion of her having a big funeral. They put their fingertips back on the pointer. Hanna asks when this funeral will be. The pointer answers when she is seventeen. Hanna and Wright stare at each other. The pointer zooms off the board and slams against the far wall. The board flips up in the air, hits the ceiling, and lands on the bed. Wright and Hanna discontinue playing with the Ouija board. Both know, the pointer's answers could be explained by the minute jittering of their fingertips and some subconscious mechanism of their minds. But even if both their legs twitched at the same time, it would not send the board high enough to the ceiling. And nothing could explain the speed and the power with which the pointer flew across the room. Electricity seems to flash between Wright and Hanna.

Now, in the Grill, Wright smiled at Hanna. He remembered that she had had screaming nightmares before the Ouija board incident, nightmares of being buried alive. She had them occasionally still, but not as often as Bennie J. and Cordelle thought.

Hanna smiled back, rubbed his arm. Wright could tell she wasn't thinking of "the incident" any more. As far as himself, he had had his fill of stepping over into that twilight zone where Greer lived.

"I'm ready for a drink of gin," he said.

"Never take that first drink and you'll never have to worry about drinking," Hanna said, mocking Cordelle. Hanna slipped out of the booth, giggled, and turned the table around, trapping Wright. She ran out of the Grill and sprinted for *Fast Boat*, which Jake had already loaded down. Hanna could outsprint Wright in a dead run. She was already in the boat by the time Wright got out of the Grill. When he got by the bait shop she had already unmoored *Fast Boat*. Wright kept running and jumped as she was pulling away from the dock.

All Wright could think of to aggravate her in return was to undo her bra through her shirt and untie her tennis shoes. But she just kicked off her shoes and pulled off her bra, lifting it out through one of her sleeves and tossing it up under the helm as she taxied out of the marina. Soon Hanna had *Fast Boat* running full throttle down the channel of the Tennessee River.

Hanna loved to drive and drive fast, loved to drive anything. Trucks, cars, tractors, riding lawn mowers, boats. For her that had always been one of the big joys of Big House—to get to drive something. She had claimed that New Orleans and Coleen's lifestyle had always restricted her to riding, riding in taxis and streetcars.

Hanna pulled up among the willow trees. She went off to find Bennie J. while Wright carried the barbecue over to Mae Emma.

A huge crowd was at the water's edge now, noisy and gambling wildly. Hanna found Bennie J. among the crowd and lured him away along the bank.

"These coon dogs?" Hanna asked and then hesitated.

"Yes?" Bennie J. said, eager for Hanna to continue. He was ready for her to tell him what was eating at her. Tell him before she exploded or it ate her up.

"They're worth a lot of money, aren't they?"

"Pure gold, a good one. More than a good horse nowadays."

"The men who own them, they love them?"

"Yeah, sweetheart. More'n anything prob'ly," Bennie J. said, sure now she was about to explain her recent strange behavior.

"Well, why do they send them out to have the raccoon drown them?"

"They don't usually get drownt. But see, if the dog gets the coon, then that dog is a lot more valuable." Hanna didn't say anything, so Bennie J. asked, "What was it you wanted to talk about?"

Hanna said, "That was all," and didn't say any more. Bennie J. thought, Shit. Shit. Shit. Why do these kids have to act so damn far-out? Just as Bennie J. was starting to think how it would take Winn to get to the bottom of all this, they heard a singsongy "Yoo-hoo!" They looked around. Cordelle walked up, stroked Hanna's hair, then put her arm around Hanna's arm. She said, "Hanna, honey. Do you want to go shopping with me now to get Winn a coming-home present? I'd like you to help me pick it out."

"Okay." Hanna smiled.

They turned their attention to some god-awful growling. Two coon dogs were in a fight. Cordelle and Hanna walked arm in arm toward her Cadillac.

They walked by the dog fight. Jerry Lee had stepped in, had hold of both dogs, pulling them apart by the napes of their necks.

Hanna said to Cordelle, "But the raccoons are so cute."

Cordelle hooked her arm around Hanna's tighter, making a hugging motion as they walked. She said, "Hanna, sweetheart! Don't you know? Why, they go straight to raccoon heaven."

II

Winn
Comes to
Big House

1

Winn locked up the brakes of her 1970 blue Corvette convertible and went into a skid. She pulled off the side of the road and parked the car. She got out and stretched her five-foot-eight-and-a-half, twenty-two-year-old body. Her hair was streaked brown shoulder-length, she wore bellbottom jeans, a faded work shirt, and sandals. She looked out across the pasture at Big House. The outside floodlights were on, meaning they were expecting her, for Bennie J. didn't normally like for Big House to be lit up. Someone had probably even been at the crossroads, had called and cued the family that she was on her way. Winn sat on her hood and stared, she wanted to get a good long look before she drove on over to the place where she had grown up.

Winn had moved into Big House when she was six years old, Wright was two and a half. She had been uneasy, not knowing what to expect from the move. Until that time she had lived in Sumpter City in a two-bedroom wood-frame house, she and Wright in one small bedroom, Cordelle and Bennie J. in the other. Mama Dog Midnight, not allowed inside in those days, slept out in her doghouse. Mae Emma was twenty-two then. She had come once a week to do the wash when Bennie J. and Cordelle first married. When Winn was born, she came three times a week to clean and cook. And by the time Wright was born, Mae Emma was working full time.

If Winn could remember the little house well, she could not remember a time the family did not have the central acreage of the farm, in the middle of which Big House now stood. She and Bennie J. would ride alone in his '52 Chevy out to the farm to see the hogs, beef cattle, and cotton Lanny Jones oversaw. She remembered riding out the day the foundation was laid for Big House. Thereafter, the trips there were daily, often with Mae Emma riding along to tend to Wright.

As soon as it was wired and the plumbing installed and long before all the construction and cosmetics were complete, they moved into Big House. Wright and Winn lived in one bedroom upstairs, Cordelle and Bennie J. in another. Midnight had the entire downstairs to herself. And only when Bennie J. bought Mae Emma a '48 Pontiac to drive out every day did Winn realize that this was a house where just they, the one family, were going to live.

One day they all loaded into the Chevrolet as if they were going on a trip to the gulf. Bennie J. drove out to the new house, pulling off the road and stopping on the gravel drive. They all looked at the house. Wright said, "Big House." Bennie J. drove on up and parked. They stared in silence at Big House as if they had never seen it before. They followed Bennie J. to the front door. He pushed the front door open. Winn walked in first. She looked up at the high ceiling, the staircase, the balcony to the upstairs, then down at the bare wood-decked unfinished floor. All the major supports were in but none of the walls was finished. It was early spring. What Winn was looking at would take until mid-autumn to finish with materials—woods, fabrics, marbles, and glass—that were still in the seven different countries from which they would come.

Bennie J. had come in next, carrying Cordelle over the threshold. He walked to the center of the vestibule and set Cordelle down. They too had looked around silently.

Then Mae Emma had walked in holding Wright, whom she had dressed up for the occasion. He broke away from her and ran straight over to a hammer a carpenter had left standing up next to a two-by-four. He dragged the hammer about four feet across the floor to where a scrap piece of one-by-four lay. He then dragged those two things over to where a sixpenny nail lay in the floor. There he sat in the sawdusty floor and commenced to drive the nail through the board and into the floor.

The noise Wright was making was the only sound in the huge cavity of the house. The large room they were now in would always be referred to as Big Room. Everyone stood there and watched Wright. After her two-and-a-half-year-old son had driven the nail in without bending it, with a hammer that looked half his size, Cordelle had said, "Oh Wright, honey. That's exactly where the marble will stop." Cordelle had been pondering for weeks where the pattern of the floor should change.

Improvement after improvement commenced. In the first few years, a four-car garage was built at the back edge of the house, the long loop gravel driveway was paved, and the big fountain was built out front.

Big House and the yard took up four acres. The hog-wire fence that kept the livestock out of the yard was soon replaced with brick wall and white fence. Shrubs, azaleas, dogwoods, and rosebushes were added to the six huge oak trees and three magnolias that had already been there when the house was built. On the back side of the lot an acre was taken in and planted in peach orchard, and on another side in a pecan orchard. The acre between the two orchards was fenced in and a stable built for Wright and Winn's horses and other pet farm animals they would have as they grew up.

The last great construction done at Big House was Big Pool. When Winn was thirteen and Wright nine, a swimming pool and pool house were built next to the peach orchard.

Winn had questioned Wright several times about something that had stuck with her through the years, but Wright never had much to add to the conversation. He had impressions of the house uptown. He could remember sitting on the linoleum floor of the kitchen playing with a big yellow cat, Mae Emma singing to him. He had a faint impression of taking a bath with Cordelle and seeing her naked. He remembered playing with Hanna there, being picked up by Coleen, being in a room where Bennie J. and Cordelle started to kiss and Cordelle said, "Not in front of the baby," giggling.

Those were his only impressions of life at Little House. Still Winn would ask him time and again, "You don't remember the cases of whiskey being stacked up on the back porch and in the kitchen, and men coming in the middle of the night to get it? It making me disturbed?" Wright would ponder it, could imagine it happening, but never could actually remember it.

Winn recognized that the move to Big House marked a new era of Bennie J.'s operation, just as Wright recognized the coinciding death of Pete as such. The only whiskey Winn ever saw at Big House was that which she or Wright had snuck into their rooms. The only people who ever came to Big House were close friends. The only business ever conducted there was farm business with Lanny Jones and, after his death, Alan Dempsey. All of Bennie J.'s other business was conducted out of the bait shop, never brought back to Big House.

About once a week during her childhood, Winn would ask Cordelle, "Mama, we're rich, aren't we?" Cordelle would always smile at Winn and reply, "Honey, we're well-to-do."

Winn liked driving by Little House when she no longer lived in it. It saddened her to find that as she grew up the house became more and more run-down along with the other wood-frame houses on the street near Sumpter College for Women. In the mid-sixties the landlord who owned all these houses died. To Winn's delight, a professor at Sumpter College bought Little House and restored it.

Of the family, Winn was the only one who held on to an admiration for Little House. She felt Cordelle liked to pretend Big House had always been there. And when Winn would mention Little House at the supper table or out on the veranda, all Bennie J. would ever say was, "I spent two thousand eight hundred and eighty dollars in rent there that I'll never see," as if that ten years of rent kept him from wealth. Thousands could be spent on the Big House wall and fence, a couple thousand on a weekend trip to see the Alabama Crimson Tide play football, but it was that twenty-eight hundred dollars he had paid in rent that Bennie J. had pissed to the wind.

Winn got back into the Vette, and slugged down the rest of what was in her half-empty Right Time bottle. She cranked the car, turned into the driveway, and headed toward Big House, driving off the driveway to go straight through the front yard. She swerved, barely missing Big Fountain, hopped back up on the drive, and came to a stop in front of the house.

She walked up to the massive front door, tested the knob, paused a moment, and stepped inside. It was dark. A spotlight from the inside balcony came on, shining on Mae Emma, who stood by the baby grand. The piano began playing, then a guitar. Mae Emma began singing "Summertime," and after the first stanza the lights came on. Jerry Lee was on guitar, Hanna on the baby grand, with Wright sitting beside her playing chords. Bennie J., who had worked the spotlight, was walking down the stairs.

Cordelle walked over. She and Winn hugged, then Winn and Bennie J., who said, "Hug line. Hug line." As the song continued, Winn walked around, hugging Wright, Hanna, Mae Emma, and Jerry Lee. Mama Dog Midnight walked out from the dining room. Bennie J. said, "Hug line. Hug line. Here comes Mama Dog Midnight for the hug line." Winn kneeled down and hugged Midnight.

Winn strutted over and began singing with Mae Emma. When Jerry Lee handed Winn her trumpet, everyone hollered. Winn intermittently sang with Mae Emma and played the trumpet. When "Summertime" ended, everyone yelled and clapped, and Winn hugged them all again. She announced, "There's nothing like coming home to Big House. You don't know how much I miss y'all."

Bennie J. said, "My little girl's home. Come on, let's eat."

Jerry Lee told Winn it was nice her being home. She hugged him again, giving him a kiss on the cheek. He put his guitar back in its case and looked at Cordelle's low-cut dress to try to keep his mind off Winn. He gracefully excused himself for the night, as he had a pressing engagement.

Winn, Wright, Hanna, and Bennie J. settled at the dining room table while Mae Emma and Cordelle brought out salads. Cordelle sat down to eat with the family while Mae Emma brought a couple of big platters of T-bone and sirloin steaks.

Bennie J. had finished off his salad by the time the last one had been dished out on the table. He always ate a salad just to be polite and ate it quickly so he could get on to his steak. He pulled a sirloin over onto his plate, asking Winn, "Well, d'ya git through all your final quizzes alright?"

Winn sighed and said, "You won't believe, Doddy, how hard those courses were this term."

Wright coughed out a piece of tomato to keep from choking. He thought those quizzes must have been rough since Winn hadn't been in Baton Rouge for three weeks prior to final exams. He didn't know where yet, but Winn had called him on the upstairs line to see if Cordelle or Bennie J. had been trying to call her. When Wright told her they had, she handled it by promptly calling the downstairs number and complaining to her mother and father how she had been studying night and day at the library and that college was no fun at all. Then she called Wright again to scrounge up $1300 to put in her account before Bennie J. found out she was overdrawn.

Cordelle said, "Wright, honey? Are you all right?"

Wright finally cleared his throat enough to say, "Yes, ma'am."

Bennie J. swallowed a mouthful of steak. He said to Winn, "I know it's rough, honey. But you got to keep that grade point average up." Then to all of them he said, "Got to git an education. One thing I know. My kids are going to get an education. That's the one thing I can give y'all that nobody can take away."

Wright said, "If you give me a Corvette, Doddy, couldn't nobody take that away from me."

Winn said, "No one could," correcting Wright's grammar.

"I give you a Corvette," Bennie J. said, "you could go out and wreck it and then you wouldn't have jack shit. Not a pot to piss in."

"Or a window to throw it out," Hanna said. She had heard all this before and knew the words by heart.

Mama Dog walked in, went up beside Bennie J., and looked at him. He reached over to one of the platters, got a porterhouse steak, and gave it to her. Midnight took it over to the corner of the room, looked back, then headed toward the door to Big Room.

Cordelle said, "Mama Dog, don't you drag that over the carpet, now."

Mama Dog paused, then walked on out.

Wright opened his mouth to say something again about the Corvette. Bennie J. had promised to buy them a brand-new car when they graduated college. Winn had gotten hers when she became a junior, leaving the green MGA at Hanna's disposal when she had moved up from New Orleans to go to Sumpter College for Women.

Wright started to say something again about the Corvette but knew if he did Bennie J. would start carrying on about "them skitters." Bennie J. couldn't talk too long about skitters before he started talking about the Depression. When he talked about the Depression that made him start talking and complaining about plunkin' gee-tars and not standing hitched. Wright didn't want to hear about the Depression, picking guitars, or standing hitched so he didn't say any more about the Corvette.

Bennie J. said, "Aw, Winn, honey, did you get your passport all right?"

"Yes, Doddy. Everything is in order."

"Well, good," Bennie J. said, then took a bite of steak. "Could I see the thing?"

"Well, Doddy, I left it with Gina. I left it with some of her things so it wouldn't be misplaced."

Bennie J. said, "I wanted to see one. I might get me one."

"Are you and Mama Cordelle going somewhere?"

"Naw. You know me. Except for going to see the Tide play, I'm not gittin' out of Sumpter."

"What do you want with a passport, then, Doddy?"

Bennie J. clanked his fork on the plate. "Now what if you git over in them foreign countries, git in trouble? You think the damn U.S. Embassy going to say, 'Oh, Winn, honey' and you be out of trouble? Shit, naw. You don't know when Bennie J. gone have to come git you out of trouble. It's a thirsty city." He went back to eating his steak.

After supper they all went out on the back veranda, where Mae Emma brought out a container of homemade ice cream. Hanna, Wright, and Winn sat on the swing eating theirs, Cordelle and Bennie J. in the wicker love seat, and Mama Dog Midnight in the middle of the floor. Mama Dog liked homemade ice cream almost as much as she liked all-meat bologna.

Cordelle ate a spoonful of ice cream and gasped as if it were the best thing she had ever eaten. But it wasn't the ice cream she was gasping about; it was the thought that had just occurred to her. She said, "I'll be glad when all y'all finish college so we can all live here together at Big House again."

Mama Dog looked up at Cordelle, gave a big burp, then went back to eating her ice cream. Cordelle said, "Mama Dog Midnight, is your ice cream good?" Mama Dog barked.

"Winn, honey, let's go up to your room," Cordelle said. "I have a present to give you."

Winn had not been upstairs yet since she had come home. As she walked up she studied the walls, the stairs, the floor of Big Room. The decor looked bare. Without thinking, she said, "Wright sure can hammer good to be so little, can't he?" It was the same thing she had said the day they had moved into Big House and she was walking with Cordelle up the stairs after Wright had nailed the board to the floor.

Cordelle said, "I think one day he may become a famous architect." It was the same thing Cordelle had replied that same day. That was before Big Jim Folsum had referred to Wright as Senator Reynolds.

By the time Winn got to the top of the stairs she was stone judge sober. She and Cordelle walked to her room, the room Winn and Gina Farrow had spent $6200 of Bennie J.'s money redecorating in French Provincial. Gina and Winn had been roommates for six years, first at Sumpter College and then the five different colleges and universities throughout the Southeast they had attended. Gina's home was one hundred miles southeast of Sumpter City. Her father was a U.S. senator and a rancher. During summers, Winn and Gina spent some time at each other's ranches.

Cordelle opened the bedroom door and Winn walked on in to find a new dress laid out on the bed. Winn held the dress, adored it. She hugged Cordelle. "Oh, Mama. Thank you. This is just gorgeous."

"I thought you might have occasion to wear it in Europe."

"I'm going to have so much fun abroad. You don't know how much I love you and Doddy."

Cordelle kissed Winn. "Oh, Winn, sugar. You don't know how much B.J. and I love you. How much we think of you and miss you."

Winn and Cordelle inspected the dress a bit more, then walked out of the bedroom to go join the others. They were about to go back downstairs when they heard voices down the hall, coming from Cordelle and Bennie J.'s bedroom. Walking back down the hall, they found the door open.

Bennie J., Hanna, and Wright were lying around at different angles on the king-size bed, their shoes off. The double French doors to the balcony were open. A nice breeze was coming into the room. Cordelle crawled up close to Bennie J. and Winn plopped herself across the foot of the bed.

Bennie J. was telling the story about his and Greer's pet rattlesnake. Everyone listened as if they had never heard it before. That's the way Bennie J. could tell any story, but especially a Depression story.

Wright asked, "What happened then, Doddy?"

Bennie J. continued, "Uncle Davy and old Cousin Greer, they's crazy in them days. They caught the snake. Biggest rattlesnake any-body ever seen. Uncle Davy and his daddy had an old country store out about where Jacobs Crossroads is now. A little bit back this side. There was another little road that cut just this side of Mud Creek and that's where the store was. What they did was take all the candy out of the glass candy case and put the rattlesnake in there. The story got to spreadin' how big this snake was. They gone charge folks to see it, don't you see. Things were tough in the Depression . . ."

"Did it ever bite anyone?" Hanna asked. She couldn't wait.

Wright said, "That part don't come yet. Just wait."

Winn said, "Doesn't," correcting Wright's grammar, but Wright thought he should be able to speak incorrect grammar if Bennie J. was.

Bennie J. went on, "It became a pet snake. To cousin Greer, that is."

"What did it eat?" Wright asked, careful to pronounce his words carefully. Winn would also correct him for slurring.

Hanna said, "It ate rats, I bet."

"Rats?" Bennie J. replied quickly. "Hell, old Dude—"

"That was the rattler's name," Wright interjected.

"Did you name Dude the pet catfish after Dude the pet rattle-snake?" Hanna asked.

"Naw, naw," Bennie J. brushed her off. "I named Dandy first. Then named Dude Dude because it kind of rhymed with Dandy. Naw, Dude the pet catfish and Dude the pet rattlesnake not kin at all."

"I see," Hanna said, pleased at the explanation.

Bennie J. said, "And naw, Dude didn't eat rats. Hell, ole Dude'd eat rabbits. Greer had to set out an extra trap just to keep ole Dude in hares."

Hanna whined, "Ugh," to which Cordelle replied, "Hanna, honey. These weren't bunny rabbits. These were ugly rabbits." And Winn said, "They would go straight to rabbit heaven."

Bennie J. said, "Ole Dude had fangs long as bowie knives."

"Were you ever bitten by a snake, Bennie J.?" Hanna asked.

Cordelle said proudly, "B.J. has been bitten by every type of poisonous snake native to the State of Alabama."

"How is it they would do for snakebite?" Wright asked.

Bennie J. said, "Back then they would throw you down and put a constriction band above the bite. Between the bite and your heart. Then somebody'd run catch a pullet and wring its neck. They'd cut the chicken open. Then they'd cut the two fang marks open and slap that fresh hot meat on the cuts."

Hanna whined, "Ooooooow." And Winn told her softly, "They went straight to chicken heaven."

Bennie J. said, "That poultry meat would draw the poison out."

Wright said, "Didn't they pack baking soda on there too till the blood kept from turning green when it hit the soda and that meant all the poison was out?"

Winn hollered, "Goddammit! Will y'all shut the fuck up?"

Startled, Wright and Hanna froze. Cordelle pretended she didn't hear anything. Bennie J. was so caught up in the story he didn't pay any attention to what Winn had said. Cordelle never let anyone cuss in Big House, except for Bennie J. But Bennie J. never said "fuck." Bennie J. just mostly said damn, shit, and hell.

Winn said to Wright and Hanna, "And let Doddy Bennie J. tell about Dude. I want to hear about Dude the rattlesnake."

Wright and Hanna slowly began to relax as Bennie J. went on, "Anyway, cousin Greer figured he could train ole Dude . . ."

2   Wright could see arcs of rainbows cast all about Hanna's room, though he only had his eyelids a bit open. He, Winn, and Hanna had fallen asleep in Hanna's bed talking the night before. He had not felt Winn slip out of bed this morning, but now he saw her in the middle of the room, stretching. She had on a pair of bikini panties and one of Hanna's deep blue "Billy Jack for President" T-shirts.

She was on the floor, her right leg straight out in front of her, her left leg at a right angle in an "L," bending with her nose to her right knee. Wright watched her stand up, bring her left knee up to her chest, hug it and slowly extend her foot above her head. She shifted and did the right leg.

Winn walked over to a chair where her clothes lay. She pulled on her jeans, traded the T-shirt for an Indian shirt with the sleeves rolled up. She left Hanna's room barefooted, quietly closing the door behind her.

Wright closed his eyes completely now, thinking of last night. He and Hanna had gone into Winn's room to help her unpack. As Wright was pulling out underwear a passport flopped out onto Winn's bed. He called to Winn, "Your passport *is* in here." She told him to take a look inside and find out why she didn't show it to Bennie J. Two pages of visas were stamped, one to Ecuador, one to Costa Rica. Then she explained how she and Gina had gotten into an argument about French, Greek, and Spanish architecture and ended up settling the argument by just by God jumping on a plane and going to Ecuador, then stretching out the trip to three weeks. And that was the reason she had had Wright go deposit $1300 in her account rather quickly. By the time they had landed in Quito they forgot what the argument was exactly, but sitting there on Bourbon Street guzzling down hurricanes, a tour of Ecuador seemed the only solution.

Shit, here he was scared to leave Big House to go to college when it was the naturalest thing in the world for his sister to go off to South America on a drunken spur of the moment, taking her time getting back, all the while not worrying, knowing she would somehow cover her ass.

Wright opened his eyes, the sunlight and rainbows intense now. Hanna's room, since she was eight years old. Though Hanna had always lived with her mother in New Orleans, she had spent most of her summers and other school vacations at Big House. Hanna would spend the entire summer at Big House this year, while Coleen spent the summer in New York doing a decorating job.

Wright felt the bed jiggle. He heard footsteps across the room and then the sound of Hanna throwing up in the sink. She had confided to Winn the night before that she was pregnant, she was sure. Her period was three weeks late and she was nauseous in the morning (Wright thought this nausea might just be because Hanna, close to the end of the night, would down 90 percent of her alcohol in about thirty minutes). Winn had said she'd help, would set her up with a gynecologist in Birmingham. But the pregnancy was not a dilemma for Hanna: She knew there was no real way for her to have a baby now because she knew she wasn't going to live to her eighteenth birthday.

Wright heard Hanna brush her teeth, pee, then there was silence. He knew she was giving herself her early pregnancy test—pulling up her T-shirt, standing sideways to the mirror, rubbing her lower abdomen and seeing if her stomach was pooching out.

He heard her walking across the bedroom, felt the bed being laid upon, then felt Hanna's skin against his. As Hanna snuggled up to him, Wright thought about sex. He thought about Big House. "Sex and Big House," Wright mumbled. They seemed to fit together some way. Wright had had sex with three different girls in his life: Kathy Lee, Gina, and Hanna.

The last day of June, when he was fourteen almost to turn fifteen, he was with Kathy Lee at a country club dance. For three years they had been close friends. After a slow song, Kathy Lee went off to procure someone's older brother's car. Soon, with Kathy Lee driving, they slipped away from the country club. Stopping at a late-night gas station, she had the tank filled while Wright went to the restroom. He looked up at the machines, a choice of three. He passed up the two twenty-five-cent ones for the fifty-cent extra-strength blue condom. The machine advertised how the colored condom added variety to your sex life and pleased your woman. Wright didn't need variety and Kathy Lee seemed as if she were already pleased. But Wright quickly deduced the highest-priced one was the best. He put two quarters in and shoved, it sounding like when Wild-1 had had a chipped gear.

Kathy Lee drove to the marina and broke into her family's houseboat that was docked there. In spite of the full moon and all their giggling, Kathy Lee was sure they had gotten in without the Redstone Arsenal Yankees, who were in the houseboat in the next slip, seeing or hearing them.

On and off for the next two years, Kathy Lee and Wright would sneak into their houseboat, one or the other's bedroom, or on a blanket in the horse stable. It seemed to Wright as though there had been hundreds of these rendezvous, though he knew it to be only tens of times. Seldom was it done fully unclothed, always with a condom.

Last summer, when Gina stayed at Big House for those six weeks, one night with only two weeks of her stay left, Gina snuck into Wright's room and seduced him, which was not a very hard thing for her to do. For the next two weeks, she and Wright had sex seven times, always at night. Their escapades lasted well over an hour; they would have long foreplay, and afterwards she would stroke Wright and tell him how pretty he was. Five of those times they showered together afterwards. Though Kathy Lee had initiated Wright into the world of sex, Gina, perhaps because she was four years his senior and more experienced, introduced him to a world that was erotic and bizarrely risqué.

Late the night before Gina was to go back home, Bennie J. was awakened by a phone call from one of the Redstone Arsenal Yankees who had a houseboat at the marina. He thought the café was on fire. Bennie J. thanked him, hung up the phone. Wright told Bennie J., "We'll handle it." Bennie J. went back to bed, for he knew what it was. Several times each year, mostly in the summer, a phenomenon occurred in the café. If the temperature and humidity changed suddenly, steam would come off the grill, forming a cloud in the café that looked like smoke.

What started out to be Wright, Winn, and Gina going out to double-check on the café, turned out to be Wright and Gina going out to the marina for one last time. They went in, checked, the cloud in the café was the steam from the grill. By the grill Gina began kissing Wright. They locked the door from the inside, closed the Venetian blind of the front plate-glass windows, and made love in the big corner booth. Then they put their clothes back on, locked up the café, and strolled around the marina holding hands. It was the coolest night they had had since May. They rolled up their jeans and walked around in the warm shallow grassy water at the edge of the marina. Gina was five-eleven, had been Miss Alabama two years earlier, had been on national TV the following year to compete in the Miss America pageant. She thanked Wright for their affair, said she had been infatuated by him, again told him how pretty he was. They kissed in the moonlight, Gina with her feet wide apart in a stance making up for their height difference.

Since early childhood, Wright and Hanna had had an intense affinity for each other, had slept in the same bed often, had spent hundreds of hours of their summers and holidays alone with each other. But mid-November, after the summer of Wright's affair with Gina, he and Hanna fell hard for each other. Late at night Hanna would slip out of the dorm, Wright would pick her up in his MGA, and they would drive the curvy mountain roads across the state line into Tennessee, leaning together so the cold wind wouldn't hit them and to be nearer and to feel the warmth coming off the engine and into the cockpit.

Hanna came to Big House for Thanksgiving vacation, and Thanksgiving night she and Wright began their full-fledged love affair. The next morning at the kitchen table, with Cordelle barely out of earshot, Hanna looked over at Wright and asked "Do you still respect me?" He choked on his orange juice, then laughed so hard tears ran down his face. Cordelle and Mae Emma looked over to see what was going on. Hanna just smiled at Wright.

Kathy Lee, Gina, and Hanna—his affairs with each made sense to Wright. It was dating that he couldn't figure out. During high school, before his midnight rides with Hanna, he had gone out with several girls, Betsy Coleman being one. Each had rubbed up against him, ate as if innocously performing sexual acts on their food, made sexual innuendoes in conversation. But when alone, each had pushed his hands out from under their dresses after he had had them there a short while, had acted offended, but then kissed him like they wanted him to do it again.

Wright lay there now in Hanna's bed thinking how all three of his partners had been of or through Big House. The world outside of Big House seemed to operate off an illogical set of rules Wright knew nothing about, nor could even begin to decipher. He wondered if Gina would have acted like Betsy Coleman if she hadn't been "filtered" through Big House. He certainly didn't plan on dating anymore, but he wondered if trying to live outside Sumpter County was going to be as strange.

3 Cordelle and Bennie J. sat at the table out on the back veranda, eating breakfast. Cordelle always got up and ate breakfast with Bennie J. and then went back to bed to sleep for an hour.

Bennie J. ate some eggs and said, "Kids. Damn near can't git 'em up in the mornings. Then they got to sunbathe for two hours. Damn if it might give 'em skin cancer the way they lay there and cook."

All Cordelle said in reply was, "Aren't those birds lovely?" But she spoke so faintly Bennie J. didn't hear her over those same birds. Cordelle finished her biscuit. "I think I'll go watch *Morning U.S.A.*"

She felt some small obligation to watch *Morning U.S.A.* because her first cousin, Ed Sanders, a lawyer in Campbell County, had given half the cast of *Morning U.S.A.* a divorce. He was well into procuring Alabama residency for part of the *CBS Evening News* staff, getting them set up for their divorces, when the Alabama Bar Association disbarred him for two years.

Cordelle got her coffee and walked back into the house. Bennie J. kept eating, thinking of last night, thinking of Winn being home. When they had been alone for a moment he had told her how Hanna had been acting strangely, had been having more screaming nightmares. He wanted to see if she could find out what was the matter. Winn had nodded, not saying a word.

Bennie J. looked around, looked at the veranda and what he could of Big House from where he sat, looked out to the pastures. He was thinking how it was Winn who seemed to make the house worthwhile. To Bennie J., the existence of Winn, a beautiful appreciative life-full daughter, justified having a big Parthenon of a house. Often he got aggravated at having so far to walk from the bedroom to the kitchen, at how much money it cost to keep it up, at people always commenting on his home to him. But when Winn was home, she reminded him that it was all worthwhile.

And then like magic Winn walked out onto the veranda and said, "Morning, Doddy." Bennie J. noticed Winn was wide awake, raring to go. He almost hollered, "There's my little girl! I'm glad you started gittin' up early. I hope the other kids grow out of laying up all morning." Bennie J. hollered back into the house, "Mae Emma! Winn out here. She needs her a good breakfast." Mae Emma hollered back for him to calm down, that she knew Winn was up.

Bennie J. looked down at her feet and said, "You still going barefoot, like ole Bennie J. when he was a kid." This pleased him. "So my little girl's going off across the big pond."

"Oh, it's going to be so much fun, so educational, Doddy."

"Nothing like a good education," Bennie J. said and remained silent when Mae Emma brought Winn some coffee. When she went back into the house, he said, "So Winn, honey, you ever git to the bottom of what's wrong with you cousin?"

"Well, Doddy. It's woman kind of stuff," Winn replied and then ventured off into a taboo subject, telling Bennie J. how ladies had monthly occurences that began quite young but sometimes when they got in their later teens it became more intense and was often hard to adjust.

Bennie J. nodded, trying to act like they weren't discussing the subject of menstrual cycles. "I figured something like that. But nothing's wrong with her mind, is it?"

"No," Winn said, took a sip of coffee. "I'd say her trouble is mostly at the other end."

"Medical, you might say?"

"Somewhat. See Doddy, when a young lady gets to be Hanna's age she should be going to a doctor once a year, a doctor that looks at those female things and makes sure all is going well. Hanna hasn't been doing that."

"Damn. Damn. Damn," Bennie J. said and slapped his hand down on the table. "Coleen hasn't been seeing to that? Coleen can be so harum-scarum! Don't even see to it her own daughter—"

"Doddy," Winn said, cutting him off. "I'll take care of it. I'll get her an appointment with the man Gina and I go to in Birmingham. Excellent doctor."

"What's good enough for the senator's daughter and for ole Winn is good enough for Hanna Belle." Bennie J. took a biscuit, sopped up some blackstrap molasses with it, ate it, then said, "Now see, you can get something done! I ask Cordelle to find out, she couldn't. Ask Wright to find out, he couldn't even see nothing was wrong with her. See, I need somebody that can do something about something. Now ole Winn, I always know you can git things done. Yeah. I need you to git through with all that school so you can come back run things."

Bennie J. smiled. Things were clicking in his mind. How Winn could enliven circumstance. Now it was falling into place. There was hope. He didn't know why he hadn't thought of this before, noticed what had happened with Terrel's family. Terrel's oldest boy, Gilbert, hadn't been worth a shit. All time hot-rodding around, getting into trouble. But when he turned twenty-five he got married and within two years was practically running Terrel's operation. Same thing with Terrel's youngest boy. He went off to college, shit around flunking out, wrecking cars. Then came back, went to work, finished straight As at a local junior college, and wasn't even thirty yet and knew more about buying out estates than anybody in the South.

Yeah, it took old Winn to get things running straight, Bennie J. thought. Just maybe they'd all—Winn, Wright, and Hanna—come back to Big House and take hold. He had no idea why college had to be four years. Why couldn't it just be two? Shit. Shit. Shit.

Mae Emma walked out with Winn's breakfast and the coffeepot.

She put the plate before Winn and asked Bennie J., "You't some more coffee?"

Bennie J. said, almost singing, "Not I, said the cat. I got to git goin', Cousin Emma. I shoulda been down at the marina half hour ago." He got up and said to Winn, "You git the other kids up later, all y'all come down to the bait shop? Everybody'll be wantin' to see my little girl."

"Of course, Doddy. We'll all be down there later."

"Hot dig." Bennie J. walked down the veranda and said, "Ponjo," some word he and Greer had brought out of the swamp that was an alteration of some foreign word that meant good-bye. He walked on through the patio and toward his pickup truck.

Mae Emma sat down beside Winn, poured herself a cup of coffee. "Bennie J. sure is glad you home, we all are. But Bennie J., he plumb tickled. All beside hisself." Mae Emma took a sip of coffee. "How you doin', chile?"

"Just dandy. How are you, Mae Emma?"

"Sweetheart, I'm gone turn the big five-oh this year. I'm still a-kickin'. If it gits too lonely after Wright and Hanna leaves Big House, I mought just go up New Yowk start sangin'. Shit, Jerry Lee had a good idea. Said I ought to go to Nashville. Be the first black female country singer. Hell, I git any older and meaner I just mought do that. Go up there make ole Tammy Wynette move on over."

Winn laughed, sipped her coffee. Mae Emma said, "Good to see ya back at Big House, honey." Mae Emma put her palm over Winn's hand.

Winn smiled, looked Mae Emma in the eye. "Thank you, Mae Emma. And thank you for always being here."

Mae Emma smiled, nodded, looked as if she were about to cry.

Winn asked, "How is everyone here?"

Mae Emma squeezed Winn's hand, then let go of it. When she did, her melancholy that had almost brought tears dissipated. She perked up and said, "Bennie J. He like always. Thank he have to hustle like hell all day long to keep from starvin' to death. He thank it still the Depression or something.

"Wright and Hanna. All they can do the last month is stare at each other. I send 'em off to town, they come back two hours later fergit whut I sent 'em off for.

"And Cordelle. She all time on some committee. The city got to shootin' the stray dogs uptown a couple months ago. Honey chile, you couldn't walk uptown fer the dogs. Don't nobody know where dey come from. If you wudn't steppin in dog shit you's havin' to walk around two of 'em fuckin'.

"When the city started shootin 'em, some them country club women they got a committee up to save the dogs. Cordelle joined up. But wudn't 'bout a week she jine up that she uptown in front of Mr. Bernstein's she got all scratched up by a couple dogs that was after another dog that they's all after, this bitch in heat. 'Bout the time Cordelle goin' to resign from the Save the Dogs Committee she done got elected while she was late gittin' all scratched up to de president-ship to this co-mittee. Now bein' president, instid of resignin' what she done was form a sub-co-mittee to the co-mittee to shoot all the dogs.

"If they's a club to preserve something Cordelle'll join it. Then she has a meetin' out here and Bennie J. gits all pissed off. You know how he don't want no committee meetin's being conducted out chere at Big House."

Mae Emma had been talking fast, smiling, Winn giggling as she talked. She paused, took another sip of coffee, then said, "Thangs been 'bout usual here at Big House, Winn honey."

4 Old man Lanson was sitting out on the dock whittling a piece of cedar. The shavings were blowing down into James Barnett's bass boat. He had a pint of wildcat whiskey covered up in a number eight brown paper sack. Every once in a while he would reach over and take a slug, did it in such a way that a passerby would never have noticed him miss a stroke on the cedar stick.

Bennie J. was in front of the bait shop looking in the ice machine to see if it was making ice fast enough. Jake walked up and said, "Mr. Bennie J., Mr. Lanson out the end of the dock drinkin' whiskey and whittlin'."

"He thinks that's his job," Bennie J. replied.

Jake said, "Mr. Lanson all time gittin' in some kinda accident. Maybe we ought to go git him off de pier 'fore he falls in the water drowns hisself."

Bennie J. leaned up, looked down at old man Lanson, then back to Jake. "Ahh, he'll be all right. He lived through two world wars. He damn near ninety. He must have some knack for knowing how to stay alive." He leaned back over into the ice machine.

Jake looked back down at old man Lanson, thought a moment, nodded in agreement, and headed back to the Grill. Hawk, came out of the Grill, headed for the bait shop. He walked over and stood beside Bennie J., looking over his shoulder to see if something was wrong with the ice machine. He said, "Hey, boss."

Bennie J. said, "Hey, Hawk. You seen Winn?"

"New, suh."

"I wanted her and the kids to go to the bank for me."

"Maybe they be here directly. You know how they is about zipping in and out in them little spootniks they got."

Bennie J. just then heard his crop duster that Jerry Lee was obviously piloting. He looked up and saw Winn, parachute open, heading for the grassy area between the parking lot and the boat ramp. "Shit," Bennie J. said. "Jumpin' out of planes agin. I hope her mama don't find out about this."

Winn landed on the grassy spot and rolled. The wind started to pull her, so she disconnected from the parachute. She chased after it as it blew across the parking lot, down the pier, and onto old man Lanson.

Wright and Hanna pulled up and parked in front of Bennie J., right by the ice machine. Hanna turned the engine off; they sat there and stared at old man Lanson trying to punch his way out of the parachute, which engulfed him. He was hollering about a ghost had hold of him, was cutting a fast deal with the Lord. Winn grabbed him just as he was about to step off the pier.

By the time Winn got old man Lanson settled back down to drinking and whittling, a crowd of employees, tenants, and hanger-outs of the marina had gathered around, hugging her, welcoming her home. Hanna stuffed the parachute in the trunk of the Vette while Bennie J. carried on how everybody was crazy to see Winn. "Yeah," he said, "when ole Winn shows up the party starts." Finally Winn, Bennie J., Wright, and Hanna went into the bait shop.

Bennie J.'s office was at the back, a ten-by-twelve-foot room with a seven-foot ceiling. The floor, walls, and ceiling were wood-decked and unpainted. On one wall was a small hatch that could be opened to look out into the bait shop—there were no windows. Opposite the door sat a large antique rolltop desk and a swivel chair. On one wall was a Pet Milk clock, a First Sumpter Bank calendar on another. Three ladderback chairs and four file cabinets were set around the room, up against the walls. A single hundred-watt bulb hung down from the ceiling above the desk to light the entire room—it shined twenty-four hours a day.

Bennie J. had often sat in his swivel chair and said, "This right here is the center of Bennie J.'s empire," and put his hand on his desk. "The center of the family might be Big House. Mama Cordelle head of Big House. But this little hole right here is the center from which Bennie J.'s empire revolves."

Once when Wright was in junior high, he and Bennie J. were about to leave the bait shop late one night. Wright climbed up onto the chair to pull the chain on the light socket. Bennie J. said quickly, "Naw, naw, son, that stays on. See, a man's work is from sun to sun. A woman's work is never done. A farmer works from kin to can't. But the sun never sets on Bennie J.'s empire." Wright stepped down off the chair, realizing that he had never seen the light off. Wondered what the sun had to do with it, for it was impossible for the sun to shine into the office. A box of hundred-watt light bulbs was on top of the desk in case the one in the socket burned out. It was then that Wright recognized Bennie J. spoke very poetically and symbolically whenever he spoke of the office or his empire.

Bennie J. led them into his office where he sat at his swivel chair. Wright, Winn, and Hanna hovered around him. He started taking sacks and envelopes of money out of the drawers and telling Winn what account he wanted each bundle of money and checks deposited in, what he wanted put in the safe deposit box.

"Well, Doddy, we're going to have to go back to Big House and get Mama Cordelle's roadster if we're going to the bank."

"All right, all right," Bennie J. motioned. "But don't waste any time, Lemay closes up at two. And don't be speedin'."

They all walked back out through the bait shop, Wright and Hanna carrying sacks of money. Wright sat in the passenger seat of the Vette, Hanna got in his lap. Bennie J. began looking at the ice machine again. He turned as Winn was getting behind the wheel, and said, "And if y'all see Jerry Lee, tell him to come down here and look at this ice machine. It ain't puttin' out like it ought to."

Winn nodded and roared away, heading for Big House to get Cordelle's canary yellow 1928 Model A Roadster and her drum-feed Thompson .45 submachine gun that had belonged to Julius. As soon as they arrived, they all ran in and changed clothes. Winn and Hanna put on flapper outfits; Wright put on a double-breasted suit. All this had started back when they were young children. Big Pete would come out to Big House in his horse-drawn surrey. He would take the kids up to the bank and then over to his house for refreshments and for Winn to look at his horses. After Pete died, perhaps to make up for the formality of riding in the surrey, Winn would get dressed up and make Bennie J. take her in Cordelle's roadster up by the drugstore for a milkshake whenever he was going uptown to the bank.

The fourteen customers, five tellers, two loan officers, and President Lemay turned around to watch the three young people dressed in twenties garb walk into the bank. Each had a sack of money in one hand and a firearm in the other.

The Henson old maids were at a table endorsing some checks. Wright overheard Mildred sigh and tell Edna, "Oh, that's Bennie J. and Cordelle's crazy kids." Edna replied, "It looks like Cordelle would make them go to the University of Alabama."

Lemay walked over to Winn and welcomed her back to town. He had a bank employee take the sacks of money. This month was Lemay's thirtieth anniversary of being with First Sumpter Bank. He had come from Nashville to begin his banking career as a teller. That first day, his first customer was Bennie J. Reynolds. Bennie J. had walked up and plopped a flour sack full of ones, fives, tens, and twenties up at the window. He promptly told Lemay he didn't know how much money was in there, that he hadn't had time to count it.

Lemay hadn't known what to do with the money but that day had become Bennie J.'s personal banker. For the next thirty years Lemay had carefully directed Bennie J.'s cash flow through the bank. Now, Bennie J. often said, and to the swelling of Lemay's pride, "Yeah, old Lemay come all way from Nashville to help old Bennie J. out with his money. Old Bennie J. would had all kind of trouble if not for Lemay." Sometimes late at night these words would ring in Lemay's ears, and Lemay would drift into a philosophical vortex, pondering if Bennie J. had willed him to Sumpter County with some common karma. These were the only nonconservative thoughts Lemay allowed himself.

Winn put her Colt .45 Goldcup in her left hand and shook Lemay's hand. She told him what Bennie J. wanted done with the money. He nodded and walked off to oversee that it was done properly. Winn turned around, and there was Bebe Marlin in her face. Bebe hugged her, started whining in a drawn-out Southern accent how she hadn't seen her in so long. Winn referred to her and her cohorts as Bebe Boo and the Dixie Do's.

Bebe said, taking hold of Winn's hand, "Winn, sweetheart, I have a most urgent matter I must speak to you confidentially about." Winn thought Bebe sounded like a bad imitation of Hanna's impersonation of her. Winn followed her to a couch in the waiting lounge.

Bebe started out, dragging one-syllable words into three: "As you know, Marty Lou Wilburn, Irene Jennings, and myself make up the Sumpter County Miss Maid of Cotton committee this year. We have a lovely bunch of contestants this year, all sweet girls, mind you, Winn, but we don't feel we're going to be able to do that well in Memphis. And as you know Sumpter's Miss Maid of Cotton has never failed to have a finalist. Thanks to you, your mother, and your aunt, we have a reputation, a heritage at stake here. Just keep this between us girls but Irene, Marty Lou, nor I feel any of our contestants this year, now as I said, they are sweet girls, but none of them have that"—Bebe paused to search for a word—"have that winner's edge."

Winn could tell Bebe loved to hear herself talk, was proud of herself for coming up with the term "winner's edge." Winn smiled at her and said, "And so since I am a former Miss Maid of Cotton, you are consulting me?"

"Not exactly consulting, Winn, honey. I'm more accosting you for a little help," Bebe said. "Irene, Marty Lou, and I feel it is clear the handwriting is on the wall. Fate holds it for Hanna to enter and win the Miss Maid of Cotton. Every girl from Sumpter who has won has been a graduate of Sumpter College for Women. Hanna is such a graduate. Her father served his country in Korea, he was a cotton buyer. Her mother, her aunt, her cousin were crown holders. It is in her blood, like a good racehorse, like a good coon dog, it is in her blood."

Winn nodded to Bebe and said, "I don't think Hanna is interested."

"I know. I have talked with Cordelle at length over the matter. But Winn, it is her duty. Would you please talk to her?"

"She's right over there, Bebe. Why don't you talk to her yourself?"

They looked over. Wright and Hanna were standing by each other. Hanna had the Thompson in her hands and was smiling at something Wright had just said to her. Wright then walked away, holding the sawed-off shotgun Bennie J. had blown off Lincoln's head with.

Winn watched Bebe walk toward Hanna, then turned to go to the safe deposit box, but now the Henson twins stood in front of her.

Edna said, "Winn, dear. Mildred and I were just talking and wondered how you think that Tide-Tiger game is going to come out this next season?"

"Well, Miss Henson, I'm afraid the Tigers are going to tear up Bear's boys."

Mildred dropped her jaw, and Winn walked on back to the safe deposit box area and signed in. She looked back into the bank. Edna was complaining to Lemay, probably telling him she had blasphemed against Bear Bryant and the Crimson Tide, that Bennie J. and Cordelle surely didn't raise her like that. Then she glanced over where Bebe stood in front of Hanna. Winn could see Hanna staring Bebe in the eye, could see Hanna's lips move, then saw Hanna chamber the Thompson, could hear it echo throughout the bank. Bebe walked on out of the bank. Winn tried to imagine what Hanna had told her, for she had been succinct. Winn imagined the way Bebe would call Marty Lou and Irene over when she got home. Bebe would say, "The nerve, told me to mind my own blankety-blank business. You know, I doubt her mother was ever married. I bet that Jerry Lee redneck of Bennie J.'s is really her father. I've heard that for years and I think it's true now. Why would a young woman in her position not want to be the Miss Maid of Cotton? You answer me that." Marty Lou would nod and say, "You have a good point, Bebe. I've often wondered why Coleen and her daughter still go by Coleen's maiden name, Remington. You answer me that. And why wouldn't Winn help you persuade Hanna to enter, huh? I heard Winn has rebelled." Irene would say, "I heard she never got over Butch."

Winn followed a bank worker to the safe deposit box. After adding a small bag of diamonds Bennie J. had just bought to some small bars of gold, Winn left the bank, her arm hooked into Hanna's.

Wright followed behind, looking at the Thompson in Hanna's right hand. Hanna had told him how easy it would be. She could walk into a large bank in Birmingham with the Thompson, take a burst of fire at the wall and at least three armed guards would be ready and willing to do what the guards had been praying for years to happen. A torrent of large-caliber bullets to the body and head. One in the cheek of the face, taking out the back of the head. Another three or four in the torso, at least one ripping through the heart. In broad daylight. Sudden. No time to be able to breathe. Hanna had said there was something about death, she wanted to go ahead and get it over, for she knew she wouldn't live to be eighteen.

But Bennie J. was right. "When Winn comes the party starts." Hanna wasn't able to contemplate more on the subject of death with Winn around.

In the courthouse yard sitting on the bench under the water oak, whittling, Lester spit out a stream of Day's Work tobacco and stared at the Model A. Wright waved; they waved back. Wright imagined Lester telling Andy T., "Don't build 'em like that no more." "A real auto-mobile," Andy T. confirms.

Hanna turned around then to get in the rumble seat with Wright. As she was crawling over, the wind caught her dress and blew it up around her waist. Winn was laughing, Hanna giggling. Wright can feel Lester and Andy T. staring at Hanna's ass. He imagines they stop whittling and stare at her ass, watch until the roadster hangs a left past Bernstein's Department Store and barrels out of sight. They begin whittling again. Lester says, "Where's Jacob Lanson today?" Andy T. says, "He told me yestiddy he's goin' down to the river." Lester says, "He misses everthang."

5 Winn lay alone on Jerry Lee's bed, looking out through the window screen to the backwaters. It was almost dusk. A breeze was coming off the backwaters through the front window, across her body, and out the side window. Winn began thinking how this felt like the most exotic place she had ever been.

Bennie J. was always saying how he was from the swamp, that not only explaining any shortcomings of his but also any great strength or esoteric wisdom he possessed. He said he was from the swamp as though Mama Bo, Bennie J.'s late mother, had only raised him, that he had been born mysteriously of the swamp. In the last few years Winn had envisioned herself, if a holocaust was extant, in her delirium trying to make it to the backwaters. Looking at the dock in front of Jerry Lee's house, she imagined this holocaust scenario, making her way into the depths of the backwater to a place she had never seen.

Three swampers finding her as though they had been expecting her and carrying her to a small civilization that lived in the midst of the swamp. They would heal her, wait patiently, looking solemnly and confidently to her. Soon she would realize she was the chosen one. That she was their leader—and was to reestablish an Atlantis-type utopian civilization.

The plank door squeaked open. Jerry Lee walked in. He was wearing a long pair of faded Levi's, nothing else. A heavy whiskey glass full of gin, lemonade, and crushed ice, a short straw, was in each hand. He pushed the door back shut with his foot as he looked at Winn's evenly tanned body, her smooth long legs. Her thick blond pubic hair had been shaven back so she could pose in any type swimwear for the modeling jobs Coleen got her. Jerry Lee imagined Winn and Coleen going out naked onto Coleen's sundeck, rubbing each other down with expensive suntan oil, sunbathing, conversing and sipping highballs. He imagined Winn's and Coleen's picture on the cover of a fashion magazine, Winn the famous model, Coleen the famous look-alike designer aunt. All more or less in the same way Wright saw Terrel's picture on the cover of *Newsweek*.

Only when his left knee touched the bed did Winn come out of her thoughts. She looked at Jerry Lee, smiled, took her drink, sipped it. "This is refreshing."

"It do quench the thirst." He lay on his stomach between Winn's legs, propping up with an elbow on either side of her hipbone. When he lay his drink on her sternum, she gave a twitch at the shock of the cold, then disregarded it.

"Why did you come back to this town after Korea and after living in California?" Winn asked.

"Cause as Bennie J. says, this is a thirsty city."

Hearing her father's name shifted her attention. She said, "Oh, Doddy wanted you to come down to the marina and look at the ice machine."

Jerry Lee said, "Ah, Bennie J., I was fucking your daughter yesterday and she happened to mention something about your ice machine." They giggled. Then he asked, "What's wrong with it?"

"I don't know. Doddy says it's not putting out like it ought to."

"Anything seldom does."

The term "putting out" made Winn think of the three men she had slept with. Jerry Lee. Butch. And Gina's older brother, Frank. Wright had confessed his experiences to Winn, and now she thought of their spooky similarity to her own. Butch and Kathy Lee, brother and sister. Gina and Frank, brother and sister. Hanna and Jerry Lee. Jerry Lee, Hanna's mother's first lover. It all connected too closely, Winn thought.

Jerry Lee said, "It's a thirsty city. And I hadn't finished my drink of it yet," and took a strong pull on the straw to his highball. He was answering Winn's earlier question of why he had come back to Sumpter County.

"It's not just a thirsty city. It's a thirsty world," Winn said.

"Nobody can say you ain't gone for your share."

Winn resisted correcting Jerry Lee's grammar. "What? Do you feel you've already gotten your share?" she said, knowing she was chirping along a string of quips that led nowhere. As Bennie J. would say, "What you talking about? Say what you mean. You ain't said shit."

Jerry Lee said, "Naw. I'm still thirsty. I just thank sometimes all the world is is a small town."

That made her jolt more than the cold drink Jerry Lee had laid on her. She took a deep breath, sighed, imagined her breath mixing with the swamp air and floating with the breeze out the other window. She said, "You were my first."

Jerry Lee grinned and said, "Yeah. And nostalgia seem to do something good for the body." He sucked hard on his drink, cut his eyes up to look at Winn's face at the same time.

"I was seventeen," Winn said, then gave him a shit-eating grin. She laid her drink over on the windowsill, took his drink off her sternum, and stood it beside hers. Her glass was half full, his empty of liquid, half full of crushed ice. The setting sun's rays were hitting the glasses at right angles.

She wiggled and said, "Drink my nectar, you thirsty son of a bitch."

6   That Saturday, Wright, Hanna, and Mama Dog Midnight caddied for Winn, who'd hustled up a game at the country club with a lawyer from Sumpter City and three of his cohorts from Birmingham. All four fancied themselves big-time gamblers who couldn't resist giving Winn five-to-one odds, stroke for

stroke, in eighteen holes of golf. Winn's only handicap was that she could only use one club, a nine iron. Wright, Hanna, and Mama Dog tagged behind Winn, one or the other taking her iron after she made a stroke with it. On the eighteenth hole Winn sunk a twenty-foot putt to win by two strokes. The four men stood there in silence, staring at the ball twirl around the edge of the cup, then fall in. They looked up at Winn, Wright, Hanna, and Mama Dog Midnight, who now had the nine iron in her mouth. Each of the four men reached into his pocket, peeled off five one-hundred-dollar bills, and paid Winn off right there on the eighteenth green. Winn handed Wright the thirteen hundred she owed him, stuffed the other seven hundred she would blow in Europe in her right front pocket.

They went down to the marina late in the day and entertained Bennie J., drinking malt liquor out of soda bottles in front of him. As soon as it was good and dark, Wright, Winn, and Hanna went to the drive-in to see *Thunder Road,* but all Wright could remember was Hanna sitting on the console with her legs across him, and he asking for another Right Time.

He woke alone in his bed, fully clothed, at two A.M. He felt like he needed to stop spinning, needed to pee, throw up, drink some water. He turned the water on in the bathroom sink, bent over, splashed his face. He threw up whole slices of pepperoni, then took the silver ice bucket off his vanity and drank the water from it. One by one he tossed the pepperoni over into the toilet, flushed them, and turned to walk out of the bathroom.

Hanna stood naked in the doorway. Her mouth was frozen open, her eyes glared at Wright. Her right hand was extended palm up toward him. It was covered in blood. Blood ran down the inside of her legs.

Wright froze at the sight. For a moment he thought he was having a nightmare, a nightmare from having seen a horror picture at the drive-in. Only when he came out of the initial shock of the sight did he realize that Hanna was actually standing there naked and bloody.

He stepped toward her. She was trying to tell him something, trying to show him something. In stark terror, she finally said, "Wright. I'm having a miscarriage."

When Wright touched her, she began sobbing, her whole body shaking. Wright was confused, didn't know what to say or do. "Hanna, Hanna." he picked her up and carried her over to his bed.

Between sobs she said, "I can't breathe."

"Breathe slower, Hanna. You're hyperventilating." When she had calmed down some, Wright ran to wake Winn.

Winn jumped out of bed and darted down to Wright's room. By the time Wright got there, Winn was at the head of the bed with Hanna's head in her hands. Hanna was telling how she had just had a miscarriage.

Winn came and held Hanna's head and listened to her talk of miscarriage. Winn rubbed the hair out of Hanna's face, kissed her on the forehead. "Hanna, sweetheart. You just got your period. That's all. You just got your period."

Hanna repeated nervously, "I had a miscarriage."

"Oh, baby," Winn said softly, rubbing Hanna's hair. "You just got your period. That's all." Winn picked Hanna up in her arms and took her to Wright's bathroom. She sat her on the commode, wet a washcloth and started cleaning the blood off Hanna's hands and legs.

"Winn?" Hanna said. Her voice was low and calm now. "I still think I might have had a miscarriage."

"Okay. But now it looks like you're having your period. That's something you can sort out with Dr. Laven." Winn stood up and turned the hot water on in the tub. "Tell you what we're going to do. I'm going to give you a hot soapy bath. Wright's going to go to my bathroom and find you a Tampax. Then we'll all go to your room and sleep."

Wright was looking at Winn. She moved about with no attention that she was naked in front of her brother. Her body was tall, strong, perfectly proportioned. She had picked up Hanna effortlessly and with grace. She had no hangover. She had known exactly what to do.

Wright watched her check the temperature of the water. Then she stood and faced him, her feet shoulder width, her back straight. She put her hands on her hips and smiled.

Wright smiled back, certain now she was no longer just five eight and a half. He walked off to her bathroom to find a Tampax.

7 Wright and Winn were alone in his bedroom, days after Hanna's incident. Wright was emitting little grunts. "Winn, I love you," Wright sighed as Winn grabbed his trapezius muscle. "I love you for a sister."

Wright's head was near the foot of his bed. He was looking through the white ornamentation of his iron bed at the dark greyish-blue color of his wall. Then to the trim. Like Hanna's room, the wood trim, doors, doorjambs, and double French glass door that led out to his balcony were all painted a high-gloss white enamel.

Winn and Wright had shared the same bedroom for two years. One day when Wright was five, Winn decided she wanted their room for her own and kicked him out. She set all his toys outside the room, pushed him out, and closed and locked the door behind him. He had tied the three banana boxes full of toys together like a train and somehow managed to drag them down the hallway, stopping at each door to peek in and consider.

Then he had come to one room that was near empty. The walls were painted, the floor bare wood decking. Venetian blinds were on the windows, but no curtains. Double-bed-sized mattress and box springs leaned against a wall. Wright drug his boxes in to the middle of the room, closed the door, opened the blinds. He went into the bathroom and looked around, inspecting it as if seeing it for the first time, even though he had been in here often to play. He filled the tub full of water for his battery-operated toy outboard boat. Then he went back into the bedroom, pulled the box springs down flat on the floor, and pushed the mattress on top of the box springs. From then on it was Wright's room.

Mama Bo, alive then, gave him one of her old iron beds and Cordelle put up some curtains. But that was the extent of the decorating. Wright didn't want anything on the floor as far as any covering. Through the years it would look more like a workshop or studio than a bedroom, reflecting whatever hobby he was interested in at that time: model planes, electric trains, chemistry lab, gym.

At the start of his dating era, when his interests in hobbies had stopped, he had lain in his bed staring at the ceiling and out of boredom decided to fix his room up. First he painted the walls, then the woodwork, had thick deep-blue carpet laid, had black velvet drapes hung, painted the bed to match the woodwork, and then bought a few pieces of furniture.

Over the last three years he had slowly decorated the walls by having different photographs custom-framed and hung. The frames were different-sized, some with mats, some without, yet all were gold-leafed. There was a photo of him and Kathy Lee dressed up to go to a dance in junior high. He and Bennie J. with a fish catch. A recent one of him, Hanna, and Winn in the swing on the veranda. A black-and-white of Mae Emma playing the baby grand, Wright sitting next to her on the stool with his elbow on the edge of the piano, his jaw resting on the heel of his hand as he gazed at Mae Emma. One of him and Cordelle in Roaring Twenties dress, leaned against the Model A. One of him and Hanna in the French Quarter when they were ten years old. One of him, Winn, and Mama Dog Midnight, all in Halloween costumes.

The most recent of the framings, a two-by-three-footer, was above the headboard of his bed. It was done from a photograph Cordelle had taken the night Wright took Hanna to the Sumpter College graduation ball. Wright was in a black tux with white shirt. Hanna had on a black formal. They were sitting side by side on the settee in the vestibule to Big Room. The shot was of from midtorso up. Hanna had actually been sitting with her legs across Wright's legs. Wright and Hanna were both looking away from the camera but in different directions.

Wright gave a long sigh and mumbled, "That feels so good." He was lying on his stomach, shirtless and barefoot, but wearing navy bellbottoms. Winn sat on top of him, giving him a back rub.

"We're all going off together to LSU." Winn said. "Everything is going to be just fine." She put her hands over each of his deltoids. She leaned forward until she was lying on him and then slid off, lying beside him. She propped up on her left elbow and stroked his back with her right index finger in little curlicue motions. "We're lucky to be together and to have been together and some way or another we'll always be together."

Wright had his chin pressed into a pillow. He turned his head; they kissed lightly on the mouths. "This place just isn't right without you," he said. Winn smiled and continued running her finger around his back. He thought of the night Hanna had come to his bathroom with blood on her hand. Of that night the image that lingered in Wright's mind was of Winn standing there, hands on hips. It wasn't so much her nakedness but the strong line of her long dark shapely legs and the neatness with which they molded into her torso. There were no weak points to her body. No clumsy tan marks, no pallid white hip or breast area, everything evenly copper brown. No vulnerable testicles hanging at the groin area. Everything powerful, sleek, functional.

"There is something about us that's very close," Wright said. He propped up on his side, facing Winn. "This is wild."

Winn smiled and nodded. With the hand she had used to massage Wright, she now rubbed around the back of her own neck and then down the front of her throat, as though she were looking for something. "Oh, Wright, honey. Would you go to your bathroom and get my necklace? I left it on the back of your commode."

Wright rolled off the bed and walked to his dressing room. A couple of empty Sun-Drop bottles, a couple of six-packs of Right Time, and the bottles lined up on his vanity counter where they had been bottling malt liquor into the soda bottles. He put a few cubes from the ice bucket into a glass, then poured in some malt liquor. The long swig he took immediately penetrated his body and made him lightheaded. He walked out of his dressing room into the bathroom.

The gold necklace was lying over on the back of the commode. When Wright reached over for it, he looked down into the toilet. He stared and then puffed his cheeks out like he had thrown up. He set the drink on the counter by the sink. "One of her classics. Goddamn."

In the toilet bowl was the biggest excretion of Winn's he had ever seen. It was about two and a half feet long. Looked like a fat cottonmouth curled up with its head cut off.

Wright hollered, "Goddammit to hell, Winn!"

When he came charging out of the bathroom toward her, Winn was grinning. She rolled off the bed on the side opposite from Wright. He ran over the bed, as if it weren't an obstacle. He went for Winn, but she just grabbed him and gave him a hip throw. Wright rolled, got up on his feet. He and Winn faced off.

Wright said, "You're going to flush it. Then clean the toilet."

Winn shook her head no. She grinned defiantly. "I wanted to leave something personal with you. Just from me to you."

Winn darted for the door. Wright sidestepped to block her way. She ran for the balcony. Wright ran and slammed the French door shut. She ran over onto the bed with him chasing her, did a turn-around, and slipped back past him.

Winn ran for the door. She almost got the key in the bolt turned when Wright grabbed her in a bear hug from behind.

They started giggling.

Winn spread her legs, squatted a bit, grabbed Wright's legs through hers, and pulled up.

As he fell back, she grabbed the doorknob with one hand, started turning the key with the other. Wright lunged for her, grabbed her thigh from behind, but his hand slipped because the boot-cut Levi's she had on were skin-tight. He grasped at her thigh again and pulled her down. They were both grunting and giggling. She fell back. As she was falling she twisted and landed on top of him, face to face.

They stopped giggling. Wright relaxed his muscles; he could feel his heart pounding against Winn's breast. Her legs that he had so admired from a distance now slid down over his. Even though all of Winn's muscles were now relaxed, Wright seemed to feel the power of her thighs. A quick kick from them could snap someone's femur, a scissor hold could crush a ribcage.

Wright could feel the heat of her crotch. To aggravate him one of the things Winn had done to Wright in the last couple of years, other than leaving her excretions unflushed in his toilet, was to wear his jeans without any underwear. Wright now realized she had on a pair of his jeans but it excited instead of aggravated him. She had on one of his work shirts, too. It had been tied at her waist, but in their last wrestle had come undone. Wright could feel her naked stomach touch and move off his as she breathed.

His hip was twisted around uncomfortably. He wiggled under Winn to straight it out.

They were very silent. Wright finally caught his breath, no longer panting heavily. Winn pulled away a little from Wright and said, "I love you as a brother, too. But please next time come back as something else."

Winn jumped up and left.

8   Early the next morning at breakfast on the veranda, Cordelle said, "Today is the day. Today is the day Winn goes to Europe."

Bennie J. said, "Don't be drinking any wine or that ole beer over there. Over yonder in them foreign countries they serve wine and beer to children. But anyway ole Uncle Davey decided to run for sheriff to save the Reynolds family all the overhead of getting pursued by the law. Between his speech making and his fiddle playin' Uncle Davey done gained the support of two thirds of the population of Sumpter County. Only trouble was Uncle Davey managed to git the support of the two thirds that was too pore to pay poll tax—"

Bennie J. stopped short. A yellow open-cockpit two-seater biplane, his crop duster, landed in the pasture off from Big House. Bennie J. said, "There he is."

Winn recapitulated: "Jerry Lee will take me to Gina's ranch. Then her mother will take us to Birmingham. We'll fly to New York, then fly off to London the next day. I'll keep in touch."

Bennie J. said, "If the senator's at his farm, tell him Bennie J. says hey. I'll see him again when the crappies start biting."

Mae Emma came out onto the veranda carrying two small pieces of luggage; Winn always traveled light. She hugged Winn and said, "You have fun, baby. I'm goin' back in 'fore I cry." Mae Emma hurried back inside as Winn assured her she would have fun.

Jerry Lee landed the plane. He climbed out and chocked the wheels. He walked to the veranda and said, "Morning," to everyone, picked up the luggage.

Bennie J. said, "You take care of my little girl, now."

Jerry Lee coughed and said, "I will."

"And take care of my cropduster," Bennie J. said.

"It couldn't be in better hands," Jerry Lee said and left with the suitcases.

As Jerry Lee was going out the gate in the wall, Bennie J. hollered to him, "And don't be spraying nobody. I don't need any lawsuits."

Shortly they all got up and walked slowly out the gate into the pasture. Cordelle and Winn hugged. Cordelle said, "Have fun, honey."

She said, "I will, Mama. Thank you for everything. I'll buy you something in every country. In every province. In every city." She walked up to Bennie J. and hugged him.

Bennie J. said, "Now, Winn. I got you some traveler's checks."

"Everything's paid for already, Doddy. And I have plenty of money," Winn replied.

Bennie J. grinned and said, "Yeah, honey. But that ain't enough. Doddy Bennie J. wants you to have these traveler's checks."

"But Doddy, you have to sign in person at the bank for traveler's checks."

Bennie J. laughed. "Not these kind." He pulled out a bundle of hundred-dollar bills and handed them to Winn, made her take them.

"Doddy!" Winn shrieked. It made Bennie J. pleased.

Jerry Lee stowed the luggage and crawled into the cockpit. Winn looked out at the plane, then pulled Bennie J. and Cordelle to her.

Winn said, "Mama. Doddy. I love you both so much. I feel sorry for all the other children in the world who don't have you for parents and didn't get to grow up at Big House."

After they hugged, she walked away with Wright on one side, Hanna the other, all arm in arm.

Bennie J. said to Cordelle, "Winn's just like old Uncle Davey. When she come, the party starts up." They watched the kids kiss each other, then watched Winn crawl up into the plane. Wright took the chocks away from the wheels and handed them to Jerry Lee. Bennie J. said, "Just because I had to do without don't mean I'm gone let my younguns do without."

Cordelle put her arm around Bennie J.'s waist and said, "Isn't it all so wonderful, B.J.?"

Wright and Hanna stood away from the plane. It rolled down the pasture; the wheels came up off the ground before it seemed to be going fast enough to take off. Jerry Lee looped around and flew back low so Winn could wave and throw kisses. Then he gained altitude.

Winn looked back down at Big House, the cotton fields, the pastures, and the Tennessee River below. Then she looked ahead, listening to the roar of the engine and the wind. She had heard so often how when someone went back to their childhood home it looked so much smaller than it did when they had lived there. She had even heard it from some of the girls in boarding school who came back from home only having lived away a few months.

But every time Winn went back to Big House it seemed bigger to her. Sitting there in the plane, she imagined Big House getting bigger and bigger until it was the size of Sumpter, and the Tennessee River feeding into Big Fountain.

Winn said, "It's a thirsty city," as if someone could hear her.

The Heart
of Dixie

| 1 |

Lou Ann was chattering away at the dinner table. Wright was wiggling around, recalling his day. When he and Hanna had been driving back through old Birmingham from her visit to the gynecologist, Hanna had pointed to an old restaurant and hotel, cried out how she loved the look of the place, suggested they lunch there. When they walked in they started pretending they were married, it was the thirties, and they lived in Paris in this hotel; they checked into a room and made love for the first time since Hanna's miscarriage incident. Afterwards they had a lavish meal in the French restaurant, lingered there drinking cappuccino, giggling, teasing each other, then went back upstairs to the old and expensive hotel room. They were loud and passionate, indulging deeply. "Decadent in a classic sort of way," Hanna had said as they sat up in the bed smoking unfiltered cigarettes and sipping expensive French red wine they had bribed the bellboy to procure for them.

When they had pulled up to the front of Big House, Cordelle had come out and yelled, "Wright! Where have y'all been? It's seven o'clock. You know y'all are supposed to be over at Lou Ann and J.C.'s at eight. I swanny, you are getting worse than your sister about appointments!" Unmoved, Wright had said, "Have you heard from her?" Cordelle said, "Oh, she called a couple of hours ago. She's having a wonderful time. They're staying at this gorgeous Parisian hotel." Wright and Hanna just laughed.

"That's the way it has always been done in the South here, isn't it, Wright?" Lou Ann Thomas said.

"Yes, ma'am," Wright answered, but had no idea what she had been talking about. He had been staring at an old painting of a Confederate officer that hung on the other side of the dining room, staring in a daze, trying to relive his day with Hanna. He looked at Lou Ann and smiled. He forced some food into his mouth, then looked down at one of his cuff links. He wiped a smudge off one with his left thumb. He looked at the initials, WR, engraved into the gold.

Winn had a habit of swiping them and wearing them with some of her French-cuff blouses, but somehow she had packed for Europe without pilfering them. All the while Lou Ann was talking, Wright was thinking, "decadent in a classic sort of way," and of his perfect day with Hanna.

Lou Ann announced to everyone, "See, Wright agrees with me." Wright then realized Lou Ann had spoken directly to him, something she hadn't done in two years. In grammar school when Wright would come over to the Thomas's plantation to play with Kathy Lee, Lou Ann would look him in the eye, grip his shoulders and say, "You're so pretty. You're so pretty you should have been a girl." At that age Wright didn't want to be called pretty or told he should have been a girl, but somehow he took it as a compliment. Then two years ago Wright had come by the plantation right before Christmas to give Kathy Lee a gift. Ida had led him into the parlor, where he sat on the piano stool playing some chords, Winn had taught him, waiting for Kathy Lee to come down. Lou Ann had walked into the parlor wearing a long dress and sat down beside him. She had a Scotch in her hand. She was not sober, nor was she drunk. Her eyes were a bit dazed; she had a drugged mellowness to her as if she had been smoking opium or heroin. She had set her drink on the piano and straightened Wright's collar, then brushed at his hair with her hand. Then she had said, "You are very, very beautiful. You have a physical mystique that only a few of each generation possess. You are half a boy and you are half a man. And you are pretty enough to have been a woman. Wright, my dear, you can be anything you want to be." She had kissed him on the corner of his mouth, risen, taken her drink, turned, and walked out of the parlor. After that evening she had not addressed him in any personal sort of way, as she often had before, until tonight.

Wright smiled at Lou Ann, who was smiling at him. He figured she was right now trying to relive that moment she had sat beside him on the piano stool, the same way he had been trying to relive his day with Hanna.

Hanna, J.C., Kathy Lee, and Eddie were also sitting there at the dining room table, had been listening to Lou Ann banter away. Wright wondered why the hell they had had to invite Eddie; things would have been fine without him. Ida walked in with a pitcher to refill ice teas. She was big, black, maternal. Wright thought about maids. Mae Emma was tall, slim, mulatto, more sibling than maternal to Wright, Winn, and Hanna. Bennie J. called her Cousin Emma.

Once when Wright was eight, a bunch of them had been eating at the café. Bennie J. looked out the window, saw Mae Emma come out of the bait shop, heading for the café. Bennie J. had said, "Here come Cousin Emma looking for me." Wright had said, "Now, Doddy, is Mae Emma our cousin on your side or Mama Cordelle's side?" Everyone in the café had laughed except Wright. Cordelle had said, "Wright, honey, Mae Emma isn't your cousin. Doddy Bennie J. just calls her cousin." It had kind of confused Wright. Bennie J. and Pete called each other cousin, too, and now Wright didn't know if he was kin to Pete either.

Wright asked Ida, "How's Horace's knee?" Horace, Ida's son, worked on the Reynolds' farm during summers. Horace had been a football star at Carver High, the black high school that had been closed last month on the federal desegregation plan. He was Sumpter High–bound.

Ida said, "It doing fine. He gone be able start football practice come August. Anxious see how he gone do at a new school. You know he got his heart set on gettin' an A&M scholarship."

"Ahh," Wright said, flipping his hand up, a cuff link flashing in the light of the chandelier. "Three years from now Horace'll be playing for the Bear. You wait and see. You tell Horace Wright says hey."

"I show will. He be tickled. He ax 'bout you las' week." Ida filled empty tea glasses and walked back to the kitchen.

Wright looked over to see Eddie give him a quick, evil glance. Wright knew it was for talking to the help. He thought it was all too typical. Of the seven human beings in the house, the last one with any right to assert behavior in an antebellum home was Eddie. Wright had often thought: Ever since Eddie started going out with Kathy Lee, he thinks he's automatically some aristocrat.

And it was a genuine antebellum home, had been built by Kathy Lee's great-grandfather in 1807, yet Kathy Lee and her immediate family had only moved in when J.C.'s mother had died—the same year Wright had moved into Big House. In his early teens, Wright would come over to visit with Kathy Lee. One of their favorite things to do was to slip into J.C.'s study, look at the Thomas family's Civil War memorabilia, and sneak bourbon out of J.C.'s liquor cabinet.

Wright saw Eddie give him another glance. Wright started to say, "What you looking at, you sleazy son of a bitch?" but didn't want to have to beat the shit out of him in front of Kathy Lee and them. Instead Wright looked over at J.C. and asked, "Do y'all still have all that Confederate stuff in the study?"

"Sure," J.C. said. "I'll show it to you again just as soon as we have dessert."

Wright wanted badly to see the study again, but knew he and J.C. would go in there alone. He didn't mind being alone with J.C., didn't mind Hanna being alone with the others. It was just he had become obsessed with being with Hanna and being able to look at her. It was something he had noticed earlier today. He and Hanna had walked out of the gynecologist's office, they had kissed there along the street, Hanna had adjusted her miniskirt, and then they walked down the sidewalk holding hands to where they had Winn's Vette parked. Along the way Wright noticed two men make double-takes at Hanna, something he was accustomed to. The second one saw Wright see him. Wright wanted to go up to him and say, "I saw you looking at her. But that's all right. Were you looking at her long black straight hair? Was it her petite ass? Maybe those long lovely legs? Those emerald green eyes? That knock-you-out face? Or were you trying to take it all in? That's what I came over to tell you. Look mister, that's my cousin. And I live with her. And there aren't enough hours in the day for me to take her all in."

Wright had opened the passenger door to the Corvette, leaned over and tossed the towel over onto the console, the towel he lay there so the seat wouldn't get scorching hot from the sun. As Hanna was getting into the car he had taken her hair and flipped it around to her front so she wouldn't sit on it; he looked at her long slim legs. At that moment as he was admiring her just for beauty's sake, he realized he had always been around beautiful women. Seldom ten feet away from one. Mama Cordelle, Mae Emma, Coleen, Winn, Hanna, Kathy Lee. Doddy, Butch, and Jerry Lee were the only men he had been around alone much. The best-looking women he had ever seen had been the ones he had grown up around. There was only one short era he had not had the company of women much, the span before he and Hanna had gotten together—when he had done his dating. When he wasn't dating, he had hung around some of his male class-mates. They would go over into Tennessee to taverns they could slip into underage. They would sit there in a cigarette fog and try to get girls to dance with them, but mostly just sat there and talked about pussy. Wright knew it was supposed to be fun, had tried to make it such, but had understood it about as much as he had dating.

But here Wright was alone with J.C. in the study. Wright was sitting in a black leather chair, a whiskey glass with a shot of straight bour-bon in his right hand. J.C. was in his chair behind the desk, facing

Wright, with a double shot of straight bourbon. Wright looked about at the antique portraits of men in Confederate officer uniforms, at the swords, pistols, rifles, and CSA medallions. The only portrait on the walls that wasn't from the Civil War period was a huge oil of Lou Ann. In fact, everything besides that portrait was military, making Wright remember that once he had been going to attend the military academy Butch had gone to. He had come down for breakfast the morning he was supposed to leave. As Wright finished the last of his breakfast, Cordelle said, singsongy, "Today is the day. Today is the day Wright goes to military academy." Wright got up, went to the stable, saddled up Thunder, and rode out in the woods all day, coming in after dark. Three weeks later he started high school in town at Sumpter City High. That morning Cordelle had said, singsongy, "Today is the day. Today is the day Wright goes to high school."

"She'll go to Rutger's next month," J.C. said and took a sip of bourbon.

"What?" Wright said, thinking J.C. was reading his mind about schools for a second.

J.C. said, "Next month Kathy Lee will go to New Jersey. He'll go to Ole Miss. That'll be the end of that." He took a sip of bourbon. "I don't like Eddie."

"You a good judge of character." Wright smiled. He assured J.C., "Yeah, that'll be the end of that," and took a sip of the bourbon that was slowly numbing his lips. "I like your study."

"Thank you. I come here to read and to be alone. I come here a lot lately."

Wright motioned to the portrait and said, "That's a nice painting of Lou Ann. She favors Kathy Lee a lot there."

"Yes," J.C. said proudly. "That was done just after she graduated from Rutger's."

As Wright looked about at the things on the walls, he thought of Bennie J.'s words: "If they keep sending ole Kathy Lee around to different schools, she's not ever gone git an education. She'll be an old maid by time she gits out of all them schools." Wright said to J.C., "My ancestors were in the Civil War but some of them got mixed up and joined the Union Army and then deserted and lived out in the swamp. Some of them got killed fighting for the Confederacy. Anyway, we don't have any stuff like this," meaning the artifacts. "All we have are the stories they passed down."

"Those are the most valuable," J.C. said and smiled. He slugged out his whiskey, leaned up, poured himself a half a whiskey glass of straight bourbon, settled back into the chair, and started sipping. "There is something I want you to think about, Wright."

Wright had drifted off thinking about Hanna. He said, "Yes, sir?"

"I know your father is going to see to it you get a college education. Your father is a good man. Your father is a smart man. He didn't build an empire from nothing just by accident. Your father became wealthy, and he has stayed wealthy. Few people can do that." J.C. took a sip of whiskey. Wright didn't know if he were just taking a sip of whiskey or was trying to accentuate what he had just said. J.C. continued, "And it's wonderful he is going to see to it you get a higher education. However, your father may only insist you earn a bachelor of science, or arts, from any college or university. I personally believe after a couple of years at LSU you could go to Oxford as a Rhodes Scholar."

Now Wright took him a sip of whiskey, wishing it was gin or vodka. He paused to think how he was barely able to leave Sumpter to go to LSU, and if he had to leave Sumpter what he really wanted was to marry Hanna and live in a gorgeous Parisian hotel. The last time J.C. gave him help with his education it was to get him accepted at military academy. When Wright didn't show up for orientation, J.C. came storming over to Big House. Wright stayed in his room, listening to the rumble of J.C. talking in the den and Bennie J. plainly hollering, "He don't want to go! Maybe he got more damn sense than you do, J.C. What he gone do, march around for four years in a wool uniform, getting brainwashed to go off to some war? What you scared of, J.C., was you scared you son was gone have to go to high school with a bunch of niggers? I not from the same place you are, J.C. I was raised by niggers, growed up with niggers, do business with niggers. Wright raised by niggers, grew up with niggers. I don't thank it gone kill him to go to school with niggers."

Wright had never heard Doddy Bennie J. say the word nigger and here he was saying it a half dozen times in a few sentences. Wright had cracked his bedroom door and heard J.C. retort in a softer voice that it had nothing to do with race or integration, but with education, then said something about Wright being one of the elite. Three years later when J.C.'s son was killed he had come back over to Big House, told Bennie J. he should have never sent him to military academy. Bennie J. consoled him and told him that to lose a parent was sorrowful, to lose a sibling or spouse was tragic, but to lose a child was beyond tragedy, was the sign of an imperfect God. It was then that

J.C. truly recognized Bennie J. for the wise and deeply religious man that he was.

Wright said, concerning being a Rhodes Scholar, "Don't you have to be a football captain or head of the Young Democrats and Honor Societies to be eligible for that?"

J.C. replied, "You have everything that's needed. The background. The character. The intelligence. I will help you."

"Thanks, J.C. Yes, sir, I'll keep that in mind. But I mean, two years. That's a long ways off."

J.C. laughed, but then just smiled when he realized Wright's statement had been sincere. "Not as far off as you might think. It's an opportunity. And opportunity you must exercise before you're twenty-five or married."

Wright knew J.C. knew Cordelle had graduated from Sumpter College after she was married. Rules were made to be broken. Wright took a slug of whiskey, trying to keep up with J.C., who had just poured himself yet another shot of bourbon. Marrying Hanna, then living in Oxford, England in a gorgeous hotel—being a Rhodes Scholar might just be the way to go. Wright said, "It's something to think about all right, J.C."

"Having been a Rhodes Scholar is one of the things of which I am proudest." He paused and added, "Butch was interested in it." J.C. slugged down his drink and began pouring another.

Wright could never catch up to J.C., he knew, even if he were drinking gin. He pointed up at the painting of Lou Ann. "Lou Ann surely is very pretty. Where'd y'all meet?"

"Yes, she is pretty. We have known each other all our lives."

"I thought Kathy Lee told me Lou Ann was from South Carolina."

"Oh, she is," J.C. said. "Lou Ann is my first cousin on my mother's side."

Wright snapped his eyes away from the oil painting and looked directly at J.C. "No, sir?"

"Yes."

Wright stood up and exclaimed, "No, sir!"

J.C. looked back casually at Wright and exclaimed, "Yes, sir!"

Wright sat back down but on the edge of the chair. "That's all right. I thought marrying your cousin was against the law or something."

"Oh, no. Historically, first cousins have often married. There have been eras and locales where it was very vogue even." Another sip.

"But we married not for the sake of history or being vogue. Lou Ann and I were, and are, madly in love."

The heavy crystal whiskey glass seemed to weigh at least two pounds, but Wright brought it up to his mouth effortlessly and killed the rest of the bourbon. "This is great!" he said. He might just go out there and beat hell out of Eddie and make it the perfect day.

2 Bennie J. thought he was going to get away without having to wear a birthday hat this year, but Winn had called from Switzerland to wish Wright a happy birthday and had made Bennie J. promise. Now Wright, Hanna, Bennie J., and Cordelle sat around the dining room table, and the excitement had lulled. They still had on their hats but everyone had finished supper. Several shirts and a couple of scuba tanks, Wright's presents, were scattered about. That morning at breakfast Cordelle had said singsongy, "Today is the day. Today is the day Wright turns eighteen."

Breaking the silence, Bennie J. said, "Winn. Winn. Good ole Winn called all the way from Switzerland."

With that Hanna raised her hand and they began singing "Happy Birthday." Mae Emma walked in from the kitchen, singing and carrying a bright yellow-and-green birthday cake with eighteen lit candles. She set the cake in front of Wright, the song was finished, and Wright blew out all the candles as everyone clapped.

Mae Emma took Wright's head in her hands and pulled it, hugged it into her side. "My little boy. My little boy done grown up to be a man." She started sobbing and ran off to the kitchen. They were all silent, only noise being Mae Emma in the kitchen screaming for Jesus to help her. When they could no longer hear her, Bennie J. said, "Wright, eighteen years ago this morning I had a brand-new hell of a son and a brand-new hell of a coon dog. Mama Dog's might near seen hers but you got you whole life ahead of you. Live it well!"

Bennie J.'s last statements were dead serious. Quiet reigned; Wright didn't fight it. He gave it a couple of minutes before he said "Where is Mama Dog Midnight? Today is her eighteenth birthday too."

Bennie J. laughed and whistled, "Mama Dog Midnight! What you got Wright for his birthday?"

Mama Dog pushed through the swing door that connected the kitchen to the dining room. She wore a party hat and came in panting, the corners of her mouth upturned, her tail wagging. She's smiling, Winn called it. A red envelope was tucked under her gold mesh strap collar. She walked toward Cordelle.

Cordelle said, "Yeah, you know who feeds you. Don't you?"

"Take it to Wright, Mama Dog," Bennie J. urged.

"Over to Wright, honey dog," Cordelle said. Midnight turned, started walking around the table. Cordelle said, "That's right."

When Midnight looked up at Hanna, she said, "Over to Wright."

"To Wright," Bennie J. said. "That's a girl."

Midnight walked over and put her head in Wright's lap. He patted her head and said, "Happy birthday, Mama Dog Midnight." He took the envelope out from under her collar. Mama Dog looked over and then walked to Cordelle. Wright slit the envelope open with the edge of a fork. The outside of the card stated birthday wishes. Inside Cordelle had written "To our darling son. Love, Mama and Doddy." A key was taped there. Wright hollered, "A car key! A Chevrolet car key!"

Wright jumped up, ran out the dining room, through Big Room, jerked open the front door. There in the illumination of the front floodlights sat a new blue Corvette convertible. He walked around it, touched it, and at last got into the driver's seat.

Hanna, Bennie J., Cordelle, and Mae Emma came out. Hanna got in the passenger seat and Bennie J. said to Wright, "I know I said I wouldn't buy you a new car until your senior year, but Cordelle and I got to talking. We had rather see you enjoy it now than wait. There might be a time for waiting but waiting's mostly from shit," Bennie J. said, then paused, not wanting to get too philosophical.

"Mama. Doddy. Thank you," Wright said.

Bennie J. said, "Damn thing's made out of fiberglass. Don't a Chevrolet engine belong in no toy. But if that's what y'all kids want. Now don't be driving fast in that little thang. Winn, ole Winn, she had the tag ordered. You see the tag?"

"Yes sir. Fast-2."

"Yeah, ole Winn, she was in on it from the start. When Winn shows up the party starts," Bennie J. said, not being able to help quoting himself.

Wright pulled away as Cordelle was hugging Bennie J., saying, "Oh, isn't it all so wonderful, B.J.?" Hanna turned on the radio and pushed in the tape Cordelle had bought. On a straightaway he pushed the car easily up toward a hundred miles an hour. Hanna turned the song on the radio down, and Wright slowed down to forty, cruising along in the hot summer night with Hanna leaning against him. She bit Wright on the shoulder and said, "Let's go to the river." There was a flat point that looked out onto the Tennessee River where he and Hanna went parking at midnight in the MGA, when Hanna was attending Sumpter College. That is where they went in the Corvette. The river was calm, lights from factories that lined the waterfront were reflected into long beams across the water. A tugboat pushed a barge along the channel.

When Wright turned to face Hanna, she held a small gift-wrapped package out to Wright. She told him it was something special and she had used some money out of her account to buy it, that she hadn't gone uptown and charged it to Bennie J. "Like somebody else we know," Wright giggled, making fun of Winn, who would often go uptown to get Bennie J. a gift and charge it to his account. Wright opened the gift to find a heavy eighteen-carat gold ID bracelet. Hanna took a flashlight, one of the essentials Cordelle had supplied the car with, and shone it on the bracelet. "Wright" was engraved across the face in capital letters. Hanna said, "Turn it over!" On the back: "To the one who's on my mind all the time. Love, Hanna."

Wright said, "Thank you so much. This is nice, very nice." Wright was good at flattery, but when it came to being lavished with presents or admiration, all he could think of to say was "nice." Hanna took the bracelet and put it on his right wrist. He wiggled his wrist, feeling the new weight on it. "Thank you, Hanna. I love the bracelet."

Hanna said, "I love *you.*"

Wright looked out to the river. This was the life he wanted. Him, Hanna, Corvettes, Birmingham Parisian hotels without having to leave Big House. He wanted the summer to last the rest of his life. But he just had this terrible feeling things sooner or later were going to turn to shit.

The next several days went smoothly, but the Fourth of July seemed lonesome to Wright. They always had a big celebration on the veranda. Winn was always there, Mae Emma and her daughter usually, and often as not Coleen with Hanna. But this year of course Winn was in Europe, Mae Emma flew up north for a couple of days to see her daughter, and Coleen stayed in New York.

Cordelle, Bennie J., Hanna, and Wright sat out on the veranda eating sirloin steak, barbecue, and blackberry cobbler out of ritual. All of them moped, speaking of the ones not present, recalling the time Bennie J. had blown up an old barn for Wright and Winn's Fourth of July amusement. The only highlight this year was when Winn called from Europe and Bennie J. lit a quarter stick of dynamite and threw it out into the yard. The resonance blew out one of the back French glass windows and made a big hole in Big Back Yard, which Cordelle fussed about to Bennie J. They all passed the phone around talking to Winn, then Bennie J. started complaining he was going to have a phone bill that even Rube Goldberg wouldn't have been able to pay. When Winn hung up, everything was that much more lonesome and quiet. Bennie J. was right, the party started when Winn showed up. When the dynamite had gone off, Midnight woke up from under the swing, walked over, and lay under the table. Now she had her head against Wright's leg.

Cordelle poured everyone some more lemonade. It was almost too hot to be sitting outside, no one hardly moved. Then Bennie J. said to Wright in a stern sort of way, "I need you to be in the meat market at seven in the morning."

"Seven?" Wright looked up, startled.

"Yeah. No need to come in before then. You gone have to be the head butcher for a couple weeks."

Wright felt like he had been hit in the solar plexus. "A couple of weeks?"

"Nita's off on vacation. Mr. Berzett wasn't going to leave till she got back, but turns out they having his family reunion down in South Alabama a week early. I told him go on take off."

"But—" Wright began.

"I got to have you be the butcher. Bennie J. can't run this empire by hisself. Bennie J. need some help. Doddy Bennie J. work all the time. Got to get back up to the marina right now. No telling what's going on up there. I tell 'em, don't drink a fifth on the Fourth if they want to be alive on the sixth." Bennie J. got up and left.

Wright was pinned down to fourteen-hour days. Not everybody could cut meat, so there wasn't anybody to pawn the work off on. If the shelves at the bait shop had needed stocking, he could have just gone up there, got Jake started on it, then invented something that was needed and been gone the rest of the day running around trying to find one. Being the butcher at the bait shop was a pinned-down immobile job. Wright said, "Shit," but not loud enough for Cordelle

to hear. Then he said, "Work, work, work. All I get to do is work."
Wright got up and went inside. As he was going in he heard Cordelle
tell Hanna, "Your cousin gets mad when he has to work at the bait
shop."

Wright stomped up the stairs, saying, "I knew the shit was coming.
My whole summer's fucked up now." He started thinking about being
away from Hanna, how he wouldn't be able to stand it. He went
straight to his vanity, pulled a Right Time out of his cabinet, laid it
up on the counter, got a glass. But the ice bucket was empty, for Mae
Emma was away. Every morning she straightened his room, made his
bed if he had slept in it, filled the ice bucket. Every afternoon before
she left she refilled the ice buckets in all the bathrooms. It was Mae
Emma who came into Wright's room the morning after Hanna's
"miscarriage," found the blood-spotted sheets, the blood-stained
washcloth Winn had used, and had secretly cleaned them. It was Mae
Emma who filled that gap for Wright, that gap between mother and
sister. She had tended to him since his birth. A bit more of a sister
than a mother. A bit more mother than a sister. And now, looking
at the empty ice bucket, he realized Mae Emma wasn't following him
to LSU. "Yeah, things are starting to turn to shit," he said, having
a hard enough time being able to get by until Mae Emma came back
in the morning.

He emptied the bottle of Right Time into a large glass, then went
down to the kitchen. After he got his malt liquor iced and sucked
about half of it down to calm his nerves, Wright got a pen and paper
Mae Emma and Cordelle kept on the counter to put the grocery list
on and started trying to figure how many hours would be left in a
day—if there would even be any hope of seeing Hanna at all. Could
he stay up all night with her, then walk around in a haze all day at
the bait shop? Then when he passed out maybe Bennie J. would leave
him alone to recover. Or, he wondered, should he just give in to the
whole thing.

Just as he had figured he needed a good seven hours of sleep a night
and had subtracted that from the twenty-four, Hanna and Cordelle
came into the kitchen and sat at the table. Cordelle was chattering
to Hanna, something about antiques and Southern heritage. She
plopped a *Southern Living* magazine down on the table and slowly
flipped through it, looking at the pictures as she continued to tell
Hanna about the antiques. When Cordelle finished telling Hanna
that, she paused and then said to Wright, while still flipping through

the magazine, "Did you know Betsy Coleman's older sister is expecting?"

"Expecting what?" Wright asked.

"You know," Cordelle said shyly. "A baby."

All of Wright's attention had been on his subtraction and sucking down his Right Time. But now it went to Cordelle. "Look, I didn't go out with Nancy. I just went out with Betsy a couple of times. I can't help what problems Nancy gets herself into." Wright quickly got up, wadded the notepaper and tossed it into the trash. He grabbed up his drink and said, "Excuse me. I'm going to the den to watch TV."

Cordelle started explaining to Hanna, "It's not a problem. Nancy's married to Dean Elroyd's son. And Dean and Mary have been wanting a grandchild for years."

When Wright closed the door to the den he could hear Hanna asking Cordelle shouldn't they do something about the shattered window. Wright flipped on the TV and eased back into Bennie J.'s big chair. "Turning to shit," he said. Wright sat there and analytically told himself he couldn't have gotten Nancy Elroyd pregnant by trying to feel of her sister's pussy. After convincing himself he couldn't, he wondered if Cordelle somehow knew he had made a fool out of himself trying to run his hand up Betsy's dress.

Wright reached over and picked up a book, was into the second page of how Gaul was divided into three parts, until he realized he was reading one of Cordelle's Latin books. Once he, Butch, Winn, Cordelle, and Bennie J. were sitting in this very den. Bennie J. was reading the paper but looked up to ask, "Does anybody know what"—then slowly pronounced some long Latin word—"means?" He had looked to each of them, everyone shook their heads "No." Bennie J. had said, "Ten years of Latin sittin' in here but don't nobody know what that word means. Shit." Bennie J. often spoke of education, but he seemed to never be impressed by it.

Hanna walked in with a bowl of strawberries and whipping cream. She saw Wright with the book, so stepped over to the TV and switched the channel. A close-up shot of an evangelist screaming out about death blared from the set. Hanna quickly turned the channel, but even from her backside Wright could see her beginning to tremble. She had talked about it so much that Wright now believed she had dispelled a fertilized egg that night. Even the gynecologist said it was possible, but just told her not to worry about it, she was perfectly normal, and he had fixed her up with an IUD. Later Hanna told

Wright how the embryo's sense of survival, through some extra sense, knew she would not live to bear him, thus committed suicide.

Wright imagined a two-inch little man inside Hanna's womb suddenly feeling he was doomed never to be born. The little man ripping away his umbilical cord, making a hangman's noose of the end, slipping it over his head. Then jumping out of the womb, through the vagina, snapping his neck. Hanna scooping the little man up in the palm of her hand, him then melting into a clump of blood. And Hanna running, holding out the clump of blood, trying to show Wright what had happened.

Wright stood up, stepped up behind Hanna, took the strawberries out of her hand, pulled her backwards until they were sitting in the easy chair. Both faced the TV, Wright's back against the back of the chair. His legs were spread; Hanna sat between them. He put the strawberries down, hugged her from behind. She put her feet up on the footstool. He said, "Let's get the scuba tanks and go lay at the bottom of Big Pool."

Wright felt his shoulder being shaken. At first he thought he was still under water at Big Pool, but then he heard his name called. He opened his eyes and saw rainbows on Hanna's wall.

He couldn't believe he had to get out of bed. It hadn't even started; he saw no way he could take two straight weeks of this. He was lying on his right side. Hanna's arm came from behind him, a cup of coffee in her hand. He took the coffee, expecting it to be the same formula Mae Emma had let him drink since he was a child: half coffee, half milk, with sugar. She had claimed straight coffee would stunt a child's growth. He propped up in bed and took a sip. It was mostly straight coffee.

"Come on," Hanna sang. "We don't want to be late."

Wright looked over at her. She was fully dressed in jeans and a cotton blouse. "We? You're going too?" he asked in disbelief.

"Yeah. Come on. Get dressed. Bennie J.'s going to pay us three dollars an hour. Can you believe it? Three dollars!"

Wright smiled. "I can't believe you're doing this for me. Going to work with me." Even in his drogginess, Wright felt a little sorry for Hanna, for the excitement she had for three dollars an hour. Winn could make that much a minute hustling golf.

Hanna pulled him out of bed and led him into her bathroom. His toothbrush lay on the sink, already toothpasted up. After he cleaned up and dressed, Hanna took him by the hand, led him downstairs and out into the passenger's seat of his Vette. She drove to the marina, he woke more, and then commented on the beauty of the recent sunrise and the dew on the ground.

The bait shop was composed of three departments: bait and tackle, grocery, and meat market. That morning, Wright, who had known how to cut meat since age eleven, began instructing Hanna. But by the end of the day Hanna, the assistant, had reorganized the entire market.

At one-thirty Wright and Hanna went to Big House for dinner, the name for the midday meal in Sumpter County. Mae Emma set the table for Wright and Hanna, saying, "Oooooooee! Bennie J. just couldn't shut up at dinner carrying on about y'all. By eleben clock say y'all done clean up the whole market. That Hanna done sculptured out the sausage in the sausage pan to look like a big fat ole hog. Stuck him some pig ears, some pig feets, some cherries for eyeballs, a little pig tail in the back end. That Hanna done learnt how to cut up a fryer and to trim out a T-bone steak. That Wright done put club steaks on sale, done solt off all them backed up club steaks. Ooooee!"

Hanna stopped gobbling down her black-eyed peas long enough to say, "Mae Emma! You wouldn't believe how much fun we've had this morning. And we're getting three dollars an hour! Can you believe it?"

Wright remained quiet. He wasn't going to admit to anything that might tie him down to further commitments.

That night they didn't get in till nine. Cordelle laid out a light supper, chattering on about how proud Bennie J. was of them, how well they had done. Hanna was too tired to go on about how much fun it was to run the meat market. Bennie J. came into the kitchen to get his plate, saying, "Ole Bennie J. does this ever' day. Done it for all his life." He walked out and into the den with his supper. Hanna ate quickly and went upstairs, while Wright sat there exhausted, humped over the table, slowly chewing his casserole. His whole body felt greasy, his scalp was itchy, and there was dried calf's blood on his forearms.

Wright was about to pass out into what was left of his casserole when Hanna put her hand over his. She led him up the stairs and into her room and locked the door behind them. For the first time Wright didn't care if Cordelle or Bennie J. saw them holding hands or going behind closed doors together. Having busted his ass at the marina had given him more of a sense of ownership of Big House. He felt bolder, tougher. If Bennie J. had knocked on the door right then, he would have said, "Yeah. I been fucking Hanna. So what? I do my work around here."

Hanna turned off the bedroom lights, but yellow light emanated from the bathroom. Soft jazz, turned very low, sounded from the stereo. She led him to the bathroom, where several candles were lit and set out on the counter. Wright could feel the heat from the bubble bath in the tub.

Hanna handed him a glass of Right Time, then began taking off her clothes. Wright sat on the closed toilet lid, sipping Right Time, taking off his shoes, and watching Hanna undress. By the time he got undressed, Hanna was sitting in the deep end of the bathtub. Wright stepped in; the water was hot. He slowly let himself down until he sat facing Hanna, who was already leaning forward to kiss him.

3 The next morning Bennie J. brought Greer to the marina to fish off the dock and do his grocery shopping. By three o'clock business was slow and Hanna was handling the meat market herself. Wright was washing his Vette out back when Bennie J. asked him to take Greer home.

Wright loaded Greer's groceries up in the trunk, and they took off for the two-bedroom frame house that sat halfway between the marina and Big House. When Wright got wound out at about sixty, Greer pulled out a bag of Bull Durham and rolling papers. "Dis de little car you and Doddy tellin me 'bout? Jest right for a young mane like you. You Doddy's a good man. Smart too. Can multiply up figures in his hade fastern they can up de bank with them addin' mow-sheens. You become half the man you Doddy is, you be a good man. Bennie J. wudn't but 'leven year old. I got down with hippatightus. I sent fer Bennie J. I sade boy you cook de whiskey fer me while I'm down I give you twenty dollah. Twenty dollah lot of money back them days. Shit, twenty dollah back then better'n thousand nowdays. I give you Doddy his first twenty dollah. He had money since."

That was a fact Wright had heard Bennie J. acknowledge: Greer had given him the first twenty dollars that started his empire, but Bennie J. always claimed he had earned it working Greer's cotton crop one season. Greer handed Wright a cigarette; since Wright was about ten or eleven Greer had let him smoke with him. Greer started rolling another one for himself. "One mo'ning we out runnin' trotlines, he 'bout thirteen. He said, 'Greer.' I said, 'What, boy?' Bennie J. say, 'Someday I'm gone be richest mane in Sumpter County and I'm gone marry the purtiest woman in the State of Alabama.' " Greer laughed. "And damn'f he didn't do both. Yeah, you Doddy do what he say he gone do." Greer kept laughing, stuck the cigarette in his mouth. When he closed up the bag of Bull Durham, flakes of tobacco whipped all around the cockpit.

He lit a kitchen match with cupped hands, got Wright fired up, then lit his own.

"Don't you never tell you Doddy ole Greer let you smoke. You know how you Doddy is about smokin' and drankin'. He have him a shit hemorrhage he know Greer let hi' boy smoke, drank beer. Maybe smokin' drankin' cut you life down like they wants you to thank. I ninety-three year old. Been smokin', drankin' since I ten. Maybe it do cut down on you years. Maybe if I never smoke, drank, I mought be a hunnert year old by now."

Wright pulled off onto a little dirt path and parked by Greer's front porch. Betsy waddled out and hollered, "Greer! You git my snuff?" She was only eighty-eight. Greer hollered back that he had gotten three bottles. She hollered, "Four-legged?" meaning she wanted for there to be four little bumps on the bottom of each bottle. She thought those tasted the best. Greer assured her they were all four-legged. Then she looked at Wright and said, "Hey, Mr. Reynolds!"

"Hello, Betsy."

"How you mama doin'?" she hollered down at him. The house was built up off the ground, the porch about chest high to Wright.

"She's doing fine."

"Good! She a good woman!" Betsy hollered and waddled back into the house.

"The deafer that woman git," Greer said, "the louder she holler. Got a set of lungs on her won't quit. Nighttime I has to say to her, 'Shit woman I sittin right here. Quit hollerin'.' "

Wright went to the rear of the car and opened the trunk. Greer took the wet tow sack with the three catfish he had caught. Wright started setting sacks of groceries on the porch. When he went to get the sixty-pound sack of sugar, the trunk was empty. He looked back and saw it sitting on the porch, and Greer making his way up the steps to the house. Wright paused: He had only had his back turned a second. When was there time for the knotty old man to have slung a sixty-pound bale from the trunk up on the porch? Wright gave into it. He knew he was in the land of Greer.

As Wright climbed the steep worn-slick wooden steps, Greer started in. "I was cookin' whiskey the night the stars fell on Alabama. Sittin' on a locust stump. Look up. Damn'f de stars didn't start to fallin'. Look like they fall to the top of de treetops and go out. Betsy she run out de back doo' holdin' out her apurn tryin' to catch one. I say, 'Shit, woman, them thang burn a hole plumb through that apurn.' "

Wright knew Greer to be as bad about telling stories as Doddy Bennie J. was. They were different, though. Greer told every story with the same tone, but Bennie J., the moment he started out, Wright could tell by his tone if he was telling a Depression story, a World War II story, a present time story, or a story his daddy had told him. Greer would start out with a story that seemed to have occured last week, and Wright would say, "Now, Greer, when did this take place?" Greer would cock his head back and say, "Well, I reckon, Mr. Reynolds, this was bout eighteen-eighty." Unlike Bennie J., Greer gave a cosmic dimension to his stories. Like when he went down to Birmingham in a Model T hauling whiskey, and Greer's guardian angel, Bo, held up the back axel while Greer changed the wheel.

Wright and Greer carried the groceries in and sat them on the kitchen table. Betsy put the fish in the sink, saying how nice they were. Then she started rummaging through the groceries, making sure Greer had gotten everything, started putting things away.

Greer started, "Me an' Betsy an' LaSalle in ne kitchen heuh eatin' suppah. Wadn't good da'k yit. We hud dis hummin' noise. Might near hu't you ears. We run out. Dis flyin' saucer come down. Ever' color in ne rainbow come out de bottom dat thang. It lit down ne edge of the cotton field back yonder." Greer pointed through the kitchen window to where he meant. He lit another cigarette. "We just stared at it. Figured somebody come out of it directly but it jest commenced hummin'. Then directly raised up 'bout thutty feet ne air and took off out toad de river like a streak a lightnin'." The cigarette went out. He picked a match off the kitchen table, lit the cigarette. "You know where dat thang landed left a bare spot out yonder like when lightnin'll strike? Didn't nothin' grow dere fuh couple yeahs. Just a bare spot out in ne cotton."

Betsy hollered, "Didn't nuthin' grow dere fuh three-foew yeahs!"

"You kin sit a spell, can't ya, Mr. Reynolds?" Greer asked.

"A little while, Greer."

"Come on in ne living room." They sat in a couple of rockers. Greer got up to get a couple of briar pipes off the mantle, handed Wright one, and sat back down. He pulled a twist of Red Ox tobacco and a pocketknife over to Wright. Wright cut off some, filled the bowl. Greer struck a big wooden match, held it out over Wright's pipe until he got it lit. Then commenced to fix up his own smoke, and out of the blue went right into a story.

"Ole Robeson woman, had her laid up fuh dade. Back them days dey just laid 'em out on a table or boa'd o' somethin. Dress em up, put a saucer of salt on their chest. Didn't embalm 'em in nem days. Naw. Anyhow, my paw made me stay over at the Robesons', sot up wid her that night."

"What was the salt for?" Wright asked and took a pull of the strong harsh tobacco.

"To keep em from gurglin' up. Made de gas subside."

Betsy walked into the room, gestured gas coming out her mouth to help explain to Wright, then brought a tin can up to her lower lip and spit snuff. She seated herself in a rocker on the other side of Greer.

"I wadn't 'bout six o' sebem." "I's sittin' up next to the ole Robeson woman. She 'as stretched out on top dis table. Folks on ne other side de room, prayin', moan cause she done passed. 'Bout that time that dade woman raised up and sade, "What goin' on heuh?"

"Was she dead?" Wright asked. He wasn't sure if this was a story that had guardian angels or haints in it.

"Shit, naw! Been layin' up for dade fuh two days. Then come to. Gone bury her next day. Dat woman live thutty mow years, didn't she, Betsy?"

"Least thutty!" Betsy hollered.

"I shot up, run half mile to our house. I scream to my paw she done rose up from ne dade. My paw told me go out de shed he's gone whup my ass fuh lyin'. Then my maw tell my paw, naw. Go see fust. Make show he lyin' fow you whip his ass. Show 'nuff she wadn't dade."

Wright wiggled, glad Hanna wasn't here to hear stories about people put up for dead.

Betsy said, "They bed Willie Coats alive!"

"Naw!" Wright said.

Greer leaned over, struck a match on the wood heater, and lit up his bowl again. When he had it puffing good, he said, "Show nuff did. I's pole bare at his funeral."

Betsy hollered, "Had a stroke! He an invulid, in a coma! His wife Dana Mae said he wadn't no better off than dade! She sade she been waitin' on him like a baby fuh fow months, that she ti'd of it! She had em put 'im in a casket and bed him! That man live when dey put him in his grave!"

Wright said, "Naw!"

Betsy hollered, "Yeah!"

Greer said, "Show did. No tellin' how many folk bed live. Some of em thank they dade, they ain't dade. Folks want 'em dade an outta da way. Most folks thank it ain't so. But it as true as me an you sittin' here."

"Boy, am I glad Hanna didn't come with us," Wright said. He had spent thirty minutes two nights ago trying to convince Hanna she wouldn't be buried alive. Her fear of dying young had lately grown into a horror of being mistaken for dead, pumped full of formaldehyde, trapped in a casket, then put in the ground. "No, sir," Wright said aloud. Hanna didn't need to be hearing about anybody being buried alive. "Well, Greer," he said. "How in heaven's name did Dana Mae justify burying her own husband alive?"

Greer said, "Hell, told me God come to her told her to do it. Shit. God don't come around here. He live way on the other side of the Big Dipper. Mr. Reynolds, you't a cole beuh?"

"Sure."

Greer slowly got up. "Now you don't be telling Mr. Bennie J. I been givin' you beuh."

"You just don't tell him I've been drinking it," Wright replied.

Greer giggled at their mischievousness as they walked into the kitchen. Wright watched him open the yellowed refrigerator door and reach into the back with his black leathery arm, the black leathery skin that Wright as a boy had asked Bennie J. if mosquitoes could bite through; it made Bennie J. laugh. Greer pulled out two longnecks. Something named "Dixie." Wright smiled, for Greer was always giving him the dog-damndest off brands of beer. Last time it was something called Jax. You could forget about Greer ever having something as simple as Budweiser or Miller's.

Greer set the beers over on the counter, opened them, handed Wright one. As Wright was taking a long pull, Greer said, "You Doddy say Winn went across the big pond. She a fine lady. She need to git around see thangs fore she git marr'ed. I over deah in Wo'ld War I."

As soon as Greer had said the word Winn, Wright remembered that Greer had once for a few years lived in New Orleans. In fact, he had been the link of Coleen moving there, had known some people there who had originally hired Coleen. Now Wright remembered seeing signs in New Orleans advertising Dixie and Jax beers. Then it all fit in—Winn had been bringing Greer beer from Louisiana that he had taken a liking to years ago. Wright stood there a moment in his own thoughts: Somehow Greer and Winn were the key to this Hanna dilemma, this dilemma of Hanna dying before she turned eighteen.

Greer took a slug of beer and said, "Bo give me one these one time."

"Bo?" Wright questioned, not sure what Greer was talking about.

"Bo one my gardine angels! He da one lifted up my Model T that time. I ax him he God. He say, 'Hell, naw. God live way over on ne other side de Big Dipper. I's an archangel. So one night 'bout twenty year go I wake up need to relieve myself off the back porch. I been shittin' blood for two days. When I wake up I notice a light heuh in ne kitchen. I walk in. There stand Bo. He look at me real serious say, Greer you got cancer. I say, "Well, Bo. What the hell you doin' standin' nere? Suck it out of me.' He float me up, lay me out on ne kitchen table here, suck that cancer out of me. Give me a beer. Say I be all right in ne mornin'. I say pulls you up a chair. He say, 'Shit, Greer. I got a lot a work to do. You thanks you the only one I has to be fuckin' with. Can't be just shittin' around all time.'"

Wright now imagined three or four ghosts and archangels floating around Greer. Wright needed to ask Greer a lot of things about fate, about changing fate, about what happened with that Ouija board that time. But Wright suddenly blurted out, "Greer, do you think something's wrong with somebody that falls in love with their cousin?"

Greer had started to walk back toward the living room. He stopped, turned, looked at Wright, and said, "Mr. Reynolds, I should think some'in wrong wid you if you *ain't done* been tryin' to git into Miss Hanna's bloomers."

Wright smiled.

Greer turned and continued walking. "I tell you 'bout the time me 'n' Jerry Lee got drunk and got ow asses throwed in jail in Birmingham? He wudn't but twelve yeah old when he sta'ted running wildcat—"

4 Several mornings later Wright woke up thirty minutes early. The room had begun to lighten. Wright was nervous. All night long it seemed he had dreamed, dreamed of the compressors to the meat coolers going out, the meat spoiling. Dreamed of all the pain-in-the-ass customers up at the counter at once demanding special orders, complaining of the prices, wanting to know why he wasn't going to the University of Alabama. Dreamed he could do nothing right; he would trim out a T-bone and then with a slip of the hand slash it in two. Worst of all, he had dreamed Eddie had come into the bait shop and invited Hanna to go waterskiing. She had yelled, thrown off her apron, and run off with him. While Wright tormented over cutting the meat right, he stood there with visions of Hanna banging Eddie and Daughtery and liking it, spending the rest of the summer with them.

Wright's awakening hadn't dissipated the sickening feeling the dreams had caused. In fact, short of Hanna running off with Eddie, yesterday had been a lower, but as frustrating, harmonic of the dreams. One after the other customers complained of prices, had picky esoteric special cuts of meat they wanted, had queried Wright at length as to why he was not going to the University of Alabama. Harvey Wiggins, an overweight middle-aged Ford car salesman, even went to the trouble of following Wright around for half an hour in his puke green sports coat assuring him that Bennie J. could probably pull some strings and get him in at the University of Alabama; no use going off to some out-of-state second-rate college when Bennie J.'s son could be right there on campus with Bear and his boys. Then Mrs. Clement had come in and interrogated Wright as to whether he was going to give up his Alabama citizenship when he went way off to Louisiana. When Wright had told Mrs. Clement there was no such

thing as Alabama citizenship, she had snapped that she hadn't seen
him at church in years and had stormed out of the bait shop.

Then several meat trucks all came at the same time delivering
meats. All the orders had been messed up, one packer sending pork
loins instead of beef loins, another completely out of the bait shop's
favorite brand of bologna. It was almost three in the afternoon until
Wright and Hanna got to go to lunch; they just walked over to the
café for some cheeseburgers. Sitting in the back corner booth, everything looked brilliant in color to Wright, all his senses seemed un-
desirably magnified. Three tables down Kent Hargrove was
whispering to his wife how Cordelle was born and raised a Republican, how she ran around with Bernstein's daughter and all them Jews.
On down two Redstone Arsenal Yankees were talking about the
isotopes of uranium and something about the properties of a
"quark."

Wright had told Hanna he was nervous, was on edge, was about
to explode. Hanna had smiled at him, pulled his hands over close to
her, gently stroked his upturned palms. Then Jem Flannagan had
burst through the front door, run over to his cousin Tanner who was
eating some barbecue, sitting on a stool at the counter. Jem hollered,
"Tanner! You heard about Dude Harper? He just went home, stuck
a shotgun in his own mouth and blowed his head off!" As Wright was
wondering if Dude had just gotten back from Tuscaloosa for electric
shock treatments, Hanna threw up in his hands.

Wright got up, dressed, went to the bathroom. Seven days without
sunbathing; he felt he was a pukish death white every time he looked
into a mirror. Last night Hanna's suggestion that perhaps they should
spend their dinner hour down at Big Pool had confirmed this feeling.
They had seven more days at the meat market, and all Wright needed
was one more day like yesterday and he would go shithouse crazy.

He walked back into the bedroom and tried to shake Hanna awake.
Three days ago she had stopped jumping around about the three
dollars an hour they were earning. Finally, she got up and started
dressing.

Wright sat on the end of the bed, still nervous. He had to figure
some way to get some more beef loins in; he didn't want to hear
Bennie J.'s speech about having stuff now when people wanted it,
about having something in a couple of days didn't mean shit. That
it was the meat packers' fault didn't mean shit to Bennie J. You had

the beef loins or you didn't, that's all that mattered. In the eighth grade Wright had obtained a newfound ability: "I tried." Every year, every teacher preached to them about the virtues of trying. Win or lose was beside the point, but to try was noble. Then one day fate found Wright in the empty hall with his eighth-grade algebra teacher. She explained how he had disrupted her class for the third time that week, now she must take him to the principal's office. The words came out of Wright's mouth: "I tried. I really tried." The algebra teacher asked, "What?" The words themselves had backed her down. Wright found a new power. He began to roll, he told her how he had really tried to control his behavior in her class. That he had an emotional problem, that often he could not control his tendency to misbehave. But he had tried, he had really tried. But now his parents would probably send him off to military academy or down to Tuscaloosa for treatments. That this would be the straw that broke the camel's back. That he was getting better at controlling his conduct, but he obviously just wasn't getting better fast enough. But he had tried, Lord knew how he had really tried. And he had tried especially hard for her, because she was such a kind and caring teacher. Sixty seconds later Wright was back in class, sitting behind Kathy Lee.

And boy, did Wright have him a newfound ability. He "tried" to do his homework, he "tried" to get there on time, he "tried" not to say offensive things, he "tried" to respect authority. Boy, did he try try try. Cordelle even rewarded him for trying. Wright had him a new passport, a new prepaid ticket to Paradise, a visa he opened that had the simple words "I tried."

One year later Bennie J. and Cordelle had been gone one weekend to an Alabama game. Winn, in Sumpter College now, had gone home with Gina. Bennie J. had given Wright about a dozen things at the marina to make sure got done. That next Monday Bennie J. wanted to know why the minnow pools didn't have any minnows in them. Wright explained about the ten other difficult things that he had gotten done. He told how ole man Tisdale had had a heart attack and he couldn't find his son to send the shipment, that there was some supplier in Birmingham but they couldn't get any up until Wednesday, that he had bullshitted the Redstone Arsenal Yankees into the idea that the crappies would bite worms as good as minnows. Then at the end of his speech Wright had added the magical words: "I tried." But Bennie J. hadn't backed down like the algebra teacher. It hadn't dissolved Bennie J.'s control. In fact, Wright would have thought Bennie J. had failed to hear those magical words had Bennie

J. not responded with, "What does trying have to do with anything?" Shit. Doddy Bennie J. didn't know a goddamn thing about modern education.

"Yeah, Doddy Bennie J., I tried to wake up and open the bait shop all last week while you were gone. Ah, it probably only meant just a handful of lost customers. You got plenty of money anyway." "Yeah, Bear. Sorry, I missed that field goal. Wind must have gotten it. Lord knows I tried. Ah, it's about time we let Nebraska have the national championship back. You know, it doesn't really matter if we win or lose. The important thing is—I tried."

Goddamn modern education. It had its limitations.

Wright and Hanna drove to the bait shop in silence, Hanna sleeping and Wright in a miserable anxiety. Wright parked behind the meat market. He got out, pushed on the solid thick back door as if to walk in, but it was still barred shut from the inside. Bennie J. usually unbarred it when he opened the bait shop up. Wright went on around to the front door, walking off and leaving Hanna. She had gotten out of the Corvette and was still stretching. Wright was anxious to handle the beef problem before Bennie J. found out.

He pulled the front door open and walked in. The first thing inside the front door was a large glass candy case, probably very similar to the kind Uncle Davy had kept Dude the pet rattlesnake in. Wright imagined a huge rattlesnake coiling up inside the case, looking at him, getting ready to strike, the front plate glass telling Wright, "I'm going to try to keep him from breaking through. I'm really going to try. But you know it doesn't matter if I succeed or not, the important thing is I'm going to try. I have me a modern education, and boy do I try."

There was only one clerk Rita, behind the counter, and she was waiting on a couple of NASA Yankees. They were buying some minnows. They had helped put a man on the moon and here they were buying minnows in the middle of July.

They said hello to Wright, he spoke back as high-spirited as he could muster. When he got back toward the meat market, he saw Mr. Berzett moving about there, getting the market set up for the day. For a moment Wright thought it was just an illusion, the same nature of a thing as he had just imagined there being a coiling rattlesnake in the candy case.

Wright cut loose and ran up to the big stout seventy-year-old man and began shaking his hand. "Mr. Berzett, Mr. Berzett. Am I glad to see *you*!" Just then Hanna ran up shrieking and hugged Mr. Berzett.

"My vacation is over!" Mr. Berzett exclaimed with delight.

Bennie J. walked back into the market, saying, "A week of vacation can get to you, can't it, Mr. Berzett?" Bennie J. walked on up and put his arm around Hanna.

"It sure can, Ben." Mr. Berzett called Bennie J. Ben. Then Mr. Berzett went on to tell how wonderful his trip had been, how he had seen all his kinfolks, but how good it was to get back to the marina and go back to work.

Hanna said, "I don't see how you keep things going back here. The last couple of days almost drove Wright and me crazy. I think we need a two-week vacation somewhere to get over it."

Much to Wright's amazement, Bennie J. said, "Aw, y'all don't need two weeks. A couple-day camping trip would straighten y'all out. Mr. Berzett, when they were little fellers, I mean no more'n six or seven, Winn, Hanna, and Wright would go off in the woods camping. Cordelle would get a little skittish. I'd look out the window. They'd be hiking off, with Mama Dog Midnight tagging along. I'd say, 'Cordelle, Mama Dog Midnight ain't gone let a thing happen to them younguns. They'll be safer out the woods with Mama Dog than they would be inside here at Big House.' "

To Wright, Bennie J. might just as well said, "Why don't you and Hanna go off fucking in the woods for a couple of days? Forget this working shit."

5 | Jerry Lee stopped his '59 Chevy pickup in the middle of the old one-lane metal-beamed bridge that went across Sumpter Creek. "Old Catawa Bridge," he said. Fifty feet long, between two dirt roads that each led off into woods. Jerry Lee took a swig of the small bottle of Dr. Pepper and thought how he had come across this bridge one time doing a hundred miles an hour, with the state chasing him. He was loaded down with a hundred gallons of moonshine. The road was a lot better then but the bridge wasn't any wider. What he was having a hard time believing right now was that that was about twenty years ago now, almost to the day.

Wright and Hanna were crowded into the back of the truck with a sixteen-foot aluminum canoe, a fourteen-foot flat-bottom wooden skiff, and a heavy load of gear and food. They looked down. Sumpter Creek was narrow and swift here at the Alabama-Tennessee line, cutting through rocks and bluffs that were the foothills of the Appalachian Mountains. The terrain gradually changed until twenty miles downstream the creek was wide and lazy, cutting through Sumpter Swamp.

The passenger door to the truck opened and Mama Dog Midnight squeezed out. She was wagging her tail, padding her feet up and down in excitement. In the last year or so, she made stomping motions with her front feet when she got excited. Due to her old age, it had replaced jumping up, but still the action made her look puppyish.

Bennie J. got out of the passenger side now and said, "You excited, Midnight?" Jerry Lee cut the engine off, got out with his Dr. Pepper in hand.

They all gathered at the downstream side of the bridge, leaned on the railing, and looked down to the creek below. "Look at all this," Bennie J. said. "Paradise. All of Sumpter County is a downright paradise. Why anybody would ever want to leave Sumpter County, I don't know. Do you, Jerry Lee? Look at the beauty." Jerry Lee mumbled he regretted he wasn't going with them. And it was beautiful, so breathtakingly so, that Wright for the first time relaxed enough to enjoy the idea that Bennie J. was going along with him and Hanna. Jerry Lee drank the last of his Dr. Pepper, then tossed the bottle off the bridge. It splashed below.

Wright said, "If Winn were here she would make you go get that bottle."

Jerry Lee laughed as if in nostalgic recollection. He said, "She don't like improper grammar or litterbuggin', do she?"

Bennie J. pulled away from the rail and said, "Come on, let's get the boats in the water, load up, let Jerry Lee git out a here." He walked to the back of the pickup. "Did y'all know there were more caves in Sumpter County than any other county in the state?"

Bennie J. had gone on about how canoes were easy to tip over and what they needed to do was bring the flat-bottomed boat, but Bennie J. ended up in the canoe with Hanna and off they went down the creek. Wright sat in the stern of the boat with Mama Dog in the bow and most of the supplies between them. He pushed away from the bank with an oar, the current caught the boat, straightened it out; Wright and Mama Dog began floating downstream. Wright looked back up at the bridge. Jerry Lee was leaning against the railing, looking down at Sumpter Creek, now with a longneck bottle of

Budweiser in his hand. Jerry Lee raised the beer up to Wright in a toast and grinned. Wright waved back, then put the oar in the oarlock at the transom and sculled the skiff around the bend.

Wright had on long navy bellbottoms, long denim workshirt, was barefooted. Although it was up in the morning and one of the hottest months of the year, August, the day was cool and pleasant. The creek was clear, the bottom of the boat cool from the spring waters empty-ing into Sumpter Creek. To his right was a fifty-foot bluff. Water seeped from the cracks of the rocks and dripped down into the creek. The air had no humidity; and tall sprawling trees kept the creek shaded.

To Wright, Sumpter County was made up of Big House, the ma-rina, the courthouse square, and the backwaters around Jerry Lee's house. This place, this week, was foreign to him. They might just as well be in North Carolina or Colorado or somewhere. When he cleared another bend he could see the canoe a piece downstream, could hear Bennie J. talking away at Hanna. Mama Dog was standing up in the bow, stepping in place with her front feet like she was going to dive out. Like Bennie J., she was excited. Hanna had told Bennie J. it was generous of him to leave his business to go camping. Bennie J. just giggled and said his money made money while he slept. That the sun never set on Bennie J.'s empire. Bennie J. seemed to be stern on getting up with the sun. Wright figured Doddy thought once the sun shone that he had to take over personal control of his empire, then when the sun set some of his guardian angels took over, made sure his money was making money.

As far as camping was concerned, Cordelle was a different story. Wright knew she would have just loved to be with them right now, would have carried on about the beauty of the place, about the wonders of nature. But come sundown she would have been ready for a jet helicopter to drop in and take her back to Big House. There was nothing that could supplant the wonderfulness of a luxury bath and bed.

Wright suddenly felt like Cordelle. The ride up to the bridge had been fun, it was fun going down the small rapids of Sumpter Creek, supper would be fun. But then Wright would be ready to head back to Big House with Hanna.

Around the next bend and off to the right, a series of flat slate rocks lay at a thirty-degree angle in the side of a mountain and formed an inlet. Water ran down, draining from somewhere in the mountainside and where the slate rock of a small waterfall poured into the pool.

There Hanna and Bennie J. floated, waiting for Wright to catch up. "Now isn't this Paradise?" said Bennie J. "Winn running around over in them foreign countries. Paradise right here under her nose." Hanna had her hands in the water, saying how cold it was. Bennie J. pointed down some twenty yards to a flat area that ran about a hundred feet along the creek. "There's the perfect place right there to set up camp."

Wright floated on down the bank some thirty feet. A tree limb came out from the bank and ran parallel to the bank some five feet, growing parallel to the water. Wright drifted past the tree, then pulled the skiff back up between the trunk and the bank. Midnight scrambled out onto the tree trunk and up onto the little plateau as Wright was tying up the skiff. When he walked up onto the area, Hanna and Bennie J. were there, having walked up from the inlet side. Bennie J. said, "Look at this. Naturally air-conditioned. Spring water flowing down a slate-rock slide to one side of us. A shady creek in front of us. A damp bluff right behind us. Tall trees all about. Everything so purty and green! Never let it be said that Sumpter ain't the Garden of Eden. Paradise, just Paradise!"

Bennie J. led them up along the outside edge of the slate rock, telling them how the bluffs on this side of the creek were the edge of one big mountain that got bigger and bigger back toward Tennessee. A cave ran under the mountain, and a creek meandered through the cave; he had gone inside it with Greer one time when he was a little boy.

At the top of the formation, they saw a narrow cave-like opening in the mountainside about chest high, where water was slowly pouring out. "Pure mountain spring water" Bennie J. called it. Hanna cupped her hands and drank, saying it was so cold it numbed her fingers. Midnight, too, was lapping up the spring water that had settled in a pool of the rocks. "That good, Mama Dog?" Bennie J. said, standing ankle deep in cool water in his old unlaced leather Hush Puppies, no socks, dress pants, short-sleeved shirt, and safari hat. Midnight stepped toward the middle of the slate rock, trying to find a deeper place to drink from. When she did she started sliding downward. She sat down on her back haunches but continued to slide faster and faster. Mama Dog looked like she was riding an invisible sled down the slate-rock drainage. She would sit down on her back haunches, lie down, then sit back up as she slid. Finally she was deposited off the end of the slate ledge and down three feet where she hit the four-foot-deep pool with a splash. She swam up by the canoe, climbed out on the bank, shook off, and started padding her feet up and down. Wright and Hanna laughed. Bennie J. said, "Mama Dog Midnight's just like Winn and ole Uncle Davy. She knows how to have a good time."

Hanna grabbed Wright, threw him down, and together they sped down the natural water slide, screaming. When they hit the pool and stood up in the chilled water, Bennie J. was sliding down, yelling, "Tally-ho!" As Bennie J. slid down, Wright thought of how the hundred-watt bulb in Bennie J.'s office was shining.

Bennie J. was hungry, so they unloaded the boat at their campsite and one by one slipped off into the woods and changed into dry clothes. Bennie J. took a long stick of bologna, whacked off about a pound, gave it to Midnight. She gobbled it up, found a splotch of sunlight to lie in, and went to sleep.

They ate sandwiches and sodas, then pitched the tent, a green teepee-shaped thing with an outer aluminum frame, zippered windows, door mosquito netting, and a built-in waterproof bottom. Wright rolled out the sleeping bags. Bennie J. dug out a fire pit at the edge of the plateau by the creek. Hanna stretched out a rope for a clothesline, squeezed out their wet clothes, and hung them to dry. They cut and collected firewood, and finally sat listening to Bennie J. tell a Depression story.

Bennie J. stood up when he'd finished, stretched, and said he and Mama Dog were going downstream a bit in the skiff, find a good place to run a trotline. "I be back in an hour or two," he said, and disappeared with Midnight down the creek.

Wright looked over to Hanna. She got up and ran barefoot toward the slate-rock slide. She turned around, said, "Come on," and disappeared out of sight. He lazily got up and followed. He tracked her into a valley that sloped upwards between two hillsides. He heard her sing for him again. To his right he saw a clearing on top of one of the hills. A huge oak tree stood near the edge of the peak, its roots hanging naked through the edge of the steep wall. He walked past the hanging roots, circled around an upgrade, and came to a clearing several times the area of their little campsite. Three huge oak trees umbrellaed the place; there was no undergrowth. There was a small slant of the land up toward the oak tree near the edge.

Wright walked toward the oak tree under which the land was a thick deep green carpet of grassy moss. In the middle of that mossy site lay Hanna, naked. Her almost-dried hair was fanned out evenly in a half circle under her and to her sides. What struck Wright the most was the intense color of her deep green eyes, which matched the color of the moss on which she lay. Matched so perfectly, her irises could just have well been a void, and Wright looking straight through her head at the moss itself.

Hanna grinned at him and said, "Welcome to Paradise. Welcome to Sumpter's Garden of Eden."

As Wright lay down with Hanna, he imagined Bennie J. in a slough downstream running a trotline, saying to Midnight, "You want some catfish for breakfast? Huh, Mama Dog?"

6 The next morning Bennie J. did fry them some catfish he had caught on his line, along with country ham and soft scrambled eggs, camp coffee, and orange juice. They all had hearty appetites, though Bennie J. had fixed them T-bones and baked potatoes for supper the night before.

Up in the morning they broke camp, loaded up, and let the current take them down Sumpter Creek. After an hour of drifting downstream, the terrain began to change—from mountains and bluffs to rolling hills and farms. They began to see cattle, occasionally a farmer on a tractor in the distance. The creek got wide, the current slower. After a couple more hours they passed under the Thomas Ferry Road bridge. "We only got two or three miles to go," Bennie J. said. "But we gone have to dig in now. Paddle most of the way."

The air became muggy, the creek mucky and hot. The banks of the creek were swampy. Wright was rowing alone in the skiff, thinking he was ready for Jerry Lee to come in *Fast Boat*, as planned. He took his shirt off, but had to put it back on because of the bugs and mosquitoes. He occasionally saw a cottonmouth swim the creek.

The creek curved into a slow bend. Wright heard dogs yelping. He looked around to find Bennie J. and Hanna had pulled the canoe over to the bank. Midnight sat erect in the middle with her ears perked up. Out in the creek a ways a man on a horse was talking to Bennie J. and Hanna, while another held two coon dogs on leashes at the bank—the dogs sniffed around frantically.

Wright rowed up beside the canoe, and saw it was Deputy Loggins on horseback, with an automatic shotgun. The deputy tipped his Smokey Bear hat to Wright. Bennie J. was a good man, he was saying, what good younguns he had, now most kids were too candy-assed to get out in the woods nowadays, all they did nowadays was lie around protesting and taking pot. Wright wasn't going to be able to get up to Washington a minute too soon, he was saying. Maybe he would get there just in time to keep the whole country from going to hell.

The dogs pulled the other man into the swampy waters of Sumpter Creek. Wright asked, "Who they after?"

Bennie J. said, "Lizard McGuire. Stopped him for speeding out on the highway. He ran out into Sumpter Swamp."

The deputy exclaimed, "We suspect he might be dranking, too. He resisted arrest. Now he's a fugitive from justice!"

"Is he armed?" Hanna asked.

"Is he armed?" Deputy Loggins repeated, laughing. He looked at Hanna and said, "Honey, he's the most armed man since Joe Willie Namath. We talking Lizard McGuire, first-string quarterback for the Tennessee Vols. Threw a forty-yard touchdown pass the last ten seconds of the Alabama-Tennessee. Cost us the national championship. I'd call that armed and dangerous!"

"What are you going to do with him if you catch him?" Hanna asked.

"If? When, honey. We take him uptown, book him for resisting arrest. They'll have to suspend him for a semester. Yes, sir, Lizard McGuire won't be throwing no touchtown passes agin the Crimson Tide this year. That'll teach him the fourth quarter belongs to the Bear. Time's a-wasting! Good day to you and yours, Mr. Bennie J." The deputy turned the horse, sloshed off toward the direction the dogs were barking.

Bennie J. and Hanna pushed off, started back down the creek with Wright behind them. Just like the sight of Hanna laying on the moss had shocked Wright though he had seen her naked plenty of times, something about Bennie J. now stunned him. Somehow Bennie J. sitting down in the canoe seemed to sit taller than the deputy up on the horse. And the deputy had chattered away, but somehow Bennie J., though he unlike usual had little to say, had actually had control of the conversation, control of the whole encounter.

Wright feathered the oars, recovered, dug in, and took a stroke. Shit, Bennie J. ought to be the one up in Washington.

Wright glanced over to see the canoe pull over to the bank. Midnight clambered out, almost capsizing the canoe; she traipsed off into the swamp. Then Hanna stepped out and disappeared behind some trees. Wright rowed up and asked Bennie J. what was up.

Bennie J. said, "Mama Dog and Hanna had to go pee."

Shortly Hanna ran back out and got in the canoe. Bennie J. started hollering for Midnight. Then they heard her howling like she had something treed. All of a sudden a man came running out of the swamp, stopped right at the canoe, stunned there was someone there. He froze and stared in fear at Bennie J., Hanna, and Wright. Bennie J. told him to calm down, relax, that they weren't part of the posse.

"They were going to kill me," was all Lizard said right away.

"They weren't going to kill you," Bennie J. said.

"No, they were. When they looked at my license saw who I was, they were going to lynch me. Kept talking about the fourth quarter belonged to the Bear."

"Ah," Bennie J. said. "All they's gone do was take you uptown git their names in the paper. Git themselves some free football tickets. Now git in the canoe before you git snakebit."

Lizard looked about him fidgity like a cottonmouth was about to strike him. He minded Bennie J., all the while saying, "I've got to get out of Alabama. But the harder I try to get out the harder it gets."

"I know what you mean," Wright said.

Bennie J. pushed away from the bank. Lizard was pleading, "If I can just get back to Tennessee I can get someone to straighten all this out."

"It's a thirsty city," Hanna said.

Midnight came out of the swamp, wagging her tail, panting. She clambered over into the skiff and Wright pushed off, following the canoe.

Hanna gave Lizard a cold piece of country ham and a Nesbit Orange. He worked on it heartily as Bennie J. explained to him how the freight train would span across the trestle, would stay stopped to load up at the lumber mill, that he could jump it, that it would stop once in Sumpter City, then the next time it stopped he would be in Tennessee.

When Wright rowed around the next bend, he turned to look. The freight train was parked across the trestle. Bennie J. was holding on to a pillar of the bridge. Lizard was climbing up the wooden beams toward the tracks. Wright kept rowing. As he passed Bennie J. and Hanna, he peered up through the railroad ties, saw Lizard disappear into a boxcar.

Wright saw Bennie J. let go of the pillar; the canoe floated on away from the bridge slowly. Bennie J. kept staring back at the trestle. But Wright could tell he wasn't thinking about Lizard or Alabama football. Wright could tell Bennie J. was thinking about Pete and the train.

Lizard McGuire stood in the open door of an empty boxcar, waving. Hanna and Bennie J. waved back. Wright stared at the train, took a stroke, glided. He heard the *blum-blum* of *Fast Boat*'s 350 Chevy taxiing up behind him.

7

There was one end of Big Pool up next to the pool house where they could lie in the sun and not be seen from Big House. Wright and Hanna now lay there nude, Wright on his stomach, Hanna on her back.

That morning Bennie J. had carried on at the breakfast table about everything they had done on the camping trip, like it was the most fun he had had in ages. "It was Paradise," he had told Cordelle.

Hanna said, "Somebody's coming!" She and Wright scampered around getting their bathing suits on and then lay back down just as the Model A rolled into sight. Cordelle had driven it down across Big Yard. She stopped the car as near to Wright and Hanna as she could without running into the low hedge that separated the yard from the pool deck.

Cordelle stayed in the car, speaking over the running engine. "Mr. Taylor called from Baton Rouge, Wright. He wants you to call him."

"Mama Cordelle," Wright whined. "I don't want to worry with renting an apartment right now. It's over a month away."

"Wright, honey. You have to get one now, while Mr. Taylor still has one available. You're going to have to take more responsibility now. You have to look after details. You just can't lie around and wait until the last minute. B. J. and I have always taken care of things, handling them promptly and properly. We expect you to do the same. You're a young man and you've got to see to these things."

"Mama, please! I could even stay with Winn until I find a place," Wright said. Shit, it would be easier to go to Washington.

Cordelle cut off the engine. "Wright. Winn and Gina will not have any extra room with Hanna moving in. Also you need to get with Mae Emma and get together all the things you'll need to set up housekeeping. In fact, it should be looked into about buying a house or duplex down there. Winn, Gina, and Hanna could stay in one side. You could take a roommate, charge him rent, and live in the other side. Then sell it for a profit when you graduate. Make money instead of wasting it all on rent. Wright, the time has come for you to be much more foresighted."

"Please, Mama," Wright begged. "I'll call Mr. Taylor. I'll call him. Please."

"Good." Cordelle cranked the old Ford roadster back up. "And Wright, honey. You're eighteen now. You have to go up to the post office and register for the draft."

"Mama. You know Doddy can get anything in this town fixed," Wright said.

"It's a thirsty city," Hanna mumbled.

"Wright," Cordelle said. "We're not sending you off to college to get into all that protesting stuff. And you need to go on up to the courthouse and register to vote. You know eighteen-year-olds may register now."

"I know. I know. Okay, okay, okay, Mama Cordelle! I'll go uptown *today* and register for everything."

"That's my young man," Cordelle sang. "Today is the day. Today is the day Wright registers to vote."

---

8 Wright told the Selective Service officer, "Well, I made straight As in my science and math classes all through high school."

She forced a smile and said, "No, Mr. Reynolds. I mean on your body. Do you have any distinguishing marks on your body?"

"Oh, on my body. I got a scar on my left foot where I accidentally shot it with a thirty-eight when I was nine."

"I'll write that down. But do you have one closer to your heart?"

"That scar is dear to my heart. Mama must have kissed on it for a week after I got back from the doctor. And Doddy still fusses about

being careful with firearms. Mama Cordelle too. But I don't think an
unloaded gun can hurt anybody. I still think it's those loaded ones
that get you."

"No. No." She couldn't quite make out if Wright were serious or
not; so she was patient. "I mean, do you have some distinguishing
mark on your body that is closer to your heart than your foot? Say
if you were in combat and had your foot or leg blown off, is there some
mark that could identify you?"

Wright barely liked the idea of himself having shot his own foot
cleanly between two metatarsals. He didn't even want to think of
somebody else blowing the whole thing off. He said, "I got a tattoo
on my ass." What Wright actually had was a stain on his hipbone of
a homemade tattoo attempt, a remnant of when he and Kathy Lee
were twelve and had given each other tattoos there of each other's
initials with a needle and India ink. Lou Ann had seen Kathy Lee's,
gotten all bent out of shape about it, shipped her down to Birmingham to get it removed, had come over to Big House demanding of
Bennie J. to explain her son's behavior. Bennie J. had just stood there
unmoved and said, in a bored way, "Well, Lou Ann. You talking to
the wrong person. Who you want to talk to is Wright." Lou Ann was
standing there in the middle of Big Room. She was taken by Bennie
J.'s presence; there was nothing she could say. Then she was taken
by the presence of Big Room. She thought she lived in the grandest
of all homes in Sumpter County, but she all of a sudden was engulfed
speechless by the presence of everything and everyone at Big House.
Then next time Wright had come over to see Kathy Lee, Lou Ann
had hugged him, stroked his hair and told him how beautiful he was.
And Bennie J., he walked around for the next few days saying,
"Wright done been tattooing on ole Kathy Lee's butt. Ole Wright's
like Winn and ole Uncle Davy. He knows how to have himself a good
time."

The lady wrote something down and said, "Describe it."

"Some say it's a little too skinny," Wright said.

"The tattoo!"

"It is of two dogs copulating."

The lady sighed and started writing it down. Wright felt he had
finally won her over. He said, "Look, lady, I don't have a tattoo on
my butt. I'm not trying to give you a hard time or anything. I kind
of like filling out forms and being asked questions. I just don't think
I have any distinguishing marks to amount to anything."

The lady looked at Wright in the same sort of way Lou Ann had looked at him that time she told him he was half a boy and he was half a man. Wright just looked back at the lady and tried to act like the boy.

Wright made his way out of the old post office without anybody noticing he was Bennie J. and Cordelle's boy. He walked down the block to where his Vette was angle-parked in front of Lipsom's Appliances. He was standing by his car door, trying to fish his car keys out of his tight front pants pocket, when he heard, "Wright! Is that your car?"

Wright turned around, saw Daughtery standing at the parking meter admiring his car. "Yeah." When he noticed Daughtery wasn't being an asshole, he added, "Yeah. Got it for my birthday."

"You lucky dog, you. That's really nice. Boy," Daughtery said.

"Want to go for a spin?"

Daughtery pointed down the sidewalk. "I'm due at work in a few minutes down at the feed store."

Wright handed Daughtery the keys. Daughtery got excited, said, "Aw, man," and got behind the wheel. Wright got in the passenger seat, pulled out his pint bottle of gin, a plastic cup, and began fixing himself a gin and Sun-Drop. "Want a drink?"

Daughtery cranked the engine, looked around smiling. "No, thanks. I'm taking some antibiotics. Had a bit of a sore throat. Eddie and I went out camping a couple of weeks ago. I think I stayed wet too much."

Daughtery pulled the car out very carefully and drove slowly the six blocks to his father's feed store. They had been such good friends in elementary school; Wright couldn't figure it out. Daughtery had turned into a Dr. Jekyll and Mr. Hyde. Sometimes he was nice, like now. Then the next time Wright saw him he might be a snide hateful shitass worthy of Eddie's company. In some ways Wright respected Daughtery, in some ways felt sorry for him. Daughtery was actually Kathy Lee's third cousin. Daughtery's grandfather had been the black sheep of the black sheep of the Thomas family. Daughtery had the aristocratic blood, but not the money. Sort of the opposite of himself, Wright was now thinking. Daughtery's parents had divorced when he was young, and Daughtery's mother had raised him. Daughtery, ever since Wright had known him, had had a job to help his mother defer some, even if little, of the cost of raising him. Despite holding down a part-time job, Daughtery had managed to become a football star.

Wright came to think of it now: Daughtery was a football coach's dream, a prodigy, an example of hard work, natural ability, and dedication. In contrast, Wright personally knew himself to be a football coach's nightmare, a physical education coach's spite. For Wright, when told to suck it up and go, wanted to know, suck up what? And go where? When he was told to put out 110 percent he wanted to explain how that was mathematically impossible.

Maybe he and Daughtery were opposites, Wright thought as Daughtery got out of the car at the back of the feed store, thanking him for getting to drive the Corvette. Wright crawled over into the driver's seat and headed up toward Courthouse Square. He had to register to vote now.

He drank half his cup of gin driving to the courthouse, then drank the other half as he walked slowly toward the building. Wright tossed the empty plastic cup into a trashcan, looked over at the two water fountains. It was the only thing he hadn't been able to get away with uptown when he was little—drinking at the "Colored" water fountain. A policeman always took him directly to the sheriff, the sheriff always trying to explain slowly to Wright how things were so the eight-year-old would understand.

Wright went to Voter Registration on the ground floor. Mrs. Victor had known Wright all his life, so knew the answers to all the questions she was supposed to ask him; she just filled it out. Soon she put a sheet of paper in front of him, told him to sign it where she had marked X. Wright, smiling, signed it. Then Mrs. Victor took the sheet back, singing some song to herself Wright didn't recognize. Then she said, "Congratulations, Wright! You are the youngest registered Democrat in Sumpter County."

Wright looked puzzled and said, "Mrs. Victor, I only want to register to vote. Not pledge a party."

Mrs. Victor gave a little smile, said, "Wright," and gave a nervous giggle. "Anyone who registers to vote in Sumpter County is simultaneously automatically registered as a Democrat."

"I don't want to register with any political party," Wright said. "I want to unregister as a Democrat."

Mrs. Victor stared at Wright. There were two other courthouse workers in the room; they stopped what they were doing to stare. Mrs. Victor said, "Let me check on this, Wright."

She walked through the doorway that was behind the counter and shut the door behind her. Wright heard her walk out into the hall of the courthouse from that room. Then the two other workers walked out through the doorway behind them, shutting that door.

The courthouse was well over a hundred years old. The door that led directly to the hall and the two doors the ladies had just shut all had translucent glass on their top half. Wright tried to see through them but couldn't. He had the feeling all the doors had been locked. He looked out the huge window that looked out onto the courthouse yard.

Wright had an intense feeling that he was about to be assassinated. He started to run for the window and dive through the glass, but he couldn't move. He might as well have been tied to his chair. He tried to think the feeling was silly, but nothing else was on his mind other than he had just been locked unwittingly in a room and shortly a gunman would come through the door, probably the one Mrs. Victor had gone through, and shoot him once in the head.

Wright could hear his heart pounding inside his rib cage.

Someone began opening the door Mrs. Victor had exited. Somehow Wright shed his paralyzation and stood straight up. As Winn would have put it, he was ready to bite bullets and kick ass.

Wayne McKinney came through the door. He walked around the counter, said, "Hello, Wright," and extended his hand. Wright shook it. Wayne, chairman of the County Commission, was one of Bennie J.'s friends. "Let's go up to my office for a little visit, Wright."

Wright followed him out the door that went directly to the hall. They walked down the wide marble-floored hall past the shoeshine stand Pops Malone had operated for thirty-five years. Wright and Wayne walked up the broad stairway to the second floor. Wayne talked about the weather. Wright looked at Wayne's blue-and-white cotton seersucker suit. Wright looked around for something that would tell him it wasn't 1955, but he couldn't find anything.

After Wayne's secretary fixed them some coffee, they went into Wayne's office. Wayne shut the door and motioned for Wright to sit down in the big chair in front of his desk. Wright sat down.

Wayne smiled at Wright as though he were going to tell him a fun secret. He said, "I'm going to go over some interesting things with you right now, Wright. Now, Wright, I want you to hear me out. We are talking about the future of our civilization as we know it today. You can take what I say and make of it what you wish. But I want you to hear me out first."

Wright said, "All right." The coffee he was sipping on now seemed to make him drunker.

A huge map of the United States was on the wall behind Wayne's sprawling desk. Wayne pointed to the map and said, "Do you know what this is?"

"That is the United States of America, one nation justice for all and the liberty for which it stands." Wright knew Wayne to be politically minded.

Wayne nodded and said, "Absolutely correct." He pointed to the southeastern states, made a circling motion with his hand to include as far north as Tennessee and as far south as Ocala, Florida. "Do you know what this is?"

"That's the Southeast."

"That's right. Also known as Dixie."

"Dixie includes Texas, too," Wright added.

Wayne nodded. "Texas is part of the Confederacy. That's true. But Texas is Texas. I'm talking about the Deep South. This is Dixie." Wayne smiled. Wright passed no objections, so Wayne continued. He pointed to Alabama. "What's this?"

"That's Alabama."

"That's right. And Alabama is the Heart of Dixie."

"It says that on the license plate, even."

"And it's for a reason," Wayne said. He pointed to the very north of Alabama and the very south of Tennessee. "And what's this, Wright?"

"That's the Tennessee Valley."

"That's one hundred percent correct." He pointed to Sumpter County. "What's this?"

"Sumpter County."

"That's right. If you will take a careful look, Sumpter is the very Heart of Dixie. Sumpter is the Alabamaest Alabama. Sumpter is the Deepest South."

After Wayne said that he sat down at his desk across from Wright. They both took a sip of coffee. Wayne was smiling. Then he grinned at Wright and said, "Wright, I didn't ask you all those questions to be condescending. I know you are a very intelligent person. If you weren't a very intelligent person I wouldn't even been talking to you, for this talk would be unneccessary. I just first want to orient you. I know you know where you are. But I just want to orient you to where you are. We are very fortunate people. I will not even ponder the question if we are fortunate because of our own will over our destiny. Or if it is by chance. I have my own opinions on that. But that is not the purpose here right now. I am not here to discuss opinions or philosophy with you."

Wayne took out his pipe, stuffed some tobacco into the bowl. Wright didn't know what it was but knew damn well it wasn't Red

Ox. Wayne lit it with a pipe lighter, puffed at the pipe, then said, "With my job I have to use a lot of different kinds of thinking. I have to use book sense, common sense, take potshots. But Wright, I deal a lot with statistics."

Wright killed off his coffee and looked out the window at the steeple of the First Methodist Church. He thought about all the parties he had been to at Wayne's house as a child. Parties where a lot of the state politicians would get very drunk.

"Wright, this is the garden spot of the nation. I won't bore you with statistics. I'm not speaking biasedly now. One only has to look at the trend. I'm talking about in black and white. I'm not talking about looking into some goddamn crystal ball. If one wants proof of the possibility one only has to look at the shoreline of the Tennessee River. Big commerce is coming."

Wright wasn't sure if that was the big secret he had seemed to be holding. Wayne was looking out the window now. He had gotten up and walked over to the window that looked to the east side of the square where Bernstein's Department Store was. Wright bet the odds were three to one that Cordelle was in there right now buying shoes, trying to get Hanna to get another pair so she would have plenty at college.

"Yeah," he said, "them Yankees coming down here polluting up the Tennessee. God's own river."

Wayne acted like he hadn't heard what Wright had said. "People like you, Wright. You have a born knack for capturing one's heart."

Wright figured there were some people like Jerry Lee that liked him, some like Eddie that hated his guts, and some like Daughtery that flipflopped on the subject. Wright did appreciate his friends, but mostly didn't give a shit what anybody thought about him. He was like Winn in that respect. "People like you too, Wayne," he said.

"Wright, you are a born leader."

Wayne stood looking out the window. Wright was noticing that what he had thought was a 35-mm camera in its case on the desk was in fact a .38 Smith and Wesson revolver in a holster, Wayne's personal handgun.

Wayne looked Wright in the eye and repeated himself. "You are a born leader."

Wright thought of how he couldn't lead jack shit. Wayne should be giving this speech to Winn. Now Winn was a born leader.

Wayne said, "You are one of the chosen. By God, by fate, by family, by chance. I will not get into that. Wright, when you are twenty-five years old there is no, absolutely no, reason that you can not be sitting in the House of Representatives in Washington, D.C."

It seemed to Wright this was part of the secret. Wayne lost his smile.

Wright felt disoriented. Like when he was little. He had pondered and pondered as he sat in Lanny Jones's bathroom. Lanny and his wife had had an ultramodern bathroom in their home in the late fifties. The walls were solid mirror. As a child whenever he was at Lanny's house, Wright would go in the bathroom to stare into the mirror at his image and image behind the image. Once Lanny had walked in while Wright was looking at this and said, "It goes into infinity. There is no end."

Wright said, "There is no end."

"That's right, Wright. There is no end to where it could lead. Wright, I'll give you a little example. An incident you are familiar with." Wayne was pacing behind his desk. "In 1937 Judge Thomas stood up and decried his jury for finding ten black men guilty of raping two white women. Judge Thomas was a good man. But he was out of place. He was out of time. What he did benefited no one. In that moment he forfeited his political career. Had he restrained himself he would have walked into Washington as a U.S. congressman less than a year later. No doubt. That is a fact. And there is a strong possibility—not even just a possibility, a probability—had the judge been a congressman and had J.C. not been so goddamn left-wing when he was representative. The nation was ready. J.C. would have been in the position to walk into the presidency of the United States of America."

Wayne stopped pacing and pointed to the map. Then he looked back at Wright.

"Wright, these things do not happen by accident." He leaned on the desk and looked straight at Wright. "Wright, you have people ready to guide you. Ready to steer you in the direction of leadership that molds, that runs the nation. It has to be a very special person. There is usually only one of each generation. Only one from this heart of the Heart of Dixie with the potential." Wayne stood up straight. "You are that one." He pointed to the map. "Those are your people who need you. You must not turn your back on them."

Wright couldn't get his mind off Lanny now. When Wayne said things didn't happen by accident, Wright remembered being told Lanny was dead. Bennie J. had said "It wasn't an accident." He had asked Bennie J. where it had happened. Bennie J. had told him in the bathroom in front of the vanity counter. Wright had wondered if Lanny was thinking about him when he had stuck the shotgun in his mouth and looked into the infinite-image mirror. As Wright thought about it now, he tried to imagine how the mirror behind Lanny had shattered, destroying the images.

As he was imagining the explosion of the shotgun, Wayne put his arms out to Wright. Throwing his arms apart, hollering in an explosion, Wayne yelled, "If you want to forfeit the destiny of the Heart of Dixie as a stronghold of the nation, you just go back down there and rebuke your Democratic affiliation!"

Wright stared at Wayne, unmoved. Then Wayne settled back into his chair, smiled, and said softly, "Wright, you have the ability to own the hearts of the Heart of Dixie. Don't pass it by."

Wright reached up slowly, got the revolver, took it out of the holster, and examined it. Wayne watched silently, smiling. It was the first time Wright had had a .38 in his hand since he had put a hole between his first and second metatarsals. After that he had switched over to .22s.

Wright aimed at Sumpter County and pulled the trigger. The blast shook the room and it was dead on. Wright said, "Sumpter." Then he said, "New York," and shot New York. "Los Angeles." He aimed at the other side of Wayne's head and shot Los Angeles. He swung the revolver back past Wayne, said, "Miami," and shot Miami. He imagined the map being made of glass, shattering and falling to the floor, leaving an empty space to represent nothing.

Wright told Wayne, "Call Birchdale if you got any problems." Birchdale was an old attorney in town who handled only his own and a few select families' legal matters. When Wright, Winn, or Bennie J. messed something up uptown they told the person to call Birchdale. That Birchdale would have it paid if merited.

Wright had been talking about the map when he spoke of Birchdale. Wright said, "You got something else you want to tell me?" He wasn't being arrogant. He was serious, acting very polite to Wayne. He wasn't mad at Wayne or anything. He had only shot his map out of boredom and drunkenness. Wright wasn't even thinking about being twenty-five. As Hanna was sure she wouldn't make it to eighteen, Wright didn't really foresee himself being able to live as old as twenty-five.

Wayne's ears were ringing somewhat. He rose and said, "No. That's all I wanted to say, Wright. Thank you for listening."

Wright rose and said, "Oh, thank *you.*" He put Wayne's revolver back in the holster, then laid it back on the desk where it had been. They shook hands. Wright walked to the door. After he turned the doorknob, he took his hand off the knob and turned back to Wayne. He held out his palm and slapped it with the back of his other hand, smiled, and held the empty cupped palm out to Wayne. Wright said, "The hearts of the Heart of Dixie are right here."

Wayne winked at him. After Wright stepped out, Wayne smiled to himself, for he was going to have an interesting story to tell the press after Wright was in the White House.

IV

Midnight
in the Heart
of Dixie

"Doddy pulled into Fred Fielding's Amoco station to get some gas one day. I was six, Winn was nine. We were riding in the back of his pickup. Sitting with our backs against the cab. Midnight was lying between us. Fred's brother Lakel owned this pit bull named Ollie, number one fighting pit bull in North Alabama. Ollie started circling around the truck, growling. Lakel told Doddy to put the kids and Midnight in the cab, that his dog would kill Midnight if she got out. Doddy told him Ollie couldn't kill Midnight. Lakel told Doddy that Ollie had killed fifty other pit bulls in a row, that he was worth thousands of dollars. Winn and I were sitting real quiet and listening. Doddy says, 'Well, if that dog leans up against that truck or gits near those kids you gone be out a lot of money.' Then Lakel says, 'You not gone shoot my dog are you?' Getting real smart with Doddy, you know. Doddy says, 'Listen, mister, I ain't gone do nothing to your dog. But I got ways of protecting my children.' Lakel eases back his agitation some, says, 'You children not gone git hurt, but I'm warnin' you that coon dog gets out of that truck, she's dead. Don't come crying to me. I warned ye, now.' The tailgate was down on the truck. About that time that pit bull jumped up on the tailgate. Midnight charged him and they rolled in the dirt. By the time they had rolled over twice, Midnight had tore his throat out and killed him. Doddy says to Lakel, 'Don't come crying to me. I warned ye now,'" Wright said and took a sip of Right Time.

Hanna said, "I guess Ollie went straight to pit bull heaven."

"I reckon. Anyway, the story spread like wildfire through the coon dog runners that Midnight had killed the number one pit bull. So she was henceforth referred to as Queen of the Coon Dogs. The end." Cruising past the site of the Coon-on-a-log, Hanna had asked if Mama Dog Midnight had ever done that. When Wright had replied that no, and that she had never coon hunted, that she had never even seen a raccoon up close to his knowledge, that Midnight rarely went out of the Big House compound at night, Hanna had wanted to know why they called Mama Dog Queen of the Coon Dogs.

Wright was surprised Hanna didn't know the story but told her he would relate it all once they got to the old homeplace that Bennie J. was born and lived in until he was twenty years old, to the roots of thirsty city.

Wright was at the bow of *Fast Boat* with a spotlight, shining it in front of the boat. Hanna cruised along slowly, dodging stumps, logs, trees; they were in shallow water, up in a swamp among locusts and water oaks. Wright told her how they had had to move the house back a few hundred yards in the thirties when the TVA had backed the water up with the dam system. Hanna had been here plenty of times when she was little, when Mama Bo was still alive, for Mama Bo had refused to ever move from this place. The house had been empty for the last eight years.

Hanna drove the bow up onto soft ground and cut the engine. Wright shined the light back into the trees. Several feet from the boat was a narrow pier of a walkway that led over the mucky ground to a small board-sided wooden house built on oak posts, making the floor about four feet off the ground.

Wright with a five-cell flashlight, Hanna carrying an unlit Coleman lantern, they had gotten out of *Fast Boat* and walked slowly down the walkway, being wary of rotten planks though it was all very solid. When they got to the front porch Wright lit the lantern. Hanna said, "Can you imagine living here in the Depression? Sitting around at night? Greer coming over? Light being that from a coal oil lantern? Telling stories? Planning going into town, getting a ride on a train to Birmingham?"

"Yeah. It must have been fun. But Mama Bo. Before she died she would say, 'The good old days, huh, you can have them.' " They laughed.

When Wright got the lantern glowing, they made a tour of the house. Two cottonmouths were laying in the front room but slithered away. An old wood heater and a couple of ladderback chairs were the only things remaining in the room. They walked on back; an old cabinet bin of a thing remained in the kitchen. Wright and Hanna reminisced how Mama Bo used to roll out her biscuits on the marble slab there on the counter, how she would make them biscuits and coffee, tell them old fairy tales. Off from the back porch, there were two more walkways, one to an outhouse and another to a well.

Wright and Hanna had gone back to the front porch. Wright cut the lantern. A full moon was rising; moonlight was coming down through the trees. Hanna went to *Fast Boat*, retrieved two Right Times and upon returning reminded Wright that he was going to tell her how Midnight had become Queen of the Coon Dogs.

They had been all excited, making this trip to the roots of thirsty city, coming open throttle down the channel of the Tennessee River in the moonlight. But now the hot muggy night had gotten to both of them. Hanna suggested they leave now, that the trip back would cool them off, then they could take a bath.

The trip back to the marina seemed short. As they were pulling away in Wright's Corvette, he saw Kathy Lee's Camaro parked in the lot by the bait shop; he wondered if Kathy Lee and Eddie had slipped into the Thomas's houseboat and were banging away at each other. Kathy Lee sure was smart, but could do some of the fucked-upest things. Hanging around Eddie. Shit.

It was around midnight by the time they pulled up to the front of Big House. The moon seemed to be right dab up on top of Big House. They quietly walked in, headed for the stairs arm in arm. Big Room was fairly well lit by the moon. Splotches of light, shining through the windows, streaked across the floor. Wright thought he was walking into a splotch of shadow but then realized it was something, and sidestepped. He whispered, "Mama Dog, I almost stepped on you."

Wright and Hanna looked down at Mama Dog; something was wrong. They stared at her for a moment, then Hanna said, "Midnight?"

"Mama Dog Midnight?" Wright cried.

Hanna ran over and turned the lights on. Wright told Hanna, "Go get Doddy." She ran upstairs. Shortly she ran back down. A minute later Bennie J. came down barefoot, wearing a pair of pants and undershirt. Cordelle was behind him in her housecoat. Bennie J. kneeled beside Mama Dog and rubbed her neck. Wright thought Bennie J. was about to cry. He had never seen Bennie J. cry before, or Cordelle either for that matter.

Bennie J. got up and said, "Cover her up. I'll wake you up before daylight. You go get Jerry Lee in the morning and y'all make a casket. I'll bury her tomorrow night. And if Winn calls, don't tell her. Don't ruin her trip. We'll tell her when she gets back." Bennie J. turned and walked back up the stairs to his bedroom.

Cordelle had walked into the dining room. She came back out with a beige tablecloth. She kneeled and lay it over Midnight. Her arms around Wright and Hanna, she said, "Let's go in the kitchen and drink some hot chocolate."

Cordelle put a stewer with milk on the stove eye. Wright and Hanna sat at the table. Wright's hands were on the sides of his face holding his head up, tears were streaming silently down his face.

Cordelle turned and saw him. She walked over to him, pulled a chair up, and sat down. She stroked his hair. "Honey, Midnight was eighteen years old. She was a dog. She couldn't live forever. I'm sorry, sweetheart."

"I don't want anything to die," Wright said. "I don't want anything that's ever had to do with Big House to die."

"I understand, honey. But Mama Dog Midnight is in heaven right this minute. Not dog heaven, but real heaven."

2 The next morning Wright woke up to a knock at the door. It was still dark outside. "Yes?" Wright said.

"Just you Doddy wakin ye up."

"Thank you, Doddy. I'll get up and go get Jerry Lee," Wright said. He heard Bennie J.'s footsteps fade down the hall, heading for the marina. Wright moved his hand over Hanna, but she remained asleep. He left her to go to the marina. Day was breaking as he went down the glasslike river, to Jerry Lee's.

When Wright and Jerry Lee got back to Big House, some lumber had already been delivered to build the casket with. By the time they set up some sawhorses and tools in front of the toolhouse in Big Back Yard, Mae Emma had fixed them some breakfast. They ate slowly and in silence on the veranda.

After they had cut all the pieces of plywood they started assembling the casket. That was when Bennie J. came around the house in his two-year-old straight-six stick-shift Chevy pickup. Bennie J. got out and walked up to Jerry Lee and Wright.

Everything was quiet and solemn for a moment. Then Jerry Lee said, without stopping what he was doing, "Are you gone bury Mama Dog in Wendell's cemetery, Bennie J.?" It almost seemed like a stupid question to ask since Mama Dog Midnight was Queen of the Coon Dogs.

But Bennie J. hollered, "Hell naw, Jerry Lee! I'm not burying Mama Dog Midnight in that son of a bitch's coon dog funeral!" Then Bennie J. hollered, "Cemetery!" to correct himself.

Jerry Lee knew he should have known that all along, should have known it when Wright knocked on his door two hours ago and told him Midnight had died, asking him to help make a casket. If Mama Dog was going to Wendell's cemetery she would have gotten one of Wendell's caskets in the deal. The caskets that Wendell's brother, the cabinetmaker, made. That his sister, the upholsterer, lined. That his wife's nephew, the alcoholic, decorated with colored tin and metal borders.

Bennie J. calmed down and said, "Y'all fix her up and then take the casket. Put it and a pick and shovel in my boat down at the marina. Come night, I'll take her to the island. Build a fire. And bury her myself. I was her master. I'll bury her the way a coon dog ought to be buried."

Bennie J. left his truck and went back to the marina in his Model A. He didn't care to drive anything but his pickup, though did enjoy an opportunity to drive the classic Ford. Bennie J. claimed it was a "real Ford," but wouldn't have a new Ford now if someone had given it to him; Fords were all fucked up now. He claimed the only car was a Chevrolet and the only outboard was a Johnson, though Mercury outdrives were all right. The only thing he ever fussed about Jerry Lee was that Jerry Lee had a Mercury outboard. At least he had an old Chevy pickup and an old Chevy car to make up for it. And Cordelle got away with having a Cadillac because they were "just high-priced Chevrolets anyway." How Wright, Winn, and Hanna had gotten away with having the MGAs was by having to hear about five times a day how "them little foreign pieces of shit stay tore up more than they work. I have to pay Jerry Lee more a month for working on them than I do the TVA for lighting up Big House." And sometimes that was true.

About the time they finished the casket, Cordelle drove up in her Eldorado with Hanna. They had gone to one of Bennie J.'s cotton gins and gotten a basket of cotton that had been seeded from last season. They put the cotton into the casket, then covered it with purple satin cloth. Cordelle shaped the cloth, recessing the middle for a place to lay Midnight. "I sure am going to miss Mama Dog," she said and left.

Jerry Lee and Wright went back to Big Room to get Midnight. She had not been touched since Cordelle had covered her. Bennie J. claimed that Cordelle kept it cold enough in Big House to hang a side of beef. Last night Cordelle had turned the temperature even lower so that Midnight wouldn't start stinking too bad. It was cold in Big House.

Jerry Lee and Wright lay Mama Dog in the casket, leaving her eighteen-carat gold mesh collar on. Hanna lay another purple satin cloth over her. Jerry Lee placed the lid on the casket. He and Wright nailed it shut.

Bennie J.'s bass boat stayed next to *Fast Boat* in a two-slip tin boathouse at the end of one of the piers. After they put the casket into the bass boat, Jerry Lee, Hanna, and Wright sat down on the dock inside the boat house and let their legs dangle down toward the water. Wright started to say something about Mama Dog, but didn't see any use in it. Instead he said, "Jerry Lee, you want me to take you back home now?" Jerry Lee said yeah, why didn't they all go to his place for ice teas.

Wright yawned as he flipped the switch that let *Fast Boat* down into the water. "Man, I got up too early this morning," Wright announced to no one in particular.

Hanna said, "Take the truck back on to Big House and then get a nap. I'll take Jerry Lee home."

When Hanna pulled up to Jerry Lee's dock, she tied up and stepped out of the boat. Jerry Lee said, "Come on in for some refreshment." They went on to his house. Jerry Lee walked on into the kitchen and opened the refrigerator. He looked back and Hanna was standing in the kitchen doorway, staring at him. He looked back at her and asked, "You't a Sun-Drop, a beer, some ice tea?"

Hanna responded, "Tell me about my father."

Jerry Lee, now knowing why he had had the feeling she was following him ever since she had told Wright to go to Big House and take a nap, repeated, "You't a Sun-Drop, a beer, some ice tea?"

"Sun-Drop. I want to know about my father."

"Like what?"

"Like everything you know. First of all, is it you?"

Jerry Lee smiled, said, "Hanna, dear, if I was your daddy I wouldn't be keeping it a secret. No sirree. Why you ask?"

"I've seen pictures," Hanna said, lost her defensiveness, walked over and sat at the table. Jerry Lee handed her a bottle of Sun-Drop, got himself a beer and sat down. "Mama's told me long ago, all she knew about Charles Aaron Rodgers. That was when I was real little. One summer when I came to Sumpter, I was twelve I think, I would look you up and down when you weren't looking. We had the same hair, the same color eyes, the same teeth, the same cheekbones. I thought maybe Charles Aaron Rodgers was some story she told me, you know, to be sheltering me as a little girl. Then I heard all the rumors about you being my father, here in Sumpter. I asked her again. She told me she had told me the truth when I was little, just that there wasn't much truth to tell. I didn't disbelieve my own mother but for some reason I wanted to ask you." She took a sip of Sun-Drop.

"I wish I was your father," Jerry Lee smiled. "I'm afraid Coleen's told you the way it is."

"But you did save his life, then, didn't you?"

"I don't know if I saved his life. I just picked him up in a helicopter. If I saved his life, I just saved it long enough for him to git back home and git killed in a car wreck. I think your daddy was destined to die."

Hanna bit her lip. "Please, Jerry Lee, tell me about my father."

"What do you want to know?"

"Everything. Tell it to me from the start. Start from where you and my mother were in love."

Jerry Lee took a sip of beer. "Well, she was twenty-two, I was seventeen. Of course I knew her because of Bennie J. and Cordelle. Coleen was at her last year of Sumpter College. We hit it off, I was crazy in love with her. Still am. She'd sneak out of the dorm at night, go haul whiskey with me. She liked drivin' fast. Boy, I was in love, ready to git married. She graduated, she went off to New Orleans. I reckon she just loved excitement, maybe liked the way I looked. But don't reckon she really loved *me*."

"Don't leave anything out," Hanna demanded.

"I'm not. It gets even shorter."

"So what happened then?"

"Then what happen was real classic. Back then in 'fifty it was real classic. Right after your heart got broken, you got drafted and sent to Korea. I had to go up git this captain that had been hit. I lit down in the edge of a field. I run up. Two soldiers were tending to him. He turned around looked at me. I thought I was looking into a mirror. If that wadn't bad enough, two days later I learned he was from New Orleans and was married to a Coleen Remington who had gone to boarding school in my hometown. Right then I knew the world was too damn small. Damn, cranks me up just thankin' about it," Jerry Lee said and killed his beer.

Hanna just watched him guzzle the beer. She had known everything he had just told her. She started to ask him about all the philosophical implications of seeing your double, of traveling halfway across the globe to see somebody that looks like you, of finding out that double was married to the woman you were madly in love with, of the woman just a couple years prior you had been raising hell and hauling whiskey with. Hanna started to ask Jerry Lee what that did to one, how that made the world too small a place, because to her it seemed to make the world too big, too bizarre, it made death seem that much closer. Her mother seemed to have a thing about a certain-looking man, maybe if Jerry Lee had never laid eyes on Charles Rodgers maybe he would have never been killed. Maybe it had been a battle of the psyches somehow; all Hanna knew for sure was that she would see her own grave before her eighteenth birthday.

Hanna considered commenting on all that had flashed through her mind, but when Jerry Lee sat the beer bottle back down, it looked like she had already spent too much time thinking about all that shit. Instead she said, "When's the last time you heard from Mama?"

"Two days ago."

"Huh?"

"Yeah. Come on." Jerry Lee got himself another beer out of the refrigerator and then led Hanna out the side kitchen door, across the yard, to his work garage, a building made of barn wood that looked like a small version of Terrel's barn. Jerry Lee took away the two-by-four crosspiece that held the two doors shut. He swung back the doors and said, "A late graduation present from one Coleen Remington to Hanna Belle Remington."

There sat the most exotic-looking car Hanna had ever seen—a shiny midnight black '66 Corvette convertible with dark tan leather interior. In New Orleans she had been around Mercedes, Ferraris, Porsches, and Jaguars, but there was something about this car; it was the sleekest automobile she had ever laid eyes on.

Jerry Lee said, "Coleen had Bennie J. find it for her. Bennie J. had me to totally restore it. Coleen paid for it. It got a rebuilt engine, new interior, all the mechanics, the brakes are brand new, reworked body."

Hanna shrieked, "This is the most gorgeous car I've ever seen! I can't believe it's mine!"

"Well start believing, Hanna, honey. Look at the license plate."

Hanna walked around to the back of the car; there was a vanity plate. Across the bottom of the plate read "Alabama," across the top, "The Heart of Dixie" with little hearts on either side. On the plate was printed "Midnight."

Jerry Lee explained, "Because it was shiny black I thought 'Midnight.'"

"I love it."

"See, Midnight used to be my nickname when I's growing up because my hair was raven black. Well, still is. Did you know Bennie J. named Mama Dog Midnight after me?"

"No."

"Yeah. When she was born, she was such a black shiny puppy Bennie J. says, 'Look at ole Midnight there. Her coat's black as your hair.' He just called her her name right off the bat. But anyway, because the paint job turned out so shiny black on this baby, and since you got raven black hair, too, I thought I'd name it Midnight."

"A very appropriate name. I love it!" Hanna said, then hugged Jerry Lee.

"Yeah, Midnight's a lucky name too," Jerry Lee said. "Mama Dog Midnight lived to be eighteen."

Hanna went into a shaking fit.

3 Wright lay on his bed, wiggling his right wrist in front of him, feeling the weight of the bracelet Hanna had given him, touching it with his left hand, looking at it. He decided he was going to start sleeping with it on. Between having cut meat for a week, the camping trip, and building the casket this morning, he hadn't worn it as much as he had wanted. Somehow his intense admiration of it now helped to make up for the lost time of not wearing it.

He had come straight home from the marina, pulled his heavy black drapes to darken the room, and lay fully clothed on his bed. He had napped for about an hour before he woke and turned on the lamp to admire his bracelet.

When he had come home from the marina, Bennie J. had told him

Jerry Lee was going to give Hanna her Corvette today. She hadn't returned yet; maybe he was giving it to her now. As he was imagining Hanna's reaction to it, the phone rang.

"Hello, Wright?"

"Yes?"

"This is Daughtery."

Wright sat up, confused. "Hello, Daughtery. How are you?"

"I'm sorry your dog died."

Wright froze; he didn't know how to take what Daughtery had just said. It almost hit him like, "I hate your guts so I poisoned your dog last night." Daughtery never called him. Wright didn't know whether to be nice, cuss him, or just hang up. He did the easiest and most logical thing. He replied, "Thank you."

"Yeah. Remember when we were little and would go swimming, we'd hold on to her tail and she would drag us through the water? We'd ride her like a horse, too. What was her name, Midnight?"

"Yeah." Wright smiled. He had called to be nice. Daughtery was referring to the era before he had turned into Dr. Jekyll and Mr. Hyde.

"Yeah. I always had a dog up until the last few years. It's a heart-breaker to lose a good dog."

"Well, thank you for your condolences, Daughtery."

"Sure. The reason I called was, I'm helping out Lou Ann. There's going to be a big party at the country club three weeks from this Saturday night. It's in Kathy Lee's honor because she's going off to Rutgers."

"Oh yeah?" Wright said. He enjoyed knowing Daughtery could be so nice to him but at the same time was taken out that Daughtery was closer connected to something that Lou Ann and J.C. were doing than he was.

Daughtery continued, "We're inviting a lot of people from our graduating class so it will be like a last party before everyone goes off to college, you know." Daughtery went on to explain how there would be a band from Georgia, that parents were going to be invited but later would go to Lou Ann and J.C.'s for a tea. They were mailing out invitations but Lou Ann had a list she wanted called beforehand.

Wright told him that sure he'd be there and they hung up. Wright was pissed; he felt he had lost clout with the Thomases. What in the hell was Daughtery knowing about a party they were giving before he did, why didn't Lou Ann or Kathy Lee call up themselves? Wright reached to dial Kathy Lee's number. There was no answer so he dialed the Thomas's downstairs number. Lou Ann answered, "Ha-lou."

"Lou Ann, this is Wright."

"Hello, Wright. How are you?"

"Fine." He started to ask her what the hell was going on with the party and why didn't he have anything to do with it. Instead he asked, "May I speak to Kathy Lee, please?"

"She's taking a bath right now."

Wright didn't know what he was hearing. If he were taking a bath and got a phone call, expecially from Kathy Lee, Cordelle or Mae Emma came and got him out to answer it. Wright started to tell Lou Ann to get Kathy Lee and get her ass to the phone. He said, "That's nice. Could I speak to her, please?"

"Well, Wright, honey, she just went in to take a bath. Could I take a message? Oh, I was sorry to hear about Midnight."

Wright mumbled, "Thank you," and told Lou Ann not to bother with a message. He hung up. Wright had the feeling he was going to walk out of his room, look down, and Big Room would be an empty shell the way it was the day they had moved in. Bennie J. would have on Levi's and an old shirt. He would say they were moving to the little house out in the swamp. That Hanna was moving back to New Orleans to marry some older man. That all their, Hanna, Winn, Coleen, and Cordelle's diplomas had been voided by the Sumpter College for Women. Wright felt he was no longer welcome at the Thomas's. That his celebrity status had just been pulled uptown and he would be jailed for any minor infraction.

Mama Dog Midnight hadn't been dead twenty-four hours and things had already started turning to shit.

There was a knock at the door like somebody was trying to beat it down. Mae Emma hollered, "Git out here, Wright! All them god-damn coon dog people are descending on Big House!"

Wright got up. By the time he got out his door, Mae Emma was at the bottom of the stairs walking back across Big Room toward the kitchen. Wright hollered at her, "What you telling me for?"

"I want you to do something about it! They gone be shittin' all in Big Yard. I don't want to be scoopin' up dog shit all day tomorrow. If ya Mama sees all them dogs on her yard she'll have the Committee for the Preservation of the Dogs out here shootin' em." She went on to the kitchen.

When Wright came through the kitchen door, he looked at Mae Emma as if he was going to say something to her, was going to argue about the coon dogs. But standing there, he forgot what he was going to talk about. He didn't even know if he was for or against all the coon dogs outside paying respect to Mama Dog Midnight.

Mae Emma looked at him, saw his distorted face, felt his confusion. She said, sympathetically, "What's the matter, baby?"

"I don't know. I forgot what I came in here for."

"I know whut you come in here for. You come in here to talk to Cousin Emma. That what you in here fuh. Come over here and sit down, baby."

Wright went over and sat at the kitchen table. He put his head in his hands. Mae Emma stood beside him and hugged his shoulders to her hips. "What's the matter with my baby?"

Wright forced a grunt laugh. "Mae Emma, I'm lost. I gotta leave Big House and I'm lost."

Mae Emma walked over to the cabinets. She bent down and pulled a little silver flask out from way behind the turkey cooker.

Wright said, "Mae Emma! You know Mama Cordelle don't allow alcohol at Big House."

"Mama Cordelle don't have to put up with the shit that Mae Emma do," she responded and poured up a couple of bourbon and cokes. She handed Wright his and said, "Suck on this." She sat down beside Wright.

Wright listened to the dogs howling outside as he sipped on the bourbon. Mae Emma said, "Listen, baby. You gone go off next month. Truth of the matter is, you git away from here ain't nobody gone give a shit who you mama is or who you daddy is. But let me tell you. You a gifted child. Folks like you. The folks that really like you like you for you. That's you and it don't stay at Big House. It go with you wherever it is you go. And it go with you because it don't go with you, because it you. It not who you daddy is, who you mama is, how much money they got. Now. Big House and who you daddy is do have something to do with something. They is shitasses in the world. They can't fuck with Bennie J. But they can fuck with Wright, they can fuck with Mae Emma. And these shitasses. I caught me a few through the yeahs. And onct I catch 'em I folds 'em up to wipe my ass with. Onct you catch 'em they folds up real easy. All the shitasses I caught, they smile real big at ye, but they look at ye out the corner they eye. When you around 'em, you feel like they got 'em a little sharp knife hid, just waitin' to stab you onct you turn you back on them. Oh, it's a thirsty city all right. This society we live in fixed up to keep just a couple shitasses pissin' in the well, so everbody's drank stays fucked up."

Wright looked over and said, "Have you been talking with Greer?"

Mae Emma said, "Baby, you think you world's falling apart. But it ain't."

"So everything's not turning to shit?" Wright asked, looking over at Mae Emma.

"Naw, baby, it ain't. You just keep on doin' what you doin'. Don't be stoppin' to thank everthang's turned to shit."

Wright felt better but had no idea what Mae Emma had been trying to say. When she saw him nodding his head, she said, "Now go out there and keep them dogs from shittin' all over the place."

Wright went to Big Room, peeked out the window. Fifteen pickups were parked along the drive. Men were milling around the yard with coon dogs on leashes. He didn't see any in the process of shitting or pissing, mostly they were just howling and sniffing around.

When Wright stepped out the big front double door, the thirty-odd men present froze in silence. He walked to his Vette, opened the driver's door, looked around, waving to everyone. Everyone waved back. He got in, started pulling slowly around the drive. Wright spotted Eb Roberts down by the side of the driveway. Eb was watching the car. Wright knew Eb as the oldest and best coon dog runner in all of Sumpter County. Eb had on some brand-new Duckhead overalls and had Queenie on a leash.

Wright pulled up by Eb and stopped. Eb stepped up to the Corvette. Everybody else went back to talking and milling around.

Eb said, "Midnight done gone on."

"Yes, sir," Wright confirmed.

"Heard you's goin' off for an education."

"Yes, sir."

"Do good. Don't forgit you friends, Wright."

"No, sir, Mr. Roberts. Don't you worry about that none."

"We need ye back here soon as ye can git back," Eb said. Queenie was smelling of Wright's door. Eb looked away and then looked back at Wright. "If ye do come back."

When Eb said that Wright wondered what he knew. Besides all the moonshine he cooked, Wright knew Eb mixed up herbs and potions. Even read cards now and again. He wondered if Eb knew something he didn't know, if Eb knew he would ever make it out of Sumpter or not.

"Thanks for coming and paying respects to Mama Dog, Mr. Eb," Wright said.

"My honor, Wright," Eb said, stepping back away from the car. "Anything I can do, let me know."

Wright paused, then said, "I tell you what, Mr. Roberts. I think everybody should be down at the marina."

"I didn't know."

"Yes, sir. Maybe if you could just get everyone, one at a time, to quietly come down to the marina. Maybe I could get the casket set out, everybody could come by pay their respects in a more reverent manner."

"Yeah! Everbody wonderin' where the body was."

"If you could just do that for me, for the family, Mr. Roberts. I think that would be best for everyone."

"Consider it done, Wright. I'll take care of it."

Wright extended his hand. Eb stepped up to shake it. Then Wright cruised on. That had been easy, he thought. Maybe he could go into politics. Maybe he could lead people, get things done. As Wright cruised away from Big House, he imagined moving the Capitol to Sumpter County. Having Big House be the White House. He might could do it that way. Have Bennie J. financial advisor and policy-maker. Winn, head of state. Hanna, the first lady. Greer and Mae Emma his personal advisors. Jerry Lee, head of defense. And last but not least, Cordelle as head of protocol.

As Wright slipped into fourth and saw the fork in the road ahead, he realized he didn't know where he was going.

4 The moon was getting on up in the sky when Bennie J. pulled his bass boat out of the channel of the Tennessee River and headed toward Hatchett Island, his favorite place on the river. It had been a high-ground hammock in the swamp when he was a young boy but the backing up of the water by the TVA dams had made a smaller island out of it, just several acres now. He had come here to hunt rabbits, and to hunt for Indian artifacts. To Bennie

J. it was one of the safest places in the world. For the family Big House was the safest place. But for him personally, just himself, Hatchett Island seemed even safer.

Bennie J. cut the Johnson motor. The bow of the boat drifted into a small coarse-sand clearing of the wooded island. In his Hush Puppy shoes and dress pants, he stepped out of the boat into knee-deep water. He walked to the bow and pulled the boat as far up on dry land as he could. With pick and shovel he walked toward the center of the island, through thickets of mosquitoes. But they didn't bite Bennie J. Like Jerry Lee, there was something in his blood or skin that repelled mosquitos.

He walked through the darkness until he came to a clearing where there was a hint of light from the moon. He collected tinder and small rotten sticks into a pile. He pulled a wooden match out of his pocket, lit it on one of his teeth, and started the kindling to burning. After adding some larger sticks, he got down and blew at the base of the flame until there was a fire going. He gathered some small logs to build up a good blaze. The fire lit the clearing as well as running off the mosquitoes that weren't biting him.

Bennie J. looked up through the small hole in the overgrowth of trees above to the moonlit sky. But as the fire grew, the sight faded. He sat down for a moment on a big log near the fire, looked around.

Shortly he got up and started digging a grave several yards from the fire. When he had the hole better than waist deep, he climbed out and went back to his boat. After tying some ropes to the casket, he wrestled it out of the boat over the bow, drug it into the woods, and let the casket down as gracefully as he could into the grave. After he'd gone down and taken off the ropes, he shoveled the loose dirt back into the grave, stopping once to wonder why there was never as much dirt to put back into a hole as you had taken out. He had to dig a small hole off at the edge of the clearing to have enough dirt to make a little mound on the grave.

Bennie J. tossed the shovel over by the pick. He pulled a half pint of whiskey out of his back pocket, unscrewed the cap, and took him a good slug, all the while looking at the mound of the grave.

Bennie J. said, "Goodnight, Midnight. You were something. You had sense, had class. Thank you for protecting the kids. When they were little you wouldn't let anybody touch them. Who's gone protect 'em now?"

He looked around as he took him another slug of whiskey. He said,

"You watched Big House at night. You had more damn sense than to chase coons. Some angel sent you, I guess. One of Greer's archangels maybe. Damn, you were good! I got Cordelle. Winn. Wright. Hanna. Mae Emma. I've had some good people around me. I must a done something right."

Bennie J. took another good long slug of whiskey and looked down directly at the grave. He wiped his eyes. "Here's to you, Mama Dog." He held the bottle out to pour a bit of whiskey onto the grave, but stopped and said, "I know you'll do good wherever you are" and took a sip instead.

5 By the time he had *Fast Boat* out of the boat house his bellbottom jeans and khaki shirt were soaked through with sweat. When he got out into the channel and opened the boat up, the hot wind felt good to him.

Near the second light buoy, he cut out of the channel and went up toward the backwaters. He slowed to a troll and used the spotlight to search the shorelines. When he got to Hatchett Island he spotted Bennie J.'s bass boat and cut toward it. He killed the motor, then hit the switch to raise the foot of the outdrive out of the water. The boat coasted to the bank right beside Bennie J.'s.

Wright stepped up to the edge of the woods, looked into the thick darkness, and hollered, "Doddy! Doddy!" He walked into the woods. He heard, "Come to the fire, Wright."

Wright walked around some trees, his face getting slapped a few times by tree limbs. He swatted at mosquitoes as he walked. Soon he saw a flicker of light and made his way into the clearing.

Bennie J. was sitting on the log by the fire. He had his elbows on his knees and his hands were dangling down between his shins. He had the whiskey bottle in his right hand.

Wright walked up.

"She's been buried proper," Bennie J. said.

Wright looked at the grave mound and said, "Good." He walked around and sat by Bennie J. on the log. Wright was startled to see the whiskey bottle. "What's that you got in you hand, Doddy?"

"A bottle a whiskey."

Wright sat there on the log thinking how on the days of burials you found out a bunch of shit you didn't know before. He was sitting there wondering what he didn't know.

Bennie J. took a slug of whiskey.

Wright said, "Doddy. You know whiskey's for selling, not for drinking."

Bennie J. said, "I found it on the side of the road."

Wright said, "You know Mama Cordelle don't allow any whiskey at Big House!"

"We're not at Big House."

They were silent for a moment. Both of them stared into the fire. Finally Wright said, "Doddy, what was wrong with Lanny Jones?"

"He was forty years old. He was experiencing—well, women at a certain age have a change of life. Sometimes men experience that. Sort of a male change of life. You might say Lanny hadn't been able to perform for a little while. It was driving him crazy. Why?"

"I don't think he killed himself. I think I killed him."

Bennie J. looked over at Wright, then back out at the fire. He took another sip of whiskey and said, "I don't think you killed him. I don't think he killed himself. I think those killer Nazi bastards that poured the juice to his brain and that shitass doctor over in Huntsville that sent him down to that torture chamber, I think they the ones killed him. Why you say that?"

"There's something I never told anybody."

"What might that be?"

"Remember before we had the wall around Big Yard? Had the back fenced in with hog-wire fence? There was a clover field right next to the yard? Lanny put that electric fence around the clover field so he could let the cows in and out?"

"Yeah."

"You know how Midnight used to bark at him? Charge up against the fence try to get at Lanny?"

Bennie J. smiled. "Yeah. Old Mama Dog didn't care for Lanny for some reason."

"Yeah. Well, I was looking out the window. The fence was on. He'd just let the cows in the clover. He had the hot fence, holding it with some lineman pliers. Mama Dog was charging up against the fence, trying to get at him. I saw Lanny look around see if anybody was looking, then touch the hot wire to the hog fence up close to where Midnight's front paws were. It sent Mama Dog yelping. I could see him laughing. It made me mad. I mean real mad. I pierced a hole through him thinking, 'You didn't have to do that. You didn't have to hurt Mama Dog Midnight. She couldn't git to you. You'll get yours. You'll git it for that.' Then he got shocked himself, then blew his brains out. Sometimes I think it was my thinking that killed him."

"Well, I tell you what, Wright. Sometimes we do think evil thoughts. What that does to us, I don't know. Probably does one's self more harm than anybody else. I don't know. I can see how that might rest heavy on your mind. But if I's you I wouldn't let it worry ye none. None of us are perfect. I even sinned once myself. Naw, you done got it off your chest, so if I's you I wouldn't worry about it no more."

Wright sighed and said, "Thank you, Doddy."

"You're welcome."

"Doddy?"

"Whut?"

Staring into the fire, Wright asked, "Does Mama Cordelle know Hanna and I are in love?"

"Mama Cordelle?" Bennie J. asked as though they needed to establish exactly who they were talking about. "Hell if I know. You know you mama. She puts in front of herself whatever it is she wants to look at. She don't want her children to have to see the things she's seen, to go through the doing without me and her's done without. She tried to build a fairy-tale world for her children. Said that was her mission in life. We built an empire. Protected y'all kids. Tried to get you grown all in one piece. But naw, we ain't built a world safe. I'm sorry, Wright. I'm not perfect. I'm not God. I'm not even one them archangels Greer talks about. I even sinned once myself."

"Y'all built an empire. That's for sure."

"Yeah. Big House was part of it. Mama Cordelle wanted to build everything strong. Even give y'all strong names."

"Strong names?"

"Yeah. Strong names."

"What do you mean, strong names?"

"Shit, Wright. Hadn't you figured that out? If ye hadn't, I'd a told you long time ago."

"I don't know what you're talking about."

"Shit, you and Winn take everthang for granted. Thank money grows on trees. That God just happen to decide to give me money. Naw, God helps those who help themselves."

"I still don't know what you're talking about."

"We didn't exactly name you Wrong Reynolds, did we? We didn't exactly name your sister Lose Reynolds, did we? I mean, we didn't even name you Billy Boo and Dixie Lou. We named you Winn and Wright. Strong names! To help you be strong."

"Aw!" Wright said and smiled real big. "I'll be dogged, I never thought of that."

"That's what I'm trying to tell you. Thangs don't just happen. You cause things to happen. That's what we been trying to tell y'all, don't you see? You stay on top of things. Plan things out. Figure out how you gone git to where you going!"

"I see. I see, said the blind man," Wright said, quoting Bennie J.

"But I don't need to be telling you nothing. You got the knack. You got the touch. You got what don't but a few of each generation have. You are blessed."

Now Wright thought Bennie J. was starting to talk like the rest of Sumpter City. "What you gittin' at now, Doddy?"

"I mean you can't do no wrong. If I'd made the mistakes you made, I'd still be back up in here baitin' trotlines. You can't do nothing wrong. Everthang you do ends up right. You do some dumb-ass thing, it turns out to be the right thing to do, got everbody in the palm of your hand, going on about ye. Naw, don't seem you can do no wrong."

"Well, thank you for naming me Wright."

Bennie J. looked over at him and laughed, slapped him on the back. Then he took another sip of whiskey and stared back into the fire.

Wright wondered how Bennie J. withstood sitting there, smothering hot from the fire and from the heat, no air stirring. Wright was wet with sweat; there didn't seem to be enough air to breathe, almost the feeling of how Hanna talked about how it was going to be down in a casket. Wright said, "So Doddy, what you think about me and Hanna?"

"I love both y'all."

"Naw. You know what I mean?"

"Wright!" Bennie J. hollered. Wright twitched. They looked over at each other. Bennie J. said, "You can stick a feather up ye ass run around naked up at Courthouse Square. Or you can get up on top of a soapbox on top of the courthouse steps and tell everbody God's coming tomorrow at a quarter till noon to burn everthang down. But if you want to make a real fool out of youself just go to meddling in somebody's love life. Shit. You a grown man. Hadn't you learned nothing?"

They looked back into the fire. Bennie J. took another taste of bourbon. Wright stood up. He said, "Well, I'm gone git back to Big House. Me and Hanna, I think we might go to the drive-in."

"Gone see you another one them ole picture shows. Nothing like going out to a good picture show."

"That Corvette Coleen gave Hanna is something else, isn't it?"

"Yeah, boy. Ole Hanna Belle. I'm glad she got her one them little scoots. A Chevrolet engine don't belong in no toy. But whatever y'all kids want."

"I'll see you later, Doddy." Wright walked around the grave, heading back to *Fast Boat.*

When Wright got to the edge of the clearing about to walk back through the trees, Bennie J. hollered, "Wright!"

Wright stopped and turned. He could make out the silhouette of his father, but the light of the fire blurred any distinct characteristics. He said, "Yes, sir?"

"Whatever ye do in this world, move through it with honor and with grace."

6   Bennie J. was still sitting on the log sipping on his half pint of whiskey. He had about half of the bottle to go. He looked over to where Wright had been some half hour ago, just staring.

Suddenly he said, "Hell, I thought some Klu Kluxer was after me."

Cordelle had a white blanket wrapped around her, including her head. It peaked out in a cone about a foot above her head. She unwrapped the blanket from around her. She had on a short low-cut white cotton dress. Had on white sandals. Bennie J. recognized the dress. Last summer Winn had gone uptown shopping with Jerry Lee and bought the dress. Bennie J. had claimed it was too short.

"What were you doing all wrapped up on a hot night like this?" Bennie J. asked.

"Why, B.J. I don't have that insect-repellent blood like you and Jerry Lee. When I stepped out of *Fast Boat,* the mosquitoes tried to eat me alive. All the briars I had to walk through. There don't seem to be any mosquitoes here." She walked over toward Bennie J. but remained standing.

He said, "I didn't hear anybody come up to the island." All he could hear was the crackling of the fire, the night noises of the bugs and katydids. He looked up at his wife. Her diamond was reflecting the fire.

He said, "You look like a twenty-two-year-old girl tonight, Cordelle."

"That's funny you should say that, B.J. I feel twenty-two tonight. That's exactly how old I am tonight. This hot summer night just does something to me. It's like it just can't be hot enough for me tonight. I want to sweat. My actions have always been innocent, B.J. But *I* am not innocent. I can feel it down deep where it counts."

"I know. I know how it is down there. It's thirsty."

"It is thirsty. It's a thirsty city down there. You know how I feel, B.J. We are alike in so many ways."

Bennie J. took a sip of whiskey, then handed the bottle up to Cordelle. She took a sip and handed it back to him. Then she turned around and flipped the white blanket out over the mound of Midnight's grave. Cordelle sat down on the blanket with her legs straight out in front of her. She put her arms behind her, stiff-armed, and leaned back at a forty-five-degree angle. She said, "Oh, the ground's nice and cool."

Bennie J. looked at her moist skin that was reflecting the light of the fire. The dress was hiked up around her hips. Bennie J. could see the side of her white bikini lace panties. He looked at the plunging neckline. Bennie J. said, "You look lovely tonight, Cordelle."

"Thank you, B.J. I feel lovely. I feel twenty-two. I think I *am* twenty-two tonight."

Bennie J. took a sip of whiskey. "Cordelle?"

"What, B.J.?"

"Things are going to change soon," Bennie J. said.

"Oh, B.J. What are you talking about?"

"I'm talking about Big House. Mama Dog Midnight is dead. Hanna and Wright will leave for Baton Rouge soon. Winn will go back there. Mae Emma may even go up to New York to live with her daughter. Big House will be empty except for us."

Cordelle smiled. "It'll be like when we first got married. Except we'll be living in a big ole Parthenon."

Bennie J. was unmoved by Cordelle's excitement. He took another sip of whiskey and said, "It was a mistake that can't be made right.

That makes it a sin. Oh, Cordelle, I'm sorry, so sorry, I sinned against us."

"What are you talking about, B.J.? You are being such a plumb cryptic critter tonight. I can't make heads nor tails of what you are talking about."

"After we had Wright, Cordelle. What you think I'm talking about? When I talked you into having two kids was enough. We should have had ten."

Cordelle changed the expression of her face. She looked intently at Bennie J., could see his pain, could feel his concern over this sin he had committed that he could not rectify. She wanted to chatter away about how she was twenty-two tonight and how Bennie J. was being such a mystic devil, but she said, "But, B.J. The kids'll come back to Big House soon. They'll get married. In a couple of years we'll have grandkids crawling all over the place at Big House."

"Oh, Cordelle. You know how those kids are. You can't depend on them for anything."

"Well, let's do it ourselves then, by God," Cordelle said. "Let's have another baby. Let's do it all over again, B.J.!"

"Another baby?" Bennie J. asked. He took a quick swig of whiskey. He had never heard Cordelle say by God before. "Mama Cordelle, I'm an old man."

"You're not an old man! B.J., I'm only forty-five. And I feel like I'm twenty-two. I'm thirsty, B.J."

Bennie J. said, without regard nor in response to what Cordelle had just said, "We did do a good job with the kids. And we didn't even know what we were doing." He took a long slug of the bottle that was getting close to empty.

Cordelle grinned at him. "B.J., you know the kids are going off soon. It'll be up to us then to give this town something to talk about."

"That's one thang we all been real good at."

Cordelle brought her knees up, leaned forward a little bit, hugging her legs. Then she extended her hand out to Bennie J. She said, "Come on, B.J. Come here. Let's have us a picnic right here on this blanket."

7

Wright was staring at the ceiling of Hanna's bedroom. She was asleep beside him. The room was semilit from the full moon. He wanted to sleep but couldn't stop thinking about Mama Dog Midnight. Once when he was nine he had gone down to the stables and found her wallowing around in some horse shit. He had yelled at her, then pulled her by one of her ears back to the house. After he had washed her off, he hurt for screaming at her, for making her yelp, for having pulled badly on her ear. He had petted and petted on her. He had fixed her bologna and ice cream with sugar on it, but it hadn't wiped from his mind that he had gone into a rage and pulled on her ear all the way from the stable to the back of the garage.

Wright said softly to the ceiling, "Mama Dog Midnight, I'm sorry I pulled on your ear." Then he thought he could hear her scratching in her casket, trying to get out. Wright sat up in the bed. There lying at the foot of the bed he thought he saw Midnight.

Wright gave a short burst of a scream. Whatever he was looking at or thought he was looking at faded away.

Hanna jolted awake and looked at Wright. "I had a nightmare," he said.

Hanna rubbed his arm and said, "Poor baby." She kissed him on the shoulder. "Are you all right now?"

"Yeah. I need to go out for a while. Just get outside."

Hanna lay back down to sleep. Wright dressed, and as he was about to step out the bedroom door, he heard footsteps coming up the stairs. He heard voices. It was Bennie J. and Cordelle. He waited by the door until he heard their door shut, then he walked quietly out of Big House and drove his Corvette down to the marina.

He got *Fast Boat* into the water and heard something popping. Heat was coming off the engine, it had just been run. He checked the fuel gauge. There was enough to get him to where he was going and back.

Wright sped down the channel, then cut back into the backwaters. Using the spotlight and going about twice as fast as he normally would, he sashayed around the trees and stumps until he pulled up onto the hammock where the old house-home was.

The high full moon made the place look spooky, full of subdued light and dark shadows. He walked, almost ran, down the gangway onto the front porch. He had the feeling Mama Bo was going to open the door and pull him in. There was going to be her, his father's father, Mama Dog Midnight, and all his dead relatives who lived in the swamp during the Depression. Uncle Davy was going to be there with Dude hanging around his neck. One of the relatives was going to call Wright a candy-ass. Another was going to spit and call him a spoiled rich little shit. Then Mama Bo would say, "You shouldn' a pulled on Mama Dog's ear the way you done."

Just as Wright started to kick in the front door, he saw something move in his peripheral vision. He looked over. There was a figure of a man sitting there.

"This place do seem to have some kind of lure to it, do it?" Jerry Lee said softly.

Wright stared at him a second before he went and sat beside him. Wright asked, "How did you get here?" He meant to ask him what he was doing here.

"Come down from my place in my rig. Pulled up in yonder between them locust trees. I know this place like the back of my hand."

"I think Midnight is trying to float out of her grave."

"Don't worry about it," Jerry Lee said. He had a can of beer in his hand. He took a sip.

"But I pulled her ear bad one time."

"Don't worry about it. If that's the worse thing you ever done you in good shape. I know what I'm saying. She don't care."

"I still think she's coming out of her grave."

"Probably is. She'll probably stay at the foot of your bed for a while."

"Yeah?" Wright started. "Well, that makes me feel real good."

"When I's little had this dog, Leech. He was a good dog. After he died he stayed at the foot of my bed for about a month. Then one night he barked, woke me up. Looked at me and disappeared. And I ain't seen him since."

"Yeah?" Wright said. He imagined Midnight being over at Greer's, lying on the floor sleeping while Greer rolled cigarettes and sat there bullshitting with his guardian angel, Bo.

"Yeah."

"What you doing here?" Wright asked.

"Aw. Sometimes I just have to come out here. Come out to the roots of thirsty city."

"I know," Wright said. When he was little, Bennie J. had called the homeplace the roots of thirsty city and talked about it with such conviction, such importance, that Wright thought Bennie J. was talking about the roots of the trees in the water in the swamp and that these actually held together the town; had they been cut all of Sumpter City would have eroded away.

"It's a thirsty city all right," Jerry Lee said, started to say something else but decided to take another slug of beer.

Wright saw a diver's watch on Jerry Lee's wrist. The night had seemed to be lasting for days. Like he was stuck in some kind of time warp. Wright asked, "What time is it?"

Jerry Lee looked at his watch and said, "It's midnight."

"Midnight yesterday to midnight now has been one long day in the Heart of Dixie."

V

The Free State

Bennie J. was sitting up on the bed in his sock feet, dressed the way he did when they lay around and he told stories. But just he and Cordelle were there now. He dumped the contents of a number ten paper sack onto the bed. Ones, fives, tens, but mostly twenties flopped out. It was cash from trailer and boat-slip rental. He started counting it out and placing it into mixed-denomination hundred-dollar stacks.

Cordelle walked into the dressing room. Bennie J. hollered to her almost loud enough for someone downstairs to hear, "Where's Hanna and Wright, Mama Cordelle?"

"They went to the drive-in."

"They musta seen ever picture show they ever made."

"It's good for them, B.J."

"What do you mean?" Bennie J. asked. He was piling some groups of twenties into five-hundred-dollar piles now.

"They get to see other places, B.J. How other people live."

"I bought 'em some encyclopedias."

"That was twelve years ago."

Bennie J. laughed and said, "Wright had read 'em all by the time he was eight." Wright, as a small child, would sit and read the encyclopedias. He would sit with five or six open volumes around him, researching something he wanted to know about. Bennie J. would ask, "Where's Wright?" and Mae Emma would say, "He in ne den readin' the encyclopedias." "I don't reckon it'll be long," Bennie J. would answer, "till he's got 'em read up and we can throw 'em away."

Bennie J. said to Cordelle, "Wright won't be satisfied till he seen ever picture show they ever made."

"Well, B.J., honey. They make a bunch of new ones every year."

"I like *Gone With the Wind* and *To Kill a Mockingbird*. They go see them ole X-rated ones where they naked and talk ugly," Bennie J. said. Anything that couldn't be shown on television uncut was X-rated to Bennie J. Cordelle had heard him say that about a hundred times. She said, "Winn will be home Wednesday week."

"I be glad. 'Bout time she got her ass outta them foreign countries. Maybe she can figure what's really wrong with Hanna. For good this time."

"Hanna's all right, B.J., honey," Cordelle said. She stood in the dressing room, looking at her body from different angles.

Bennie J. said, "You mark my word. Somethin's' eatin' at her. Underneath all that sweet darlin' stuff somethin's eatin' at her. And it's all gone to come to a head pretty soon."

Cordelle stepped back into the bedroom, wearing only a slip. She was holding a dress up beside her. She asked Bennie J., "Do you think this is too dark for summer?"

Bennie J. glanced up but paid no attention to the dress really. He said, "Shit, naw."

Cordelle stepped back into the dressing room. Above her hung Winn's dress she had worn last night. She liked the dress, wanted to wear it again. She wanted to wear it to go uptown, and she wanted to drive around in the Corvette at night wearing short slinky dresses. Cordelle felt twenty-two.

Cordelle said, "B.J., we should take a short trip to New York. So I can buy some new clothes."

"You got more clothes than you can wear now," Bennie J. said. But saying "New York" reminded Bennie J. of all his stocks, bonds, and banknotes. New York had been very good to Bennie J. Reynolds. He called New York City the greatest city in the Union. But Bennie J. had never been there nor had any intentions of ever going. When the notion of going to New York was mentioned, Bennie J. thought of grimy vacant apartments with people lying around shooting heroin into their arms. To Bennie J. the whole world was Sumpter County. To Bennie J. New York was the trade capital of the world. But the purpose of New York being in New York was so all the heavy trading was done at a great distance from Sumpter County; therefore there wouldn't be congestion and crime near Big House.

Cordelle decided when there was no one upstairs at Big House she was going to walk around with some of Winn's dresses on. Practice wearing them, watch herself in the mirror. See what it looked like when she turned, when she bent down. She wondered what it would be like to start wearing her hair up. She held her hair on top of her head with her left hand, most of the strands slowly falling back down.

Bennie J. looked down at the money he was trying to count, stopped counting it. Cordelle walked back into the bedroom with her nightgown on. Bennie J. started throwing the money back into the sack. He said, "Hell! I'll have the kids take this to the bank in the morning. Let them at the bank count it. That's what they get paid for. I don't get paid for counting money. I only get paid for making it."

2 | Mae Emma was milling around in the kitchen trying to work. Bennie J., Cordelle, Wright, and Hanna sat at the kitchen table having their midday dinner; it was too hot to sit outside. Wright and Hanna had on their banking clothes, as they had spent all morning conducting Bennie J.'s business at the bank and running other errands for him.

Cordelle said, "It's lonesome without Midnight and Winn."

Bennie J. grunted. He was eating quickly so he could get back to the marina.

Cordelle added, "But Winn's in Europe and Midnight's in heaven and they're both having fun. So we shouldn't be lonesome for them."

Wright wondered how Midnight could be in heaven and sleeping at the foot of Hanna's bed at the same time, unless she was commuting back and forth.

Mae Emma said, "Yeah. It lonesome all right. Lucky though, Winn'll be back purty soon."

"That's the truth, ain't it, Cousin Emma," Bennie J. said.

"Show is. If you't some pecan pie for dessert it gone be another good quarter hour," she said.

"Naw," Bennie J. said, standing up and slugging down the rest of his buttermilk. "I got to get back to the marina. Ponjo, everybody." He walked quickly out the back way to his pickup truck.

Wright said, "So I think Hanna and I might go out riding the rest of the day. You know, take the rest of the day off. We've been working all morning. Then tonight we might go to the late drive-in, so we won't be back until late."

Cordelle looked up from her plate, smiled at Wright, and said, singsongy, "Okay, honey."

Wright got up, walked quickly to the door. He turned and saw Hanna sitting there eating slowly. Cordelle's back was to him. He started waving his arms frantically to get Hanna's attention, but she didn't look up. Goddammit. He had to get the hell out of Big House. Bennie J. would cruise along at thirty miles an hour all the way to the marina, looking along at the pastures and crops, running off the shoulder now and then. He would be back at his office in about fifteen minutes, maybe thirty if he ran into someone outside the bait shop and started bullshitting. But in those next fifteen minutes Bennie J. was more than likely going to come up with some dumb-assed job he wanted Wright to do. Wright had gotten Cordelle's agreement that they wouldn't be back until late. Now he wanted to get Hanna and get away, or he might be spending the rest of the day cutting meat or boxing worms or some shit.

Finally Hanna looked up and saw Wright waving. He gave her a stern come-the-fuck-on hand motion. She took another bite, then followed him. Upstairs they quickly loaded up two beach bags full of Right Times and towels. On the way out they ran into Cordelle in Big Room. Wright explained how they might go swimming or water-skiing. She thought that was nice.

They got in Hanna's Corvette, Wright at the wheel, and drove to Fielding's Amoco so Wright could charge the gas for Hanna's Corvette to Bennie J.'s farm account. Old man Fielding walked up, hollering, "Hey, younguns!" He pulled the hose to the back of the car. "That was bad about Mama Dog Midnight dying the other day. I shore do hate it. I know y'all feel bad. It was right there." Fielding pointed between the kerosene tanks and one of the outside car lifts. He made sure Wright and Hanna were looking to where he was pointing before he continued, "Right there that Mama Dog Midnight killed Ollie, King of the Fighting Pit Bulls. And it didn't take her long."

Wright said, "I know, Mr. Fielding. Winn and I were in the back of the truck."

Mr. Fielding looked at Wright, then continued as if he were the only one qualified to tell the story. As if anyone else around hadn't actually seen it, or was dead. And now that Mama Dog Midnight had died, Mr. Fielding thought the story had more credence and was now solidly part of the history of Sumpter County. Had, with the passing of Midnight, passed over that line from story to legend.

He stopped telling the actual story long enough to say, "You hear all kinds of stories, but I was standing right there. It was my oldest boy's birthday, he was gone be twelve, and I's mad 'cause Tate hadn't come by to take over for so I could run out the house. If Tate had a been on time I'd a missed it . . ."

Wright and Hanna left Old Man Fielding telling the legend to the back end of the Corvette and went into the store to buy a Styrofoam chest, crushed ice, sodas, potato chips, and the brand of cigarettes Mae Emma smoked. Wright and Winn had been buying cigarettes at Fielding's ever since they could drive. They always said, "Oh yes, and a couple of Viceroys for Mae Emma. I almost forgot."

When Wright and Hanna went back out, Old Man Fielding had the hood raised, saying to the air filter, ". . . soon as Ollie's paws lit up on that tailgate . . ." Wright assured Mr. Fielding it was certainly a day to remember and certainly a victory for all coon dog runners. He finally got Mr. Fielding to close the hood and step out of the way so they could drive on.

Hanna popped them open a Right Time. Wright had the car cruising along a curvy paved swamp road at about seventy-five. The only traffic much was a tractor outfitted with wide sprayers now and then, the tractor having to pull off into the ditch some to let them pass.

"Do you ever think about Campbell County?" While Wright was thinking what to answer, Hanna added, "I mean when we were little." She was referring to the part of their childhood spent with their Remington grandparents in Campbell County for a few weeks during the summer.

"Not much," Wright said. "It seems like another world."

Wright hadn't been back to Campbell County or to Danbridge, the small town where his grandparents had lived, since his maternal grandmother had died four years before. When Wright thought of his childhood he thought of Sumpter County and Big House. Only occasionally would something make him think of Campbell County and staying with his grandparents. Anything in his past that didn't have to do with Big House, Cordelle, or Bennie J. seemed unreal to Wright, an invented past, like a lingering rememberance of an unimportant dream.

Wright took a slug of Right Time, handed Hanna back the bottle, and said, "Yeah, Campbell County. That was like living in a different country."

"Let's go there!" Hanna said.

Wright cut back through a swamp road and got onto the highway. They crossed the Tennessee River bridge, and drove through three counties. An hour later they passed a small sign: ENTERING CAMPBELL

COUNTY. A few hundred yards further was another sign almost the size of a billboard: WELCOME TO THE FREE STATE OF CAMPBELL.

The road was narrow, wound through mountains and timberland, a forest. Wright and Hanna had to swallow to pop their ears as the altitude changed. They were in a land now where they had great-uncles and aunts and probably scores of third cousins. But Wright and Hanna knew they could walk around downtown Danbridge and run into those kinfolks, and, except for a couple of great-uncles, not recognize them or be recognized.

As they were driving on through the forest, Hanna noted that a lot of movie stars came from Campbell County. Two of the most famous character actors from the heyday of Hollywood, still kicking around working, were from here. Three current TV celebrities were natives of Campbell. Hanna went on to discuss how strange it was that such a sparsely populated and relatively isolated area would produce so many film stars. She wondered what the significance of that was. Wright had no answers to that, only suggested that it probably left the impression to the folks in Campbell County that all you had to do to be a famous movie star was to go out to Hollywood and sign up. But that most folks from Campbell just didn't have the inclination, hadn't had the calling for stardom, or didn't want to have to travel all the way to California.

They came to a mountain peak. In front of them the road went straight down toward a gorge, then straight up again to a peak almost the height of the one they were on. At the bottom was a small bridge. It was where Papa Lucius had lost it in the state trooper car.

Wright took the bridge at a hundred miles an hour. On the other mountain peak the road again twisted and wound. Wright passed big trucks loaded with timber, passed pickups with Confederate flags for front license plates and rifles in the gun racks. As they drove on into Danbridge, Hanna observed that folks in Sumpter County mostly carried shotguns in their gun racks. "Look, don't these people know that Campbell County has never been part of the Confederacy?"

Wright thought maybe they did like Cordelle and fixed history to suit their own convenience. He said, "I guess when Alabama was forced to be part of the Union again Campbell seceded from Alabama again so had to switch flags." Wright and Hanna chuckled, but Wright was chuckling at the thought that perhaps Campbell County natives had the inalienable right to switch history as they so desired.

Hanna said, "Maybe they're behind a hundred years politically. But I don't see any slaves. In fact, I don't see any black people." They were driving through the streets of Danbridge now. "You know there aren't any cotton farmers here, no black people. No Democrats."

"Yeah. It's almost as strange as New Orleans."

Wright turned down a street and drove by the house where Mama and Papa Remington had lived. Wright and Hanna both stared but had nothing to say about it at the moment. Wright drove on to the business section, through the downtown strip, then passed back by where their grandparents had lived. Having seen it didn't seem to give either one of them any particular joy.

As they passed an old grocery store Hanna said, "That's where we used to go buy candy!" Wright said, "Yeah!" It was the first thing they had seen on the whole trip that had really amused them. Wright pulled in and parked; he and Hanna got out. As they walked in, Hanna got the feeling of feeling foreign.

They recognized the store owners, Mr. and Mrs. Adams, but were not recognized, as they had not been in here since they were eleven or twelve. Neither Wright nor Hanna felt compelled or even obligated to introduce themselves. Two men sat in some ladderback chairs whittling. Over at a little table toward the back, four men were playing dominoes.

Mrs. Adams said hello. Wright and Hanna spoke back, then milled around the general store looking mostly at the hardware-type items. Wright came across a half-bushel basket full of new uncrimped bottle caps. He knew these were for people who bottled their own beer. The caps Winn had bought with the capper were unpainted, generic. But the ones Wright was looking at now were an assortment of name-brand soda logos. He saw a lot of Sun-Drops caps in among the Coca-Colas, Pepsis, RCs. He went over and got a small paper bag from Mrs. Adams, then went back and began fishing through the basket for Sun-Drop caps. Hanna walked up and asked him what he was up to. He said, "Look, Sun-Drop caps. We can use these, then they'll be exactly like Sun-Drops. We can put the Right Times downstairs in the refrigerator. Mama or Doddy don't drink sodas. Mae Emma just drinks those six-ounce Dr. Peppers."

"Oh, goody!" Hanna said. "I was beginning to think it looked a little suspicious, us running up to our rooms and coming down with a Sun-Drop all the time."

After they collected a good half sack full, they got a couple of ice cream sandwiches from the freezer. After Mrs. Adams took their money for the ice cream and the caps, she handed them some napkins like she expected them to eat the ice cream there. There were a couple

of empty chairs over by the whittlers. One of the old men pointed
to a chair with his knife and said, "Y'all hippies kin sit chere if ye's
want to."

Wright and Hanna walked over, sat, and started eating their ice
creams. The other man said, "Y'all folks goin to the wrasslin' match
tonight?"

Hanna noticed all the people in the store had the same ashy skin
tone that their grandfather had had. She said, "We didn't know there
was a wrestling match."

The first man who had invited them to sit pointed to a poster on
one of the wooden four-by-four interior supports of the building.
Wright and Hanna glanced over to the poster, which showed four
different groups of bull-looking men in wrestler outfits. The man said,
"It's the tag-team match of the century. At the Campbell County
National Guard Armory."

"Oh," Hanna said.

The second man said, "Y'all not from around here, are ye? You got
a little bit of a Yankee twang to ye speech."

"No, I'm from New Orleans," Hanna replied.

Both men nodded like that explained everything. The first man
said, "That promoter from Nashville ain't got no damn sense." They
both whittled as they talked.

"What you mean, Red?"

Red said, "Hell, Kyle, he's got it on a Satdy night. And on the first
Satdy night of the month at that."

Wright and Hanna watched one, then the other, as the old men
took turns speaking. Kyle said, "I'm goin' to go to the wrasslin'
match. I don't give a rat's ass."

Red asked, "Y'all goin' to the wrasslin' match or the dance?" He
was asking Wright or Hanna but looking at neither.

Wright just said, "Probably both." He remembered now. In the
country, near the county seat, there was a dance every Saturday night.
But every first Saturday night of the month was the biggest one. And
every third Sunday of the month was the day that all the Methodists
in Campbell, who religiously were as predominant as the Republican
Party was politically, had a big picnic and decorated the graves at the
cemetaries, calling it Decoration. Wright remembered it all now:
Every Saturday night, the dance. First Saturday, the big dance. And
third Sunday, Decoration.

Hanna said, "Yes, sir. We thought we would go to one for a while.
Then go to the other one. Try to take in both."

"Y'all purty smart," Kyle said. "Why didn't we think of that, Red?" Red said, "Might have if you hadn't rushed me into a decision."

The men whittled in silence. Wright and Hanna ate the last of their melting ice cream sandwiches. Mr. and Mrs. Adams stocked the shelves. There were domino players in the back whooping about some play. Finally Red looked over at Wright and said, "Whut kind of knife you tote there, feller?"

Wright grinned, knew he had the best of Red and Kyle now. He knew Red thought he wasn't carrying a knife, that he was too hippy. Usually he didn't, even though Bennie J. gave him hell for it all the time, telling him, "Two thangs a man ought to keep on him all the time. Some change. And a good pocketknife," like both were not only a convenience but something one day one's life might depend on. But as he was dressing to leave Big House today Wright had grabbed his pocketknife to later cut some of the strings off the end of his bellbottom jeans. It was the pocketknife Lucius Remington had had on him when he died. Mama Remington had given the small two-bladed stag-handled Winchester to Cordelle, and Cordelle had given it to Wright. A score of different knife traders had offered Wright over a hundred and fifty dollars for it, it being some kind of special model.

And here was Wright being called upon by an old-timer to present his pocketknife. Wright had a smirk on his face, for he had on him the king of pocketknives. There were three things an old-timer liked to admonish a young whippersnapper for: no pocketknife, a shitty pocketknife, and a dull pocketknife. Not only was Wright carrying the king of the pocketknives, but Greer had honed it razor sharp for him. Wright pulled it out of his jeans pocket and handed it with pride over to Red, saying, "I carry this little ole thing here."

Red put his own knife down on his knee, took Wright's Winchester, opened the larger blade, touched it for sharpness. Red said, "Yeah. That's a mighty fine knife. I used to own that knife." He said that like it was the commonest thing in the world for a strange longhair, or longer hair than Campbell County was used to, to walk in and show his pocket knife and it be one that he had owned.

"What?" Wright asked quickly in disbelief, sort of confused.

Red closed the knife to hand it to Kyle. Hanna noticed this knife etiquette: If handed a closed knife, hand it away closed. If handed an open knife, hand it away open. Also: Never give a knife away. It's bad luck. If you want to give one away, you have to at least get a nickel, a dime, even a penny, some exchange of money.

Red picked his own knife up again and resumed whittling. Kyle inspected the Winchester, saying, "Uh-huh. Yeah."

Red said, "I's up in Jasper, Alabama. Bought this off a mule trader up there. Had it a week. I's sittin' in this very seat, whittling with it like I'm a-whittlin' now." Red nodded up to the front door. "Ole Lucius Remington come through the door, drunk, wild as an Indian. Calmed down long enough to sit down where you sittin' right now." Red nodded to the seat Wright was sitting in. "Lucius offered me a hundret-dollar bill fer it. I sold it to him. He put it in his pocket. Lit outta here. I heard a siren. I stood up. Looked out the winder. He's in a po-lice car. He screeched and screamed and roared and threw gravel outta here. Next thang I knowed tell he had run off the Sipsey River bridge into the gorge."

Hanna and Wright were both stunned. Hanna wondered what it meant that they had ended up here in this very place, in this very time, to meet these very people.

Kyle closed up the knife and handed it to Wright. Red said, "I reckon I's the last living person to talk to Lucius Remington. I'm never ever gone sell a pocketknife fer a hundred-dollar bill agin as long as the good Lord lets me walk his land, breathe his air."

Hanna felt dizzy, spooked. She knew they hadn't come to Campbell County or stepped inside Mr. and Mrs. Adams' general store in this exact time by accident. Hanna was sure the eighteen that would never come was right around the corner.

Wright and Hanna walked out without hardly saying good-bye. And before the door shut behind them, they heard Red say, "If I'd a went off with Lucius like he'd wanted me to I'd be dead today."

---

3 Wright drove aimlessly out of town. He and Hanna remained dazed, trying not to think, as if they had made contact with a ghost or one of Greer's archangels.

They passed a roadside sign that read: BIRMINGHAM—46 MILES. They went from sullen to wildly excited at the prospect of checking into their Parisian hotel, having dinner at the French restaurant, and bribing the bellboy to bring them expensive wine.

When they got there, however, the lobby of the hotel was crowded. The clerk told Wright, "Monsieur, we have no rooms." Wright turned to Hanna and said, "Madame, they have no rooms," making fun of the man calling him "Monsieur." The man explained that they were often booked on the weekends and that even now the restaurant had an hour wait. He suggested some other hotels and restaurants in the area. On the way out Wright found the bellboy, gave him ten dollars to sneak him out a fifth of gin to the Corvette, that he'd give him ten more upon delivery.

On the outskirts of Birmingham, they stopped at a drive-in for chili dogs. After Wright mentioned how disappointed he was about the hotel, Hanna said, all excited, she wanted to go back to Campbell County to the dance, to listen to bluegrass and see them clog.

They stopped at a filling station and got directions. After following the six-mile route that had been drawn out for them on a torn-open paper bag, they arrived at a big wood-frame building on top of a hill way out in the country. Cars were parked in a big gravel parking lot beside the building, which looked like one of the beer halls Wright had been to on the state line. Groups of people were sitting about on fenders and tailgates. Campbell, too, was a dry county. A lot of brown bags were being passed around.

Wright pulled into a tight space next to a hotrod Mustang with mag wheels and a metal-flake paint job. A teenage couple were sitting on the hood kissing.

Country music was blasting out of the open windows of the old building. It wasn't the country music played at the wild beer joints at the Tennessee state line, but the old type Hank Williams used to play.

The only country music Wright had been exposed to was at the Tennessee beer joints during his strange dating era. And sometimes when he rode with Bennie J., who kept his AM radio tuned to WSM in Nashville. After the farm market report, a country song would come on and Bennie J. would tell Wright how in the Depression he and his kin would gather all around the radio at the old homeplace on Saturday night and listen to Roy Acuff and the Grand Ole Opry. Bennie J. would go right on in to a Depression story, but Wright would sit there wondering if they were all so poor in the Depression how they managed to buy a radio.

Hanna looked about the parking lot of the dance hall. The pickups were mostly forties models, the automobiles of the fifties and sixties. Even if the vehicles were of a later era, Hanna had the feeling they had driven into the Depression. A Roy Acuff song was being played. Hanna took a sip of gin and Sun-Drop. She said, "I think something is going to happen tonight."

Wright smiled at her, told her something was always happening. He watched the light reflecting off her eyes.

The guy sitting on the hood of the car three feet away from Wright turned around. He couldn't have been over fourteen years old, and the girl about the same. The boy said to Wright, "You not from Campbell, are you?" He spoke in a dialect different from Sumpter County's. Not as Southern but more country, a more mountainish dialect.

"No," Wright said. "Sumpter."

"I know where at is. That's a nice Corvette. I knowed you's from somewheres else. Nobody in Campbell has a shiny black Corvette. Lawyer has a brand new Lincoln. Nobody got a black Corvette though. What? Four twenty-seven?"

"Yeah. Four twenty-seven," Wright said. He was glad to hear his great-uncle had a brand-new Lincoln. But more glad that nobody here knew him or Hanna. He felt invisible, and liked the feeling. He could have told the guy who his grandfather was, but that would have moved Wright from invisible status to celebrity status, for all the hotrodders of Campbell County recognized Lucius Remington as the father of stock car racing, held the stories of his carousing and wasting tens of thousands of the taxpayers' money, held those stories as legend. For not only had his life but his death had been glorious. Going off the Sipsey River bridge at a hundred and fifty miles an hour—no one had matched it since.

The boy asked, "What compression ratio you get?"

Wright didn't know, but didn't want to say he didn't just like he didn't want to get into the fact that it wasn't his car but was Hanna's. Wright was watching the girl rub her hand all over the boy's hairless chest. Wright said, "Stock. Just stock."

"I got eleven."

"Eleven?" Wright asked. He thought the boy meant he had eleven stock cars.

"Yeah. Eleven-to-one ratio," he said proudly.

"Damn," Wright said like he was impressed, but he didn't know what it meant.

"My name is Rusty. This here is Dewdrop," he said. Dewdrop nodded to them. Wright and Hanna nodded back.

Wright said, "Hanna," nodding to Hanna. "And my name is Wright."

Rusty said, "Wright. Like in not wrong?"

Wright said, "Wright. And I wish as in not wrong." He liked Rusty and wondered if Dewdrop had made him rusty, as in oxidation. Wright imagined him turning fifteen and Dewdrop turning fourteen and them going across the Mississippi state line and getting married one night.

Rusty said, "I got some corn liquor in the trunk. We can all take a nip later if you want."

"That would be nice."

"Y'all go to the wrasslin' match tonight?"

"No," Hanna said.

"Aw, man! Y'all missed it. The Masked Monster Mashers had doubled up on Pretty Boy McAnn. My cousin, Elmore. He's crazy. Elmore and Henry jumped up in the ring started beatin' hell out of the Masked Monster Mashers. Police came in. Purty soon the whole armory was a free-for-all. Somebody knocked hell out the side of my ear. I thank my ear's all swole up. But I got a few good punches in. Aw, boy, did y'all miss it!"

"I'm sorry we weren't there," Hanna said.

"We can't git married yet, but when we turn fifteen me and Dewdrop's going across the line and get married. You don't have to be but fifteen and thirteen to git married in Mississippi. The man fifteen. The girl thirteen."

Wright smiled. He knew it.

Rusty said, "Dewdrop French kisses."

Hanna smiled at him.

"Johnny Cane'll probably come by tonight. Sometime we talk engine. I might be mechanic for him next year or two," Rusty said.

"That's nice," Hanna said. She didn't know much about stock car racing, but knew Johnny Cane was some national stock car racer from Campbell County. She was sure Johnny Cane and Lucius had known each other.

"You know who Lee Fergesun is?" Rusty asked.

"Yeah," Hanna said. "He's got that variety show on NBC on Tuesday nights."

Dewdrop slapped Rusty on the shoulder. She said, "Don't be stupid. Everbody knows who Lee Fergesun is." She had a mountain dialect neither Wright nor Hanna could hardly understand.

Rusty said, "He's got a Ferrari. Him and Johnny Cane come by in it about a month ago to the dance. Both of 'em was drunk'n bicycles. Lee. Ole Lee can drink more whiskey than an Episcopalian preacher."

Hanna was trying to imagine a drunk bicycle but wasn't doing much good with it. Wright said, "Tell you what. We'll see you later. We're going to stick our heads inside."

Wright and Hanna walked arm in arm to the front of the building, paid their admission, and went on in to the dance hall. They stood by the wall observing. Everyone, the hundred-odd people crammed into the hall, was clogging to "Rocky Top Tennessee." Hanna said to Wright, "It seems like we've been in Campbell County forever." Hanna noticed people glancing at them. She felt a kind of violence in the air. Like everybody was waiting for something to break loose. The way they had obviously waited for a couple of big guys to pick on a smaller guy at the wrestling match.

When the band finished "Rocky Top," everyone began hollering and clapping. The lead singer walked away from the microphone, then stepped back up. He said, "Now if that didn't git ye blood to pumpin', just go on and check yeself in to Robert Tisdale's Funeral Parlor."

Everyone laughed like that was the funniest thing they had ever heard. The lead singer stepped back to talk to the drummer a moment. Then he stepped back up the mike, wiping his face with a red kerchief. He said, "We got a request we gone play fer ye now."

The band started playing a song about not smoking marijuana or taking LSD or letting your hair grow long. Hanna wondered if they had played it for her and Wright's benefit. But she didn't give a rat's ass. Right then she felt good.

At the last chord, the crowd clapped like it was their county anthem. The singer said, "Thank ye. Thank ye very kindly. We gone take us a little break now." The crowd started moaning. "Naw. Naw. It's just a little-bitty break. Ruddy back there got to go powder his nose." The fat drummer raised a drumstick up to the crowd. Everybody laughed like what the singer had just said was the second funniest thing they had ever heard.

The dancers milled around and then went outside. It was sweltering hot. Wright looked over and saw Red. Red and Kyle were slowly working their way over toward them. Two women, apparently their wives, followed. Kyle said, "I see yaw made it to the daynce."

"Yes." Hanna smiled.

While the little group engaged in small talk, Red put his hand on

Wright's shoulder and pulled him aside. He said, "I got to figuring after ye left today. If I was the last living person to see Lucius Remington before he got killed, how come is it you got his Winchester knife?"

Wright looked at Red; Red looked differently now, a little less at ease, as if he had a mission to accomplish. He knew Red must have gone over it all, figured everything. Wright knew Red had wondered whether Lucius had made another stop at the edge of town, maybe picked Wright up hitchhiking, gave him the knife, and then let him out before he went off the gorge. But Wright could tell Red had concluded that Lucius Remington had died with the Winchester knife on him.

Wright started to lie. He looked over to Hanna. She was talking with one of the women. Even though Hanna was an armlength from him, Wright couldn't tell what she was saying or even hear her voice well. He felt detached from her, like he was being drawn away by some force, a force that Red maybe had something to do with. Possibly the knife.

Wright started to lie. He started to say he had bought the knife from somebody at a store. That he didn't know what had happened, if it were the same knife. That it was probably a different knife. But he knew Red knew Lucius had died with that knife.

Wright knew he could have made Red think he was some mystic and he had walked into West's Grocery Store to select him for some mission. He could have told him Lucius had a message for him from the other side. Red would have believed that. But he wouldn't believe that wasn't the knife he had sold to Lucius.

Hanna reached back to hold Wright's hand, but still Wright couldn't hear her voice.

"Lucius Remington was my grandaddy. That knife ended up being given to me by my grandmother and my mother. It's interesting to me to know how he got it. Thank you for telling me," Wright said. Wright hadn't known what to do but to resort to the truth. He hoped he hadn't disappointed Red.

All Red said was, "Well, I'm glad somebody didn't steal it or it git lost." Red walked over to where Kyle and the women stood. "Nice meetin yaw." The group waved, broke away from Wright and Hanna, and walked out of the dance hall.

Hanna swung around and put her free hand on Wright's stomach. She said, "I feel good. I'm ready to ride!"

When Wright and Hanna went outside they were able to slip by without talking to Rusty because Johnny Cane had come, was leaned against his late-model factory Camaro. Rusty was right beside him. Dewdrop was hanging onto Rusty. A small crowd had gathered around, talking with Johnny.

Hanna cruised out of the congestion slowly while Wright fixed them up a Right Time on ice. He lit a Viceroy for Hanna, then put it in her mouth. She was taking the Vette around the curves at eighty miles an hour. Wright was leaning over the console against her. He felt his own sweat-dampened hair on his neck and against his face. Hanna leaned over, pressed her warm body against Wright's. She took a last drag off the cigarette and threw it out the car.

They went down into a dip, were on and across the Sipsey River bridge before they realized where they were. Hanna zipped past a sign, FOREST WATCHTOWER, and hollered to Wright, "I missed the turnoff."

Wright hollered back over the turbulence of the speed, "Just take the next road that comes into this one from the left. It'll lead back to the highway." Hanna slowed, took a left. Ahead on a hilltop, cars were parked along the side of the road. There was barely enough space for one lane. To their right was a huge tent from which came a constant roar they could hear now. Hanna locked the brakes up, fishtailing to a stop in the middle of the road, the car facing the other way now. Hanna shifted into first and slowly cruised back up. There was singing now, almost like a chant. She parked between an Oldsmobile and a pickup truck, got out, and began walking toward the tent and the noise. Wright slugged out the rest of the bottle of Right Time and caught up to Hanna.

Hanna could feel heat coming from the tent. As they were walking under the tent, two men cut in front of them carrying little cages. Hanna looked. Inside copperheads were curling around in globs as thick as, but many times bigger than, the worms Bennie J. sold at the marina for bait.

They stepped on into the crowd. A tall man stepped up onto the stage. The crowd was swaying with their hands reaching toward the sky. The man on stage was carrying a huge rattlesnake in one hand and had a bottle of white liquid in his other.

"Looks like my kind of guy," Wright said.

Hanna looked about, smiling. She felt as if she had walked into a grotesque yet magical forest. She was thinking maybe this had been the dance hall a moment ago, but she had driven them at a hundred and fifty miles an hour across the Sipsey River bridge and through a warp of space and time. Everything had dropped its cute, sweet facade. No longer were fourteen-year-olds in love sipping on innocent corn liquor, no longer were they buck dancing to a song about long-haired hippies. The man holding the snake was about six-six, 250 pounds of hard muscle, shoulder-length hair, piercing eyes. This man seemed to have no vengeance for long-haired hippies. Hanna could feel it. This man had a dedicated vengeance against death itself.

Wright said, "I wonder if that's ole Dude he's got there." He didn't understand what he was looking at, tried to make fun of it, tried to pretend there wasn't a man standing up there holding a rattlesnake, and everyone staring not like spectators at a carnival but like they had something to do with it. Wright slipped into fear. He wondered how the hell he had gotten here, wondered why he wasn't back at Big House taking a bath with Hanna or skinny-dipping in Big Pool. Goddamn, he had more sense than to come to the Free State of Campbell. Shit. And what scared him the most was that Hanna didn't seem to hear him, that she was drifting off into some other world; and it hadn't started with the man with the snake. He had even noticed it back at the dance. Wright brought his right arm up to take a sip of Right Time, but found his hand empty. He was soaked wet with sweat. He stared at the man on stage. The man talked with the same power as Bennie J. Bennie J. could make an oak tree shake with the quality of his voice, not even needing the volume of it.

Wright soon found out there wasn't moonshine or vodka or gin in the snake man's bottle. It was arsenic. After slugging down the contents of the bottle and tossing it aside, the man took the rattlesnake in both hands, then let go of it behind its head. The rattler struck his forearm.

Wright said, "He's one mean son of a bitch."

The man threw his head back. His face and neck were glistening. He screamed, "Live! Free! Truth! The Spirit!"

Hanna mumbled, "Free. Live."

A big fat woman beside Wright put her hands up into the air, started speaking in tongues, then dropped to the ground and began flip-flopping around. A small group near the stage was swaying and hollering in a circle. Wright saw copperhead snakes being thrown up from the center of the circle. Everyone grouped off into small circles. Hanna put her arms around Wright from his back side and spread her hands out over his stomach. She slowly slid her right hand down into the right pocket of his jeans.

For a moment Wright started grinning; this had to be a joke. The preacher up front making the place tremble and vibrate with his voice. The lady speaking some kind of funny language. People grouped around hollering, getting the spirit. Copperheads being tossed around, biting people. The real believers sucking down arsenic like it was Jack Black. And in the midst of all that, he imagined Hanna and him down on the ground making love.

A cold sweat suddenly came over Wright and he no longer could imagine anything funny. He felt Hanna drifting away from him to a place he couldn't reach. The harder he tried to reach, the further he realized she had drifted. He wished Greer were with him.

Hanna brushed at the Winchester knife until she had it in her finger crooks. She pulled it out of Wright's pocket, opened the knife, cut the left sleeve out of her shirt, switched the knife to her other hand, and cut the right sleeve out of her shirt. She handed the open knife to Wright, but he hollered, "No! No, Hanna! You have to close it! You took it closed so you hand it back closed!" Hanna extended the knife to him more until he automatically took it. She let go of the knife. Wright looked at it and had no idea why he was so worried about her closing it. But he decided to leave it open; he might need to stab a copperhead with it, or make little Xs on a snakebite.

Hanna walked away from Wright to go stand in a circle next to the woman who was speaking in tongues. A slim dark man opposite her threw his head back, dropped to the ground, and started vibrating.

The man from the stage walked into the middle of the circle carrying a tow sack. He reached down in it, pulled out a glob of copperheads, and tossed them into the air.

A three-and-a-half-foot-long copperhead landed in Hanna's raised hands. She held it at the middle of its body with her right hand, holding both her arms straight out in front of her. The snake slowly drew its head to Hanna's left wrist like it was going to smell the wristband of her Bulova watch. It struck her on the underside of her forearm.

Hanna felt lightning come out of the snake and go up her arm through her neck and into her head. It felt good, felt like she was doing something about something. The others in the circle had their hands to her, were shaking snakes at her, making moaning noises at her.

Hanna put the snake in her other hand. It instantly struck her halfway between her thumb and elbow. Hanna felt as if the Winchester knife had been stabbed into her arm, pulled up to her elbow, the bone inside the elbow scraped, the knife pulled up to her shoulder, her shoulder socket scraped, then pulled up to her neck and stuck there.

Hanna tossed the snake away. She felt her muscles trying to swell out of her skin. She wanted to get back to Wright. Sound and motion were no longer synchronized. The fat lady was waving around like she was under water. Her mouth moved but formlessly, like she was trying to subdue an itch on her face without touching it. Then a tirade of incomprehensible words came out of her mouth at Hanna.

Hanna saw the people in the circle staring at her. She held out her hands, then fell to the ground.

Wright had been conjugating Latin verbs and spinning around making sure there weren't any copperheads about to land on him. But then he caught a glimpse of Hanna and saw her fall.

He ran over and fell on top of her. He turned her face to him. Her eyes were withdrawn, her lips blue. Her whole face was ashen. She said, "I hurt."

Out in the middle of the circle Wright spotted the two sleeves Hanna had cut off her shirt. They were being stepped on, but he crawled quickly across the sandy Campbell County ground and pulled them out from under somebody's feet. A copperhead landed on the ground right in front of him. He froze; someone whisked it away.

He dove back to Hanna and tied the sleeves below her elbows on each arm. He looked about her body for more snakebites, but she whispered, "That's all. I hurt." Wright took the still-open knife and started to cut the swollen fang marks. But he paused, then jumped up, yelling, "Help! Help! We got to get her to a doctor! Help! Over here!" Someone tossed him a snake. He made a backhand block and sent it sailing toward the stage.

Wright closed the knife and put it into his pocket. He picked Hanna up, getting his left arm tangled up in her long hair. He dodged gyrating people to get her out of the tent area, then quickly carried her to the Corvette.

Wright headed back down the road, laying rubber. He knew he should have cut the bites and sucked the poison out. But there was a new treatment where you put the patient in ice, trying to slow the metabolic rate down until the body itself broke down the poison, and Wright wasn't sure what was best. He did know where he could go. Toward Danbridge, at the edge of the forest, was McCandless Hospital. When his Remington cousins would get drunk and go out turkey hunting in the forest and shoot each other, that's where they were always taken.

Hanna lay back moaning a bit. Wright floored it, came across

Sipsey River bridge at a hundred miles an hour, and headed up the steep incline ahead of him. He glanced into his rear view mirror; there was the blue flashing light of a state trooper car.

There were a lot of things Wright knew he could do. He could start tossing gin and Right Time bottles out of the car. He could stop, let the state trooper radio ahead to the hospital as they traveled there in the trooper car. But for the first time tonight Wright was in control. He knew the best thing to do. He pushed the accelerator to the floor.

4 Cordelle was sitting on the bed, leaned back against the headboard. Bennie J. was pacing the floor. He stopped and pointed at Cordelle. "I told you something was wrong with her."

Bennie J. looked at Cordelle a moment; she didn't say anything. He resumed pacing down at the end of the bed. He would go to the far wall, turn around and come back even with the settee, then turn back. Bennie J. made two more rounds and kept talking. "Letting snakes bite her on purpose! And Wright letting her do it. I don't understand these kids. Used to I spent half the time trying to keep from getting bit by cottonmouths and rattlesnakes and copperheads. Had to wear denim that showed you was poor and under my every breath swearing someday I wouldn't have to wear patched-up dungarees. Back then you's lucky to have a skitter to ride in. But the only reason you had a skitter was because you couldn't have a real car. And here these younguns are. If driving skitters and wearing patched-up dungarees ain't enough, they have to go let snakes bite em."

Cordelle said, "Well, B.J., we're lucky Hanna isn't dead. She has recovered lovely in three days. She'll get to come home in the morning. She'll probably still be able to go to Kathy Lee's party. Then Winn will be home."

Bennie J. waved to let Cordelle know he had heard her, but it didn't have anything to do with the matter at hand. He said, "I work hard so they won't have to go through all the shit I went through. Damn it to hell, I'm not puttin' up with that shit anymore." Bennie

J. slapped the dresser as he walked by it without interferring with his pace. "Winn overdrew her bank account three times last spring. By God, I'm cuttin' her finances in half. They don't give a shit. If they overdraw, it's ole Bennie J. He the one that has to go up to the bank and say 'I'm sorry, Lemay. I'm sorry I sent my little girl off to school before I taught her how to add and subtract.' By God, I'll tell you this changing her major bullshit is coming to a halt. All she's gone take next semester is arithmetic. Learn how to add up a damn bank account. Supposed to be a senior and she's still shittin' around changin' her major. What's she changed her major to last anyhow?"

"I don't think you're allowed to change your major, B.J., unless you have one," Cordelle answered seriously.

Bennie J. had stopped for Cordelle's answer, then kept pacing back and forth. "All I know is her ass is gettin' down to work. All she gone be doing is studying till she graduates. All this goin' uptown doin' what they want to do to tickle their sweet little candy-asses has just come to a screaming halt. Old Bennie J. just call a halt to all that shit. And Wright, his ass is going to work. He ain't done a half a day's work all summer. When he's not in school for now on, he's gone be working. There's a fifty-slip marina, a bait shop, a grill, a meat market, five trailer courts, a thousand acres of cotton, a thousand head of beef cattle, a cotton gin, and Big House that needs tended to. And old Bennie J. just all of a sudden got sick and tired of doing it all hisself. I work night and day, God knows how many years so they won't have to put up with the shit I had to go through. And the little spoiled sons of bitches don't even appreciate it. Let snakes bite 'em. Shit!"

Cordelle just watched Bennie J. go back and forth. She said, "Well, B.J., it was Hanna who let the snake bite her. Perhaps you should just let Coleen deal with it as she deems."

"As she deems? Hell, she thought it was funny! She's worse than the damn kids. You know how harum-scarum Coleen is. Running off to New York to work." Bennie J. paced a moment, then continued talking. "They gone end up worse'n them Yankees. Got big jobs, got big paychecks, got big boats, big houses. But middle of the month if they git a Co-Cola they have to git it on credit."

"B.J., I think Hanna has emotional problems," Cordelle said, like she had just revealed the whole problem.

"Hell, I know she's got emotional problems!" Bennie J. screamed, having stopped and thrown his arms out to Cordelle. He resumed his pacing. He was on a good roll now. "They all got emotional problems.

They in the streets all time. Won't stand hitched. Don't do no goddamn work. Look at Ruth Ray Leonard. She inherited a fortune. Had
the world whipped. What'd she do?"

Bennie J. stopped, extending his hand to Cordelle on the last and
rhetorical question. He resumed pacing and answered his own question. "Took them damn pills, had nervous breakdowns, in and out
of the insane asylum till she finally managed to kill herself. Look. It
ain't them kids' fault."

Bennie J. stopped pacing; he realized the real matter of the crisis
with these last words he'd spoken. He leaned over on the foot of the
bed, looked down as if he had gone from being mad to saddened. He
said, "It's old Bennie J.'s fault. If all this money is gone end 'em up
like Ruth Ray I'll, by God, give all this shit away and drag their giblet
asses back out in the swamp where I come from and show em what
it's all about."

"Oh, B.J.! I don't think that would do anybody any good!" Cordelle responded quickly. She sat up stiffly, thoroughly paying attention to Bennie J. for the first time that night.

"Them kids don't even know what it's all about. They never had
to do shit. And can't blame them. Poor things. I just hope it's not
too late."

"Oh, they do know what it's all about, B.J. That's why they go to
the drive-in all the time. To see what the rest of the world lives like."

Bennie J. went over, sat on the settee with his head down. Then
he looked up, still not understanding it all. "And what's been all this
shit?" he said. "Wright could have gone out with any girl he wanted
to. I don't know why he don't want to marry Kathy Lee. Nice family.
Pretty girl. Family had money for two hundred years. They learned
good how to keep it."

Cordelle said, "They're just eighteen. They could still get married."

"Nah. Wright and Hanna just want to cling on to each other."

"Oh, B.J. That's just puppy love. Innocent little ole puppy love.
Didn't you ever fall in puppy love when you were a child?"

"Naw. I ain't no dog."

"Kathy Lee got to dating someone else. Wright's been running
around with Hanna," Cordelle said, trying to explain why Wright and
Kathy Lee weren't getting married yet.

Bennie J. said, "Nah. Not just that. Even before. Now, like Wright
and Winn. Why'd they just sit out in the swing and talk? Go out in
the boat together all time? They could associate with anybody they

wanted to, but most the time they just stayed together off to their selves. What could they talk about that long ever' day, that many years? Look like they'd a got tired of each other. Seems like there's only so much you could say to one person."

"Well, we don't associate with much of anybody ourselves," Cordelle said.

"Yeah, but we married. And we all time doing something. Working," Bennie J. said. He was tired of sitting down and acting sad over the matter. He stood up, resumed pacing. Then he raised his voice back similar to when he was fussing about the kids acting like a bunch of beatniks.

He said, "By God, they can run some of this shit and we'll sit on our asses and go uptown and act like little darlings!"

Cordelle perked up. "Oh, B.J., that would be so much fun! Do you think the kids would mind?"

5	Wright had come home from the hospital late that afternoon and gone by the marina to tell Bennie J. how Hanna was doing. Bennie J. had been nice to him. Too nice almost,

so Wright was sure something was coming down, that Bennie J. was saving it all up to get all bent out of shape again like he did the first night at the hospital. Asking Wright what the hell they were doing, why he let the snake bite her, and what the hell they were doing in Campbell County anyway. But what had scared Wright the most two nights ago when Bennie J. had raged at him was that Bennie J. had sounded exactly like the snake man, the same earthquake voice and cadence. It had scared and confused Wright.

Around nine, Wright finally came out of his room, went downstairs. All the lights were on, but he saw no one nor heard any noise coming from the den. When he walked into the kitchen, Cordelle was standing at the sink cleaning out a bowl. Obviously Bennie J. was upstairs reading the paper in his room and Cordelle was cooking one of her dessert recipes.

Wright went to the refrigerator and got one of his special Sun-

Drops. With the new caps he had put on the bottles last night, he had started storing a few of his Right Times in the kitchen refrigerator. No one would know the difference.

Cordelle turned around and smiled. "Hi, honey. You got the old blues?"

Wright made a whining sound as he filled a glass with ice. "Little bit."

"What about, darling?"

"I don't know. Hanna. Doddy getting mad. Winn being gone. Mama Dog gone."

"Honey, I know what you mean. Wouldn't it be nice if we were all here at Big House all the time?"

Wright just grunted. He plopped down at the kitchen table, opened the bottle, and poured some malt liquor into his ice, hoping Mama Cordelle wouldn't notice that it foamed a little bit more than Sun-Drop.

Cordelle said, "Well, don't worry. Hanna will get to come home in the morning." She got a glass, walked over to the refrigerator, poured herself a glass of pineapple juice, came over, and sat at the table. She took a sip and said, "One time Coleen and I went to one of those meetings and a snake bit her."

"Yeah? Really?" Wright said, perking up.

"Oh, yes. I was only fifteen. Coleen was just a little skinny thing. We slipped the Model A out for a ride on a terribly hot summer night. Out of curiosity we stopped at one of those tent meetings and began meandering around amongst the folks. Oh, it was a terribly hot night. Somehow or another a copperhead snake bit Coleen right on the ankle. She had some yarn holding her hair back. I tied it below her knee, picked her up, carried her to the roadster, and took her into Danbridge to old Doc Teddlesen. He tended to her, and I took her back home that night. She was a little sick for a few days."

"Wow," was all Wright could say. But his mind was ticking away. The similarities were too great. Papa Remington's Model A; Cordelle had taken it to Nashville ten years before to get it restored. He could see the whole thing, see it like a movie. He could see Cordelle all beautiful and slim, dressed up like some silver screen star. Coleen, preteen, a skinny bright-eyed firecracker of a girl. Cordelle gets her into the Model A and pulls out onto the dirt road. When she makes the turn at the intersection the road that goes through the forest is gravel. Cordelle grabs the big steering wheel with both hands, white-knuckled. The Sipsey River bridge is steel girdered with wood planking, narrow and one-lane. Cordelle takes it at fifty miles an hour, then floorboards it.

Wright let the scenario go. He started thinking of Coleen. He had almost forgotten she existed, though he knew she was living a fine life in New York City and come fall would be living again in New Orleans. Last summer she had lived on the coast of New England. Coleen, it seemed, was destined to live in places that started with "New."

Cordelle sipped on her juice. "Oh, back then Campbell was so different. I couldn't get over it when I came to Sumpter County to go to school. Leah lived in that house her father, Mr. Bernsten, lives in now, still, on Saunders Street. They had a maid and I thought they had to be the wealthiest family in all of Alabama. Leah would come back with me some weekends to Campbell County and she couldn't get over that place. She loved the hills and mountains. We had such fun then. It should have lasted longer."

When Cordelle paused to take another sip, Wright said, "Time do change," just to be saying something.

The phone rang. Cordelle said, "Hello? . . . Speaking of the devil. I was just telling Wright about how we had such fun when we were going to Sumpter. . . . Oh, thank you so much, Leah darling. But Hanna is going to be just fine. Wright's going to bring her home in the morning. . . . She and Wright went over to Campbell County and she had a little fainting spell in that terrible heat we've been having the last few days. The last couple of nights have been much cooler. . . . Yes, I know, and all your children will be in high school this fall. How time flies . . ."

Wright listened to Cordelle talk on about nothing. She had nothing to say, he suddenly realized, to her old college roommate. And he saw that she herself realized she had nothing in common with her own generation. Wright knew how she felt.

Winn would be home next week, but that was too far away. Wright knew there was no telling what Bennie J. might come up with by then. He thought of every bad thing that could happen, having to haul hay on the farm until he went off to school, Hanna going back to New Orleans. Wright just couldn't seem to think of anything that was bad enough to account for this feeling of doom he had. Even Mae Emma, instead of making fun of the trouble he and Hanna had gotten into, spoke very firmly to him, saying, "Bennie J. on the warpath for sure. If I's you I'd tighten up my ass a notch. If I's you my asshole be squeakin' when I walked." There had been only seriousness in the tone of her voice.

He felt, sitting there, that the doom hanging over him had gained an immediacy to it. Wright knew he needed to do something about it. And what he had to do was get to Jerry Lee.

Wright got up, took the Sun-Drop bottle by the neck in one hand, his glass in the other. Cordelle was listening to Leah, saying "Uh-huh" every once in a while. Wright wiggled his fingers good-bye to Cordelle, Cordelle smiled and waved back. Wright walked out.

6 Wright parked beside Jerry Lee's '57 Chevy. He started to run up onto the front porch, and only then did he notice the back of a baby blue two-seater Mercedes 250 parked on the other side of the Chevy. Wright looked up to the doorway; the screen door was kicked open. There in the lighted doorway stood Coleen. She was leaning against the doorjamb with her left shoulder and left hip. She wore a brilliant blue minidress, a pair of dress sandals. Her blond hair was a bit longer than shoulder length.

In her coarse, raspy, alluring voice she said, "Here he is. The love of my daughter's life." Her accent was similar to Hanna's, and she spoke clearly and distinctly. Coleen took a drag of her Winston.

Wright walked on up to the front porch. Coleen pushed herself away from the doorjamb, took Wright into her arms, and kissed him on the mouth. "How the hell are you?"

"Fine. Fine. I didn't know you were coming." Wright paused a moment. "Do you know about Hanna?"

"Yeah, we just got back from the hospital." Coleen took Wright by the arm and led him into the house. "I got back from New York. Walked into the apartment in New Orleans early this morning. The phone rang. It was Bennie J. having a shit tizzy about Hanna. I told him hell, calm down, B.J., just a fucking snakebite." She gave her raspy laugh, took a drag of her cigarette, then put it out in an ashtray on the coffee table. There was a bottle of Amaretto sitting there with two empty but used glasses. "So I got in my car, drove up. She's fine."

Wright looked at Coleen. Coleen looked like Cordelle but was as skinny as Hanna and moved about like Winn. Jerry Lee walked in from the back room and said "Hey, boy." Wright said, "Hello." The sight of Jerry Lee all of a sudden made Coleen seem out of place. The last person in the world Wright expected to find at Jerry Lee's was Coleen.

Wright looked at Jerry Lee. Jerry Lee looked back at him. Wright could tell Jerry Lee knew Wright was confused already about Hanna. And now Wright didn't know Coleen was going to be here. Jerry Lee said, "You all right, Wright?"

"I think Doddy is going to send us all to Tuscaloosa."

Jerry Lee said, "He does want you to go to the university, but he says you can go to any college you want. No reason he won't let you go to LSU. Why do you think he won't keep his word?"

"I don't mean Tuscaloosa as in the university. I mean Tuscaloosa as in Brice's Mental Institute."

Jerry Lee and Coleen laughed, but then saw Wright didn't. Coleen said, "Wright, sweetheart. Aunt Coleen will cool Bennie J. out for you. You just get your ass down at the marina, act like you're doing some work so he can go on about how smart his boy is. Haven't you caught on yet, Wright? You don't even have to work. You just have to be visible. He just wants to see you, that's all. All Bennie J. cares about in the world is Cordelle, Mae Emma, Winn, Hanna, me, Jerry Lee, Greer, and you. Don't you see?"

Wright sat down and started crying.

7 | Aunt Coleen was right. Wright went to McCandless and got Hanna the next morning, and that afternoon they hung around the marina with Bennie J. and Coleen. Bennie J. was all beside himself, hugging on Hanna, saying, "Hanna Belle, ole Hanna Belle. You trying to get the Spirit, wadn't you? I tell y'all about the time I was back up in Sumpter Swamp during the Depression got hit by two big ole cottonmouths at the same time. Boy, don't ever let nobody tell you a snake can't hit you in the water . . ."

The next day Coleen left for New Orleans. Late that afternoon Bennie J. and Cordelle walked down to Big Room, Bennie J. in a suit and Cordelle in a long dress. They were going over to J.C. and Lou Ann's. They were all going to crowd into Alan Depsey's big Lincoln and ride down to some big statewide cattleman's banquet in Birmingham. They wouldn't be back until after midnight.

Hanna and Wright were alone at Big House. Hanna was playing the piano. Wright was sitting on the floor of Big Room watching her. She was playing the song she said she had been learning and practicing for him for the last month.

The song was as fluid and dreamy as the long white low-cut cotton dress Hanna wore. She was not sitting on the dress, but had it pulled up and draped over the piano stool. She claimed it was more comfortable that way.

Wright had watched her dress. He knew she was wearing white stockings, a garter belt, and a pair of hundred-dollar white lace bikini panties. Cordelle had given them to her. Cordelle bought her lingerie at a boutique in Birmingham, paid exuberant prices for them. Once Wright had been in the bedroom with Cordelle and Hanna when Cordelle had come back from a shopping spree. She was laying the lingerie out on Hanna's bed, giving Hanna some panties and bras she had bought for her for a gift. Cordelle was ecstatic, explained they must not tell Bennie J. the kind of money she paid for them. That he would have a hemorrhage if he knew. Then she said, "A lady's dress begins with her lingerie. To be richly dressed, a true lady should have on the finest pair of panties money can buy, or wear none at all," and then giggled. Wright had been stunned and embarrassed that his mother would say something so bold in front of him.

Hanna, with her long black hair falling about her white dress, looked chaste. Wright thought it was ironic that having been brought up by a single mother in a large liberal city, Hanna did not have a voluptuous sexual past. Wright thought beautiful Hanna would have been seduced in her early teens by one of her mother's lovers. But Hanna's sexual history, prior to her involvement with Wright, consisted of a single experience with a boyfriend.

At fifteen and a half, Hanna had gone with her sixteen-year-old boyfriend one night into a shabby section of New Orleans to an old apartment, the apartment of his older friend who was gone for the weekend. They pushed open an unlocked window and crawled in, rolled some marijuana with a piece of brown paper sack for a rolling paper, smoked it, and then had sex in the dark room with an eight-track of what Hanna thought was the Band playing over and over on the stereo.

Wright found amusement that both their first sexual experiences had begun by breaking into a place through a window—Hanna through the window of an apartment, Wright through the window of a houseboat.

Hanna finished playing her song. Wright was sitting up on the floor with his legs crossed like an Indian, leaning back a little, propped up with his arms locked behind him.

He sat up straight now and clapped. Hanna turned and looked at him, smiling, proud of the job she had just done, but a little embarrassed at his praise.

Hanna got up and walked over to Wright. She threw the bottom of her dress over him with a flair, and sat down on top of his head, giggling.

VI

The Social Graces of Dixie

1

"I don't want to go," Wright said.

Cordelle said, "Wright, don't be like that. It's for Kathy Lee. Y'all were good friends all through school. Hanna went to SCW for two years with her. J.C. and Lou Ann think the world of you. You ought to be ashamed not wanting to go."

Wright said, "I don't mind honoring Kathy Lee. But why don't J.C. and Lou Ann have a little supper or something over at their house? Why does J.C. and Lou Ann do that invite-every-country-club-type to a party? I don't like those country club types."

Wright was sitting at the kitchen table with Cordelle, Hanna, and Bennie J., eating midday dinner. He was still a little peeved about having been invited by Daughtery. If it was because of all those years of friendship with Kathy Lee that he should go to the party, he felt, then Kathy Lee should have had the dignity to invite him. "It looks like Kathy Lee could have at least called me to invite me if she wanted me to come."

"Wright, honey," Cordelle said, as if he wasn't getting the point of the matter. "They're giving the party *for* Kathy Lee. If it had been given *by* Kathy Lee, then yes, she should have called you."

Wright got the point, but wasn't pleased with the whole deal. He didn't want to argue about it anymore. He just said, "Ah. It sounds all too whoop-de-do for me."

"You got to have all them monkey-face women pulling up in them big old Oldsmobiles looking through the steering wheel, driving like a monkey climbing a pole. And then they can stick out they little finger when they pick up a teacup and go 'Oh, dawling,'" Bennie J. said, imitating the old society ladies. He was laughing.

Mae Emma walked by and slapped Bennie J.'s upper arm for making fun. Wright said, "Hey, why don't Doddy have to go? Doddy never has to go nowhere he don't want to. I don't think I ought to have to go if Doddy don't have to go."

Bennie J., quick with a defense, said, "I have to put up with folks' bullshit all day long. Work hard from kin till can't. We got to rest at night, don't we, Baby Dog Midnight?"

Baby Dog Midnight, a two-month-old black Plott hound Jerry Lee had given Bennie J. two days earlier, right before he went off to New Orleans, was over in his cardboard box in the corner, tearing the hell out of an old sock. Baby Dog sat up on his hounches, howled, then gave a couple of sharp barks. When Bennie J. started giggling Baby Dog jumped out of the box and ran over to Bennie J.

"Baby Dog," Bennie J. said, "Mama Cordelle'll get mad if you shit in the floor."

"I mean it," Cordelle said. "I want you to keep Baby Dog in his little pen on the veranda. I don't want him running around messing things up, chewing on things."

Mae Emma walked over to set a bowl of mashed potatoes on the table. She said, "And I'm not cleaning up his pee or his doo-doo."

"Baby Dog, they all givin' you a hard time, ain't they?" Bennie J. said down to the puppy. Baby Dog made little bark-growl noises, running around in circles.

Wright said, "Well, if I have to go I'm gone dress like I want to and act like I want to."

Bennie J. said, "Now, you don't be hurtin' youself too much for society there, Wright," and laughed.

Bennie J. handed down a piece of beef to Baby Dog. Baby Dog started licking on it. "Shit. Where is it Kathy Lee's going to school?" Bennie J. picked up Baby Dog and put him in his lap.

"To Rutgers in New Jersey," Wright said.

Bennie J. said, "I don't know why they want to ship these kids from one school to the other till they thirty years old for. Sending Kathy Lee up north to New Jersey. Shit."

Cordelle said, "B.J., she went to high school at Sumpter College. And like Lou Ann, she'll probably go on to get her B.A. at Rutgers."

"Rutgers? That sounds like some trade school to learn how to make pistols," Bennie J. said. "I don't know why those Thomases have to go off to those strange schools. Naw, if Bennie J. was a young man, wouldn't but one place I'd go. University of Alabama. And I'd major in karate. That's something nobody could take away from you."

For the first time, Wright wondered if Bennie J. really believed you could major in karate. He said, "Doddy! You can't major in karate."

"If you went to the University of Alabama you could. It's a big fine school. You can major in anything you want to down there. Yes, sir, I'd go straight down to Tuscaloosa. Wouldn't be shittin' around with changin' my major. I do down there, load up ever' course I could take, go to summer school. I'd finish in two and a half years. Go in, root hog, get the hell out of there fast as I could. Come back up to Sumpter, start making some money. I wouldn't shit around. Then when Alabama played Auburn, I'd be sittin' on the fifty-yard line. Why come? Cause I'd be a University of Alabama alumni and I'd be able to git all the tickets I want."

"But Bennie J.," Hanna said. "When Alabama plays Auburn you *are* sitting on the fifty-yard line."

"Yeah. That's because Bennie J. works hard. Can get anything in this town fixed."

"It's a thirsty city!" Hanna said.

Bennie J. said, "Mama Cordelle. Lookie here! Baby Dog Midnight done peed all over my new britches."

2 Late that afternoon Wright came in the back kitchen door. Hanna was still up at the bait shop helping Mr. Berzett process some beef. For the last three hours Wright had been unloading and loading sixty-pound bales of sugar. A tractor-trailer truck had pulled up to the back of the bait shop. He and the driver had unloaded over three hundred bales. Soon after the tractor-trailer pulled away, Terrel's trucks pulled up to load the sugar and take it back to Tennessee to make whiskey out of it. Wright wanted to raise hell why didn't they coordinate it so they loaded Terrel's trucks straight from the tractor-trailer, that it would have saved a lot of worthless motion, but didn't, since Bennie J. had let up about him letting the snake bite Hanna. Wright did, however, feel he needed to slug down a Right Time in protest.

A couple of strange cars were out front at Big House, so Wright just pulled around back. He opened up the refrigerator to grab a Sun-Drop bottle, but didn't find any, only Mae Emma's Dr. Peppers. Mae Emma must have moved them. He had put seven Right Times, in Sun-Drop bottles, the last of his stash, in the refrigerator. He opened the bottom crisper but it was empty. About the time he was shutting the refrigerator door, Mae Emma walked into the kitchen from the dining room.

Wright said, "Mae Emma. I had about ten Sun-Drops in the refrigerator. Where'd you put them?"

She said, "Them society women is here."

"What society women?"

"Them that Winn likes to make fun of," Mae Emma said.

"What are they doing here?"

"They wudn't satisfied until they had Cordelle as an advisor for that beauty contest," Mae Emma said. She was moving about quickly, fixing some finger food on a silver platter.

"Where'd you put the Sun-Drops?"

"Them society women is sucking 'em down like a bunch of field hands."

"Mae Emma! Those were my Right Times! Like the ones I used to keep up in the bathroom vanity."

Mae Emma had her back to the swinging door, about to go out. She stopped, giggled a few seconds, then walked on out.

"Goddamn, if Bebe Boo and the Dixie Do's don't get you one way, they'll get you another," Wright said out loud. He walked up to the door that Mae Emma had just gone through, cracked it a bit, and peeped into the dining room. Mae Emma set down the tray and said, "Here you go, ladies." She walked out toward Big Room.

Bebe, Marty Lou, Irene, and Cordelle were sitting around the dining room table. Irene and Cordelle were drinking coffee. Marty Lou and Bebe had glasses of ice full of Right Time. Empty Sun-Drop bottles were scattered about on the table.

Wright mumbled to himself, "Their last ditch to try to get Cordelle to make Hanna join the Miss Maid of Cotton." He eased the door shut but stood there listening.

Marty Lou was giggling. "Then Cordelle, what do you think?" she said. "We play the state song while the girls come out one more time in antebellum formals. And while 'Dixie' is playing . . ."

Hearing this, Wright thought about Mrs. Goodwin's class in the ninth grade. He had sat behind Kathy Lee. At the beginning of the second semester, in which they studied Alabama history, they were to have read the appendix in the book that had such information as the state song, bird, flag, and so on. They had been given a pop test on this. The next day Mrs. Goodwin had passed out the graded papers, then stood at her lectern. She had said, "From your test scores, I would say that every one of you in here read the appendix the other night. There are thirty-three students in this class. On question number eight, thirty-three of you answered the state song of Alabama was 'Dixie.' Alabama is the Heart of Dixie. But the state song of Alabama is not 'Dixie.' The state song of Alabama is 'Alabama'! It is right there in black and white! So class, your next assignment is to memorize verbatim every stanza of the Alabama state song. Which is 'Alabama'!"

Five weeks later, on their six-week test, thirty-three of the students had answered to question number twenty-one—"What is the state song of Alabama?"—"Dixie." It had infuriated Mrs. Goodwin so that she had gone to the principal, Mr. Henry, who had said, "Huh, Louise? I thought 'Dixie' *was* the state song. Maybe the textbook is wrong. Maybe it's a misprint."

Wright stood there thinking about how he used to pass notes to Kathy Lee, encoded, with plans of where to meet that afternoon, for the era in which they had studied Alabama history was also the era of their sexual escapades. The Alabama history era had been good to Wright Reynolds.

Wright walked into the dining room and announced to the ladies, "Alabama is the Heart of Dixie. But the state song of Alabama is not 'Dixie.' The state song of Alabama is 'Alabama.'"

Bebe looked up at Wright and said, "Oh, Wright. You are one good-looking thing of a young man, but the state song is 'Dixie.'"

Marty Lou giggled and said, "Wright, if I were ten years younger I'd eat you up like some cotton candy!" She giggled in delight at the thought.

Irene said, "Marty Lou! Get hold of yourself!" She turned to Wright and said, "Darling, the state song *is* 'Dixie.'"

Bebe said, "Cordelle. Do you have some encyclopedias here so that I can show your charming son what the state song is? And could I have another one of these Sun-Drops? They are so good."

Cordelle said, "Bebe. 'Alabama' *is* the state song."

"No," Marty Lou said and burped. "Oh my, what fun."

"Yes, 'Alabama' is the state song. It goes"—Cordelle sang—"'Alabama, Alabama, we will aye be true to thee.'" She said, "We had to learn it in junior high school."

Bebe said, "Cordelle, with all due respect, but you *did* go to a

Republican junior high. You must remember they do not even give proper respect to the great Franklin Delano Roosevelt."

"He did make his mistakes. Like giving away Berlin," Cordelle commented.

"Oh, my!" Marty Lou gasped.

"Now, now," Irene said. "We didn't come here to talk about politics or religion."

Bebe said, "Oh, me. Dr. Turner gave me some pills for my back yesterday and I *do* believe they are making me lightheaded. Cordelle, dear, could I have a glass of water?"

"Surely," Cordelle said, and walked to the kitchen. Wright followed her. As she was pouring the water, Wright said, "Mama Cordelle! Those women are doped up or drunk or something. You know you don't allow any drinking at Big House!"

Cordelle whispered, "Wright! I couldn't tell until a couple of minutes ago. I have no idea why they came out here when they've been drinking. I don't condone it!"

Wright walked out, went into the den, and found his old Alabama history book in the library. When he walked back into the dining room with it, Cordelle was seated again and Bebe was sipping the water.

Wright opened the book to the appendix and lay it on the table beside Irene. Irene looked at it and said, "Oh, my God! If the state song isn't 'Dixie' . . . what are we going to do? Cordelle, we've got to form a committee right this minute! Cordelle, you've got to help us get the state song changed to 'Dixie.' Like it should be. You know, like that lady from south Alabama who loved camellias. She got the state flower changed from the goldenrod to the camellia. Yes! That's it! We've got to form a committee right this instant!"

"Oh, Irene. Let me see," Bebe said, pulling the book over to herself.

Marty Lou pulled the book from her, looked down at it. She started crying, then sobbing and gasping. "I can't believe it." She hiccupped, then threw up into the book.

Bebe said, "Oh, Marty Lou. Don't get so upset. That has to be a misprint."

3   Early that night, Wright was alone in his Vette, following Cordelle's Cadillac. Hanna was riding with Cordelle. They were in separate cars because after the dance part of the party began all the older guests were going out to the Thomas plantation for a tea. It took Lou Ann to think something up like that, Wright thought.

As they pulled up to the country club, Wright was thinking of Bennie J. One night at the dinner table in the dining room, when Winn was a year away from enrolling at Sumpter College for Women, Winn had told Doddy she wanted him to get the family into membership at the country club. Bennie J. had stared at Winn, then gotten up and started pacing the dining room floor and giving a speech, a fairly loud speech. He said, "Join the country club?! Join the goddamn country club? Hell, y'all live on a country club. I've been out to the Sumpter Country Club. Seen it. Y'all's pool's bigger'n theirs. Big Room's a lot nicer than their ballroom. Y'all got stables and horses. They hadn't got stables and horses. Got a thousand acres of pasture right around Big House to play golf in. Got a damn marina. Boats. Do you realize it? Do you realize what you got? If we lived in the middle of New York City, yeah, old Bennie J. might consider joining up to some country club so y'all could git ye some fresh air. But y'all don't live stuffed up in some damned old apartment. Y'all live at Big House. Look around you, goddamn it! And see what's there. I don't know if y'all can't see it, don't know what you got. Or if y'all just not satisfied unless y'all pissing my hard-earned money into the wind."

Winn hadn't said any more about joining the country club. She and Wright had gone and hung out at the country club when they wanted to as Kathy Lee and Butch's guests, and nobody said anything about it. She and Wright would sneak in nights to the pond of the golf course, diving for golf balls. Winn would hit them around the pastures with her nine iron until she got good enough to sucker the old men golfers into betting against her. Wright had always thought that had been Winn's revenge for not ever having gotten to be a member of the Sumpter Country Club.

Wright parked and got out. He adjusted his cape. He was wearing an old black tuxedo with a black satin cape. His hair was brushed out; he had on dark eye makeup.

He stepped on up beside Cordelle and Hanna. Cordelle was wearing Winn's low-cut white minidress and was combing out Hanna's hair; on one side down one side of her face, in front of her, on the other side behind her shoulder.

Hanna had on a long black satin dress, long-sleeved to cover up the snakebites and the rotten skin around them. A small ladybug was painted on her right cheekbone.

Cordelle put up her comb and the three of them walked around the building. The doorman opened the door, and they went on into the vestibule, Hanna first, Cordelle next, Wright last.

Standing there greeting people as they came in were Lou Ann, Kathy Lee, and J.C. J.C. had on a navy blazer, red silk tie, and grey slacks. Lou Ann was all dolled up in a long white sleeveless dress. Kathy Lee was in a long dress, too; just a sundress, but the way she wore her makeup and jewelry and had her hair pulled around made it all look formal.

Lou Ann hugged Hanna. Hanna thanked her for the flowers she'd sent. Lou Ann said, "Yes, I was so sorry to learn you became the victim of our awful August heat."

Cordelle hugged Lou Ann. Then Lou Ann looked at Cordelle and her dress. Lou Ann was breathless for a moment, then said, "Cordelle, dear. You look very lovely. But beholdingly risqué, I must say. I hardly recognized you. You look so young."

"Thank you, Lou Ann. I do feel twenty-two. You and your family look very charming yourselves. The hot summer is on its last legs. I thought I may as well live it dangerously." Cordelle went on to be greeted by J.C. and then Kathy Lee. Cordelle told Kathy Lee, "Darling, I wish you the best at Rutger's. You know you should come out to Big House for a little get-together before you leave for up north and the kids leave for Louisiana."

Lou Ann hugged Wright, then stepped back. She said, "How stunning, Wright. But this isn't a costume party."

Wright looked seriously at Lou Ann and said, "Lou Ann, this isn't a costume." Wright stepped on, as someone came in behind him. He shook J.C.'s hand.

J.C. smiled and said, "Where's that ole Bennie J., Wright?"

"Aw, the sun never sets on Bennie J.'s empire," Wright said, like that explained the matter. "I saw that movie on television about your father again the other night. He must a been a good judge."

"Yes. He was a good man," J.C. said.

Cordelle was over talking to J.C.'s great-aunts. Wright and Hanna sauntered on into the ballroom. A large cocktail party was in progress, a couple of hundred people at least, half of them Kathy Lee's old schoolmates. People were mingling, talking, sipping on punch or cocktails. Supposedly each person brought his or her own bottle, and the bartender fixed a drink from that bottle. That was the way country clubs managed to serve alcohol in dry counties.

Wright and Hanna aimlessly meandered around, greeted here and there by sundry people, many of whom took double takes at their outfits. Most of the guys their age had on casual dress slacks and a dressy knit shirt, a few had on sports coats. Some wore their hair long. The girls had on sundresses or miniskirts. Most had dark tans. Hanna made the observation that it looked as though this was the first time anyone of the young here had put on dress clothes all summer. As if everyone, since spring, had been running around barefoot, in cutoff jeans, hot pants, and halter tops. Wright called it an "astute observation," a phrase he had learned from Winn.

As five long-haired rock musicians were setting up on a small stage in the corner, Kathy Lee came by and took Hanna away with her. Wright watched the musicians for a few minutes, then looked around the ballroom. All the cocktail partiers looked distorted and grotesque; the whole place looked dangerous to him.

His old classmates huddled at the other end of the ballroom. He stood amid the parents in their semiformal wear. Jo Ann Simpson's mother walked up and said, "Hello, Wright. I heard you were going to LSU. What are you going to major in?" Wright told her he wasn't sure yet, smiled at her, thinking how he had to get the hell out of there before they started on him. He wasn't in the mood at all.

Wright walked toward the back of the ballroom, down a little corridor, and through the kitchen door. A black man with an apron on was working alone in the kitchen. He looked up and said, "Hey, youngblood! How's my main man?"

"All right, Bud."

Bud picked up a bottle of whiskey, took a slug. He handed the bottle over to Wright. Wright took a long, hard pull, wiped his lips, and handed the bottle back.

Bud said, "That a mean lookin git-up you got on there. Look like you gone whip up on somebody's ass or fuck somebody or somethin'."

"I ain't takin' no shit off nobody tonight."

Bud said, "That good. I all time been worryin' bout you and you sister. The ways y'all all time takin' shit off'n folk. I glad to hear that."

There was a little serving window on the other side of Bud, between the kitchen and ballroom. Through that opening Wright could hear J.C. telling everyone over the microphone that the dance for Kathy Lee's classmates would soon begin and the tea for the parents would commence at their house soon.

Bud commented, "I don't know why the hell they didn't just go straight out yonder in the first place. Half of us out yonder. I here. Everthang got fucked up."

Wright could hear the drummer warming up, heard the microphone giving feedback. He said, "I guess this'll be the last fuckin' shit deal I have to come to at this place."

Bud said, "Git you ass back out there, man. It's too short. I've showed myself a good time, boss. St. Louis. New Orleans. Tampa. I lived all around. A life you wouldn't believe. But it's too short. Ask you daddy. He lookin' at it, too. Git you ass back out there. It's too short."

One of the band members could be heard welcoming everyone and saying they had come all the way from Macon, Georgia, to play a little rock and roll for the fine folks in Alabama. Wright heard everyone cheer and whoop.

Wright and Bud shared another slug of whiskey and then Wright said, "Yeah, see you later, Bud." Wright walked back out to the ballroom. The band had started playing some Southern rock. About three fourths of the party was dancing. He saw Hanna standing with Jenny Sutton, one of her SCW classmates. They were both sipping drinks, occasionally touching at each other and talking, though Wright didn't see how they could hear each other over the music. He walked over and told Jenny hello, then hollered at Hanna that he was going to give his best wishes to Kathy Lee. Hanna nodded and gave him a kiss. Wright walked on toward the dance flooe. A couple of girls Wright had gone to high school with grabbed him and kissed him on the cheek. Guys were hollering out his name, pointing to his outfit, giving him an "okay" sign. Everybody seemed to be having a big time. But Wright just wanted to give Kathy Lee well wishes and get the hell back to Big House.

All of a sudden someone grabbed Wright's arm from his blind side. He looked around to find Kathy Lee had hooked her arm in his. She was laughing, kissed him on the corner of the mouth in the same place her mother had a couple of Christmases ago. But Kathy Lee wasn't in a state of mellowness; she had a wildness to her. She had two large cups of punch. She handed Wright one.

On one side of the ballroom was a wall of French glass windows and doors that opened out onto the patio next to the golf course. Kathy Lee led him in that direction, but she and Wright were stopped every few feet to be kissed or hugged or shake someone's hand. They finally made it onto the patio, now holding hands. A short hedge went around the perimeter of the patio. They walked off and sat on a stone bench on the other side of the hedge. They looked out at the darkened golf course.

Wright realized he was now sitting beside the person who used to be his best buddy and had been his first of just three lovers. Kathy Lee was sitting there bronze-tanned with her long wild sun-streaked hair. The same girl he had been with constantly in junior high school, searching their own and each other's souls.

They started talking and giggling about having broken into J.C.'s liquor cabinet when they were twelve, about horseback riding, sneaking off to the stables and cotton fields with a blanket, about all the shit they had gotten into for cutting up in the library and in Mrs. Goodwin's class. Wright thought of Greer, and how he could have but wouldn't have made fun of two eighteen-year-olds reminiscing.

The band started playing louder. Wright and Kathy Lee instinctively got up and sauntered out onto the golf course, away from the music, where they could hear each other better.

Kathy Lee told Wright that they were different, had been different from the rest of their classmates. Wright told her that was an understatement. Kathy Lee said, "God, Wright. I would have never made it without you during those tough times." Wright knew she was talking about everything, all the things that worked over and over, all the things they couldn't understand, couldn't make light of when they had had all their soul-searching talks. Wright couldn't help thinking that while Butch's guts were being splattered out in a foreign jungle, he and Kathy Lee were half naked in the front lower deck of the houseboat banging away.

The alcohol was starting to work on Wright. It was making him foggy, but not high, like his body was fighting it. To Wright, there was some kind of bizarreness about him, a feeling that things were out of sequence. He took another swallow of his drink. All the reminiscing shit seemed to be over. He said, "So, you going off to Rutgers? Eddie's going off to Mississippi."

Kathy Lee sipped on her drink. "Mississippi's a good place for him to be."

"I thought y'all were in love," Wright said.

"I don't know. Sometimes I think there's something just a little strange about Eddie. But I never can put my finger on it. All I know is I'm getting the hell out of Sumpter and having as much fun as the law allows."

They both made a snort laugh, then walked along the golf course silently. Wright wondered about Kathy Lee, tried to imagine a future for her. If she would get married in her early twenties. If she would come back to Sumpter. If she would turn out to be a wild, unmarried Coleen sort. Sauntering along, he could almost imagine any type future for Kathy Lee. Wright looked over at her. Sure she looked taller, looked older, but there seemed to have been no time between their escapades in the houseboat and tonight. Yeah, something was bizarre and he was ready to get the hell back to Big House.

4 Jenny and Hanna had walked out onto the patio to talk, away from the immediate loudness of the band. Daughtery came up and asked Jenny to dance. As they went in, Eddie came out and stood by Hanna. "So you'll be off to LSU soon?" He was drinking something that looked like Scotch and water, was dressed in a sports coat and had on chestnut-colored loafers, looking all Ivy League.

"Oh, yes," Hanna answered and smiled, knowing he knew very well where she was going to college.

Eddie craned his neck around. "Oh, that must be Wright and Kathy Lee out there walking around on the green. But I could care less. Just a moment ago, someone asked me wasn't I jealous, how could I bring myself to be Kathy Lee's date tonight. I'm very mature when it comes to matters like that."

Hanna looked over at Eddie. "What are you talking about?"

"Oh, I thought you were staying at Wright's house," Eddie said. He reached out and stroked the back of his hand down the front of Hanna's hair, lightly touching her face also. "I don't want to bore you with my life. But last week for several days I didn't see Kathy Lee.

Supposedly she was busy with her family, getting ready to go to Rutgers. But later, from three different reliable sources, I heard rumors she and Wright had had a last little fling. Oh, I don't begrudge Wright at all. Oh, I could have pitched a fit, not escorted Kathy Lee tonight. But why be so petty? Why spoil the whole party? I'm beyond that. Kathy Lee and I are both free spirits. I don't begrudge her a last-minute fling with an old flame. I'm not even going to bring it up to her. I'm just surprised, you and Wright living under the same roof, that he didn't mention it to you or brag about it. Who has Wright been dating this summer, anyway?"

"No one," Hanna snapped. She had been staring at Eddie but now was looking away, fidgeting with her drink, feeling like she had just had the wind knocked out of her.

"Forget that. Who have *you* been dating this summer?"

"No one," Hanna said quickly.

"No one! You must be kidding me? What do you say to the guys when they ask you out?" Eddie asked.

"No one has asked me out."

"I can't believe that! You are so beautiful. You know, I bet all the guys think you wouldn't go out with them because you are so pretty. You know, that's common with exceptionally beautiful girls like yourself. But that will all change once you get to college. Oh, once you get to college you won't be able to beat the guys off with a stick. I tell you what, if I had been a free man this summer, or even knowing what I know, oh, I would have asked you out."

"Thank you," Hanna said quietly.

"I better get back in here. Listen, I hope later I get the honor of dancing with you. I'll be around," Eddie said and walked back into the ballroom.

Hanna looked out onto the green. She could see Wright and Kathy Lee's silhouettes. They were holding each other's hands. Wright moved in closely to Kathy Lee. They appeared to have kissed. But Hanna couldn't tell what kind of kiss it had been. She slugged down the rest of her drink, tossed her glass over into the hedge, and walked in just as the band stopped.

The lead singer was at the microphone, introducing the members of the band. Everyone in the ballroom had moved up close to the stage. Hanna stood at the outskirts of the crowd watching, but in a stunned numbness, thinking of what Eddie had said, trying to decipher what she had just seen.

The singer said, "This next song we gone do is about this feller that runs moonshine whiskey. Some of you may or may not be able to relate to that." The band members were all pointing to one another, the crowd giggling at them. "Now wait, we come to play for y'all, not for me to talk. But ole Bogo back there done broke his gee-tar strang. After ole Bogo gits his ax sharpened we gone start playin' this song real soft and purty for you so you can slow dance. But then the song's gone build up and cut loose. Then we gone play about two hours of nonstop driving in the left lane with the headlights out Southern rock and roll."

Everyone in the ballroom whistled, clapped, or whooped. When they quieted down, the singer continued, "Anyway, this song is about this feller his girl run out on him." The crowd oohed and ahhed. "Yeah. Terrible as it sounds. But this feller done spent all his money on her. All that kind of shit. This feller down to rock bottom is what it amounts to. He down to this silver dollar his granddaddy give him that he totes for good luck. So this feller gone make the biggest haul he ever made. He got to make this haul or, man, that's the end of him. He makes this haul he have enough money to make him a comeback and all that good shit. He got his '57 Chevy all hopped up, all checked out, got plenty oil pressure, all that shit. He a little nervous. Then he takes a suck of bonded whiskey and he eyes light up and he know it don't matter now. I mean he don't give a shit no more!

The crowd whooped on, not giving a shit. He said, "I mean it ain't nothing as dangerous as somebody don't give a shit no more. He is one mean son of a bitch and he don't care what happens!"

Tony DuBois was a few years older than most of the kids. He had just finished at the University of Alabama and had been denied entrance into the law school there. He was whooping and hollering, "All right! All right!"

Bogo was ready. The lights dimmed, and they began playing slowly and softly. The people moved back out across the dance floor, paired up, and began to slow dance. Daughtery walked up to Hanna and asked her to dance. She said, "Sure," put her arms around his shoulders best she could with his size and height. He put his arms around her waist and held her closely; they began to slowly sway with the music. Daughtery rubbed the side of his face along Hanna's forehead. She looked up at him, and when she did her lips were right at his. He kissed her. Hanna didn't know why, but she automatically started kissing him back.

All of a sudden from behind, Wright grabbed her by the arm and jerked her back, hollering, "What the fuck you think you doing?"

Daughtery stuck out his chest and said, "What the fuck you doing jerking her around?" He grabbed at Wright's lapels, but Wright blocked Daughtery's arms out of the way and jabbed him right under the nose. Daughtery staggered back a bit, but Wright had not landed hard enough with the snap punch.

Steve Leonard grabbed Wright to restrain him, but Wright threw his elbow back, caught Steve under his right cheekbone, and knocked him down. Two other guys rushed Wright in an attempt to subdue him. Wright just brushed them aside, tripping them up.

Danny Hargraves hollered, "Hey, cut it out!" Tony hollered, "Fight!" Several people screamed. Pandemonium broke out. Someone threw the light switches on. But the band continued to play. They were used to this, especially up near the edge of Tennessee. Sometimes they played behind chicken wire to protect themselves from flying beer bottles.

Hanna somehow had been pushed to the back of the crowd, near the doors to the patio. Kathy Lee came running in, her sundress flopping around as she ran and catching on the door hinge. The dress tore some, so she pulled it off over her head; she kicked off her shoes and stood in only her body suit as Hanna hollered to her what had happened, what Eddie had said. Kathy Lee grabbed Hanna by the arm, told her to come on, they would get to the bottom of this, that Wright could take of himself.

Hanna and Kathy Lee pushed themselves through the crowd. Wright and Daughtery were still trying to get at each other. Robert Elridge and Ken Jacobs were trying to hold back Daughtery. Wright was fighting off two guys Hanna didn't know. Another guy came charging at Wright, as if to tackle him from the side. Hanna stepped in and gave the guy a hip throw. The guy slid across the floor, stood back up, and landed against the punch bowl. He, the punch bowl, and the table fell over in one great crash.

Kathy Lee grabbed Hanna's arm again. "Come on, he's not in here." Jenny was in the middle of the dance floor swinging a broom around in a circle. The lead singer was trying to tell her to break the broom end off it. She started stomping on the broom, trying to break the handle off.

Kathy Lee bumped into Tony. He had the security guard in a head lock. He said, "Kathy Lee, you want to fuck?"

"Huh?" Kathy Lee asked. She couldn't hear him on top of all the fighting. And the band had just gone into the loud fast part of their song.

Tony followed her, dragging the security guard along. He said, "Do you want to fuck? You know, fuckin' and fightin' seem to go to-gether."

Kathy Lee smiled and said, "Fighting does tend to make me horny." Tony gave a *yee-ha*, but Kathy Lee and Hanna broke away and ran down the corridor by the kitchen. Bud was coming out of the door, sipping on some whiskey, shaking his head, saying, "Bennie J.'s younguns show do know how to have a good time. Don't take no shit off'n nobody."

They ran on down the corridor. Kathy Lee pushed the door to the men's restroom open. There stood Eddie combing his hair. Hanna saw his face in the mirror. He had glanced up, horrified for a split second, then went back to combing his hair as if he were unmoved, bored.

Kathy Lee stood in the doorway. She said, "There's a fight going on out there."

"I'm a lover, not a fighter."

"There's about fifteen guys out there getting the hell beat out of them, trying to keep Wright and Daughtery off each other," Kathy Lee said. She and Hanna walked on in, getting on either side of Eddie.

Eddie smirked snidely. "I've always thought they had a bent for violence."

"I just thought it strange you not out there 'helping' all your friends."

"I don't have to engage in their redneck ways," Eddie responded to Kathy Lee. Eddie had only been looking at his own self in the mirror, occasionally glancing over at Kathy Lee. He only now no-ticed she had her dress off. He commented, "You got your dress torn off?"

"Yeah. This guy out there, this wild redneck guy, ripped it off and tried to feel me off. That's why I've come to find you. Go out there and defend my honor."

Eddie gave a nervous laugh. He said, "Come on, let's get out of here."

Kathy Lee said, "Yeah, let's do," and punched him in the face. Hanna grabbed his fingers and twisted his arm behind him. They marched him out of the bathroom, down a hallway, and out to the pool. All the way Eddie was hollering, "What the hell are y'all doing? You're hurting my fingers, my shoulder! Stop! This has gone too far!"

They got him alongside the pool. Kathy Lee kicked him in the back of the knees to get him lying down. Hanna knelt, put her knee in the small of his back, still holding him. Eddie was on his stomach along-side the pool. Kathy Lee bent down, got him by his hair and pushed his head under the water. He squirmed, but Hanna had him good. Bubbles came up beside his face and broke the surface of the water.

Kathy Lee pulled his head up. He gasped for air. She said, "You're such a shithead." Eddie was hollering for help. Kathy Lee said, "Tell me what you're up to."

"Daughtery wants to beat Wright up in front of everyone tonight," he said very quickly. Kathy Lee told him she didn't buy it, that that sounded like his idea. She shoved his head back under the water and after a moment brought it back out.

Eddie was gasping, out of breath, and terrified. Then he began talking frantically. "Wright is dangerous. He was out to get me. I could tell. Couldn't you tell? I could tell. He didn't like me going out with you. He was jealous. He was still in love with you. I could tell. He wanted to kill me. I was trying to protect you."

"You're sick," Kathy Lee said. She got up, Hanna pushed Eddie into the pool, and the two women reentered the ballroom.

Daughtery and Wright were squared off. The band finished their song. The ballroom was quiet. Everyone was gathered around, look-ing at Wright and Daughtery. Daughtery threw a body punch to Wright. Wright twisted to the side, but the punch caught him and caused him to lose his balance. But Daughtery didn't close in; he backed off and moved around with his fists up in the old Irish boxing stance.

Wright got back up and staggered around. He felt like he had been fighting for days, felt like he had fought every seventeen- to twenty-year-old in Sumpter County. He wished he had kept going to karate classes after Winn had gone off to college. He should have taken Bennie J.'s advise. "It was something nobody could take away from you." Wright thought he should start training again. Start jumping rope to build up some endurance, start stretching, start doing his katas down in Big Room. Get out his old *gi* and everything.

But Wright knew none of that was going to help him right now. He stumbled around, straightened up his cape. He could taste bour-bon and gin in his mouth.

Danny Hargraves, the smallest guy and the leading clown of Wright's class, was standing on the inside of the circle of spectators. The top of his ear was cut away a bit from his head, blood was running down the side of his face. He was holding his ear. Danny, despite his size and his lack of fighting technique, had somehow managed to start beating the hell out of David Kelley, who had told on Danny in the eleventh grade for cheating on a physics test. Just as Danny was really pouring it on, he had stepped into the path of the jagged edge of Jenny's swinging broomstick.

Danny hollered, "Hey Daughtery, maybe you ought to let somebody tire him out a little more. You asshole!"

Wright tried to concentrate on Daughtery, but Danny was distracting him. He thought it was ironic that Danny was defending Wright now, because all through the eighth, nine, tenth, and eleventh grades Wright had stood up for Danny. Had kept guys from picking on him. Had always stood up for him until he found out Danny had a ten-inch dick. Wright figured anybody with a ten-inch dick didn't need anybody looking out for him.

Wright mumbled, "It's a thirsty city. And somebody's thirsty for my blood." He charged into Daughtery, hit him with a backhand punch to the side of the face. Daughtery staggered back. Several cheered, but most were just looking on in shock. Wright stepped on into Daughtery, but Daughtery got him with a punch. Wright turned his head, getting not direct impact, but enough to send him rolling back. He got quickly to his hands and knees, but stayed there panting.

Wright looked around, foggy-eyed, at all the guys with torn clothes, bleeding noses, who had tried to drag him out of the ballroom. Wright smiled, but it opened a small slit of a cut in the corner of his mouth. He tasted the salty blood.

He kept his eye on Daughtery, who didn't have enough sense to attack right now. That was the only thing saving him now. But Wright felt too heavy, too exhausted. He eased up but slipped on his cape, falling down flat.

Something caught Wright's attention out of the corner of his eye. Daughtery was coming in toward him. Wright saw high heels step up beside him, saw them being kicked off. Daughtery was hit in the chest with a front kick. He staggered back, his arms out. As he took a big gasp of breath, another front kick hit him in the solar plexus. It knocked the wind out of him, along with staggering him back ten feet against the back wall. He kept his knees from buckling. He covered his chest, midsection, and groin.

But with a spinning-wheel kick, Winn's foot hit him right in front of his left ear. Daughtery fell. The whole ballroom yelled. The fight was over.

Winn turned around and looked at Wright. Wright looked at her. She had on tight shiny black leather pants and a long-sleeved white peasant blouse. An eighteen-carat gold mesh strap choker was around her neck. She looked very tall and exotic. She *was* tall and exotic.

The band started playing again.

5 Bennie J. stopped laughing and said, "So I called old J.C. this morning said, 'J.C. this Bennie J. What you doin' inviting my kids to wild reckless parties? Least you could a done's moved the damned old punch bowl somewhere else. But call ole Burchdale anyway.' " Bennie J. laughed and took another bite of steak. "Took J.C. ten minutes before he figured out I's just funnin' him. Now ole J.C. and Lou Ann they do get all serious about their parties runnin' smooth."

During the fight, Winn and Kathy Lee put a good thumb hold and performed another poolside head bobbing on Eddie. He cowardly confessed he had told a few guys that Wright claimed Daughtery was a fag, and had told Daughtery that Hanna had told him he wanted her to dance with him, that she was hot to trot. That she stayed stuffed up in the mansion all the time. That Wright was a fag but didn't want her to go out with anybody.

Hanna had loaded Wright into his Vette. Kathy Lee had loaded Daughtery up into her Camaro. Winn and Gina, using lighted cigarettes for delay fuses, had set up a bunch of cherry bombs on the eighteenth green. They all began going off just as the police drove up. Meanwhile, the two Corvettes and the Camaro were speeding through the golf course, getting away out the back side and onto Harper Road. Tony DuBois ran out onto the golf course chasing the Camaro on foot, with the misunderstanding that Kathy Lee had promised him a fruitful date later in the night. He walked back all disappointed, saw Eddie staggering around all wet beside the pool. He picked up Eddie and threw him back in just for the hell of it, but it so lifted his spirits that he went in, asked Jenny to dance, and commenced romancing her. The police were so confused, and were unable to find anyone willing to stop dancing long enough to interrogate, that they just took Bud uptown and arrested him for drinking.

They drove to Big House. As they were walking into Big Room, Bennie J. was walking up the stairs to go to bed. He grabbed the railing and looked down at them. Winn told him it had gotten too wild at the party, that they had come out to Big House. Bennie J. said, "I'm glad y'all did. I been trying to tell y'all ain't nothing but a bunch of drunks out there." He noticed Kathy Lee was clad only in a body suit. "Kathy Lee. That's a good idea. Night's the time to go swimming. I try to tell Winn Big Pool's better than that ole swimming hole they got out at the country club. Country club don't give a damn for a good pool. All that place is is a place to go drink." He said, "Y'all have fun now," and walked on up to his bedroom.

Wright woke up alone in Hanna's bed. There weren't rainbows on the far wall, but a faded splash of color on the wall to his side. He jolted up, every muscle aching. The clock read a little past noon. He had been in a long deep sleep. His stiffness was overcome by hunger pains. He lay back down, staring at the ceiling. He could remember fatigue setting in at Big Room. He couldn't exactly remember, it seemed dreamy, he had lived it through a haze of exhaustion. It seemed Gina had been there. And Daughtery, that Daughtery liked him now like back in grammar school. Daughtery was all excited, like he was celebrating something. The others had gone running down to Big Pool but Hanna had walked slowly with him down there. And when they got there everyone was in the pool splashing around. It seemed he remembered Hanna taking off her clothes, then taking off his clothes, getting him into the water, then putting him on an air mattress. That seemed to make sense.

He had the definite sensation he had floated around on the air mattress, resting, while everyone else splashed and dived. Yes, he seemed to remember Gina. He could recall her naked, diving off the diving board. Kathy Lee was climbing out of the pool naked on the ladder at the deep end. She was giggling and Daughtery was on the bottom step of the ladder, had hold of her hips, trying to pull her back into the water. Kathy Lee's grip broke loose and she fell back bare-assed onto Daughtery's face and they fell back down into the water. It seemed Wright could remember Winn with only her gold choker on, wading around in waist-deep water with Baby Dog Midnight, letting him swim and then picking him up out of the water. And it seemed Wright could remember Hanna getting him off the air mattress, sitting him in the shallow end of the pool, kissing him.

The more Wright though about it, lying alone there in Hanna's bed and now staring at the faded rainbow on the wall, the more he was certain that that was exactly what had happened.

Wright thought about the breakfast Bennie J. had cooked the morning of the camping trip. He would give anything for that break-fast right now. He got up and walked around. He was stove up. He was determined to wait until he was sure the family had eaten and left Big House before he went down. He couldn't face it all. J.C. and Lou Ann had certainly told Bennie J. and Cordelle by now all the damage that was done. All the guys he had fought were probably after him. Letting the snake bite Hanna and now this—Bennie J. was probably fit to be tied. Wright was sure he was going to be shipped out the next day to some military academy junior college. Or maybe the Army! He could hear Bennie J. saying, "A couple of years in Vietnam'll straighten your ass out." Wright was eighteen years old, and for the first time ever he thought of the threat of being drafted and shipped off.

The paradise Wright wanted seemed planets off and centuries away. He pulled on a pair of jeans but then just plopped back down on the bed and moaned.

What sounded like an explosion brought Wright out of his delir-ium. Winn and Hanna had barged through the door and now were flying through the air, screaming. They landed on either side of Wright and started giggling. Wright saw no humor in it, though. It was obvious Bennie J. wasn't mad at them. He was about to get the talking-to of his life and then shipped off to hunt for Butch's ghost and here they were giggling. Wright mumbled, "I guess Doddy's just mad at *me*, huh?"

"Mad at you? He's been bragging ninety to nothing all day long. You a hero, son," Winn said.

"Hero?"

"Yeah. Walking around bragging about you, then saying, 'See

there, see there. I been tryin' to tell Wright karate was something nobody could take away from him. Maybe he'll believe me now. Done been cleaning up house.' "

"I can't believe it," Wright said.

"Yeah," Hanna said. "J.C. and Lou Ann are all excited you flushed Eddie out as a bad egg. Saved their daughter."

"You and Kathy Lee did that."

Winn said, "Oh, but you were the one who brought it about. J.C. was down at the marina. Bennie J. was prancing around, saying, 'See, I taught my younguns to be able to do something about something. You can send them around to colleges to they thirty years old, but if you hadn't taught 'em to do something about something you ain't taught 'em shit!' "

Wright could hear Bennie J. saying that, could see him saying that, could see how he had moved. But he couldn't believe all the years he had pounded into them the value of a higher education, all the while knowing it was mostly bullshit.

Wright said, "I can't believe it." He plopped back down off his elbows and stared at the ceiling. "Did I hurt anybody last night?"

"Every guy you tussled with came by the marina this morning looking for you," Hanna said.

"Oh, fuck. A Sunday morning and they're already after me. My problems are just beginning."

"No, no," Hanna said. "They were all bragging about it. You should have seen Danny giving Bennie J. a play-by-play description. You know how Bennie J. thinks he's so funny."

"He is funny," Wright commented.

Hanna continued, "After they were all gone, Bennie J. kept saying how popular you were with your classmates. He was so proud. Oh! And I forgot! Jenny's folks called Bennie J."

"Oh, God! That frail little squeaky thing. I saw her swinging that broom around scared to death. They have to send her down to Tuscaloosa to the crazy house?"

Hanna said, "No. It brought her out of her introversion. She has a date with Tony DuBois! Jenny's father is going to see what he can do about getting him into law school."

Wright chuckled. Winn and Hanna were laughing. Wright just stared at the ceiling, thinking about Bennie J. the night he had buried Mama Dog Midnight. Thinking about how he told him he couldn't do anything wrong. "You do some dumb-ass thing, it turns out to be the right thing to do, got everbody in the palm of your hand, going on about ye. Naw, don't seem you can do no wrong." Now for the first time Wright thought it might be true. Chills ran down his spine. Maybe Wayne was right. Maybe he was a chosen one.

Hanna said, "Yeah. And Bennie J.'s all excited that Winn's home."

"Me, too," Wright said. He leaned over and kissed her on the cheek.

Hanna said, "Yeah. And he's all excited Winn's quit dressing like a hippie."

Wright looked over and took note of Winn. She had on sharkskin pants and a silk top. He said, "Wow. That looks nice. You looked *great* last night."

"Thank you." She kissed him back. "Yeah, over in Europe, I decided, fuck this shit. I'm tired of wearing old fucking patched-up blue jeans. It's kind of stupid when you come to think of it."

All three were stretched out side by side, all staring up at the ceiling now. Hanna's right ankle was lying over Wright's left ankle. Winn's left ankle was lying over Wright's right ankle.

"Was Gina here last night?" Wright asked.

"She still is. She's staying here until we go back," Winn explained.

"I thought so. Boy, I was one tired mother last night. Everything seems hazy."

Wright paused, then asked. "Daughtery was here, too?"

"Yeah," Hanna said.

"He seemed changed. Like he liked me like back the way it was in grammar school."

"He is changed," Winn said. "He found out Eddie's been fucking up his life the last six years. Fucked up your relationship. Says he feels like a new man. Claims it was all at your expense. He was walking around, saying, 'I've got to do something for Wright. He changed my life.' " Winn giggled and then said, "Yeah, and I think Kathy Lee gave him a little pussy in the poolhouse last night. So Daughtery was one happy man."

Hanna giggled and Wright said, "Kathy Lee? Gina's a little more his size."

"Oh, Gina's in love. Bad," Winn said.

"Yeah?" Wright asked.

"Fell in love with this guy from New Orleans on the tour. He's a senior at LSU. They *bad* in love. They'll probably elope in a couple of months."

"Well, good," Wright said.

Winn imitated Bebe, "Hon, his family are very well-to-do cotton buyers down in New Awluns," then switched into her regular voice. "No, for real. They are. So Robert Samuel Richardson the Third is the only guy going to be getting her pussy any more."

"Pussy is the ugliest word in the English language," Hanna said and giggled.

"Pussy, pussy, pussy, pussy," Winn said.

"No," Wright said. "Piss is the ugliest word there is."

"Piss was dripping from my pussy," Hanna said and then giggled at herself.

"Hanna!" Wright reprimanded. "You don't talk like that."

6 Bennie J. took another bite of steak. Mae Emma walked in, sat down, and began eating. She had stayed late at Big House today for Winn's coming-home supper. Bennie J. said, "Well, Mae Emma. They're all home." He handed down Baby Dog a bone that was almost as big as Baby Dog was. Baby Dog dragged it across the dining room floor and started gnawing on it over in the corner.

"B.J., Baby Dog got grease on the floor," Cordelle said.

"Baby Dog Midnight, Cordelle after you again?" Bennie J. said.

Wright came out of his thoughts of lying with Hanna and Winn on Hanna's bed earlier in the day. He looked about. He, Hanna, Winn, Gina, Cordelle, Bennie J., Mae Emma, Kathy Lee, and Daughtery were sitting at the long dining room table.

Bennie J. had already explained to Daughtery how he was about to go play football for the greatest coach that had ever lived and the greatest team that had ever been put together. That that was some honor. Daughtery had said, "Mr. Reynolds, I'm going to get you fifty-yard-line tickets for any game you want to go see."

"Hot damn! See there, Wright. You want Alabama-Auburn tickets you got to go to the University of Alabama."

After they finished eating, the kids left in Kathy Lee's station wagon en route to the drive-in. Kathy Lee was driving, Daughtery was scrunched up in the middle with Winn sitting beside him. In the back seat were Wright, Hanna, and Gina. It wasn't good dark yet, so they were just riding around aimlessly until the drive-in opened. Winn had been talking about Eddie, was trying to explain how if a lot of shit was coming down, you had to investigate, that there was some shitass behind it. She had done some investigating today, she said, although they already knew who the shitass had been in this case. She had Kathy Lee go uptown to Pine Street.

Winn directed Kathy Lee down the shady street and had her park inconspicuously on the side of the road in this sparsely populated residential section. It was just getting dark. Winn started fixing every-one drinks, though Wright nor Hanna wanted any, claimed they thought they had had their quota for the summer.

Winn said, "Now just keep looking at that brick frame house two doors down. We'll hang out here until time to go to the movies. Something may or may not happen."

Kathy Lee said, "Hey. Isn't that . . . oh, you know . . . that queer who has the tailor shop."

"George Howard," Wright said.

"Yeah. I think that's George Howard's house," Kathy Lee said.

Winn said, "Doddy gets George to make him a new suit every spring and every fall. Doddy says, 'Yeah, George's wrist is a little limp but he makes a fine suit. Only trouble is you got to keep an eye on him when he's measuring your inseam.'"

Everyone chuckled. Winn kept making drinks from a fifth of vodka she had. Gina said, "Hey, the front door is opening!"

A middle-aged man walked out of the house with Eddie, let Eddie into his car, walked around, got in, and backed out of the driveway, to head the other way.

Daughtery had his hands up on the dash. Kathy Lee's mouth was gaped open. Daughtery said, "That son of a bitch! He's been giving George butt service."

"So that's where he gets his clothes and money," Kathy Lee said. "Shitass."

Winn said, "Come on. Let's go to the drive-in. Daughtery and Kathy Lee went on all the way to the movies about what a sly, slimy, sneaky, double-crossing bastard Eddie was. The whole time Wright was thinking about Mae Emma telling him how there were shitasses in the world who tried to piss in your well, but once you found them they folded up real easy, that she used them to wipe her ass. Now it made sense to Wright what Mae Emma had been trying to tell him and teach him.

Once they got parked at the drive-in, they changed their seating

arrangement. Wright and Hanna sat in the front seat, actually watching the B movie and eating popcorn. Gina and Winn sat in the back
seat drinking, Gina talking softly and constantly about her love for
Robert Samuel Richardson the Third. Kathy Lee and Daughtery lay
in the back of the station wagon, necking, Daughtery all curled
around trying to fit back there.

About a third of the way into the movie, Kathy Lee announced,
"Y'all. Y'all," getting everyone's attention. "Do y'all want to go out
on our houseboat?"

They all thought that was a great idea. Hanna cranked the station
wagon and headed for the marina. In some thirty minutes Winn
was at the helm heading out into the channel of the Tennessee
River. Gina was sitting next to her in a captain's chair, sipping wine
and telling Winn about her longing for Robert Samuel Richardson
the Third. Kathy Lee and Daughtery were up on the top deck
under the stars. Wright and Hanna went down into the front lower
deck.

It was not until Wright felt the boat being turned around that it
struck him he was lying with Hanna in the exact place he had first
made love, but with Kathy Lee. And the only three girls he had ever
had sex with were on the boat. And the boat was being steered by
Winn. Add to that the fact that his long-time estranged early childhood buddy was up on top of the boat making love, probably, to the
first girl he had had sex with. All of this seemed to be indicative of
something, prophetic in some manner, but of what Wright did not
know.

7

Bennie J. was ranting and raving the morning after next.
He had Wright and Hanna come into the kitchen. Winn
and Cordelle were already there. Bennie J. was pacing the
floor. He was obviously upset in general and peeved in particular at
Winn. He would turn to her and say, "How could you let her do
that?"

Soon Wright found out that Gina had eloped in the night with

Robert Samuel Richardson the Third, complete with escaping down Winn's bedroom balcony with a rope. Finally Cordelle got the senator in Washington on the phone. She handed the receiver to Bennie J. and as soon as he put it up to his mouth, he said, "Look, Senator, I don't have bars on Big House. I can't—"

But he was obviously cut off by the senator. Soon he was laughing and talking about fishing. And how aren't these kids something.

In her phone conversations from Europe, Gina had spoken of Robert Samuel Richardson the Third in such a way that her mother knew she was in love and had had the Richardsons investigated and to her delight had found them to be wealthy, respected, and Robert Samuel the Third to be bright and hard-working. The senator and Mrs. Farrow couldn't have been more delighted with whom Gina had fallen in love. Gina had called them at three o'clock in the morning last night to tell them they had gotten married. Mrs. Farrow had cried the rest of the night, sobbing how she had been planning Gina's wedding for years. But the first thing the senator had said to Bennie J. was, "I already know they eloped! Hot damn. Ole Gina's done saved the Senator one chunk of money!"

When Bennie J. hung up the phone, he told Winn, "You were right. When someone makes up their mind to get married, there's no use in getting in their way."

After Bennie J. had paced around laughing, saying how wasn't Gina a card, Mae Emma said, "It coolish out this mornin'. We gone have breakfast out on the veranda." The phone rang. Mae Emma handed it to Bennie J., saying, "It the bait shop."

Bennie J. took the phone, said, "Hello," and listened. "Aw, hell," he said finally, "I reckon go ahead and let him have it. Shit . . . yeah, I be down the marina just as soon as I eat breakfast."

Bennie J. hung up the phone and said, "Ole Lummy Stanton come in the bait shop crying and wringing his hands. His coon dog died. He buried her out in his field but couldn't sleep, says she ought to be buried in the coon dog cemetery. He done dug her back up, put her in the back of his truck. Come up to the bait shop, trying to borrow five hundred dollars so he could buy a casket and plot from Wendell Laves. I told Margarette to go ahead and let him have it. It's stupid. But he's not gone be able to rest easy until he's given the best for Bluina. Nothing like a good burial to ease the live folks' souls."

The days had been so hot and humid, it felt like a cool, crisp autumn morning on the veranda, though it was still August. The season was changing a bit, the nights and mornings were cooler and less humid. After breakfast Cordelle left to do some errands uptown. Winn and Hanna left with Bennie J. in the pickup truck.

Wright sat at the table of the veranda alone, sipping his half-and-half coffee. The houseboat ride night before last had been prophetic, a portent. Wright felt like Big House was gone. Everything was leaving, and not only leaving but not coming back. Kathy Lee was going off to another life. So was Daughtery. Gina was married and would probably live in Louisiana. She would never come back to Big House and swim naked in Big Pool. Winn had quit wearing jeans and patches. She would graduate college in another year or so. Wright had no idea what she would do; Coleen had said she could get her modeling jobs in New York. Jerry Lee was off with Coleen. Wright was thinking all this stuff was fine and good, but it didn't change the fact that everybody was leaving and wasn't coming back. And pretty soon he was going to leave, too, but he didn't know, couldn't understand, that he was leaving to *somewhere.*

For the first time Wright got nervous, got a churning in his gut actually, that Hanna might be right. That it wasn't just one of her idiosyncrasies like peeling her toast in half to eat it. For the first time, too, Wright had the fear, the feeling of impending doom, that Hanna actually wouldn't live to her eighteenth birthday. But more than Hanna, Wright felt that everything was going to just *end.*

Mae Emma walked out with a cup of coffee and sat beside Wright. She lit up a Viceroy, starting puffing and sipping coffee. Wright said, "It's all over but the crying."

"I know, baby. I hates to see y'all go. My baby's going to college."

"So, Mae Emma, forget about all those utensils and shit. Hanna and I will just move in with Winn. Since Gina won't be living there and all."

"All right," Mae Emma said. She took a sip of coffee and said, "Hadn't you better call that real estate son of a bitch up, cancel your other apartment?"

"Nah. I never did call him up to get one."

"Hell," Mae Emma laughed. "You won't do!"

"You know, Mae Emma, this has been the perfect summer."

"Thangs has to end. New thangs has to start."

Sitting there, Wright thought of the summer he had just had. Of the childhood he had had. Of going down the channel of the river with his three and only lovers and his childhood buddy, and the boat being steered by his sister. He had known in that a perfection, a wholeness, and it was something that could not be experienced again.

All that was over. Wright just wanted to put his head down on the table and cry. But he gave it up. Unlike Bebe Boo and the Dixie Do's and the Committee to Preserve the South, Wright gave it up. He knew an era of his life was over.

VII

The Roots of Thirsty City

1 | Bennie J. steered through the backwaters, but just like he didn't need any mosquito repellant, he didn't need a spotlight either. He ran his bass boat up onto the hammock, right up along side a wide flat-bottom wooden boat. He looked straight up. It was a clear moonless night and the stars seemed to be right above the treetops.

Bennie J. got out and walked along the gangway to the homeplace. Greer stood up from where he had been sitting on an old crate. He shook Bennie J.'s hand. He had a home-rolled cigarette hanging out his mouth. Greer said, "Happy burfday, Mr. Bennie. What is it? You fifty-seven year old today?" Bennie J. watched the red dot of the lighted cigarette dance up and down as Greer spoke.

Greer sat back down on the crate. Bennie J. sat on another one several feet over and leaned back against the wall. "Yeah, fifty-seven. Should have seen it. Should have seen all the shirts and ties the kids got me."

"You got some fine younguns. Yessir, Mr. Bennie. You's elebem years old. Right on nis very powch. What that be? That be forty-six year to the day. Yes, sir, on your elebemth burfday you told me, Greer, one day I'm gone be the richest man in Sumpter County."

Bennie J. leaned forward, now sat with his elbows on his knees. "Yeah, forty-six years ago today you give me my first twenty dollars."

"You had money ever since."

"Yeah, it all started forty-six years ago, Cousin Greer. Right here on this porch."

"On nis very powch," Greer echoed.

"Ain't nothing like oak," Bennie J. said, stomping his feet a bit. "Poplar would have been rotten long time ago."

Greer laughed. "On you eighteenf burfday, too, we's right chere on nis very powch. I tole you you had you whole life ahead of you. That you a young mane. You says, 'Cou'n Greer?' I says, 'What, my boy?' I had got you them fancy britches from Nashville. You had 'em on. You says, 'Cou'n Greer, I ain't wearin' dungarees no more. And you gone see Bennie J. a rich mane. You gone see Bennie J. ma'd to the purtiest girl in the State of Alabama. We gone have us the sma'test, purtiest younguns. Dey gone be able to go uptown do what dey want, say what they want, can't git arrested. Why come? Cause they be Bennie J.'s younguns. That why. They gone git to go to college. They gone go git 'em an education.' " Greer laughed and said, "Yeah. Bennie J. show do do what Bennie J. say he gone do." Greer slapped his own leg, laughing, then picked up a bottle of Jax, opened it with his teeth, and handed it to Bennie J. He opened another one for himself and took a long pull off it.

Every night on Bennie J.'s birthday, since he had been eleven and Greer had given him the first twenty dollars that had started his empire, Greer had come by and they had sat on the front of the homeplace and talked. It was as if this talk kept the homeplace there, kept it standing, kept the iron-hard white oak boards from rotting.

The first year Bennie J. had been married, Greer had come up to Little House, they had sat on the front porch. But it didn't seem right, so they loaded up and went to the old homeplace. At first Mama Bo had thought it was prowlers and had blown the front door out with her pistol-grip sawed-off double-barrel twelve-gauge shotgun. Mama Bo called it her derringer, thought it was a derringer. Had been told by her Aunt Pearl that a vulnerable defenseless lady should always keep a derringer with her.

Bennie J. took a sip of Jax, looked over to Greer, and asked, "You need anythin', Cousin Greer?"

"What might you mean by that, Mr. Bennie?"

"I mean, you need a car, need anything done to your house? Anything?"

"No, sir. But thank you, Mr. Bennie. House just fine. All them fools they got drivin' ne roads nowdays, I should think I best leave drivin' to other folk. But I should think if I do wants or needs anythang I could buy it myself."

"That's good," Bennie J. said. He took a stingy sip of beer. "I never did ask you what'd you do, if it's any of my business. I's always curious. What'd you do with all that money we were making right after the war?"

"I should say that might be some of your bidness, fer curiousness sake," Greer said, taking a long suck of Jax. He sat the bottle down and pulled out his sack of Bull Durham, started rolling another one. "Now, 'course, I sent LaSalle through Brown University. Dat took some ne money. Then I built her dat house. Dat took some more. Most de rest uf it I bought fi'e-dollah gold pieces at thutty-fi'e dollah ah ounce."

Bennie J. chuckled. "Ah, Cousin Greer you won't do."

"I brung ye somethin', Mr. Bennie. Brung you somethin' fuh you burfday."

Bennie J. looked over and said, "What might that be?"

Greer reached over into the darkness with his right hand and retrieved a twelve-gauge Browning double-barrel over-and-under shotgun. He handed it to Bennie J. Bennie J. took it, twisted it around in what starlight there was. He said, "Greer, I'm plumb tickled to death," grinning. He rubbed his fingers across the inlaid gold. "Aw, Cousin Greer. Aw, Cousin Greer," Bennie J. said, suddenly realizing what it was he was holding. "This is ole Uncle Davey's superimpose! Where'd you git it?"

"It mine, Mr. Bennie. Or was mine. Now it yours. That shotgun give to me by your Uncle Davey."

"Over-and-under," Bennie J. laughed. "Count on ole Uncle Davey to have something odd."

"When ole Uncle Davey show up, the pa'ty sta't," Greer said.

"And ole Uncle Davey give it to you?" Bennie J. said.

"I reckon he did," Greer said. He reached in and pulled out a box of matches from his pocket to light his Bull Durham. "One night— dis back a couple yeahs 'fore Uncle Davey passed on. One night, I's headed to you granddaddy's place. You know dat path in ne woods we had? In them woods back of my house?"

"Sure. I walked it many a times," Bennie J. said, but knowing Greer knew that. Knew Greer was just establishing the setting and time good and firm, making him feel there, be there in that time and place.

"It 'bout da'k. I's walkin' long 'at path to'd you granddaddy's. When I come down ne crook in ne path dat led down along the bank of de branch, there up agin nat oak tree was ole Uncle Davey. He was sot down, leaned up agin the tree, had his shoes off. He bout half drunk. I stop says, 'What you doin here all bare-footed, Uncle Davey?' He says he takin' his own life. I says, 'You is?' Then he showed me he had his shotgun. He'd put the end of it agin the top of his nose, had it sidewise so's one barrel on one side his nose, other barrel on ne other side. He had de shotgun stretched out in front of him, along his legs. He took his big toe, stuck it on ne trigger, pushed. Gun go click. He put his toe on ne other trigger, gun go click. I tell him,

'Uncle Davey you ain't go' no shells in ne gun.' He says he know. That he out a shells. Then he ax me I got any shells. I say, 'Yeah but not on me, got bunch of 'em back up de house.' He ax if I loan him some.''

Greer stopped to take a pull of beer and to relight his gone-out cigarette. He got it lit and took a long puff. He said, "You know I's a fool back in nem days. Well, you know how I was." Bennie J. laughed. "I git around you granddaddy, or git around Uncle Davey, I didn't have no more damn sense they had. Anyhows, Mr. Bennie, I told Uncle Davey I said, show I loan him some shells. I ax him how many he want to borrow. He said all he needed was two. One fuh each barrel. I ax him what kind shot he want. He ax if I have some double-ought. I say shore, I got some double-ought. And Mr. Bennie J., like a damn fool I walk back to de house, git him two three-inch double-ought shotgun shells, come back give it to 'im. I just stand there, he load up the shells into the chambers. Then he look at me, tell me this personal, for me to git on. So like a damn fool I just forgit about it, go on to you granddaddy. I at you granddaddy couple hours I git to thankin' about Uncle Davey. I git to thankin', I shouldn' give that crazy drunk mane them shells. He liable to kill hisself. I tell you granddaddy I got git back home. I come back down ne path. I git to worryin' 'cause ole Uncle Davey hadn't been too long he lost the sheriff election. Ole Dude, the pet rattlesnake, he was feeling mighty poorly from all the folks that'd been lookin at him. I git to thankin' how ole Uncle Davey been havin' ne blues lately and he didn't have no mo'e sense than to blow his brains plumb out." Greer took a long drag off the Bull Durham.

Bennie J. was grinning, had the gun in one hand, had the Jax beer in the other. He took a slug of beer, held the gun across his lap now. He knew Uncle Davey hadn't blown his brains out, because one night Uncle Davey had built Dude a new cage, had gone to bed early one night feeling a little tired and had never woken up. But Greer had the power, Greer had the archangels—it was like Greer didn't tell the past but created it. Could recreate it at his discretion. Like he could change Uncle Davey's cause of death from cerebral hemorrhage to suicide. Therefore Bennie J. had no idea how the story would turn out.

"I come round ne crook in ne path not knowin' what to expect. It good dark then. I seen a figure laid up agin the tree. I don't know if he done blowed his brains out or whut. I call out, 'Uncle Davey?' He stir around, say, 'What?' I say, 'I thought you all sot to shoot youself.' He says he was. Says dat he load de shells in, but couldn't git his toe on ne trigger just right. Took the shells out, put his toe back on ne trigger, it go click. Other trigger it go click. Put de shells back in but can't git his toe inside the trigger guard agin. Says must be somethin' wrong with my shells. I says must be. He stir around, sot up, take him another sip of whiskey. Unbreech de gun, give me back my shells, tells me much obliged anyhows. I take the shells, thankin' what a fool I acted, that it a wonder he not sittin' there drankin' whiskey wid his hade blowed half off. I look at de jug of white lightnin' he got, tells him he gotta load there, that maybe I ought to take the shotgun, tote it back to my house fer him. That he come by git it tomorrow. I took de gun. I jist try git it away from 'im till he sobah up. He come by next day, but wouldn't take de gun, says he been meanin' to give me dat shotgun fuh ten yeahs." Greer commenced to laughing, strangled, and coughed the cigarette out into the swamp.

Bennie J. held the gun firmly with his hand that was free of the Jax beer and said to Greer, "Thank you. Thank you. Thank you. I'm so proud to own this gun. Take somebody like Uncle Davey to have a double barrel with the barrels on top of each other instead of side by side."

Bennie J. started to say something, started to lay it all out for Greer. Started to tell how all the kids were leaving Big House, going off to out-of-state schools. Bennie J. even started to brag about his kids, tell how Wright couldn't do anything wrong, tell what had happened out at the country club. Started to tell how Winn had quit dressing like a hippie, how she was making a fine young woman. How despite her overdrawing her checking account, she somehow had a good business sense to her. And Hanna, how beautiful she was, how she had the IQ of a genius, and despite her quiet ways and unassuming manner, he bet she figured out what it was she wanted to do with her life and ended up happy, prosperous, and thriving. Maybe somebody else couldn't see that, her letting snakes bite her the way she did, but Bennie J. knew it, that Hanna had this dynamic potential underneath it all. Bennie J. wanted to brag about Cordelle, that hadn't she raised a fine household, didn't she have a fine business sense. She could go up to Bernstein's spend fistfuls of money go to Birmingham spend more fistfuls and still her money made money so fast you couldn't even tell she was spending it.

What Bennie J. did was take a sip of Jax and tell Greer, "Cousin

Greer, some eighteen years ago I talked Cordelle out of having more younguns. Said we had all we could take care of. That we'd do good to get these two raised proper. Should a had ten. Don't see nothing I can do about it now. It's a straight sin. You get you a sin you can't do nothing about what you got you is a regret."

"Now Mr. Bennie, don't you go moaning about no regrets. Thangs did work out awright. If you'd done thangs differ'nt, that change, that change no tellin' how many thangs. Might change for the good, but just might change fi'e thangs to de worst. Naw, dat some'in I learnt from my archangel. You want to change somethin', look out in front of you. Don' be lookin' to de past. Shit."

Bennie J. nodded his head, then said, "I got some fine younguns. Don't I, Greer?"

"Show do, and got the purtiest wife in ne State of Alabama." Then Greer said, "You got ye whole life ahead of ye, boy. You got the stars wid ye. You kin do anything you wants."

It was the same thing Greer had told him when Bennie J. was eleven years old, when he was handing Bennie J. his first twenty-dollar bill.

2 | Winn slapped all the papers and forms down on the desk in front of Bennie J. She was standing beside him. He was sitting in his wooden swivel chair. Bennie J. glanced up at the hundred-watt light bulb but didn't stare because it would blind him. He looked back down at Winn's tan hand that lay spread out across the papers. The hand that at eight years old could stretch an octave on the piano.

Bennie J. was grinning like a little boy, grinning like he was embarrassed almost. Embarrassed he couldn't keep a poker face. "My little girl's going back to the University of Alabama. I knew you would come to your senses. Oh me, I don't know what I'm gone to do! My little girl's going down to Tuscaloosa to Bear's school. Down there with the winners."

Winn had just gotten through explaining to Bennie J. if she continued on at LSU it would take her another year and a half to graduate. But if she transferred all her courses, and she had investigated this and found they would fully transfer, to the University of Alabama and took a heavy load this semester she could graduate at the end of the semester with a B.S. in political science.

Bennie J. stood up, unable to wipe the embarrassed-looking kind of grin from his face. He said, "We got to go tell everybody. Come on, we got to go to Big House. We got to have us a shindig. We gone have to kill the fatted calf. Come on." Bennie J. was sort of walking around in circles like he didn't know exactly what to do even though he had just given the battle plan.

Finally he took Winn by the hand and walked out of his office.

They pulled up to the front of Big House, Winn driving her Corvette, Bennie J. riding in the passenger seat. He was talking about how smooth the thing drove, that there wasn't anything like a Chevrolet car as they got out. When they walked into Big Room, Cordelle was coming down the stairs, putting a bracelet on as she walked. She looked up to see Bennie J. and Winn in Big Room. Bennie J. had this look on his face. If there was one thing Cordelle could do after twenty-five years of marriage, it was read his face. But she was a bit taken aback. She could tell he was excited about something, but when Bennie J. was excited he paced and talked, ranted. Bennie J. now was quiet with a stupid grin on his face, a look Cordelle couldn't read.

She stopped in her tracks and said, "What?" Bennie J. told her the news about Winn. Cordelle shrilled and said, "This is the year! This is the year Winn graduates from college." Cordelle came on down the staircase, put her hand above her breast like she was out of breath. She hugged onto Winn. She stood there stunned. Then said, "Oh, congratulations, dear. What are you going to major in?"

Winn said, "Political science. With minors in marketing, geology, and sociology.

"How wonderful!" Cordelle said. "What a happy day!"

Mae Emma came into Big Room, saying, "What's going on in here?"

Bennie J. said, "Ole Winn's going down to Bear Country. Ole Winn's transferring to Tuscaloosa to the University of Alabama. Down with the Crimson Tide!"

"Again?" Mae Emma said, stopping with a rag in one hand, a ladle in the other, letting them droop at arm's length. She turned to walk back into the kitchen like she had just wasted ten seconds of her life by walking into Big Room.

"She's going to graduate, Mae Emma!" Cordelle announced.

Mae Emma turned around and stared. Bennie J. started into a quick-paced spiel of how all her credits would count at the university. Mae Emma was over hugging onto Winn and crying how her little girl was going to be a college graduate. All the while Bennie J. was saying, "Two hundred years the Reynolds been livin' in Sumpter County. Been livin' in Alabama before it was a state. And now for the first time a Reynolds is graduating. And right here in the fine state of Alabama! Down there with the Bear!"

Two gunshots could be heard. "Come on," Bennie J. said. "We got to tell ole Hanna and Wright." They all went out through the back veranda, across Big Back Yard toward the peach orchard.

Wright and Hanna were back next to the peach orchard, shooting skeet with the over-and-under Greer had given Bennie J. Baby Dog Midnight was running around, running by at Hanna, trying to grab the bottom of her sundress, but she always lifted it up out of the way, and Baby Dog all in a tizzy would just keep on running. The shots had no effect on Baby Dog, and it made Bennie J. proud that Baby Dog wasn't gun-shy.

Wright had the shotgun now, had it unbreeched in the crook of his left arm. He had on a long-sleeved white shirt with the sleeves rolled back. It was a hot day, but breezy and dry, comfortable. Wright had on a pair of Winn's boot-cut Levi's. She had given him a bunch of her jeans. Wright liked wearing them, the Levi's, they fit fine and he too had tired of wearing raveled navy bellbottoms. He was barefoot, something he had taken a habit to since he had resumed karate training.

When Baby Dog saw Bennie J., Baby Dog started hauling ass out across the back yard toward him. Bennie J. picked him up, telling him he better not pee on him. Bennie J. hollered down to Wright and Hanna, "Guess what ole Winn's going to do?"

Wright and Hanna walked over to each other, leaned into each other side by side in the shade of a peach tree. They looked back up and awaited the small group walking toward them, laughing, almost as if in celebration.

In the crook of Wright's left arm was the shotgun; he had his right hand around Hanna's waist. Hanna's right hand was up on her hip, right under the bracelet on Wright's wrist. Her left hand hooked onto Wright's left shoulder. Her hair was blowing all about herself and Wright. Bennie J., Cordelle, Mae Emma, and Baby Dog walked on up. Bennie J. announced the news to Wright, but Wright and Hanna seemed unmoved. Bennie J. looked at them in a questioning sort of way.

Then Wright said, "We know, Doddy. We're going there, too." Bennie J. sat down Baby Dog without taking his eyes off Wright. Wright added, "If it's not too late to get accepted."

Bennie J. mumbled, "It not too late. I'll call Birchdale, git everthang fixed. It's a thirsty city." Bennie J. stared at Wright and Hanna in disbelief. The air of celebration had not dissipated but was certainly frozen for the moment. There was a quietness that caused the sound of the wind through the peach and pecan trees to seem loud. Cordelle and Mae Emma looked at Bennie J. Bennie J. asked Wright, "What are you going to major in?"

"Karate," Wright said.

"That's something they can never take away from you, son," Bennie J. said solemnly.

A couple of nights before, Winn, Wright, and Hanna had laid on Winn's bed. She was talking about Gina getting married, how Europe had been. She talked about how she dreaded going back to LSU, that she was tired of college, that she was "through" with college. Wright knew what she meant. That was when he suddenly realized he was "through" with it too, yet had never even been. Wright thought how college might have been fun when he was fifteen or sixteen, but now it had nothing to offer him in the way of a lifestyle.

Winn had calculated the only way she could rid herself of college was to graduate. And the easiest way to graduate was to go to the University of Alabama. Wright and Hanna wanted to go wherever Winn went. Wright figured the easiest way for him to get out of college was to go to the university for two years and then go over to England and be a Rhodes Scholar. At the university Wright could find some way to bullshit his way through, spend most of his time away from campus life, spend it mostly with Hanna and with karate training. By the time he went to England he could be a black belt.

Wright stood there now, thinking of the chain reaction Gina had set off by getting married. When they had made love in the corner booth that night at the marina and then walked around hand in hand, even then he had felt there was something pivotal about Gina, about how she fit into Big House.

Bennie J. sat down on the grass. "All my children are going to the University of Alabama!"

Cordelle and Mae Emma were on either side of Winn, standing

back of Bennie J. with their arms all around each other. Cordelle said, "Isn't it all so wonderful?"

Baby Dog Midnight ran over and got into Bennie J.'s lap. Bennie J. picked the puppy up in his hands and stood up. "Hot dig! Heuh, Wright. Let me have that gun show y'all how to shoot!"

3 The last few days Bennie J. had taken to eating breakfast with Mae Emma at Big House on the veranda and then drinking his coffee while watching Winn. Early in the morning Winn would come down to Big Room in her *gi* and do about ten minutes of kata. Bennie J. liked to watch her; he would be entranced by the way she moved. Just like listening to her play the piano. Bennie J. wasn't given to sitting down and watching any live performance, but Winn had always been the exception. At age nine she was playing ragtime on the piano, and at nights he would sit and listen to her as long as she felt like playing. And once, when Winn was fourteen, he had come out of his bedroom, walked to the top of the stairs, looked down, and there was Winn, in the early morning streaks of light coming through the French glass windows; she was practicing a kata. He had sat down on the top step and looked down at her, entranced, entertained, moved that such competence could be attained.

But this morning Bennie J. didn't go back in to see if Winn was doing katas. He was bursting out with excitement so he had to get to the bait shop. One day everything was one way, he went back to the roots of thirsty city, had him a talk with Greer, and now everything was another way. All his younguns were going down to the University of Alabama to Bear country and get an education. Wright was going to major in karate. Just like if he, Bennie J., was a young man, he would have done. He was going to get him an education, an education in something nobody could take away from him.

Bennie J. had found out that Wright might only be going there for a couple years. But that was all right with Bennie J. Just get Wright started in the right direction. J.C. had come over talked about he wanted to start working on getting Wright a Rhodes Scholarship in England. Bennie J. had told him Wright didn't need a scholarship, that he could pay for Wright's education. J.C. had just smiled and said that wasn't exactly what he had in mind. But in the end Bennie J. confessed that that might be a good idea, Wright going over and living in England for a while. Europe, as bad as Bennie J. hated to admit it, had done wonders for Winn. She wasn't over there two months and she had given up being a hippie and wearing patched-up bellbottom jeans. She was now spending thousands of dollars of Bennie J.'s hard-earned money on exotic clothes, but Bennie J. didn't mind. It was worth it to see Winn dressed up like a sleek young lady.

Europe had probably been such a decadent and degraded land that it had woken Winn up, made her open her eyes to see where it was she lived, what all she had. Bennie J. was glad she was going to hurry up and get the hell out of and away from college. And Bennie J. bet letting Wright get over in England for a couple of years might just straighten his ass out.

He was driving along to the marina now, excited, but still only going thirty-five miles an hour, running off the shoulder every once in a while, looking out at the cotton that would be opening soon. But Bennie J. didn't pay much attention to anything he was looking at, there was too much going on in his head. Almost as much, or maybe even more, excitement than when he and Pete had the Train.

Everything would have been perfect, except for what Cordelle had brought up last night. Cordelle had been propped up at the headboard, reading a book. Bennie J. was pacing back and forth, talking about how his younguns had finally come to their senses and were going to the University of Alabama, home of the Crimson Tide, where they would be in the company of their own state, in the company of winners, in the company of the best, of the competent, where they would be able to get fifty-yard-line tickets to Alabama-Auburn games.

Cordelle announced, "I'm worried about Hanna, B.J."

"Worried about Hanna?" Bennie J. stopped pacing and looked at Cordelle. "Hell, she let them snakes bite her, got that out of her damn system. She's going to the University of Alabama. She ain't been dressing up so much like a beatnik. She can outshoot Wright with Uncle Davey's old over-and-under. Somethin' wrong with her the first of the summer, her just finishing the Sumpter College for Women and all. She seems cured to me now. Musta just had to get a bunch of shit out of her system."

"No, B.J. Haven't you noticed? You know how bright and energetic Hanna was through the years."

Bennie J. took thought and realized what Cordelle was saying. He said, "A little bug she was, running around here at Big House, gittin' into shit, scheming around. Remember the time she was about twelve, she drug Wright into it, had those Hanna River Tours? She'd sell tickets, take folks out in the runabout up the river, up into the backwaters, back downriver into the swamp. Hell, and them Red-stone Arsenal Yankees didn't have no more damn sense than to take 'em."

"Those were very nice tours she conducted, B.J.," Cordelle con-tended, as if she were taking up for the idea that Bennie J. seemed to be poking fun at.

"She never could get her pricing fixed right, though. Poor ole Hanna Belle. Always into something."

"That is exactly what I'm talking about, B.J. Doesn't that strike you as odd?"

"What you talking about, Cordelle? You usually the last person to claim something's wrong with somebody."

"Look at all the excitement going on. Gina got married. Winn decided to go to Tuscaloosa and finish school. She may come back and run the marina during the summers, may do some modeling. Wright's going to the university, going to be a Rhodes Scholar, may run for representative if he has to. They all have these plans, B.J. Except Hanna. She is just following Winn and Wright. And you know Hanna's true nature. She's not a follower. She's a leader. Yet she has no plans whatsoever. Not only does she have no plans, she—" Cor-delle paused, a strained look on her face, then put the book down. "I don't know how to say it exactly. But you know the time Coleen made an attempt on her own life? Well, there was a strange air about her. And now, not only does Hanna have no plans, but she acts as though there's nothing to plan *for*."

Bennie J. made a pace, stopped again at the foot of the bed, looked intently at his wife, and said, "That's why come you Queen of Big House. That's why come you and ole Bennie J. have an empire. Why come? Because you all time got your eyes open staying on top of thangs."

Cordelle picked her book up, looked at it as if about to resume reading, looked back up at Bennie J. to grin and say, "It's a thirsty city all right, B.J."

4 By noon Bennie J. was all out of the 8 × 10 glossy photos of Bear Bryant walking across the water. He hadn't really sold out of them, but had given them all away. Bennie J. wasn't much for giving stuff away or running loss leaders, he never could see the sense in selling something at a loss; it violated all logic. But the photos of the Bear were a "limited edition," Paul Webb called them, that usually you had to buy at the games. It was sort of against Bennie J.'s better judgment to sell something that was going to run out and you couldn't get another supply of. It tricked people, Bennie J. said, and he didn't like tricking people. When somebody came back to Bennie J. Reynolds to buy something, he by God, wanted to be able to have it to sell to them.

It was funny how fate worked, Bennie J. was thinking that morning before noon, waiting for Winn to show up. It was fate that made him hold on to the old homeplace. There was something a little magical about it. Not that Bennie J. was superstitious or anything. Bennie J. didn't believe in superstition, thought it was hogwash. Everything had a scientific explanation. Not that he was going to go putting his left shoe on before the right or something stupid like that, but there was a thing with fate, and it was this fate that caused Bennie J. to keep the old homeplace.

It wasn't twenty-four hours after Bennie J. had been talking to Greer at the old homeplace that all his kids—Bennie J. when he referred to all his kids included Hanna in the group—had up and decided to go to the University of Alabama. And it wasn't twenty-four hours after his kids had decided to go to the University of Alabama that Bennie J.'s wholesaler of lures, artificial baits, paddles, fishing line and poles, and fishing tackle in general had driven to the marina and unveiled to Bennie J. a whole line of Alabama Crimson Tide and Auburn Tigers paraphernalia. Bennie J. had told Paul Webb, the wholesaler, that he ought to have more sense than to be driving into the marina with any kind of Auburn Tiger shit. Hadn't be heard? All his younguns were headed down to Tuscaloosa.

Yeah, there were just some things that couldn't be explained.

After Bennie J. and Margarette had displayed all the Alabama Crimson Tide caps, T-shirts, cups, and calendars about the bait shop to Bennie J.'s satisfaction, Bennie J. had taken one of the 8 × 10 glossies and was headed to the café but saw Oscar Cantrell's Cadillac parked over in the lot, which meant Oscar and his wife were on their houseboat. Oscar was Bennie J.'s favorite Yankee. Called him a Redstone Arsenal Yankee, but actually Oscar was an engineer for NASA. Oscar, at sixty years old, worked hard, played hard. He drank Chivas Regal whiskey and Schlitz beer and spent at least two hundred dollars a month alone at the bait shop for fancy cuts of meat. Bennie J. even got caviar for him.

Bennie J. stopped in his tracks, looked over to the slip at the end of the dock, and saw Oscar walking into his houseboat. Bennie J. almost never went to anybody's slip; he believed in giving a body his privacy. But Bennie J. grinned and beelined for Oscar's houseboat. As Bennie J. approached the boat, he hollered out Oscar's name. Oscar, in Bermuda shorts and a knit golf shirt with a Notre Dame logo on the left breast, walked back out, Schlitz in hand. Bennie J. told him he had a present for him and handed him one of the 8 × 10s.

Oscar looked at it, took a sip of beer, and said, "Thank you, Bennie J. A picture of Ari Parseghan."

"Goddammit to hell!" Bennie J. hollered at him, then said, "Looks like they'd make you Yankees git a college education before they let you go to messing around on them sputniks," knowing Oscar had graduated from Notre Dame. Bennie J. walked on back over to the bait shop, stood out front, leaning over into the ice machine, trying to check out how it was doing. He was a little leery of it; Jerry Lee had just put a little Freon in it. Bennie J. didn't like putting Freon in it. You put Freon in it, then two weeks later it needs some more and keeps fucking up. Bennie J. would have been more satisfied if Jerry Lee had put a new motor in it or something. It'd be just like things for it to go out while Jerry Lee was down in New Orleans running around with Coleen. Coleen and Jerry Lee were both harum-scarum and didn't neither one stay on top of things. If they were going to be messing around together, Bennie J. thought, they should have done it fifteen years ago, got married, so that Hanna would have had a daddy and now maybe she wouldn't be all in a mess with something eating at her. Coleen and Jerry Lee never did think of nothing until it was too late.

And if Jerry Lee had just half-ass fixed the ice machine, it wasn't him but ole Bennie J. that would have to get Leo Edwards or some of them refrigeration men from uptown that didn't know their ass from a hole in the ground to come down work on the machine. And if they did Bennie J. didn't want to hear any shit from them how it just needed some Freon, put some Freon in it, see what that did. All the while two or three of Leo's employees standing around, dressed in little service uniforms with their first names stitched above the pocket. Them standing around, not doing shit for Leo, maybe going to his big service truck and getting some kind of gauge. Bennie J. wondered why he needed two or three helpers around him that didn't know shit. If someone don't know shit it doesn't do any good to have three more around that don't know shit. Don't know shit times three equals don't know shit.

All Bennie J. knew was if they came they better, by God, fix the thing for good. It pissed Bennie J. off. He just stared down into the ice, leaned over into the machine, wondering why people, if they were going to do something, didn't just do it. If you going to fix something, fix it. Not poke at it, put a little Freon in it, see how it was going to do now. But handle it for good, forever. There were some things about people that Bennie J. just didn't understand.

Winn barreled around and parked by the side of the bait shop with the nose of her Corvette almost right up next to the ice machine. Bennie J. stood straight up and watched her get out of the car. She had on heavy white cotton pants, a top, and a hat that was all a French Navy design. Bennie J. smiled, was sure glad she had quit dressing up like a beatnik, thought she looked real smart in the outfit she had on now. He hollered, "There's my little Crimson Tide girl!" Winn walked on up and they gave each other a quick hug. Bennie J. asked, "Where Wright and Hanna?"

"Oh, all they can do is shoot that damn gun," Winn said.

Bennie J. laughed. "Them kids are something else." He closed the lid on the ice machine. As they walked into the bait shop several people hollered over to Winn, congratulating her that she was going to graduate at Alabama. She followed Doddy Bennie J. around and soon realized she was being led "back to the office."

Bennie J. closed the door. He sat down in his swivel chair and turned around to face Winn, who was now sitting in one of the ladderback chairs. Bennie J. was silent. He looked up to the ceiling, back down at Winn, and at last blurted out "Something's wrong with Hanna. She don't seem to have things planned out like you and Wright do. Cordelle says don't seem like she got anything to plan for." Bennie J. stopped talking, meaning he wanted Winn to say something to this.

Winn said, "I don't think Hanna has let go of something of the past."

Three months ago if Winn had said that Bennie J. would have told her to say what she meant, not chirping out some bunch of way-out beatnik bullshit that he couldn't understand. But things were different now; Bennie J. knew what she was getting at. Winn wasn't sitting there looking like a beatnik, but sitting there in some high-fashion sailor-looking outfit. But what really made Bennie J. think what Winn was saying was right was something Greer had said after handing over Uncle Davey's old over-and-under. Something about only looking out ahead of you. Bennie J. said, "Yeah."

Winn nodded. Bennie J. looked back up at the ceiling, then back to Winn. "Winn," he said, "I'm counting on you to find out what this thing is that's bothering Hanna. I don't want you coming back to me whining that you tried, that you really tried, that shit that Wright tried to do to me that time. Sometimes he can come up with the damndest bunch of shit."

Winn said, "Yes, sir," meaning she promised to find out.

Bennie J. leaned forward. "But I don't want you to find out. Don't do no good just to find out. What's that shit? I don't even need to know what it is that's bothering her. But what I *do* want is for once you find out what it is, I want you to handle it. I don't care how much of Bennie J.'s hard-earned money you have to spend. I don't care what extremes you have to go to."

"I understand," Winn assured him.

Bennie J. threw his hands about, gesticulating. "I don't want you to just fill it up with neon, see what happens. I want you to handle it."

Winn knew what he meant about the neon, knew that he actually meant Freon. She knew Jerry Lee had put in whole compressors to Bennie J.'s meat coolers before when it just needed some more gas, but had put in the compressors to make Bennie J. happy. He hadn't wanted to tell Bennie J. they needed to wait and see how that worked.

"I'll handle it, Doddy Bennie J.," Winn said.

"Good. I want you to handle ole Hanna good. Whatever it takes. Anything would be better than for her to stay in the state she's in. Anything. So fix it so it stays fixed *forever!*"

5 It was the largest graveside service there had ever been in Sumpter County. People covered the south end of the Sumpter City Municipal Cemetery, trying to get as close to the graveside as they could without stepping too terribly on top of anybody's grave.

The preacher was standing at the casket, holding a Bible. He was saying something about Hanna.

Bebe, Irene, and Marty Lou were standing over to the side about fifty yards away from the preacher. Irene whispered, "A lot of people always show up at a suicide funeral."

Marty Lou said, "Yes. But this is the biggest ever. I believe there are more people here than there was at Betty Jean Daniel's wedding. I hope somebody, the police or somebody, took a count."

Bebe said to the little group, "I heard she left a note and everything. Kellie told me the turtles had already eaten on her face by the time they got her out of the water. That's why they had a closed casket and no viewing. This service is very nice, though."

Marty Lou said, "No, Bebe. You act as though she drowned. She shot herself with a double-barrel over-and-under shotgun and *fell* into the water. Wright was there when it happened, but it was too late. Mr. Lanson called the police. She committed suicide right out at the end of the dock where he fishes every morning."

"Poor man," Bebe said. "I bet it messed up his little fishing spot."

"An over-and-under?" Irene questioned. "Those Reynolds *are* different." Then she said, "Did you know she was at McCandless last week?"

"No?" Marty Lou said. "I can't believe I didn't hear about that."

Bebe said, "Oh, God. The poor thing was probably on dope and everything. She must have been a very disturbed soul."

Irene said, "I saw her at the country club just a few nights before she died," as if there was something extrasensory about that.

Bebe said, "I heard she helped start the riot they had there."

"Wasn't that terrible," Irene said. "Daughtery Adams did the best he could to stop it. I hope he didn't get bunged up any. The Crimson Tide needs him." She knew the three of them had a lot to talk about. She regretted they hadn't been able to get together before the service.

Marty Lou said, "Cordelle and them were so good to her. Treated her like their own daughter. It makes you wonder how a young beautiful girl with everything in the world going for her would do such a thing to herself."

Irene said, "I just wished she had run for Miss Maid of Cotton."

Bebe stated quickly, "If she had run for Miss Maid of Cotton she would be alive today," and was proud of herself for thinking of that. It was so powerful it had put a conclusion to their whispering conversation. She knew her last statement was still echoing through Marty Lou and Irene's heads, both wishing they had been the one to say it.

The casket was being readied to be let down into the grave. Six of the guys who had fought at the country club were serving as pallbearers. The coon dog men were over on the other side from Bebe, Irene, and Marty Lou. Wendell Laves said very low, "First Mama Dog Midnight. Then Bluina. Now Bennie J.'s niece."

Gene offered, "Comes in threes."

"I's wondering who was gone be next when Bluina passed away," Red said.

"Heard she done it with a Browning over-and-under," Olan said, but was mostly mumbling as he had just put a fresh cut of Day's Work in his mouth. "Count on a Republican to have a caddy-wampus double-barrel."

Wright was near the casket, staring at it. The preacher said, "Let us pray." While the entire congregation was praying, Bennie J. said to Cordelle, not being especially careful how loudly he was talking, "Well, I guess she finally got what she wanted. I just hope her mama don't find out about this."

"Well, B.J.," Cordelle replied, "She's going to have to find out sooner or later."

Cordelle, Bennie J., Winn, and Wright were sitting in the first row of chairs by the gravesite. The preacher finished the prayer and went down the row consoling each one. Several people came by to pay their respects. But the crowd was so great that out of courtesy most just stayed where they were and waited for the begrieved family to leave.

Bennie J., Cordelle, Winn, and Wright walked toward Cordelle's Cadillac. Bennie J. was walking along with Cordelle on one side of him and Winn on the other, Winn holding on to Bennie J.'s arm. Wright was behind them.

Bennie J. said, "I told y'all something was gnawing at her and she was going to bust."

Winn said, "You sure did, Doddy."

Bennie J. said, "How could we have known she was scared to die? Scared of death. How could we have known the thought to be put in a casket would give her screaming nightmares? Thangs some people don't even give a thought somebody else spends their ever' breath in fear of." Bennie J. shook his head.

Cordelle pulled nearer to him. She had on a short silk low-cut black dress. She patted Bennie J.'s shoulder, then broke away from him to go around and get in the driver's seat. Bennie J. and Winn slid in beside her, and Wright closed the door behind them. His Corvette was parked a few yards away.

Bennie J. pushed the automatic button and as the window was coming down, Wright heard him saying to Cordelle and Winn, "The one good thing about all this is, I don't reckon it's bothering her now." The window was completely down now. Bennie J. turned to Wright and asked, "You be home directly?"

Wright nodded.

Bennie J. reached out and embraced Wright's forearm. He said, "Don't worry, son. Everthang's gone be all right. Don't worry about what's done. What's done is done. You just handle what's out ahead in front of you. And don't worry. Everthang's gone be all right. Everthang's gone be all right because it's a thirsty city."

Bennie J. pushed the automatic button. The window went up and soon Wright could not see into the car, only his reflection on the window.

6 Wright was sitting in one of the funeral home's velvet-draped folding chairs up next to the gravesite. He slowly looked about. The entire place was deserted now except for the two black cemetery workers who had just begun to shovel dirt into Hanna's grave. He recognized them as friends of Jake's, Tommy and Kenneth. Wright had seen them down at the marina to pick up Jake.

Wright stood up, took off his jacket and laid it on the back of the chair. He walked up to the two workers. Normally he would have said, "Hey ya, Tommy. Kenneth. Glad to see you got yourselves some summer jobs with the city. Gettin' any pussy? Hey, what about that ole Jake? He's all right, ain't he?" Instead he held his hand out for Tommy's shovel and said very softly, "I want to do this. It's my job."

Tommy handed him his shovel and mumbled he was sorry. Kenneth threw his shovel up on his shoulder, patted Wright on the shoulder, also mumbling he was sorry for him. They walked away.

Wright slowly began to shovel dirt into the grave, thinking with each shovel stroke about how he'd had to fill his grandfather's grave in Campbell County that time. Wright stopped shoveling, looked down into the grave, and wondered for the first time how Bennie J. had told Winn about Mama Dog passing away. He knew Winn's return from Europe had been with Gina, driving up to Big House in a taxi. Everyone but Bennie J. was at Kathy Lee's party. Winn and Gina must have come in, walked into Big Room and hollered. Bennie J. must have come out of the den, they hugging and carrying on. Then she wanting to know where everyone was, Bennie J. telling her about Kathy Lee's party out at the country club, where all them drunks hung out. Then Winn hollering for Mama Dog. And at that point, Bennie J. looking very serious, saying Winn's name. Winn looking at Bennie J. and Bennie J. not having to say another word, Winn seeing it in his eyes. Maybe Bennie J. saying, "I buried her good and proper on Hatchett Island."

Off at the far end of the cemetery, Wright could see Kenneth and Tommy's service truck drive slowly out onto the road and pull out of sight. Wright let the shovel handle drop to the ground. He looked at his bracelet, rubbed his left index finger across the engraving of his name, "Wright," then took the bracelet off, looked at the inscription on the back. He mumbled to himself, "To the one who's on my mind all the time. Love, Hanna." He put the bracelet back on.

The wind was blowing his tie around and messing up his hair. He took his tie off and stuffed it into one of his pockets. Wright leaned his head back and ran his fingers through his hair; it was still long, but last night Winn had cut it into a shag. Mae Emma said it made him look like a Kennedy, but Wright couldn't remember any of the Kennedys having hair down over their ears, almost shoulder length. He stood there staring off into the blue sky. It was still August, but there was the feel of autumn coming. The breeze felt good.

He looked down into the grave and jumped, landing on the concrete vault top. There was not all that much dirt, as Tommy and Kenneth had only begun. He stepped down between the vault and the wall of the grave; there was about a foot of room all the way around. He lifted the top up and pushed it over.

After getting his Winchester knife out and opening it, Wright lay stomach down on top of the casket. He ran the knife blade along the underside of the lip of the casket until it hit a latch. He prized the latch open, put the knife up. He slid himself down to the bottom two thirds of the casket, lifted the lid up, then pulled himself back up a bit toward the head of the casket.

A white veil covered the opening. Wright ripped it out. Hanna reached up and grabbed him. She gave him a wet kiss.

Hanna pulled herself out of the casket, stood up, and stretched. Then she lifted the scuba tank up out of the casket and set it on the ground. Wright and Hanna stood up on top of the casket, kissing. Then Wright said, "Let's get out of here." Hanna had on a long white lacy dress. She started giggling. Wright made a stirrup out of his hands. She pulled her dress up, stepped into his hands, and climbed up.

Wright was looking up. He said, "Hanna, you don't have on any underwear!"

Hanna said, "Mae Emma says, 'Miss Hanna, I think I seen Mr. Wright trying to look up your dress at your drawers.' Well, I'll fool him. I won't wear any drawers." She giggled. "And Mama Cordelle herself told me to wear the best panties money could buy or wear nothing at all."

She reached down, gave Wright a hand. He hopped up out of the grave, thinking that for such a short time back into karate he was already much more agile.

Hanna reached her arms out in the air and twirled around. "Oh, it's a beautiful day," she said. Wright grabbed the scuba tank and by the time he got to his Corvette, Hanna had it cranked and was ready to ride. He got in. As she shifted into gear, she looked back at Wright and said, "Fucking fate is fun."

Wright didn't catch it in the first instance, but as soon as he realized she was using "fucking" as a verb, he stared at her and said, "Yeah, yeah, it is. It's a thirsty city." He realized that—fucking fate— was what he did best.

Hanna gunned the Vette and pulled on out of the cemetery. She said, "Boy, Winn sure is good at finding loopholes. She should be a lawyer."

Wright smiled and nodded. He was inventing a scenario that just started rolling, and he let it go; he just leaned his head back to the sky, enjoyed the speed of the car as they headed for Big House, and let it roll:

Greer and Winn are sitting in Greer's living room. They are drinking Dixie beer. Greer thinks a moment before putting the match to his hand-rolled Bull Durham. He lights the cigarette, puffs, shakes the match out, throws it out across the floor. He says, "Now, Miss Winn. Seem like dese visions Miss Hanna's had since she be seven year old. Dese visions so strong even ne wheggie boa'd pick up on it. So strong she dream 'bout it." Greer paused to take a suck off the Dixie beer. "But looks to me like all 'ese visions is about is about biggest funeral ever in Sumpter. Just folks standin' 'round a casket. Shit, Miss Winn. Willie Coats had him a fun'ral, he wadn't even dead. Seems we is talkin' funeral, but we ain't necessarily talkin' dade folk." Winn slaps the black leather of her pants leg. She steps over, hugs Greer, sits back down. She tells Greer that Bennie J. says to handle it, he don't care how much it costs, what extreme she has to go to, he just wants it handled, and he don't want her whining about how she "tried." She tells Greer that Bennie J. says it's a thirsty city and he can get anything in this town fixed. She says she doesn't see but one thing to do. Greer giggles, coughing his cigarette out into the middle of the floor. They clink their Dixie beer bottles together in a toast and take a slug of beer. Greer says, "Did I tell you 'bout that time me and Jerry Lee hauled a load of white lightnin' all the way to Bourbon Street . . ."

7 | "A good bitch who can find? She is far more precious than jewels," Wendell Laves was saying at the top of his lungs. He had his arms reached up to the clear blue sky. Cordelle looked up at the sky, as if Wendell was pointing for everyone to look up there. But everyone else in the congregation, the hundred-odd men, were looking at Cordelle. She had on the same black minidress she had worn to Hanna's funeral, but now she wore darker hose and a wide-brim black hat.

Wendell Laves jerked his arms back down and carried on about how Bluina was a good bitch and how she never did bark up any wrong trees. Then the six pallbearers lowered the small casket down into the grave.

Cordelle was looking down at the grassy ground. It finally came to her; she had gotten her period when Bennie J. had thrown the quarter stick of dynamite into Big Back Yard. That was the Fourth of July. She silently counted out each day. Her period was over three weeks late. She gave a sly grin.

Olan Massey and Red Stinnet were standing to the back of the crowd, dressed in khakis and open-collar shirts. It was Saturday. Bennie J. had kept Bluina in a fish freezer until a custom casket could be made. Wendell's cousin had been on a drunk so things got postponed, but the delay added suspense and got things talked up until it had resulted in the biggest coon dog funeral in the history of Sumpter County, probably in the history of the State of Alabama, possibly the biggest coon dog funeral in the history of the world.

Her master, Lummy Stanton, had wanted to lay away Bluina right. A man was lucky if he had one good coon dog like Bluina in his lifetime.

Olan said to Red so that nobody else could hear, "Bennie J. wife all the time come."

Red said, "Somebody got to bring Baby Dog Midnight, Prince of the Coon Dogs."

"Yeah. Bennie J. too busy. And Wright, he done gone off to college down in Bear country."

"Wright?" Red said. "He harum-scarum but he got a good ear on him."

"Yessirree. Heard his cousin scratching down in that casket. He saved her life."

"Yep. She's lucky her mama's from Campbell County."

"Why's that?" Olan asked defensively, as if nothing could be so absurd.

"You know how them folks are from Campbell County. They don't believe in embalming. If her blood had been drained she'd be dead today."

"I wonder what doctor it was pronounced her dead?"

"I don't know. It don't matter," Olan said. "I don't trust none of 'em these days. Hadn't trusted none of 'em since old Doc Stuart died. She 'as lucky the signs were in the bowels moving down."

"Why's that?" Red said, pulling out a plug of tobacco and cutting a chew off.

Olan said, " 'Cause. She fell in the water at the marina, drownt.

If the sign had been in the bowels or chest and movin to'ards the head, she never would come to. She's lucky the signs were movin' down that day."

"All them Reynolds is lucky," Red said, putting the chew in his mouth. "I thought she tried to shoot herself. With an over-and-under."

"Naw. Over-and-under? Only so much Bennie J.'d put up with," Olan said, like Red was having a bad case of the dumb-ass. Then he looked intently at Red. "Bennie J.'s niece has the biggest funeral in Sumpter, turns out she's not dead. Now Bluina has the biggest funeral Wendell's ever done. I's wonderin' if when Bluina thaws out, maybe she ain't dead."

"Lummy's already buried her once, dug her up. She's still dead."

"Yeah," Olan decided. "And them Reynolds is just plain lucky anyhow." Red and Olan looked over at Cordelle.

Baby Dog Midnight had on a gold mesh collar. He was running around in circles, then would run out the length of the leash and try to nip Gerald Turner's black-and-tan on the heel. Baby Dog made another run at her and this time nipped her on the back leg. The black-and-tan let out a yelp that started all the coon dogs to howling.

Cordelle picked up Baby Dog and walked back to her Eldorado. The congregation's eyes followed Cordelle. Grit Adams stepped over and opened the door for her; Cordelle thanked him kindly. He shut the door for her.

Cordelle set Baby Dog over in a cardboard box on the floorboard. She undid the leash and he started scratching at the box, stretched out, trying to pull himself up over the top. Cordelle said to him, "Baby Dog, you have to stay in the box. I can't have you peeing in Black Car."

Wendell Laves coon dog cemetery was north of town. On the way back to Big House Cordelle drove into Sumpter City. She drove down the old section of town, down a street lined with huge oak trees. She pulled up in front of Little House and parked across the street from it, leaving the engine of her Eldorado running.

Down the street she could see the huge columned antebellum front of the main hall of Sumpter College for Women. A group of freshman girls were standing in the middle of the front yard, looking back at the historic facade. The mistress of the school was telling them how in the Civil War the Yankee troops had come to burn the four-story building. How all the girls of the school had stood firm on the steps and along the balcony of each story. How the mistress of the school had pleaded with the Colonel to petition President Lincoln for the school to be spared.

Cordelle looked back over at Little House. Baby Dog Midnight finally climbed out of his cardboard box and up onto the front seat. He ran over into Cordelle's lap and started pawing at her breast.

Cordelle shifted the car into drive and headed for Big House.

ABOUT THE AUTHOR

PHILLIP QUINN MORRIS was born and raised in Limestone County, Alabama. He has worked as a meat cutter, engine rebuilder, house painter, and mussel diver. He lives with his wife, Debbie, in Coral Gables, Florida. His first book, *Mussels,* was published last year.